AETHER SPHERES
BOOK TWO

VOID SPHERES

Faolan's Pen Publishing
22 King St. S, Suite 300
Waterloo, Ontario
N2J 1N8 Canada

For paperback sales information, visit faolanspen.com. For special events, release alerts, and more books from the author, visit glynnstewart.com.

ISBN-13: 978-1-989674-89-5 (Trade Paperback)

ISBN-13: 978-1-989674-90-1 (Amazon Paperback)

A record of this book is available from Library and Archives Canada.

1 2 3 4 5 6 7 8 9 10

First edition

First printing: October 2025

Faolan's Pen Publishing logo is a registered trademark of Faolan's Pen Publishing Inc.

Read more books from Glynn Stewart at faolanspen.com

AETHER SPHERES
BOOK TWO

VOID SPHERES

GLYNN STEWART

FAOLAN'S PEN
PUBLISHING
faolanspen.com

CAT GREENTREES OF THE HOUSE OF FORESTS KNEW THE RULES OF the spheres. He could sense the currents in the aether he needed to guide a ship between worlds, find the straits between different spheres by instinct. His skill at command was half instinct, half training—the product of dozens of dances as an officer in the Navy of the High Court of the Elvar.

The space he looked out into defied all of the rules that defined the spheres. A sphere was made of five things: aether and air, dirt and stone, all illuminated by a light source of some kind.

The current sphere had *light*, certainly. It was an outerlit sphere, a piece of open space surrounded by a globe of gentle light some eighty thousand leagues across. There were even dirt and stone; he could *see* the light reflecting from worldlets in the distance.

But there was no aether. The connecting fabric of the spheres, the underlying medium that *defined* the spheres, was missing.

The void was the medium of the space *beyond* the aether spheres, where even elvar like Cat could not breathe or live. But there, *something* had consumed all of the aether in this sphere, leaving behind only void.

Only hunger.

The ship he commanded was as strange as the space she occupied. A cylinder driven by fire instead of a hull carried by aether sails, *Void Flyer* was built for void spheres like this one.

He stood in *Flyer's* control room, a very different space from the wheelhouses and command decks he was used to, and considered the new sphere. Cat knew, with little modesty, that he was among the greatest navigators of their age.

But the void spheres were new to him.

"Well, Captain?"

Alloy Bellowforge was a new addition to his crew—as new as *Void Flyer* herself, in fact. The squat darvar artificer was studying him as he prodded, looking at the elvar Captain through his monocle like Cat was another of the strange var's devices.

"Well, what, artificer?" Cat replied. He had *patience* for his crew, but he wasn't quite sure how the darvar mage-artificer fit into the delicate balance of his people. Like Cat himself, Bellowforge was now sworn to the Archmage Armand Bluestaves.

"I *built* the *Flyer*," Bellowforge observed. "I know *how* to fly her. But I'll be frank, Captain, and confess that I have no idea what is in this sphere. Or of where we're going. Or of how to find that *out*."

Cat surprised himself with a laugh. The last few days had been stressful, but they had been *successful*. Cat was still learning to fly Bellowforge's strange ship, but he'd already learned enough to know he *could* fly her anywhere he wanted.

So long as they had fuel. Which was, now he finally realized it, the problem.

"Forward, Master Bellowforge," he told the other var. "Forever forward. But *this* clock-day, I think we need to convene with Brushfire, at least.

"We have few charts of this sphere and less information. Anything you can tell myself and Officer Hammerhead about it will help—and I need some time with the charts regardless."

Taller and gaunter than his darvar companion, Cat knew he was more refined-appearing in every way, from his build to his uniform to the fact that *he*, unlike the artificer, carried both a sword and a focus carved for him by the archmage himself.

But while Cat knew he was a better officer than Bellowforge—and that the other var wouldn't survive a single clock-day in the politics of

House and Plate of the Elvar High Court—Cat knew he needed the other var's expertise.

And that he'd be *far* more comfortable asking for it with his first officer, Brushfire, present.

Cat wasn't sure at what point Brushfire Hammerhead's presence had gone from *necessary annoyance* to *solid support* to *critical for major decisions*.

He'd hired her entire tribe of gobvar aether-ship crew to manage the aether ship *Star*, the ninesail that had delivered them this far, and appointed her as first officer to manage the gobvar crew. Since his career had been spent *fighting* gobvar, having them aboard the ship had grated.

Somewhere between launching their ship from Blueswallow and fighting the murderous fanatics of the god of death and betrayal to steal *Void Flyer*, his gobvar crew had become simply *his* crew, and Brushfire Hammerhead had become his first officer in every sense.

In comparison to Cat's delicate elvar build, she was the opposite of the captain in every way. She *towered* over both Cat and Bellowforge, broader across the shoulders than either of them, with immense horns bearing inlaid silver circles marking her as a gobvar shaman.

With her size, Cat left an entire side of the chart table to her as he spread out the papers Armand had brought them.

"Where did you *get* these charts?" Alloy asked, staring at them. "These are... ancient."

"Archmage Bluestaves has a family archive going back over a thousand dances," Cat told the darvar. "His family are halvar, so it was the only way they could make sure the Ironhand Imperium wasn't forgotten."

Especially since it appeared that *Cat's* people, who lived five hundred dances to a halvar's hundred-to-hundred-and-fifty, had been doing everything they could to make sure the empire that predated the High Court *was* forgotten.

"These are... incredible," Alloy murmured. "Does this show... all of the Clan and Court spheres?"

"Most, I think," Cat agreed. He traced his finger down the chart to the sphere that had thrown him the most the first time he'd seen Armand's chart. "Here's the High Court."

That sphere, with one of the most powerful life crystals known and the sixteen interweaving plates of lodestone whose dance of orbits gave the High Court its measure of time, was the current center of civilization as Cat knew it—the Court and Kingdoms.

On the ancient charts, it was a backwater with a couple of symbols and notes around its unusual structure. The center of *these* charts was, in fact, the spheres they had entered.

"You wanted to know our course," Cat reminded Alloy. "Can you see it?"

Alloy laughed.

"First, I can barely read regular charts. This is something else again! Second, I was *kidnapped* by His Dark Brothers, remember. I don't actually know where we are."

Brushfire added her own deep laugh, shaking her head at Cat across the table before she reached out and tapped a sphere on the gorgeously illustrated chart.

"This is Brokenwright, the home of the Seventh Ward," she told Alloy. "That's where His Dark Brothers had their fortress-monastery and where they were keeping you."

"Ah, I see." The darvar studied the chart for a moment more, then traced a line. "So, this is the strait we took. Now a void strait, but not one on this map. How..."

"That's the key to our mission, Alloy," Cat explained. "These spheres here"—he traced a section of the old Ironhand map—"are *gone* now. Something happened to turn them to spheres of the void, but their straits remain.

"So, we can pass through these four spheres." He tapped each of them in turn. "Brushfire, can you show Master Bellowforge the current chart?"

It took them a few minutes to get the chart set up, and Cat knew they needed to change the room's layout. The chart room took up about a quarter of the "deck" beneath the control room, making it the second-highest of *Void Flyer*'s thirty decks, but the ship's previous owners had only been flying her on voyages through one strait. They had barely *used* the chart room.

It was a permanent space, so they could probably leave the current navigation chart pinned to a bulkhead.

"I think I see," Alloy said, studying the chart. Cat had drawn the key void spheres in on the chart himself while planning the mission. "So, we're going into gobvar spheres?"

"We pass through four void spheres, spaces no one else can travel, and enter the Clan Spheres where they won't expect us," Cat agreed. "Thanks to Brushfire and her tribe, we should be able to *quietly* investigate affairs in gobvar territory at that point."

"The archmage saved my family. I will do whatever he asks," Alloy told the other two mages. "But..." He traced the path on the chart. "We have a problem."

"Fuel," Cat guessed.

"Fuel. *Flyer*'s tanks weren't full, and we burned almost half of what we *had* trying to escape the Seeker. We could still make the journey, but it will be very slow. Two hundred clock-days or more."

"I didn't expect the journey to be *possible*, so that's better than I'd feared," Cat admitted. "We only have, what, two hundred fifty days of food, though?"

"About that," Brushfire agreed thoughtfully. "We transferred everything over, but we lost hands in Brokenwright."

Including members of her tribe, var Cat knew they hadn't had a decent chance to mourn yet.

"So, we'd be well served to stock up on fuel and food before heading deeper in the void spheres," Cat observed. He reached down to pull out a surprisingly critical tool of navigation: an oracle deck.

He was no seer, but some level of divination was key to navigation.

"Fortunately," he continued, pulling out the cards and shuffling them absently, "we know what straits remain from this sphere—*Warden of Fire*, the Ironhand called it—and one of them links to the Bright Steel sphere.

"It's a darvar sphere, but under the High Court's protection," he continued. The *impolite* description of the spheres on this side of the border with the Clans was *Court and Protectorates*, after all. The High Court of the Elvar didn't *rule* the two hundred–odd spheres they'd tied into their economic network.

The *polite* term was *The Kingdoms*, giving an illusion that the darvar and halvar kingdoms enjoyed more freedom to operate than anyone *actually* thought they had.

Cat paused, studying the local chart. They had *some* information from the old charts, but their main map of Warden of Fire was stolen from His Dark Brothers, and it didn't show *any* void straits except the one back to Brokenwright.

"This will show us the way," he murmured, flipping the top card off the oracle deck with a touch of magic to guide it. It landed and slid across the paper, guided by his magic and the oracle deck's own spark of power.

The card should have landed in the location of the strait he was hunting, but *that* thought fled his mind as he saw *which* card he'd drawn: the broken aether ship and lightning-struck clouds of the Aether Storm.

A card that predicted, with very little uncertainty, complete disaster.

CHAPTER

2

BRUSHFIRE COULD READ CHARTS AND POINT AN AETHER SHIP IN roughly the right direction, but her training as a navigator was very basic. Her training in the *divination* that went alongside navigation in the unknown was nonexistent.

She'd been trained in gobvar shamanic divination. Despite the focus she wore at her belt—carved from a black grazer horn and matched to her personal magic by Archmage Bluestaves himself—her training in "regular" magic was still fresh.

She was a good student and remembered basically everything she'd been taught, but neither Cat nor Armand had spent much time teaching her divination yet. Neither of them were *good* at it, from what she understood, but she still needed to learn.

For all of Brushfire's lack of knowledge of oracle cards, though, even *she* knew that the Aether Storm was bad news.

"I'm guessing," she observed, "that wasn't what you were expecting to draw."

Cat was staring at the card like it had bitten him.

"The actual card drawn for that particular trick is... usually irrelevant," he told her. "It's just a marker; any object with divination magic would work. Oracle cards, of course..."

"Aren't known for refraining from commentary," Alloy said gruffly, looking up at Brushfire. "You're the first officer, aren't you? You don't know the trick?

"I am still learning many things," Brushfire admitted. "Navigation, beyond the most general, I know divination about as well as I know this ship."

The darvar snorted and nodded.

"Fair. We're all learning all sorts of things." He gestured a stubby hand at the card. "I'm going to say, Captain Greentrees, that that card suggests we should consider an alternative plan to refueling in Bright Steel.

"I was hoping to leave my family there, but…"

"We can't take a unique ship crewed almost entirely by gobvar into *anyone's* territory and expect things to end well," Brushfire said. Cat seemed to have grown out of his own prejudices—and he'd always let habit and intellect override those prejudices *anyway*—but the rest of the elvar would not be so enlightened.

"No," he agreed slowly. "Bright Steel is guarded by both mercenary elvar in the employ of their Five Kings and by a squadron of the High Court Navy. Neither… would see *Void Flyer* as anything but a threat.

"Even the blue pennant of an archmage wouldn't clear us through showing up with a gobvar-crewed void ship."

Brushfire looked at the chart of the spheres and reached over to point at one of the worldlets. The Ironhand charts didn't have *much* detail on the individual spheres, and they'd copied most of what there was over to *Void Flyer*'s original charts.

The notation she touched wasn't one of the bits copied from the old charts. *Those* were in either her hand or Cat's, but this note was in script she didn't know and written in a hand blockier than Cat's but much more elegant than her own.

"What does this mean?" she asked.

Alloy and Cat both looked at the icon.

"Another answer," the darvar artificer said. "I was about to say: His Dark Brothers moved a lot of fuel into this sphere that they didn't bring back or burn. They might have wanted to gaze on the death and destruction of the void spheres, but they don't seek death for *themselves*."

"A depot," Cat observed. "Would it have enough fuel to make the full trip, Artificer?"

"Like I said, Captain, we can make the trip. More fuel means we make it faster. Unless the Brothers were fools—and I *told them* enough that they shouldn't have been that foolish—there should be enough fuel to refill *Flyer*'s tanks completely.

"That should get us through the spheres in maybe fifty clock-days? Depends on details of the straits that I can't tell from these charts."

Brushfire looked to Cat. The elvar Captain had an extraordinary ability to carve time off courses that should have taken half again as long.

"Without aether and currents, navigating like this is strange to me," he admitted. He stabbed a finger down at a note written in his hand. "Our exit is *here*. The depot isn't on our way—right now, our course has us in this sphere for a dozen clock-days, but it will take us eight just to get to the worldlet with the depot."

"We'll be able to go much faster with fuel, Captain," Bellowforge told him.

"He knows this ship better than any of us," Brushfire reminded Cat. The Captain had already made his decision, she could tell, but a bit of extra support never hurt.

"Indeed. Master Bellowforge, I feel we need to make your place on this ship clear to everyone," Cat murmured. "How does *Engines Officer* sound to you?"

"New and shiny and confusing to anyone who doesn't know what you mean," Alloy said. "Does it come with a salary?"

"I'd say I'd ask Armand, but every time I've asked him about money, the answer has been *yes*," Cat replied drily. "Let's say you'll draw comparable pay to First Officer Hammerhead."

As opposed to *Master of Decks* Axfall Hammerhead or *Master of Sails* Windheart Hammerhead. Of the two hundred gobvar aboard *Void Flyer*, nearly a hundred were Hammerheads.

Strangely, no one seemed particularly confused by that. The gobvar knew how to handle extended tribal families, and the hundred-ish elvar aboard the ship just... *managed*.

"I have no idea what that number would be," Bellowforge admitted cheerfully. "But yes, I would like to remain in charge of my engines. I will train the crew, of course, but *Void Flyer* is my masterwork."

"She is a masterwork," Cat agreed. "And the fate of all spheres and all var may ride on her, Alloy. For now, let's get to this depot and fill her tanks."

Brushfire nodded her agreement—not that Cat needed the confirmation. She'd made her opinion clear, she hoped, and she suspected the Captain would have explicitly *asked* her to argue her case if he hadn't thought she agreed.

"This entire sphere makes me nervous," Brushfire observed. "Do we know..." She paused, reconsidering her question.

"There's no aether in this sphere," she said. "Do we know if there's *air* on the worldlets?"

"There are armor suits aboard intended to let people breathe in void," Bellowforge said slowly. "But... well, they're sized for darvar and aren't going to fit anyone bigger. His Dark Brothers never *said* anything about the worlds here, but..."

"But what?" Brushfire asked.

"There are four suits," the artificer told her. "I'm not sure they could have set up the depot with just four suits.

"I do not *know*, my friends, but I suspect that the surface of the worldlet may be more hospitable than we fear."

"It can't be less," Cat said grimly. "In the worst case, we have enough mages on this ship to make it work regardless. We'll get that fuel."

GREAT MAGICAL POWER DID NOT MAKE IT ANY EASIER TO GIVE UP habits when circumstances changed. Armand Bluestaves, Archmage of the Towers of the Great Red Forest, certainly possessed the former.

The rotund halvar commanded the base magic of the spheres, a link to the fundamental underpinning of reality that he felt as a second heartbeat. That was the power that had fueled his duel with the Seeker of Her Dark Brother, the priest-archmage who had originally owned *Void Flyer*.

Drawing on that power was more a *loan* than a gift, however, and Armand had paid for the power he'd commanded in that duel with clock-days of fatigue and muscle pain.

In theory, he could have climbed the steep stairs that rose the full height of *Void Flyer*. The exercise would have done him good, on the clock-days when he had the energy. But habit spoke louder than intent, some days, and *Void Flyer* was a strange ship.

A halvar like Armand couldn't breathe aether. Neither could a darvar like his newest sworn servant, Bellowforge. But the elvar and gobvar who made up *Void Flyer*'s crew could, and so, on an ordinary aether ship—like *Star*, the ninesail that had delivered them to Brokenwright— most of the ship was open to aether.

Only the quarters for special guests—like halvar archmagi—and the medical suite were sealed to contain air. So, Armand had been basically trapped in his quarters aboard *Star*. He was *not* so trapped aboard *Flyer*, but habit kept him out of the way of his crew.

He felt it was… excessive that an entire deck of the void ship had been set aside for him. The deck—one of four with magical windows that looked out into the void around them—had *already* been set up as luxurious personal quarters, probably for the Seeker, but Armand still felt that he should have shared the space with someone.

Still, it meant they'd had room to bring not only his books—all copies of tomes in his personal library, just in case *this* library was lost—but his *oven*.

And another habit that Armand had *no* intention of ever giving up was that he baked when nervous or exhausted. The current batch of sweetrolls didn't taste quite right, and he leveled a sad look on the glaze he'd made.

The sweet cinnamon icing he'd made would be too much on these rolls. They needed *something*—they were both too dry and too sweet—but the different temperatures and vibrations of *Void Flyer* compared to anywhere else he'd ever baked had turned the sweetbark nuggets into a pervasive flavor.

He was about to give up entirely when Cat Greentrees knocked on the door. Armand couldn't identify *everyone* aboard *Flyer* by their knock, but he knew he could pick out Cat and Brushfire. His two senior officers had been recurring visitors on *Star*, and only the nature of the door had changed.

"You know you can come in," he told Cat. "Captain Greentrees."

"Armand."

The elvar Captain crossed the room swiftly to stand across the table from Armand. The archmage took a moment to, hopefully covertly, enjoy the sheer grace and agility of his subordinate's movements.

His own frame couldn't have managed that even if he *hadn't* happily consumed the majority of his own baking over the dances.

"We're changing course," Cat told him. "Talking to Alloy, we don't have enough fuel to make the full journey. I tried to plot a course to a sphere in the Kingdoms, but…"

He shook his head and Armand waited patiently.

"The navigation cantrip I used calls for a divination tool," the Captain explained. "I have an old oracle deck—nothing like yours—and the card I drew was the Aether Storm."

Armand had his suspicions about what *an old oracle deck* meant to a senior scion of one of the central bloodlines of the House of Forests, a Great House of the Elvar High Court. On the other hand, his own oracle deck was a gift from the Shining King, the master of his home sphere.

Each card was a hand-calligraphed work of art.

"So, we do not take that route," Armand agreed. "What course did you and Brushfire agree on?"

The elvar smirked, silently acknowledging that, yes, the first officer had been involved in the discussion.

"The largest worldlet, Flame's Gem," Cat concluded. "Thanks to Alloy and the charts from His Dark Brothers, we know the Brothers had a fuel and supply depot there. While we do not know if Flame's Gem has, oh, *air...*"

"Any work done by the darvar there was done with the tools we have," Armand agreed. "We should be able to access the fuel depot, yes?"

"Yes. We may need to use more magic than they did," Cat warned. "The suits aboard *Flyer* would fit Bellowforge or his wife. They are made for darvar, and the Bellowforges are the only adult darvar aboard this ship."

"A risk, I think, we should hesitate to take," the archmage said. "I believe in Alloy's oath of service, but he has spent a full dance or more in the hands of His Dark Brothers."

And His Dark Brothers regarded lying, manipulation and torture as sacred rites, holy sacrifices to Her Dark Brother, their god.

"He also lacks a focus," Cat pointed out. "I did not think to lay in a supply of spare general foci, which leaves him limited in the magic he can command."

Armand nodded, glaring down at his failed sweetrolls.

The ability to make a focus was what differentiated an archmage from a regular mage. Cat, for example, was a fully trained Captain of the High Court Navy, empowered by the blood of his Great House and equipped with a personal focus made for him by Armand himself.

There were few regular mages who could face Cat Greentrees. Brushfire Hammerhead might be more powerful—even Armand wasn't sure!—but she lacked the Captain's extensive training.

But Cat could not make a focus, and without a focus, he would be drastically weakened. The elvar *also* bore a brand on his right hand that was supposed to keep him from using magic, but Armand had broken that as part of his payment.

"You want me to make him a personal focus." It wasn't really a question.

"I am *suggesting* it, yes," Cat agreed. "What I *want*, though I do not know if it is an option, is to have personal foci for all of my officers."

Armand nodded slowly. There were three junior officers aboard *Void Flyer*—all elvar who had proven their worth on this mission but had been hired through ordinary channels originally.

He had to be careful with personal foci. A mage with a focus attuned to them was easily twice as strong as a mage with a general focus. There were levels in between—family and House focuses, tied to family groupings of differing sizes—with increasing power with the increased alignment of the mage to the focus.

Of course, the *main* reason to be careful with making foci was the judgment of his peers, and they were outside the Kingdoms now.

"There is a difference," he warned slowly, "between a *personal* focus and an *attuned* focus." He gestured to the wand Cat wore at his hip. That had been carved from the wood of the ship he'd learned to sail aboard. Both its magic and its construction were intimately linked to Cat.

"We stand aboard Alloy's masterwork," Armand said. "I am confident I can find something to make him a true personal focus from. For the other three, I can attune a focus to them more tightly than any other, but without materials that are meaningfully linked to them, I cannot make a true personal focus."

Armand wasn't sure anyone other than an archmage would notice the difference.

"I don't think they will complain," Cat replied. "I presume such work shouldn't be done on *Flyer*?"

"I would hesitate to try, not least because a failure in the process is… energetic," Armand said. He'd used a munitions bunker as a workshop on Blueswallow to make Cat and Brushfire's foci.

Just in case.

"We're some clock-days from Flame's Gem, but I imagine the fuel depot is near a city or something similar," Cat said. "We can set up an air envelope for you to work in."

"Then I see no true barrier," Armand said, nodding firmly. He took another bite of the sweetroll and sighed, sliding an untouched roll to Cat. "Try this, Captain? I fear they may be irretrievable."

Cat hesitated, then shrugged and took a bite of the roll.

"*Irretrievable* is… harsh," the elvar said after a moment. "They are very dry. I could tolerate the sweet if it was a touch softer."

"I must learn how *Void Flyer* impacts my baking." Armand smiled. "Among other things. She is a strange ship, though as one unable to breathe aether, I see advantages to her."

"Takes less lodestone, if nothing else," Cat noted. "I wasn't sure, so I checked. There is a single plate at the base of the ship which weighs far less than the keel of a ninesail. The highest decks are a bit light but no worse than the rigging of a ninesail."

Lodestone was the strange metal that cored worldlets and anchored lodeplates. Even a tiny chunk of lodestone exerted a clear pull of *down* toward it. Aether ships had central keels made of the metal, drawing everything toward the center of the ship.

Void Flyer had a single base plate, more like the lodeplates of the High Court—vast continents that floated in the aether, one side forever to the life crystal of at the center of the sphere.

"I have one request, when you make the foci," Cat said quietly.

"Oh?"

"Allow Brushfire to watch."

Armand stared down at the sweetroll in his hand and considered the suggestion.

"You know what that leads toward," he observed softly. He knew that Cat would have watched a focus made at some point. "She has mastered every magic shown to her even a single time. There is a danger to that."

"It is the path to archmage," Cat agreed. "And I believe it is a path she can walk."

Armand was silent for a long time.

"She is a gobvar," he finally said. It wasn't an objection. Just a statement.

"And one of the most powerful *non*-archmagi I have ever met," Cat pointed out. "And…" He paused, then shrugged. "It is an open secret,

I believe, that the Academies of the High Court are better at judging archmage candidates than the Towers of the Great Red Forest."

Armand wanted to argue, but he knew that was true.

"They still lose two Trial petitioners for every archmage they raise up," he pointed out softly. An Archmage Trial could have four results: the petitioner could become an archmage, they could have their pathways of magic forced further open to make them a more powerful ordinary mage, they could lose their magic, or they could die.

The Academies had a far smaller number of the last three options than the Towers of the Great Red Forest. But they still buried more failures than they celebrated new archmagi.

"And that is why I am forbidden the test," Cat noted. "My sister is an archmage; you knew that. I have passed all of our pre-Trial examinations and would otherwise stand, but the odds suggest that I would die."

"And those are the odds Brushfire would face. Plus the risk of losing her magic entirely."

"I am trained in things I cannot share," Cat said quietly. "Things I know from being of a line of archmagi, Armand. Like myself, Brushfire would either pass the Trial or die."

Armand let the silence sit in the room, closing his eyes as he processed Cat's words.

"How many of your family have you lost?" he asked slowly.

"My eldest half-brother died. A cousin died. Two lost their magic forever. Another was lucky and channeled instead of burning out." Armand *heard* the shrug in his Captain's voice. "Once Hearth passed the Trial, of course, no more of my generation were permitted the attempt."

"We are less… organized, I think," Armand admitted. "Our lives are shorter, so perhaps we regard the risk as lesser. I do not know."

The elvar rule—law? Tradition? Armand wasn't sure of the exact form—allowing no more members of a family's current generation to attempt the Trial after one had succeeded made *sense*, in a cold-blooded way. Certain lineages tended to produce archmagi; that much was known. The rule both allowed those lineages to produce archmagi and preserved those lineages to produce *more* archmagi.

"My sister was never interested," the halvar murmured. "Gods bless her, she *wanted* a family, and the path to archmage didn't permit that. My father never had time, according to him, but his mother's sister was an archmage.

"It runs in families for us, too."

"But we would never know what families it runs in among the gobvar," Cat pointed out. "My people would not permit a gobvar to be trained to face the Trial. Yours might allow it, but I suspect the Academies would find a way to stop it before the Trial took place."

"We would be no better."

Despite Cat's allowance for any impression that Armand's var were less bigoted than the elvar, he was probably wrong on *that* point. Armand had no illusions about halvar tolerance. The long dances of the border war between Kingdoms and Clans had been *fought* by the elvar, but when the High Court Navy failed, it was halvar and darvar worlds that felt the blades and fire of Her Crimson Sisters.

The hatred those raids spawned toward the gobvar and the Clans was, Armand suspected, part of the *point*. Her Crimson Sisters—the warrior-priestesses of Her Crimson Sister, the sibling to Her Dark Brother and mistress of bloodshed and murder—*wanted* the Clans and the Kingdoms to hate each other.

As lies and torture were sacred to Her Dark Brother, strife and hatred were sacred to Her Crimson Sister.

"And even if you were, my people would stop it," Cat repeated. "The Academies and the High Court would *break* a mage academy that raised a gobvar." He snorted. "It is rare enough that anyone would take a gobvar as a student mage. The path of the archmage would be closed to them."

"Which brings me to another thought, I suppose," Armand asked slowly. "If Brushfire is as powerful a mage as you and I know her to be, the rest of her family and tribe should not lack for magical power."

His Captain was silent for longer than Armand expected, then took another bite of the dry sweetroll to conceal his thoughts.

"Petal," he said grimly. "I didn't think of it until you spoke, but there were signs in her *cooking* for those with the eyes to see and the wit to think." The Captain snorted. "The latter I appear to have lacked.

"Unfortunately, His Dark Brothers killed her."

Seven of Hammerhead Tribe had died in the desperate battle to seize *Void Flyer* and the Bellowforges from the Seeker and His Dark Brothers. Seventeen dead and eleven missing in total, with the heaviest weight falling on the elvar storm-stave crews.

Even Cat and Armand hadn't been willing, initially at least, to train gobvar to manage the magical storm staves that armed a ninesail. They didn't *have* any of the weapons aboard *Void Flyer*, so the remaining elvar crew were learning new tasks.

But so were the riggers and deckhands, from what Armand understood.

"Curses." Armand sighed. "I have spent too little time among the crew, I fear. I don't have enough exposure to pick out who should be trained."

"Fistfall. Brushfire's first-brother."

Armand didn't pretend to understand the complexity of *anyone's* family relations. Even Cat's family structure and its position in the greater House of Forests was odd to him—nothing like the simple, if sprawling, connections of blood and history that made up the Bluestaves.

But Fistfall was definitely Brushfire's brother by any standard Armand understood. He was probably the biggest gobvar on the ship, physically powerful if, well... a touch dim.

"I would not have guessed him to have the gift," Armand admitted. "He is..."

"Not as stupid as *he* thinks he is," Cat countered. "He is two and a half yards tall and nearly as broad. I believe he has played the kindly lovable oaf so long that even *he* has forgotten that the *oaf* part was an act.

"And he is not his sister. I do not believe he could be trained as a shaman, from what little I know of that path. But given a focus, he *can* be trained as a mage."

The Captain smiled thinly.

"Which would help him and my fourth officer sort out some things, I suspect. Though Petal's death will cause problems there regardless."

Armand understood about... half of what Cat referred to. In the battle inside the Seventh Ward, Fistfall had taken a blast of magic meant for Bogsong Smallwolf, Cat's elvar fourth officer.

Smallwolf had healed him from a fatal blow on pure instinct. That, Armand knew, took a powerful emotional connection. Being saved from certain death might have been enough. *Maybe.*

"Fistfall and Petal were a couple," Cat explained after a moment. "I wonder now if their shared unknown gifts were part of what tied them together."

"I have been a teacher for longer than I have been an archmage," Armand pointed out. "I have never commanded ships, but I suspect that the approach to relationships among our subordinates should be much the same as I once had to my students.

"Unless there is a *problem*, we keep our noses out of it!"

Cat chuckled.

"Agreed. But if you are willing, my lord archmage, I think some general focuses and perhaps even a handful of family focuses for Brushfire's tribe would serve us well.

"We do not know what is in front of us, except that *something* wiped life and aether from these spheres. I…"

"*I* fear that the center of whatever calamity shaped this void is in the center of the old Imperium," Armand finished his Captain's hanging thought. "Which means that we will pass right through it."

"I am no seer," Cat said softly. "I can do enough divination to navigate, little more. But even *I* can tell that we are going to learn more about these spheres than we ever wanted."

"We need to pass through them. We will learn what we must to survive and reach the other side," Armand told Cat calmly. "The answers *we* seek lie in the Clan Spheres."

Because while Armand was also no seer, he was an archmage and he had reactivated a tool *built* by an archmage seer. He had been shown the future—a future in which dragons and gobvar spilled out of the Clan Spheres and conquered *everything.*

They could not let that happen.

"Well, Master Bellowforge, now is the time for a question I should have thought about long ago," Cat said calmly, watching Flame's Gem grow through the magical crystal windows of the control deck.

"Just how, exactly, do we land this thing?"

Flame's Gem was a midsized worldlet, a smooth-looking sphere roughly a thousand leagues across. About half of it was covered in water, which shone brilliantly blue in the spherelight, but the land surface was a dead brown color Cat had never seen before.

Lodestone rocks tended to come in two varieties: those with water and dirt, and those that were *just* rock and lodestone. The former were alive and had air; the latter weren't and didn't.

Gem was a worldlet of water and dirt, but there was no color to suggest anything on it was alive. Like the sphere around it, it was *dead*—and Cat felt no more aether from the world than he did from the void around them.

"Right now, the sextant says we're about two hundred leagues out, moving toward her at around half a league a minute," Bellowforge noted. "So, in about a quarter of a clock-day, the *Flyer* will land herself quite handily, won't she?"

"I have seen aether ships crash at such a speed," Cat replied. "While *Void Flyer* is sturdier in some ways than a ninesail, I would not lay coin on her surviving that."

"No, she wouldn't; you're right," the artificer conceded. The darvar chuckled as he surveyed the control. "The first thing is to turn us around. Would you care to do the honors, Captain?"

Cat had spent the days since they'd captured the ship learning to fly her. *Landing* the ship was still a strange thought to him. Aether ships, with their spars and sails sticking out in every direction, *didn't* land. They docked at piers suspended out into the air to meet them.

Void Flyer had been placed on her side in a custom cradle inside a cavern on His Dark Brothers' fortress-monastery asteroid. From Alloy's complaints, that had been a *terrible* idea and the Brothers had badly damaged the ship trying to land her in there at least once.

Still, Cat was confident in his ability to turn the strange ship. He knew how to fly an aether ship, using the main wheel to turn sails and magical lift crystals alike.

Aboard *Flyer*, the lift crystals were key. The engines could do a *lot*, but for small maneuvers, the magical crystals and their push against the spheres themselves were more than enough.

Magic flickered from Cat's hands and focused into the *Flyer*'s interlinked lattices of crystals, waking the ship's arcane devices and pushing against the universe.

Void Flyer turned. Her motion toward Flame's Gem didn't change, but she gently rotated under Cat's touch and power. It wasn't a fast process, but it took only a couple of minutes by the clock for the ship to be pointing away from Gem.

"Have you worked out where the depot is?" Alloy asked.

"You know as much as we do, Engines Officer," Cat replied. "None of us have a voids-cursed clue where His Dark Brothers put it. I *presume* near to landmarks to make it easy to locate, but who knows what the landmarks on a long-dead world are?"

"A more accurate destination than *the planet* might help, Captain," the darvar told him.

Cat glanced around the control deck. The ship was small enough that very few people were ever alone at any given moment, but his fourth officer, Bogsong Smallwolf, was studiously ignoring the argument between the other two officers.

The pair of gobvar helping Smallwolf check over the spare sextant were giving an equal appearance of complete deafness, which Cat appreciated.

"Let me see."

Cat drew his focus, channeling a portion of his magic into a glorified telescope. An image of Flame's Gem appeared in front of him, a thousand-league rock compressed into an illusory clone a yard across.

"Here." He stabbed his finger down on the illusion of the worldlet. "Do you see?"

"A harbor, a city, and a mountain," Bellowforge said. "Somewhere in the city. But why there?"

"Because where water and mountains meet is where we put aethership docks, Alloy," Cat told the darvar. "If we have to crash a ship that missed the dock or has a problem, water is better than dirt.

"And I don't see that combination in many other places on Gem, which tells me this was their main dock and probably their main city."

"His Dark Brothers' ego will not have let them set up in anything less than the old capital," Bellowforge observed. "I agree, Captain."

"So, now can you land us?" Cat asked.

"I could always *land* us," his new subordinate pointed out. "The question was whether I was going to land us anywhere *useful.*"

As he spoke, Bellowforge crossed to the sextant and started taking another set of readings. The clockwork and magic of the device chimed softly under the darvar's hands, as if happy to be touched by the var who'd made it.

"If we make the right adjustments to our speed, we will come down perfectly above the city," he noted. "That will minimize the adjustments on final approach."

"I have sailed aether ships for as long as you've been alive, artificer," Cat pointed out. "*That* much I know."

"I figured. I'm going to burn the engines for about ten minutes now," Bellowforge told him. "That will slow us down, give us more time to manage the approach."

"And the approach?" Cat asked.

"Vertical and careful. We need to shed speed as we approach, but once we enter the lodestone field, we need to make sure we don't *gain* speed from the lodestone pull. It's a careful balance, and quite different for *Flyer* than for an aether ship."

"Plus, *Flyer* actually *lands*," Cat said slowly.

"We'll need to get the crew to extend the support struts, but at the right moment," Bellowforge warned. "They can take the flame of the engine, but not for long. The less time the supports are out while the engines are firing, the better."

Cat was learning, but it was very clear that he *needed* Bellowforge to land the ship.

This time, at least.

"Captain, there's *air* down there."

Smallwolf's quiet interruption drew Cat's attention. He turned away from where he was watching over Bellowforge's shoulder, following every movement and making the darvar explain every thought, and studied his fourth officer.

Elvar fell between halvar and darvar in height, making them—on average, at least—the second shortest of the var. Cat was tall for their var. Smallwolf was *not*, barely a fingersbreadth taller than Bellowforge himself, and she was small with it, too.

She was young, barely forty dances, and still had some time to fill out. Houseless and from a family of no grand name, her mage gifts had elevated her to officer and given her a chance to make a career of sailing aether ships.

She was also, in Cat's quietly considered opinion, very bright.

Even if what she'd just said made no sense.

"What do you mean, *air*?" he asked. "There's no life in this sphere, Officer Smallwolf. No aether. Nothing *lives* here, from what sense and magic can tell me."

"Air is required for life, but life isn't required for air," the young var replied carefully. "If my magic found *life* here where yours didn't, I'd presume I'd made a mistake. But I didn't hear any of the officers speak to *air*. Only life and aether.

"And I wondered."

"So, you checked," Cat said. He smiled. "*Well* done, Officer Smallwolf. Well done indeed. I had assumed that without life, there was no air."

He turned to Bellowforge.

"Engines Officer, it appears our destination has a regular air envelope," he told the darvar. "Does that impact the landing?"

"Yes," Bellowforge said exasperatedly. "Why did we... No, wait, I didn't ask, so why would anyone check. We're going to hit that envelope in, what, ten minutes?"

"Eight, Master Bellowforge," Smallwolf said instantly. "Envelope is ten cables deep; just covers the mountain at our landing site."

"Yeah, yeah, *that* impacts the *cursed* landing," the darvar confirmed. "Firing the engines. We need to shed less speed *later* but more speed *now*."

Cat was listening and learning, taking mental notes as the massive rockets at the base of the ship awoke again. Sparks of magic would ignite the stream of pure alcohol, turning fuel into flame—and flame would become, via the basic laws of the spheres, *push*.

"Watch the sextants, please, Captain," Bellowforge asked. "Our speed and distance to the envelope?"

"Distance is six cables," Cat reported. "Speed is one-seventy-five yards a minute."

They'd been *eight* cables away and moving at a cable a minute when Smallwolf had corrected their assumption. They were still over six minutes away, but they were coming in faster than Cat would have preferred in an aether ship.

The delicate sails that caught aether currents did *not* handle hitting air at speed well.

Of course, the lodestone core only reached about ten cables above the surface. Some of the highest mountaintops could easily lose a var who jumped too high—and often didn't have much air of their own.

Right now, the only thing pushing them toward Flame's Gem was the velocity they hadn't yet shed of their travel across the sphere from

Brokenwright. The whole process was making some sense to Cat, but it was still new.

"Lodestone pull before we hit the air envelope," he murmured aloud. Bellowforge probably knew that, but he wanted to be sure.

"Got it. Keep the sextants aligned for me," the darvar told Smallwolf. "We do not want to get this wrong."

The vertical orientation of the ship threw Cat's instincts off. Dances upon dances of training were telling him he was on the wrong part of the ship, that the lodestone keel should run the length of the ship and they should be landing on their side if they had to land at all.

Still, there were advantages to the design that he could see. Not, true, for a proper aether ship—but not all vessels that traveled the spheres were crewed wholly by the aethervar, the gobvar and elvar.

"Got the lode," Bellowforge declared. Cat felt the engines rumble to life again as the darvar spoke, slowing their descent further even as the worldlet tried to pull them to it.

"Speed one hundred yards a minute," Smallwolf declared. "Air envelope in one minute."

That felt fast to Cat. Aether ships sliced into air at an angle if they didn't stay above it entirely. The mountain a few leagues away was home to at least one dock he'd have aimed for if they'd still been sailing *Star*.

But *Star* was an aether ship and there was no aether. And Bellowforge insisted that His Dark Brothers would have gone for a wider, flatter landing surface than any mountain could provide—and there was a massive central plaza to the long-dead city that met his description.

"We're in the envelope," the fourth officer said. "I... I didn't even feel that."

Neither had Cat. Now that Smallwolf had reported it, he could. There was a different feel to *Void Flyer*'s motion now, a new heavy ponderousness that even the lodestone hadn't imposed on her.

"Ten minutes," Bellowforge declared aloud. "Then you can get out and look around. For now, everybody can just shut up and *wait*."

Cat suspected that the first time *he* landed *Void Flyer*, it wasn't going to be nearly as smooth. Bellowforge touched the cable-high void ship down in the broad flagstone plaza with barely a tremor.

"I'm going to check over the ship," the darvar declared. "Let me know if you need anything from me."

Cat chuckled.

"You've done more than enough, Engines Officer," he replied. "Small-wolf, stay up here and use the mirrors to keep a watch."

Several of the younger Hammerhead gobvar trooped into the room, someone having clearly realized he was going to need couriers to carry his orders through the ship. One of the two gobvar Masters—Axfall or Windheart, two elder gobvar who appeared to be in a relationship that didn't slow either of them down—had almost certainly sent the youths up.

"I need messages carried," he told the four young var, who came to a crisp-if-amateur impression of High Court Navy attention in response.

"One of you find Brushfire, one of you find Paintrock—and Axfall and Windheart," he ordered. Paintrock was the Master of Staves, who also served as the closest thing they had to a boarding-troop commander.

Because Hunter Paintrock was most definitely *not* a pirate. Anymore. But the skills he'd picked up in a "prior life" served Cat well.

"I'm going to collect the archmage and we will all meet at the exit ramp," he told the youths. "Paintrock is to gather a party. He knows what I mean."

Paintrock, Cat suspected, knew what kind of armed party should accompany the Captain and archmage onto a strange worldlet better than his *Captain* did.

After all, Cat had followed a conventional career path for the HCN until very recently.

CHAPTER

5

Bʀᴜsʜꜰɪʀᴇ ᴡᴀs ᴀʟʀᴇᴀᴅʏ ᴀᴛ ᴛʜᴇ ᴇxɪᴛ ʀᴀᴍᴘ ᴡʜᴇɴ ᴛʜᴇ ᴍᴇssᴇɴɢᴇʀ found her. She gave Statuebright a grin as the young gobvar emerged from the stairwell.

"Captain sent you for me?" she asked.

"Yes, elde—Officer Brushfire!"

"*Eldest sister* is still fine, Statuebright," Brushfire told her cousin. "What were his orders?"

"Meet him, well, here, sister," the young var said. "He was gathering the archmage and sent other messengers for the Masters of the ship."

"Thank you, Statuebright." Brushfire managed to *not* smile indulgently. Statuebright and the other teenagers were providing a valuable service, even if she seemed so *very* young and eager.

"You told me," Fistfall said. Her younger brother was the only other person in the storage well that held the folded ramp. "Should I get this unfolded?" He gestured at the ramp.

None of the Hammerhead Tribe were short for gobvar, an already-tall race, but Fistfall had fingersbreadths over most of the tribe. The only thing keeping Brushfire even *close* to matching her younger brother's height was that her horns curved more sharply up than his.

There was no question in her mind that Fistfall could get the ramp unfolded on his own through sheer physical size and strength. It would just be safer, faster and easier with the half dozen sets of hands it was designed for.

29

"No, brother, we'll wait for the Captain and the rest," she told him.

Fistfall had always been eager to please, but the loss of his on-again, off-again lover in Brokenwright had changed something in him. Brushfire couldn't put her finger on it, not yet, but she was worried that he'd lost some key support that kept him going.

The next arrival was the reason why she was less worried about her brother than she otherwise would have been. Blue-skinned, long-eared and clad in a set of crossed bandoliers *full* of battlewands, Hunter Paintrock managed to always stand *just* on the right side of insubordination.

And given how *vague* the concept of insubordination was on a private ship run by an archmage, that he even *found* the line was impressive to Brushfire. He'd also, however, become fast friends with Fistfall despite their different species and had clearly recognized the same issue Brushfire had.

"Big guy, help me with this, will you?" Paintrock asked. He was dragging a heavy, clanking bundle behind him. Brushfire didn't realize what the halberd-wands *were* until Paintrock and Fistfall unrolled the bundle to reveal the weapons.

An upsized version of the battlewands that filled Paintrock's bandoliers, the halberd-wands were also lengthy polearms with wicked striking heads.

"I didn't think we had any of these," Brushfire murmured to the Master of Staves as the rest of the landing party trooped in—about half-and-half elvar and gobvar, a mix that spoke to both Paintrock's agreement with the officer's attitude to the crew *and* the Master's ability to get the two var to work together.

Void Flyer's crew gave Brushfire hope for the future of gobvar in an elvar-dominated universe—and she knew *almost* as much of that hope rested on Paintrock as it did on Cat Greentrees.

"We didn't," Paintrock agreed. "I picked them up on the Ward. They were just *sitting* there while we were all getting onto the ship, and I figured they'd come in handy."

"Sitting there," Greentrees said, the Captain seeming to materialize with Bluestaves in tow. "In a locked armory behind an armor plate? I don't think the Brothers would have left weapons lying around."

"Something like that, I'm sure," the Master of Staves agreed brightly. "I've been giving these var"—he gestured at the dozen hands around them—"as much training as I could in the space we had. They'll do okay."

That gesture, Brushfire judged, included her brother. Who hadn't mentioned any such thing to *her*—but then, she was pretty sure Paintrock had been training Fistfall to use a storm stave back on *Star*, and that was most definitely *illegal*.

It hadn't stopped many pirates from training their gobvar crew on the arcane weapons, she was sure, but it was still against the law in all of the spheres of Court and Kingdoms for anyone to train gobvar how to use storm staves.

In case someone had *missed* that her people were tolerated at best in the Court and Kingdoms.

"The other Masters should be..." The Captain trailed off as two of Brushfire's oldest tribe members entered the room. The ramp's access point was a full quarter of a deck, but it was getting crowded.

"Ah. Thank you, gentlevar," Cat greeted Axfall and Windheart. He gestured around the gathered var.

"Office Brushfire, Archmage Bluestaves and myself will be leading a landing party," he told them. "Master Paintrock will accompany us, leaving the ship in the capable hands of yourselves and the other officers."

"Has anyone told Streamwater this?" Windheart asked carefully. "If the second officer is in command..."

"I spoke to Faith on my way down, before I tore the archmage away from his oven," Cat continued.

Brushfire, who had been as exposed to Bluestaves' insistence on handing everyone a muffin, cupcake or other baked good upon entry to his quarters while the halvar was "thinking," concealed a chuckle.

"I wasn't baking at this moment," Bluestaves said with a grin of his own. "I'd prepared that sweetroll especially for you, Captain. *I* knew I was going to need a few moments to finish getting ready."

Brushfire found it *fascinating* that the two men were slowly beginning to tease each other. Both, in their own way, had been extremely stiff when she'd met them. Some of that had been their interactions with *her*, but Cat especially had been stiff with *everyone*.

"If Officer Streamwater knows she's in charge, we'll make sure everything moves smoothly, Captain," Axfall promised. "Do we know what's here?"

"No," Brushfire said before anyone else. "Only what we've seen from the windows. This plaza was the best place to land *Flyer*, so we're figuring it's where the Brothers landed her, but that's all we've got."

"What about threats?" Paintrock asked.

"We know nothing," Bluestaves warned. "My divinations suggest it is not *safe*, but also that there is nothing alive in the city.

"Come. Let us get the ramp open and see what we shall see."

It wasn't until she walked onto the flagstones of the plaza and looked around that Brushfire truly understood what *nothing alive* meant. The plaza was easily a cable across in every direction, a gleaming expanse of white stone that had probably been used for celebrations and grand events once.

Around that two-hundred-yard white expanse of stone, however, was a half-cable of dirt with smaller paved avenues leading through it to the rest of the city. That, too, had been part of the plaza—but it had almost certainly held shrubs or grass or *something*.

Now it was brown and lifeless. The wind had claimed whatever life had once filled those fields.

"Over here, sir," Paintrock said. The Master of Staves had been second off the ship and had led two of his halberdiers off in what felt like a random direction.

Given the way he'd stopped and was inspecting the stone at his feet, Brushfire realized it hadn't been that random.

She followed Cat and Bluestaves over to the Master and saw what Paintrock had seen instantly.

"We guessed right," she told the Captain. "That looks like someone landed *Flyer* here, doesn't it?"

It was strange just how gleaming and clean the plaza still was. It was like even the lichen and weeds she would have expected to take over the place were dead.

It was *exactly* like that. *Everything* was dead.

It was creepy.

Still, that same extraordinary cleanliness made it impossible to miss the scorch marks. *Void Flyer*—she presumed, since Brushfire didn't know of any *other* void ships—had landed and taken off from there.

"Can we track where they went from here?" Brushfire asked.

"In this place? No," Paintrock said flatly. "There's no dust, Officer. No moss, no animal leavings… nothing." The blue elvar looked around and shivered. "I've never seen anything like this."

"No one has, Master Paintrock," Bluestaves noted. "These spheres are something unique in all the known universe. I do not know what created them, only that it has left nothing behind."

That wasn't entirely true, Brushfire suspected. She knew the other mages could feel it too. There was *something* there.

Hunger, the Seeker of His Dark Brothers had warned them. Only hunger awaited in the void spheres they were traversing.

"We are not limited to our eyes and the skills of tracking footprints in the mud, Master Paintrock," Bluestaves continued. He held out his hand, and a translucent image of a cat-sized flying lizard settled into it out of nowhere.

"My little friend," the archmage told the oracular spirit. "You know what I seek. Show me the way."

With a cheerful trill, the spirit leapt into the air. It circled the scorch marks three times, then took off toward one side of the plaza.

"I believe they went that way," Bluestaves said, gesturing after the spirit. "Shall we?"

The depot was both easier to find and far less imposing than Brushfire had anticipated. The oracular spirit circled around it and trilled victoriously, but the gobvar shaman wasn't entirely sure the creature was *right* in its claim.

It looked like nothing so much as an outdoor brewery, four massive tuns laid on their side and dug slightly into the dirt. Brushfire could see framing where some kind of cloth cover *had* been rigged over the supplies, but it had been long blown away by the chilly winds of the dead world.

"Perhaps we should have brought Bellowforge," she observed. "I *think* what we're looking for is a liquid, but I was expecting… more."

"From what my divinations tell me, it no longer rains here," Bluestaves observed. "The wind is the only danger, and the fuel barrels seem heavy enough not to be blown away."

"Paintrock, check the boxes and look for threats," Brushfire instructed with a sigh. She glanced over at Cat.

"Good call, Brushfire," he told her. Despite everything, his approval *still* sent a thrill of warmth down her spine.

She'd never get used to being the first officer of an elvar Captain—let alone to said elvar Captain treating her with respect and friendship!

"May I borrow some of the halberdiers?" Bluestaves asked. "I would like to investigate some of the surrounding structures. I have other work to do while we restock the ship."

"Fistfall, take three and accompany the archmage," Cat ordered instantly. "Brushfire, let's take a look at this 'fuel.'"

She nodded and fell into step behind Cat as her brother indicated three of the crewvar to follow him. Two of the var who fell into step with Fistfall, she observed, were *elvar*—elvar who didn't even blink at the big gobvar stepping into the nebulous role of "senior crew but not a Master."

"We need to talk about your brother, too," Cat murmured as he led her away from the landing party to check the closest tun.

"My brother?" She swallowed a moment of worry. She'd spent her entire *life* worrying about Fistfall—or, at least, *his* entire life—but she didn't think Fistfall had done anything to anger the Captain.

"Not a bad thing," the elvar assured her. He considered the big sideways barrel in front of them for a few moments, then delicately leapt to the top of it.

Brushfire wasn't sure if he'd used magic for the leap—but she doubted it. She didn't need it to follow him—but shamanic training covered many things. Cat *might* have needed it, but she suspected much of his agility was just years of practice.

"What has Fistfall done?" she asked, balancing on top of the tun as Cat knelt at a small spigot, tiny against the multi-yard-wide barrel.

"Nothing." Cat snorted. "Okay, a lot of things, but nothing I *mind*. No, Brushfire, the question is about what he *is*, not what he has done."

"I don't understand."

"Smell this," the Captain instructed. "Smells like high-proof liquor to me, which I think is what we want."

Brushfire swapped places with him, still concerned about what he meant about Fistfall. The "fuel" smelled much the same to her as Cat had said. She'd drunk her fair share of rotgut, liquid whose only virtue was its alcohol content, and she still wouldn't choose to drink this.

She wasn't sure *anyone* would survive drinking this—but *Void Flyer* ran on pure alcohol.

"I can't see anything else His Dark Brothers would have put in giant barrels here," she told her Captain. "How do we get it into the ship?"

"That's a question for Bellowforge, I suppose," Cat allowed. "Sorry, I didn't mean to leave you hanging on Fistfall. Did you know he was a mage?"

She stared at her Captain for a long few heartbeats. Fistfall, a mage? The big dumb lovable hunk of muscle who'd tried to take care of everyone almost as determinedly as *she'd* taken care of *him* since he was ten dances old?

"You're certain." Brushfire knew that her Captain had skills she lacked. Her training as a mage had been focused on the immediate skills of being first officer of an aether ship. They'd expanded it a touch now that they were aboard *Flyer* and not sure what magical skills would be useful, but she didn't have the breadth of training a proper mage would have.

"Yes. There are a couple of others in your tribe as well," Cat warned her. "Fistfall is the strongest, I think. Not quite up to you or me but definitely worth training.

"I didn't want to present that to him without asking you, though."

"Who would teach him? Who would make him a focus?" The answer to the second question was the same as the first, she realized.

"Our archmage was a teacher before he was an archmage," Cat reminded her. "And training young mages like Smallwolf has always been part of the Captain's job." He was looking away from her, but she could *feel* his smirk.

"And I should be doing a better job of training *you*," he continued. "The two Bellowforge teens are mages as well but too young for me to want to train them. Armand has to make Alloy a focus, and I've asked him to make personal foci for the other officers.

"He's going to make a few others," Cat noted. "Some general, a couple tied to the Hammerhead Tribe. But I want to put Fistfall at the front of the line, so to speak, and have him receive a personal focus as well.

"I *won't* pull your brother into that without your permission."

Brushfire shivered. She didn't know of *any* gobvar trained as mages in the Court and Kingdoms. The shamanic tradition thrived amidst the scattered gobvar communities, but it was born out of the need to work without foci.

The only people who trained gobvar as mages were the gobvar mages of the Clans… and *they* answered to the Quadrumvirate. Usually through Her Crimson Sisters and the First Crimson Sister.

"If we train gobvar as mages, they will be in danger back home," she said. She'd known that when she'd accepted a focus for herself.

"They will." Cat clearly wasn't going to argue *that* point. "But we're also going into the Clan Spheres. I don't know what your people's home spheres look like or what fate and challenges await us there.

"But I suspect that having more than one mage among our gobvar will serve us well. I *should* have assessed your tribe for mages when we first recruited them, but I was still blind."

"You saw more than most," Brushfire said quietly. She considered their precarious position atop the tun of void-ship fuel and chuckled. "I don't know, Captain. Fistfall is…"

"Very good at pretending he's as dumb as he is big," Cat told her, forcing her to stop and consider her words.

"He is my little brother, Cat," she said after a long moment. "I trust him to be many things, but it's not an act that he isn't smart."

Cat gestured for her to follow and hopped down onto the ground. Now she was *sure* there was no magic to him leaping and dropping distances twice his own height. Just wiry muscle and a *lot* of practice.

She followed him down, much less softly or lightly, and shook her head at him as he looked back at her.

"I know how he acts," Cat told her. "But I also know more about what Paintrock is teaching him than I think either of them realize."

Only as First Officer had Brushfire even *begun* to conceive just how much of an aether ship's magic could be turned to watch over the crew. Cat seemed to have an almost preternatural instinct, beyond even magic, of when to admit he knew what was going on versus pretending ignorance—and she suspected that he didn't even let *himself* realize many of the things he was ignoring.

"He's almost as fast a student as you are, Brushfire, and while his gift isn't as strong, the spheres still sing in his veins. I would offer him a focus and training, but you are his sister and the head of his tribe. If you would prefer that I do not, I will not."

And *that*, Brushfire realized, would be entirely unfair to her little brother.

"I'll talk to him," she decided aloud. "He is my brother and the choice should be his."

"Of course."

Cat nodded to her and turned away to call the landing party over.

They had work to do.

CHAPTER

6

"Watch out, milord," Fistfall rumbled. "Windhook, check the doors."

Armand started as the big gobvar cut in front of him before he could touch the door. He figured the building on the edge of the plaza was a warehouse of some kind, which meant it should have the space and some of the tools for the work he needed to do.

Windhook, a wild-haired elvar crewvar with void-black skin, stepped forward at Fistfall's orders. The other two members of the archmage's party took up covering positions, their halberd-wands aimed at the wooden doors.

Armand swallowed his original inclination to remind Fistfall that he didn't need *that* much protection. The crew wanted to keep him safe— and if the threat was something they could handle, that *was* the best use of resources.

And if it wasn't something four var with wand-halberds could handle, well, there was an archmage right behind them.

The door was closed but not locked. It only took Windhook a few heartbeats to work out the strange-looking angled lever to release the latch, and the elvar pulled the door open, stepping back with it and using the heavy wood panel as a shield.

Only silence answered them as they all looked into the dark interior. If there had been any lights, they'd long since run out of fuel or magic to keep running. The only reason the interior of the building wasn't the darkest thing Armand had seen recently was because he'd been looking out into the void.

"I think whatever is inside is as dead as everything else on this rock," Armand told his escort gently. He sent a trickle of power through one of the focus rings he wore, conjuring up a trio of tiny sparks of light that he sent flying into the warehouse.

"We go first, milord," Fistfall insisted.

Armand suspected the gobvar was keeping his comments simple out of a fear of embarrassing himself, not a lack of vocabulary. He didn't know the young gobvar *well*, but the fact that two *elvar* were taking Fistfall's orders without hesitation or question told him everything.

The second of those elvar, Sky, walked into the warehouse at Fistfall's side. Windhook and Catcher Hammerhead, a cousin of Fistfall's, stayed outside with the archmage.

What Armand *didn't* tell his escort was that the sparks he was lighting the room with were the same sparks he'd conjure in battle. They were bright enough to light the entire open area inside the building, but they were also both clever and dangerous.

If anything tried to hurt Armand's people, *he* was going to lay a sphere or two's worth of hurt on *them*.

"Looks clear, milord," Fistfall called back. "Just junk."

Junk, Armand realized swiftly, wasn't the *right* word. Everything in the warehouse was intact and probably quite useful for its intended purpose. It was just that said intended purpose was *decorating the square for festivals*.

"Well, I certainly don't need any of this," Armand said with a chuckle. "But I think the space is big enough and hardy enough for my work. Fistfall, can you get this cleared out?"

The gobvar surveyed the warehouse with a measuring eye and shrugged.

"I'll talk to the Masters and Officers," he said. "We'll want the resupply started, but then I figure we'll need to keep hands busy, and this will serve. Take a few hours, but we can get you space."

"Thank you, Fistfall."

Armand didn't pretend to understand the process of loading more fuel into *Void Flyer*. Setting it up had taken half of a clock-day—though it wasn't like worldlets in an outerlit sphere had *night*.

That, he suspected, was part of why the warehouse he'd taken over had no windows. The handful of outerlit spheres he'd been to had visibly tended toward fewer windows—and a greater ability to completely block off the ones they had—than his own home sphere, the Shining Eye. The titular Eye was one of the larger and brighter light crystals in the Kingdoms, though not *quite* in the realm of the handful that rivaled the High Court's central crystal.

Still, at least worldlets around the Eye mostly turned on their axes and had day and night. Outerlit spheres weren't so lucky, with the light from the outer sphere shining on them from *every* direction.

It did keep them from needing to worry about nightfall, at least, and allowed them to work for hours.

Once the tuns and *Flyer* had been brought together, the heavy-lifting part was done, and the Masters had sent a dozen crewvar into the warehouse to clear it out. They'd been somewhat excessive, Armand realized as he reentered the space.

He'd only *really* needed an area about ten yards on a side to set up the table Windhook and Sky were carrying in behind him. He wasn't entirely sure *why* he'd ended up with two elvar crew carrying his working gear... but he suspected that the slimmer and more lightly built var were actively avoiding letting the gobvar do all of the heavy lifting.

Pride did funny things.

It had also likely contributed to the fact that the warehouse was now *completely* empty. The main storage space was fifty yards wide and seventy deep, an echoing void lit only by the half dozen sparks Armand sent up into the air around them.

"Set the table up in the middle," he instructed. "My tools will be joining us in a few minutes."

"May I ask a question, Archmage?" Sky asked, their voice carefully respectful as they hauled the table past him.

"Of course, crewvar."

"Why are you setting up outside the ship? If you have all of your tools aboard *Flyer*, why not work there?" they asked.

"Because while archmagi don't like to admit to mistakes, the mistakes we *make* are spectacular," Armand said with a smile. "This process should be entirely safe for everyone, inside and outside my workspace. But if I *do* make a mistake, this building will... go away.

"And we can't afford to lose the *Flyer*."

He saw the var swallow as they put their end of the table down and glanced over at Windhook.

"We'll, uh, check in on your tools, milord," Windhook said quickly. "Should have everything here in a few ticks."

"This part seems easy enough," Brushfire observed.

She was whittling for Armand, carving a piece of wood down to match two others sitting on the table by her. There was quite a bit of wood around, for all that there were no living trees on the planet. Even dead trees were hard for wind to carry away, and the usual processes that consumed unliving wood didn't seem to be present there. So, doors and furniture and lampposts and decorative signs and such remained.

Even Armand had difficulty reading the script on the signs. He was *reasonably* sure the city they had landed in had been called Luminary Fire, but anyone who had known it by that name was long, *long* dead.

The strangest part of the city, to Armand, was that there didn't seem to be anything much *smaller* than trees left. The remains of trees and wood and a dozen other things told him nothing had consumed the dead, but there were no bodies. No shrubs or grasses or animal remains.

As far as var went, it was like they'd all left. But the absence of every *other* kind of life told a darker story.

"*Usually*, making the physical focus is the easy part," Armand agreed. He was working with metal for his part, a piece of spare hull panel that Bellowforge had removed to make a repair. Both part of the ship that the darvar had designed *and* something the artificer had handled repeatedly, he could feel its resonance to the other mage.

Unfortunately, metal wasn't something he could handle with a vise, a foot-lathe and a knife. So, the wand hung in the air in front of him, its temperature carefully controlled by his magic as he shaped it to his will.

"I am not sure if I am observing or being taught here," Brushfire told him, laying the third focus down.

"Yes," Armand replied. "Whether you *do* anything with the lesson is a very different question, but no one sits in on this process unless we are teaching them. And no one sits in on the binding of a focus who did not see it made."

He shrugged, a twist of his fingers finally forcing the last piece of metal into the place he wanted it. The binding process would reshape it yet again, but it needed to be close. *Especially* with metal.

"The binding is... also the Trial, isn't it?" Brushfire asked. She started work on a fourth focus, clearly able to both work wood and talk at the same time. "Fistfall or Axfall would be better at this part, in truth. They're carpenters. I just know roughly how to work wood."

"The Trial is more than that, but... yes, that's part of it," Armand confirmed. He carefully checked that the focus for Bellowforge was cool enough to touch before putting it on the wooden table. A fire from putting hot metal on wood would probably be the least damage he could cause in this process, but it would still be foolish.

"But it is easier to do the binding—both parts!—with a focus you've worked on yourself," he told her. "That's why you are *refining* wands I already carved. These will all need to be refined again in the binding to the users. They will be personally attuned foci."

Armand regarded the wands with a momentary hesitation. "Not the best kind," he conceded, as he'd warned Cat. "This one, for Bellowforge, is the only one that's *truly* personal."

"What do you need for a true personal focus?" Brushfire asked. "And what will these be if they're not personal foci?"

"Something of meaning or sympathetic connection to the intended mage," Armand explained, fully in lecturer mode even as he summoned a piece of wood to him and began to work it into the shape he needed.

"For Cat, a piece of *Star*. For Alloy, a piece of *Void Flyer*. For you, that horn—and no, I have *no* idea why it has sympathetic resonance to you."

His student chuckled.

"I was going to ask. But one of these will be for Fistfall, right?"

"Alloy, the officers, and Fistfall will be receiving personal foci," Armand confirmed. "I'm also planning to make two that are bound to your tribe, as backups and potential training tools, and four general foci because we should have had them on hand all along."

Brushfire was silent for a moment.

"I can get you something for him," she finally said. "But... that's a *king's ransom* in foci, isn't it?"

"And, given access to the five var I'm attuning personal foci to, less than a day's work," Armand replied. "Personal foci are expensive because they need an archmage to make them and bind them and attune them to their mage.

"Ready access to them is a perk of serving an archmage," he concluded. "Now that all of our var have proven their worth and loyalty, I wish them all armed and equipped to protect me and serve our cause as best as I can make happen."

He smiled. There was a reason archmagi were never short of money. He couldn't quite mass-produce general foci—while he knew archmagi who would have artisans prepare the blanks, requiring minimal work from the archmage, it still took time to make each one—but the eleven foci he was planning on making there would pay for half of a ninesail warship.

Possibly the *entire* warship, depending on who the personal foci were for.

"I'm going to work through these"—he gestured to the blanks—"but we're at least an hour from being ready to start binding. If you want to grab something for Fistfall's focus, go. We have time."

And while the difference between a true personal focus and a "mere" *attuned* focus might seem irrelevant to anyone who'd never wielded either, it was enough that Armand wanted as many of his people to have the real thing as possible.

CHAPTER 7

CAT COULDN'T PUT HIS FINGER ON WHAT WAS WRONG. EVERYTHING he *could* put a mental handle on was under control. They'd moved the tuns of pure alcohol over to where Alloy could hook them up to the *Flyer's* fuel tanks. The archmage was set up in a solid-seeming warehouse, and Cat had officers he could rely on at the peak of the ship, with eyes in every direction.

But the white stone city still felt *wrong*. There were no signs of violence, no signs of mass evacuation. Everyone was just *gone*. The city had to have held a quarter-million var or more, and there was no sign of *any* living thing.

So, he stood back from the work crews keeping the fuel flowing and watched the square and his ship, trying to put his finger on what was bothering him. Like a loose tooth, he kept poking at his unsettled feeling until it finally clicked into place.

There was no aether there at all. He was used to being able to feel the currents and draws of the aether around him—it was how he navigated. Even on worldlets, there *was* aether. It was lost in the background of the air and the lodestone pull, but he could still feel its currents and navigate with it.

That was how lighter ships and even full ninesails navigated inside an air envelope—but there, an aether ship would crash to the surface without its lift crystals. There was *nothing* for an aether sail to catch on.

What had *happened* there?

"Part of me wants to see something move," Paintrock said quietly. The ex-pirate had positioned himself by Cat, weapons readily to hand in case some strange enemy attacked his Captain. "Even if it was an *enemy*, at least there would be *something*."

"The Seeker said this place had been... consumed," Cat told his Master of Staves. "That all that was here was hunger."

"I can feel it," Paintrock said grimly. "Feel like fresh meat in the black market, being sized up by the kind of var that take and sell slaves."

That was not a situation Cat was familiar with. It wasn't a situation he had thought *anyone* in the Court and Kingdoms would have been familiar with, but he knew better than to think Paintrock was lying.

Paintrock was a strange var by Cat's standards, someone he would have arrested or even killed without a second's thought in his prior life—but he also owed Hunter Paintrock his and his archmage's life.

"All I feel is a hole where I should feel aether," Cat admitted. "It might even be the hunger. I can't believe I'm saying this, but I think I will be happier once we're *back* in the void."

Paintrock was silent for a few heartbeats, leaning heavily on the halberd-wand as he surveyed the approaches to the square.

"I have to agree, sir," he finally said. "I don't like t'void either, but out there, we can see what's coming. Here..."

"'*Ware to the north!*" Streamwater's voice suddenly projected out from the tip of the ship. "Something is *moving*."

Cat shared a long look with Paintrock.

"Archmage said there's nothing alive, didn't he?" the Master asked.

"He did. And I'll believe Armand Bluestaves over my own *eyes*. Which means whatever is coming... isn't alive."

Cat took a second to process what he'd just said, a hard shiver running down his spine as he drew his wand focus.

"With me, Master Hunter," he ordered. "Whatever this is, we need to get between it and the others."

As he stepped onto the north boulevard, Cat shivered at a sudden chill. For the first time since they'd entered the Warden of Fire sphere, he felt something more than emptiness where he could normally feel aether. A strange pressure rippled along his nerves, a feeling that wasn't his.

A *hunger* that wasn't his.

"I don't see anything," Paintrock told him, the elvar surveying the broad roadway at his side.

"And yet you know there's something coming, don't you?" Cat asked. "You can feel it?"

There'd been something in the Master of Staves' tone that warned him.

"Yeah. I can feel *something*." Paintrock turned back to the work crews and bellowed. "I need six with halberd-wands, *now*."

"Stay here," Cat ordered. "I'm going to go—"

"Not a chance," Paintrock cut him off. "You do remember who the Captain and sworn servant to the archmage here is, right? Because *that* elvar isn't particularly expendable. T'rest of us, on t'other hand, have jobs to do."

"And if you run into something swords can't kill?" Cat asked.

"Much as I'd like to leave you behind, Captain, I remember that shielding-everyone trick you pulled on the Ward. And I would be *delighted* if you came along," his subordinate said with a wide grin. "Just... *behind* the rest of us, please."

Cat considered *ordering* the other elvar to hang back, but one of the things they'd taught High Court officers along the way to Captain was *Don't give an order you know won't be obeyed.*

The High Court Navy had... *other* solutions to that situation, few of them pleasant. Cat's former life had been very hierarchical, though, and he'd *never* encountered a crew that would quite so bluntly tell the Captain to fall in behind the landing party to stay safe.

Somehow, he suspected he didn't want to *discourage* that level of loyalty. Regardless of his uncertainty of what was coming toward the square.

Seven of his crew spread out in front of him, with Paintrock in the center. The Master of Staves was the only one not carrying a halberd-wand, but Cat had seen the other elvar with both the battle-wands he carried and the sword at his waist.

Cat was deadlier, but Cat was a fully trained mage. Hunter Paintrock was an ordinary var, if a touch faster than most.

"It's getting bigger," Streamwater shouted down from the top of the ship. "I can't... I can't make out what it *is*, but it's getting bigger and moving down the road."

Cat didn't give any orders. Paintrock and the other crewvar were moving ahead, and he followed, weaving magic for exactly the spell Paintrock had half-jokingly referenced. The shield wouldn't stop much, but it should protect them all from the first strike or two from anything short of a ship's storm staves.

And he didn't like his second officer's confusion. He couldn't see anything himself, but Streamwater was a full cable above the plaza. She could see things he couldn't—and if she wasn't sure what she was look-ing at, that was concerning.

The first sign that they were approaching the oncoming strangeness was when the colors started to wash out around him. It could have been clouds, except that Flame's Gem didn't seem to *have* any clouds.

Cat blinked, wondering if he'd got something in his eyes, but the impression didn't change. There weren't many colors *left* in the long-dead city—mostly disturbingly clean white stone—but even the white was fading toward gray.

He drew his wand.

"I don't know what that is, but I really don't like it," Paintrock said softly.

"It feels hungrier, too," Cat agreed. He ran more magic into the shield, trying to protect his people not just from a physical attack but from the growing mental *pressure* trying to crush them down.

"Still not seeing anything moving, but there is something here, sir," the Master told him. "Crew, close up, ready halberds."

Six two-yard-long polearms leveled into a solid wall of points in front of Cat. He doubted his crew were well-enough trained with the weapons to hold that position for long, but there was *something* there.

"Move up," he ordered.

Paintrock now had a battlewand in each hand too, a half-step at most behind the halberdiers and two steps ahead of Cat.

Everyone in the party moving up the north boulevard was on edge—but Cat couldn't see anything. He could just *feel* the presence growing closer. He could feel his magic struggling against the strange pressure too, the world continually graying out and then regaining its color around him.

He wasn't sure what he saw first. There was no *conscious* recognition of a threat, but he felt *something* and swept his wand across the boulevard in front of them, conjuring a wall of fire to guard his people.

Moments after the flames took shape, the enemy hit them. Shapes in the smoke more than any physical presence, they were visible for the first time as Cat's power tried to drive them back.

And failed.

"Volley! Now!" Paintrock snapped. Six halberd-wands and the Master of Staves' own two battlewands cracked as one, hurling bolts of magical energy into the flames as the smoke highlighted the creatures.

The oncoming wraiths didn't even blink. The power of the wands cut through them and did nothing, sending a chill down Cat's spine as he summoned more power.

First, to *see* the enemy. Now he conjured a *field* of flame that draped itself across the dirt and stone alike, igniting everything it could and spewing up both magical and natural smoke in billowing clouds.

And in those smoke clouds, the wraiths of the Warden of Fire were clear at last. Even there, they were indistinct, caricatures drawn of var rather than full people. The flame itself barely seemed to slow them, and the halberd-wand blasts did nothing at all.

"Fall back," Cat ordered.

"We can't leave you to them," Paintrock objected.

"You're blocking my aim," he told his Master of Staves. "And the wands do *nothing*. Fall back!"

Paintrock almost physically yanked the other var directly in front of Cat out of the way, pulling the rest of the party back behind the Captain.

"And... *now*."

The focus Cat carried now was the most powerful he'd ever wielded, an extension of his will and magic forged by his new master. As a High Court

Captain with a House Focus, one restricted only to members of the House of Forests, Cat Greentrees had been a powerful and dangerous mage.

With a personal focus in hand and the lives of his crew on the line, the hunger of the Warden of Fire did not scare him.

The smoke let him see the wraiths, but the fire was only slowing the creatures. There had to be dozens—maybe hundreds?—of the creatures swarming through the smoke toward his people.

Where flame failed, he figured *light* could serve. He summoned power and channeled it through his focus, calling forth a wall of light and energy to block the road between him and the wraiths.

The half-visible swarm collided with the light barrier, and he felt the blows like they struck *him*. He fell back a step, the barrier moving with him, but it was *working*. He could feel the wraiths breaking apart as they struck his barrier, the light burning through shadow and hunger to shatter whatever power held them together.

But for every wraith his barrier burned away, two more replaced it. Each spirit that hammered into his wall of light felt like a punch to the gut.

He fell back another step. And another. The flames were flickering, the smoke fading, and he could *see* less of his foe than he had before—but he could feel their hunger and he could feel the impacts as each of them drove into his shield.

He was one mage holding an entire hundred-yard-wide boulevard alone. He wasn't sure just what was pushing against his will and power, but he knew he was holding it back.

Two more steps backward, almost involuntarily. He nearly stumbled, but Paintrock was there. The strangely colored Master of Staves had sheathed his own wands and caught Cat as he tripped, helping his Captain stay standing and keep the barrier up.

"I can't see them, cap'n," Paintrock admitted. "And I can't hurt them. But I *can* see that line of yours."

"They're pushing," Cat warned. Leaning on the other elvar, he straightened and faced the wraiths. Holding his wand parallel to his body, he concentrated on his spell and strengthened the wall.

"My kingdom for a stave gallery," Paintrock said grimly. "Because I don't think steel will serve where battlewands failed."

"Send for the other mages," Cat half-whispered. "I can hold them. For now."

"Sure, sure." Paintrock turned, not releasing Cat's shoulder as he shouted orders back to the rest of the party. "Get the officers! Smallwolf should be with the fuelin' party!"

Brushfire and Armand were working on the foci, Cat knew. Those were the two he *wanted* for backup, but there were stages in that process that could *not* be interrupted.

Smallwolf, Crane and Streamwater were his officers, and while he might *rather* have the first officer and the archmage, none of them were *useless*. And any support could make the difference there.

His barrier cracked. Just for a moment before he shored it up—but *something* got through.

"I can *see* that one," Paintrock snarled—and Cat realized he was right. He'd held the line against the insubstantial wraiths, but a handful of visible ones were now appearing in the push.

And the first of those to meet the barrier had cracked it, slipping through before Cat resealed the barrier. The lesser spirits had ignored the battlewands—but his warning to Hunter Paintrock died unspoken as the elvar charged the wraith with sword drawn.

Wands, magical tools forged for the use of the many, had done nothing against the lesser spirits. Steel, forged by "merely" advanced metallurgical processes, shouldn't have done more.

The *wraith*, a thing of translucent gray and washed-out sickly green light, certainly didn't expect it to. It ignored Paintrock, surging toward Cat at a speed no living thing could match.

Surging forward until Paintrock's curved blade struck where a living var would have kept their guts. The blade sliced through the creature, splattering its strange gray-and-green substance in a dozen directions and halting it in place.

For a moment, Cat thought that it was about to reassemble itself and tear apart Paintrock for daring to touch it. Instead, it held together in two pieces for a few moments and then collapsed, dissipating into nothingness as the pieces of its strange form hit the ground.

Another of the solider wraiths forced its way through a moment later. It didn't seem to be *walking* forward so much as *drifting*, the elusive impression of a var *so* vague that it could have been any of the four species.

Paintrock took several steps back, positioning himself in front of Cat and to the right, waiting for the wraith to come for the mage. For Cat's part, he *had* to focus on the wall of light. The solider wraiths might manage to push there where a dozen insubstantial ones had flashed to nothingness, but the lighter wraiths were still *there*, still *pushing*.

And the hunger he'd felt since landing on Flame's Gem rippled out from them in an unending wave that pressed on Cat's nerves and will. He'd found a balance now, one he could hold against all but the strongest of the wraiths, but he couldn't spare a drop of attention or power for the ones that broke through.

But the ones that broke through found Hunter Paintrock waiting for them. The Master of Staves lacked his Captain's magic, but he had a fine blade and an indomitable will. Cat suspected it was the elvar's *will* that mattered, more than the sword, but as he saw Paintrock dodge around the strikes from the second wraith and slice it open from ground to helm, he knew that few mortal var could match Paintrock's moves.

A third wraith tried to take advantage of Paintrock's distraction, only for a halberd-wand to stab from out of Cat's vision. The gleaming blade embedded itself in wraithstuff, and if, for a moment, it looked like the sword wasn't enough, the fist that followed *was*.

Fistfall Hammerhead was, after all, the biggest gobvar Cat had ever seen, and the pinned wraith had no chance against the young var's size, strength and will.

A blow that would have broken a mortal's skull off their neck *splashed* as it plunged into the creature's form. Between blade and blow, the creature seemed to recoil from Fistfall and then shatter.

Cat grinned, but two more wraiths broke through his barrier as he did, and a chill ran through him. These *things* weren't creatures, not really. They were a manifestation of something—something he *couldn't* fight.

Something he wasn't sure he could outlast.

"On your left," a young but determined voice told him. Bogsong Smallwolf stepped into his view, her own focus raised high. Power flowed from her to join his own channel, reinforcing and aligning with his spell.

"And your right," Crane added. The tall elvar doctor was, though Cat would never *say* so, the weakest mage of *Void Flyer*'s officers. Still, the power of mages didn't add strictly. Three mages together were far stronger than merely the sum of their parts.

And his officers knew how to follow his lead. The two wraiths between them and the barrier were outmatched by Hunter and Fistfall, and Cat stepped forward as his crew cleared the way.

His officers stepped with him, and *this* time, when the barrier hit a trio of solider wraiths that had been about to breach it, the wall of light highlighted those wraiths in power—until they simply came apart.

Then, as strangely as it had begun, it was over. There was no pressure on the wall, nothing moving in the smoke, and color slowly began to seep back into the world.

"Is that... it?" Crane asked.

"I hope so," Cat replied. "See to Fistfall."

He gestured to his first officer's younger brother.

"I'm still not sure what those things were, but I *am* sure that he shouldn't have put his *fist* in one of them!"

BRUSHFIRE AND ARMAND JOINED THE OTHER OFFICERS IN THE AFTER-math of the chaos. The work parties handling the fuel kept going, but there were a lot of worried-looking crewvar scattered seemingly randomly around the square.

Leaving Armand to talk to Cat, Brushfire gestured the three ship's Masters over to her.

"Crew and family are bothered, Officer Brushfire," Windheart said before she could speak. "They need to be put to work, but the things we know how to do on Flyer can't be done while fueling."

"We can put up barricades," Paintrock suggested, the Master of Staves sounding surprisingly subdued to Brushfire. "But I'm not sure they'll do much."

"They need to give the crew something to do and give us a place to set up watchvar," Brushfire told the three Masters. "Get me walls, chest-high to a gobvar. Rig up towers, ten yards high at least.

"Get eyes on each road coming into the square," she continued. "We need to know what's coming."

"Wands and bows won't do much," Paintrock warned. "Took magic to stop the last bunch."

"And we have less than half a dozen mages, Master of Staves," Brushfire said. "So, having the crew see them coming means we can be in the right places."

"Aye. Aye," he repeated slowly, then shook himself like a wet dog and put on his usual unstoppable grin. "A shock to the spirit, whatever the voids that was. We might be done with them?"

Brushfire shook her head silently.

"I'm not the Captain," she noted. "But I can feel this place. It *hungers*—and it's the hunger that came for us, isn't it?"

"Aye," Paintrock repeated again. "Steel works, but I think it's as much our *will* as our *steel* that held them off the Captain. And *I*, for one, have will to spare."

"I know, Master of Staves." She looked at the two older gobvar. "Brothers?" she asked them softly, their first officer but also their tribal shaman… and their niece.

"It's a good plan," Windheart said swiftly. "Axfall, do we have the wood to build that?"

"We hauled a bunch of signs and similar out of the warehouse we cleared for you and his lordship," the carpenter said. "We might have to choose between towers and barricades, though. Or maybe break open some more buildings."

"Watchtowers first, then barricades," Brushfire told her tribesvar. "And break open whatever you need to, my friends. No one here is going to complain."

"Except the dead," Paintrock said, his cheerful tone ringing ever so slightly false. "But your brother and I already beat *them* off once."

"Fistfall?" she asked.

"Yeah. *Wand* part of halberd-wands didn't do much, so he joined us and stuck the *pointy* bit in one of the wraiths," Paintrock said, his enthusiasm solidifying back to his usual self. "Then punched it, which seems a tad less smart, but, well, Fistfall."

Brushfire chuckled. She'd had that conversation with both Armand and Cat, and only the archmage *really* seemed to think her little brother was smarter than he tried to appear. And yet…

"It worked?"

"It worked," Paintrock confirmed. "Like I said, it's *will* that matters, not steel. And like a few of us var around here, Fistfall Hammerhead has *will* to spare."

And power, too, which would have helped. Brushfire had to wonder if even an untrained mage's fists would carry a spark a regular var's wouldn't.

"Get the crew moving," she ordered. "If we get things set up *right*, no one else is going to have to punch the things.

"Whatever they are."

"They are not actually the spirits of the dead."

Armand Bluestaves' precise tones laid that statement out like a law of reality as Brushfire joined the conversation.

"They sure as spheres *looked* like it," Cat countered. "Half-translucent forms of var, charging down the street."

"I'm not clear on what they are, Cat, and I won't pretend I am," the archmage replied, giving Brushfire a nod as she approached. "But I *have* encountered true undead before. Ghosts or animated corpses... neither match what you met today.

"More, there is a *feel* to necromancy that this place does not have."

"This place feels fucking awful to be in," Brushfire told him. "Necromancy is worse?"

Armand laughed bitterly.

"I cannot believe I am saying this, but no. This feels worse. Necromancy feels *different*. This is..."

The archmage trailed off into silence as Alloy joined the three of them.

"Just what have you brought my ship into?" the artificer demanded.

"The void spheres," Cat said grimly. "I suspect, Officer Bellowforge, that we are going to find these *things*—these wraiths, I suppose—in every sphere of this journey. Whatever tore aether and life from the heart of the Imperium created them in the process."

"Yes and no," Armand argued. "They're part of the hunger that defines this place, but I don't think they were created by the spell. They're... an afterimage."

He sounded surer of himself now, and Brushfire gave her archmage a prodding look.

"Armand?"

"A big-enough spell leaves fragments behind," he told them. "Really, *any* spell does, but for most magics any of us work, those fragments dissipate in breaths. Making the arcane devices that maintain our civilizations is a continual effort to find ways to make spells survive the casting.

"This spell wasn't *meant* to survive, I don't think. But it was so large, so powerful, so destructive... it created an afterimage with a life of its own."

"The hunger we all feel," Cat guessed.

"Exactly. The wraiths aren't part of the spell, I don't think," Armand concluded. "They are pieces of that hunger made manifest. They take the form of var because that's what the spell consumed, so those are the forms the afterimage knows.

"These spheres are still hungry, despite all that was destroyed here. And we have been... attacked by that hunger."

"Which means it doesn't matter how many wraiths we burn or drive off," Cat said grimly. "Because it will just generate more."

"I *presume* the manifestation has only a limited ability to send forth pieces of itself like that," Armand replied. "But... yes. It will marshal whatever resources it has, and we will come under attack again."

"Then I will see to the fueling and find out how long we have," the Captain told them. "You should finish your work, Archmage. But I suggest we should, perhaps, not start anything new."

CHAPTER

9

THE FEELING OF HUNGER AND PRESSURE WAS STARTING TO WEAR ON Armand. It was getting heavier, growing with each passing tick of the clocks aboard *Void Flyer*.

He was beginning to realize that he perhaps shouldn't have started a process as delicate as making foci on a worldlet he knew nothing about, but everything they had seen and done had said that Flame's Gem was dead and empty.

And *dead and empty* was unpleasant but should have been safe.

"Brushfire, keep one ear for trouble outside," he instructed as he laid out the foci he was *definitely* going to finish before they left. Alloy and Fistfall's foci were almost done; a few tweaks and then he'd empower them.

None of the broader-use foci were getting done. The three foci he'd prepared to be attuned to specific individuals were almost ready, so he'd finish those if he could. None of the five he was going to complete would be bound to their user there—there was a far lower risk of catastrophe doing that than empowering them in the first place.

It was this stage, where Armand linked the objects he'd made to the underlying magic of the universe, that was dangerous. The links would be quiescent, silent, until he bound them to the users—and both stages required an archmage's hand—but once the link was *created*, they could move the foci safely.

"And you?" Brushfire asked.

"You're here to watch me," Armand said with a chuckle. "Because two of these foci are now at the stage where we must either complete them or abandon them. And I *can* complete the three for the other officers.

"The rest can and clearly *should* wait. But those five, I must now begin the process."

"And once begun, you cannot be interrupted?"

It wasn't really a question, but he nodded acknowledgement as he turned back to the magically shaped metal that would become Bellow-forge's focus.

"I will watch and stand guard," Brushfire promised.

"Thank you."

Armand concealed a smile as he lifted the focus from the workbench with a touch of magic. He had never doubted, for one moment, that Brushfire would find the right balance between learning from him and watching over the crew.

This moment was the dangerous one. This was the line that divided mage from archmage, the Trial that killed most of those who attempted it—and then became a regular, somewhat ordinary-if-dangerous, task for the archmagi themselves.

He reached into himself, to the pulsing magic that he registered as a second heartbeat beneath his own. There were a hundred names for the energy he was touching. The Song of the Spheres. The Weave. The Veil. The True Power.

Armand called it the Source, the remaining power of the creation of the universe, the energy that sustained and created *everything*. Even there in the void spheres, where some dark magic had torn away life and aether from every world and stone, the Source remained.

He became a link between the beat under his heart and the metal wand in front of him, until the enter room seemed to *thrum* in time with the rhythm of the Source of all magic. Then, half instinctively and half guided by practice and training, the fingers touching the focus twisted.

A portion of the Source plunged into the focus, and he pulled his own power back. As his own power and link retracted, a softer beat remained. One he'd never mistake for an archmage's link or for a var's heartbeat, but one he could sense nonetheless.

One down.

There was a risk to rushing the process. A steady rhythm, smooth and safe, was both the easiest and safest way to complete his work—but Armand also knew that he needed to complete the five foci he'd decided on swiftly.

No one except *maybe* Alloy knew how long the fueling process was going to take—and Armand hadn't garnered the impression that his artificer had more than an educated guess. They didn't know how much alcohol was in each tun. They weren't even entirely sure how much fuel was *left* in *Void Flyer*.

Armand hoped that his foci work wouldn't trap them on Flame's Gem after the fueling, but he had a grim feeling that he would regret not completing personal foci for the officers and Fistfall.

And archmagi learned not to ignore any feelings that were *that* explicit!

He had completed Streamwater's, the third of the batch, before he realized that Brushfire had left and he was alone in the warehouse. The foci for Crane and Smallwolf were hanging in the air, the final preparations complete.

With the rhythm of the Source ringing through his workspace, Armand was even more stuck than he'd told the others. He couldn't leave. Brushfire *could*—and he could hear the sounds of fighting outside, shouting and the crash of magic.

The hunger of the Warden of Fire still pressed in on him, like *he* was the meal the leftovers of the ancient spell wanted to consume. It challenged his link to the Source, making the rhythmic beat that filled the impromptu workshop harder to sustain.

Not only could dropping the link cost him the last two foci on the spot, but Armand also wasn't sure he could reestablish it. The Warden of Fire was broken in more ways than he'd ever realized. He needed to research the strange wraiths and the hunger that filled the sphere, but he didn't know if he'd even brought the right books.

The plain, easily adjusted wand focus he'd picked for Crane drifted into the air in front of him as he heard the chaos of battle magic through the rhythm in the warehouse.

He *needed* to focus, to complete the work in front of him. The line would be held to keep the resupply going. He knew, in his bones, that Cat and Brushfire had this under control.

There was a strange power to this world and sphere. The hunger of the ancient spell was unlike anything he'd ever known, but *there*, in the Warden of Fire, it didn't have the strength to overcome those two.

The rhythm grew louder in his ears, the steady drumbeat drowning out the sounds from outside the warehouse as he concentrated on the fourth focus. An unheard *click* slipped a piece of the Source into the wand, and it settled delicately to the work table.

The cadence quieted as his magic lowered from crescendo, and Armand studied the last focus with scant favor. He was half-tempted to let it go—but that same niggling thought that told him he'd needed to make the officers' focuses at all told him that Smallwolf's focus was at *least* as important as the others.

Even an archmage, he suspected, wouldn't be able to tell the elvar first and second officers of their ship that he was giving the *third* officer a personal focus first. He needed to finish the last wand—and, thankfully, he realized the sounds of struggle outside the warehouse had faded.

Whatever assault had hurled itself against his people had been beaten off as he'd expected. His sworn servants, even if Bellowforge was still lacking a focus, had the strength to stand off this danger.

There.

He knew very little of what he faced, but he suspected it was weak there. As they drew closer to the center of the spell, to the center of the old Ironhand Imperium, it would get stronger.

It was their *next* stop where they would face the greatest danger, hence the stop where his people would need the foci he was creating.

A moment of rest and internal attention, leaning into the beat of his link to the Source, and he felt as much as heard Brushfire return.

"We're still loading the ship," she told him. "Alloy estimates another two hours at least. There is time."

"I need to finish the last of these," Armand said. "Then bind them. If I can do that here, it will be better.

"How bad is it?" he asked.

"We lost two crewvar this time," Brushfire told him flatly. "They came from the west and we were figuring them to come from the north again. If the next attempt is stronger still..."

"Then I must finish my work so that I can join you," he told her. "Come. Hold the light for me. I am tiring but this *must* be finished."

CHAPTER

10

Three times more, the wraiths hurled themselves against Cat's people. Three times more, the watchvar at the top of the rocket or in the hastily assembled watchtowers gave warning, sending Cat or Streamwater rushing to bar the way.

Barricades of wood and stone and dirt proved as useless as the watchtowers proved critical. The wraiths had no issues rising over mounds or even sharp inclines. Whatever they truly were, the pull of Flame's Gem's lodestone core was more of a *suggestion* to them than a requirement.

Four times, now, Cat and Streamwater had conjured barriers of light and power that had hurled the strange attackers back. After the first time, neither of them had worked alone. Cat wouldn't have wanted Crane or Smallwolf to hold the line on their own, but they could definitely *help* the senior officers stand off the enemy.

It wasn't perfect. An elvar and a gobvar from his crew were dead, their flesh seemingly untouched but their life essence *torn* from them by the strange magic.

"How much longer on the fuel, Alloy?" he asked the darvar.

"Not much," Bellowforge told him. "I *did* design better methods for tracking fuel than just tapping on the tanks, you know."

"I wondered," Cat said dryly. "And?"

"His Dark Brothers didn't care. Or understand." The artificer growled. "They were clever and sneaky and powerful, but void take me before I'd call them *smart*."

"I suppose I know what you mean," Cat allowed. It was much how he'd describe his old superiors in the High Court Navy, especially after they'd cashiered him for disobeying orders to save his ship and warn them of a new threat.

Not that he'd describe them that way to anyone else. He might have some separation from the game of status and face that defined the Great Houses and the elvar's Navy, but sooner or later, he'd be back in that game.

Even if he stuck with Armand Bluestaves, well, archmagi lived longer than other var, but halvar were the shortest-lived of the four var. He'd lose Armand in a hundred dances or so—longer than he'd been exiled for—and then the law of House and blood and face would define his life again.

"Keep things moving," he ordered Alloy. "I'm going up the watchtower."

"Lord Bluestaves!"

Cat turned as he heard Paintrock's shout, a sense of relief filling him as he saw Brushfire and Bluestaves emerge from the warehouse. That meant *their* work was done and only the fuel was keeping them there.

And they were both safe, which was only so certain when dealing with foci and the Source.

"Armand," Cat greeted his master, crossing to the two other mages and trading warm nods with Brushfire. "You're done?"

"I didn't feel that spending the time on general foci was worth it this day," Armand said. "Alloy, come here!"

The artificer turned back to them from his focus on the hoses, visibly sighing before he walked over to them.

"I'm not seeing any clever ways to speed this up," he warned.

"But there is still no time for ceremony. Draw blood and smear it along the focus," Armand ordered, drawing a strangely perfectly formed shaft of steel from inside his bag.

There was no silk or similar wrapping as there had been when Cat had received his focus from their master, simply the focus. *Simply* an arcane device built for and attuned to the darvar.

Alloy was clearly familiar with the concept. He took the metal rod and weighed it in one hand.

"This is from *Flyer*, isn't it?" he asked.

"Started as the discarded plate from one of your repairs after we fled the Ward," Armand confirmed. "Now mark it with your blood, Alloy, if you would be my var as you swore."

"Aye. I swore it and I meant it. I didn't ask for this."

Bellowforge wasn't really objecting, and he pricked his thumb on a knife, smearing a streak of blood along the wand. Cat watched with interest as Armand placed his hand on the focus, both var now touching the steel.

He'd been a tad distracted when Bluestaves had attuned his own focus and the one for Brushfire. Now he *felt* the magic flow from some hidden well inside the focus—and Armand's will flowing into it, matching it to Alloy's power as the darvar wondered at the process.

It took moments, but when it was done, Alloy Bellowforge was a true mage-artificer again, with a personal focus to summon his power.

"Oh," he sighed heavily. "It's been... a dance, at least, since I held a focus, Lord Archmage. I did not ask for this," he repeated, "but *thank you.*"

"I would have you fight by our side at your full strength, Alloy Bellowforge," Bluestaves said. "You are either my var and arming you with that focus is to my advantage, or you are not and I am fucked anyway."

Cat swallowed an uncharacteristic snort of laughter at the archmage's unexpected crudity.

"The other officers. Fistfall," Armand continued. "Do we have ti—"

"*'Ware to the north!*" a watchvar bellowed. "More movement. *Big* movement."

"That's what I was afraid of," Cat murmured. "The attacks were getting weaker. Which meant either they were running out... or gathering strength for one *big* push."

He grinned at the other three.

"Ready to stand with your archmage, Officer Bellowforge?" he asked. "Because if the wraiths waited to put together a heavy blow, I think they waited too long."

"*'Ware to the west!*" another watcher bellowed, and Cat's confidence shivered.

"*'Ware to the east!*"

"*'Ware to the south!*"

The wraiths had taken as long as Cat would have hoped to put together their heaviest blow, but they might have gathered *enough* strength.

Cat considered the situation for a few more precious moments. They *now* had four senior mages, including their archmage. Except that Armand had just made half a dozen personal foci, and Cat honestly did not know how much that took out of him.

"Can you fight, Armand?" he asked.

"As well as anyone here," the archmage replied. "Do you have a plan?"

"Maybe." Cat glanced back to the ship and saw Streamwater leading Crane and Smallwolf over toward them. He gave his second officer a grateful nod, then turned back to the others.

"We have six mages and an archmage," he reminded them. "Can you fight *alone*, Armand?"

Armand chuckled.

"If I cannot, none of you can stand in my place," the archmage reminded him. "I can hold a path."

"Okay. You go north," Cat ordered. "Brushfire, you take Crane and go west. Smallwolf, you're with me at the south. Streamwater, Officer Bellowforge *just* got his first focus in dances. Can you keep him alive while he fights with you?"

"I am not helpless, Captain."

"But you are out of practice," Streamwater noted. *Flyer*'s second officer was one of the oldest var in the crew—the two gobvar Masters were older than her, but Cat wasn't sure if anyone else exceeded the second officer's two hundred–odd dances. "I can watch your back while you remember the steps."

"Go," Cat urged them all. "Our people are depending on us!"

His youngest mage fell in beside him as he watched the other mages scatter. He gave Smallwolf a reassuring smile and then set off south. He was guessing as to where the heaviest blow would fall—he was, in fact, guessing that the blows at each quarter would be roughly equal.

If his suspicions about what they faced were correct, it wasn't like the wraiths were being gathered from somewhere. They simply *existed* when the underlying hunger of the sphere had the energy to create them.

So, if whatever intelligence was behind this had decided to come at them from every direction, it would probably simply split its energies four ways.

Assuming, of course, there *was* an intelligence behind this.

Cat wasn't sure, and he hadn't had a chance to ask Armand what the archmage thought.

"Here they come," Smallwolf told him, and he shivered as light and color slipped out of the world around them.

C H A P T E R

11

G HOSTS, AS B RUSHFIRE UNDERSTOOD THEM, WERE USUALLY LITTLE
more than visual memories. A manifestation of memory and emotional
energy, given shape by magic or by the sheer *amount* of emotional energy,
they couldn't actually *do* anything except repeat a given series of motions.

She knew there were other, less-harmless forms of undead. Very
little beyond their *existence* was common-enough knowledge to have
been included in the education of a ship's hand turned shaman—and
if Armand and Cat knew more, it hadn't been important enough to
include in her abbreviated and condensed training as a mage.

From the reactions of those two, though, Brushfire suspected that
the wraiths of Flame's Gem were something else again. As a renewed
host of insubstantial creatures surged toward her along the west boulevard, all that *really* mattered was that her crew, her tribe and her *friends*
were in danger.

Her focus was carved from a black grazer horn that *something* had
told Armand Bluestaves would work for her. She wasn't entirely sure
what the connection was herself—a horn for a var with horns seemed a
bit *too* on point—but she couldn't deny it.

Power flickered through the wand, though the horn was cool to her
touch.

"Are you ready, Officer Crane?" she asked the other mage. Crane was
the ship's doctor, the elvar augmenting relatively weak personal magic
with the specialized training of a mage-healer.

This was not Crane's specialty, but only magic could really hurt the wraiths. The half dozen crewvar who took up position around them with swords and wands were to protect the two mages doing the real fighting.

"I am ready," the elvar intoned, their own focus—a red-painted staff as long as Brushfire's arm, quite distinct from the forearm-length wands Armand made—held in front of them with both hands.

Brushfire watched the red fade out of the staff as the wraiths approached, the entire world losing color and fading into shades of gray, then summoned her own power and faced the horde.

The last time she'd fought the things, she'd reinforced a barrier already being drawn in the air by Faith Streamwater. The second officer had followed Cat's lead, conjuring a barrier of light that held the wraiths back.

Now, *leading* the defense, Brushfire saw the issues with Cat's tool. It had been the plan of desperation as the crew's attack had failed, and since it had *worked*, they'd repeated it. But it wasn't an efficient use of power, and their defenses had drained their mages badly.

Instead of a wall of light, she conjured a *source*. A gleaming half-orb, its flat surface facing toward her and her var, that hung in the air before her and projected wave upon wave of brilliant light toward the onrushing horde.

"That's not—"

"It's working," Brushfire cut Crane off. "Back me up, Emberlight."

The elvar looked oddly bothered by Brushfire's use of their first name, but their staff reached to touch the half-sphere of light, the doctor's power adding to Brushfire's as their light blazed out.

Brushfire focused on her half-orb, extending and shaping it so that its light swept the entire width of the western boulevard, highlighting and then annihilating the wraiths as they approached.

There didn't seem to be much thought or tactics to the enemy. Even animals turned back from dangers they couldn't face. The wraiths just kept coming, trying to push through the blazing light Brushfire and Crane filled the road with.

They had learned to breach Cat's wall, but there *was* no wall for them to push through this time. Only light, streaming out from a spell that Brushfire realized was taking more out of her than she'd expected.

As her muscles spasmed with magical fatigue and she found herself forced to kneel to stay upright, she realized she might have misjudged which spell was more inefficient.

Still, she and Crane held their impromptu ember together until the light no longer silhouetted half-visible forms. Whether the wraiths had given up, retreated or all been destroyed didn't matter.

They weren't coming from the west anymore.

The light from the Warden of Fire's outer sphere felt like it was burning down on them all when Brushfire returned to the center of the plaza, limping against muscles drawn taut by overuse of her magic.

"I have ideas," Bellowforge said flatly as the mages gathered again. "I think, with some time and the tools I brought aboard *Flyer*, I can make lamps that will recreate the power of the walls. They will not be perfect or as powerful, but with some help, I should be able to make a dozen or more of them."

"Anything that allows the rest of the crew to fight these things," Cat said wearily. "Please tell me we are done fueling. Even with Armand with us now, I do not know if we can stop another attack like that."

Brushfire looked around, swiftly counting the crew. They hadn't lost anyone else, but the mages looked exhausted to a var. Her particular trick had drained her more than she'd expected, but it had also *worked*.

"We're done."

All nine mages turned as one as Fistfall spoke.

"You're sure?" Alloy asked.

"I'd like you to check so we can be, yeah," the young gobvar agreed. "But Treevoice got herself covered in alcohol when it overfilled, so I think so."

Brushfire couldn't help snorting in laughter at the image.

"Sounds right. I'll check anyway."

"Please," Fistfall confirmed. The big var looked around the mages as Alloy took off toward the ship. "If we're fueled, are we good to go?" he asked. "I think I speak for everyone when I say this sphere has…"

"Lost any appeal it had," Cat finished. "It was good to get out of the *Flyer*, but Flame's Gem seems determined to *eat* us."

Brushfire saw Fistfall's eyes flicker to the shoulder bag Armand was carrying. She'd spoken to him about the possibility of training as a mage, but from his eyes, it looked like she needed to check in.

"You have a beat, brother?" she murmured.

"Yeah," he agreed. "Back on the ship?"

"Go," Cat urged her. "It will be some time before the wraiths return, if they do. We should be gone by then."

"Are you all right, first-brother?" Brushfire asked him once they were away from the others. *Void Flyer*'s spaces were both continuously connected to each other through the pillar of ladders and landings that rose her complete height, and also easy to find a corner in.

"Two more dead," Fistfall said. "I... I'm not used to losing friends, sister. Nor to some of those friends being elvar, but that's another problem."

"You're telling me that this crew are the first elvar you've got on with ever?" Brushfire asked. She knew him better than that. Some, maybe even *most*, elvar were prejudiced bigots, but she knew her brother. He'd always found a way to charm people and make friends.

Some of that appeared in his face as he chuckled.

"Fair," he allowed. "But most elvar *friends* I've made have been for a night of drinking or maybe a few days in port. Or ship's crew, where we *had* to be friendly, at least.

"This lot seem that much more... willing to look at us and think of us as var, not beasts."

"Especially Paintrock," Brushfire suggested.

"I'm not gonna say the pirates seem better than most," Fistfall counted. "But yes, Paintrock never saw any of us as anything but var and crewmates. I can see how so many of our var end up with pirates."

So could Brushfire. But Brushfire had understood that, at least in theory, a *long* time earlier.

"Another mage would have saved lives today, wouldn't it?" he asked her, switching topics like a falling mainmast.

Brushfire swallowed, but if Fistfall deserved *anything* from her, it was the truth.

"Aye. If we'd had another mage to cycle through while Bluestaves was occupied, we might have been able to keep everyone safe," she admitted. "But we didn't *have* another mage today, my brother. We couldn't."

"Because I—"

"Would never have been measured by, let alone welcomed into, any academy of Court and Kingdoms," Brushfire said harshly. "Only now, when Cat and the archmage *need* power, do even they think to look at our tribe.

"I don't want you to feel you must," she told him. "You'll be Bluestaves' var if you take that focus from him, brother."

"As you are," Fistfall pointed out. "As the Captain is. Bellowforge, too. And I thought the rest of us were too?"

"The rest of you are the archmage's *employees*," Brushfire told him. "That isn't nothing, but it isn't a lifetime oath of service. What Cat and I are to him? What Bellowforge chose to become? We are Armand Bluestaves' var. He can release us from that bond, likely plans to if he even realizes it ties as tightly as it does, but it has real meaning—legally. Morally. Magically."

"And if I take a personal focus from the archmage's hand, that binds me?"

"It does," she confirmed. "The officers... don't care. They know, but they are more aware of the advantages than the costs. If you are Armand's var, brother mine, and he and the tribe part ways, he must either release you or you will go with him."

"Sister mine... I go with *you*," Fistfall told her gently. "So long as you are the archmage's var, I'll take the same oath and walk the same path. If it helps me protect the crew and our family? A thousand times again."

Brushfire sighed.

"I worried when I saw you looking at the bag of foci," she admitted. "I want you to have that focus and the training they promised. But I want you to know what taking it means."

"I get the feeling, sister, that being a gobvar mage in the Kingdoms is going to be ugly," he said quietly. "But if I can protect our tribe, I'll do it. Told you that before."

"I know." Brushfire pulled her brother in a rough embrace. "And there's no one I'd rather have watching my back, little brother."

CHAPTER 12

ARMAND KNEW HE WASN'T AS TUNED IN TO THE FEELINGS AND morale of the crew as Cat and Brushfire. That was part of what he *had* the elvar and gobvar mages for, to run the ship that was meant to get him into the Clan Spheres.

Somewhere in the Clan Spheres, after all, was the source of the dragons that had burned every ship in Cat's squadron except his. The dragons that Armand's visions had shown conquering and enslaving *everyone.*

So, Armand's duty drew him to the spheres of the gobvar, where a halvar couldn't pass unnoticed. Worse, Her Crimson Sisters controlled the border spheres on the gobvar side. Even without exposure to Brushfire and the rest of the Hammerhead Tribe, Armand had assumed that the gobvar were not lost to all reason as a race.

The problem was that the First Crimson Sister was one-quarter of the Quadrumvirate that ruled the Clan Spheres. So long as the First ruled, with the Warlord, the Blood King, and Old Bloodscale, Her Crimson Sisters would control the border.

And violence and war were sacred to the Sisters. There would be no peaceful crossing of the border while they guarded it.

Armand didn't know how dominant the worship of Her Crimson Sister truly was among the gobvar of the Clans. He suspected that the *form* of it was almost omnipresent—not least because casually murdering someone who disrespected Her was well within the "worship" of the priestesses—but he suspected true worship was rarer.

Just like he suspected true loyalty to him wasn't as all-pervasive among the crew as his officers might pretend. The crewvar aboard *Void Flyer* were, he was reasonably sure, committed to the mission. Whether or not they *believed* in it, well… Armand didn't need them to.

But as *Void Flyer* lifted away from Flame's Gem on a pillar of semimagical fire, he *knew* the crew was glad to see the rock shrink behind them.

Armand certainly was. The journey in front of him wasn't going to be easy, but it seemed that each step proved stranger than the one before it. His Dark Brothers were murderous backstabbers, but they'd at least been *people*, var that the crew could see and understand and fight.

Well, with the exception of the Seeker, but divinely chosen champions didn't play by everyone else's rules. Even divinely chosen champions of gods of treachery.

If only he thought the Seeker was the *last* divine champion they were going to meet on this trip. He'd given Cat one copy of the ancient map from his family's archives, but he'd brought two. The other now hung on the side of the wardrobe the crew had *somehow* brought over from *Star*.

He'd have to ask Cat or Brushfire how long it would be before they entered the IronHome, the home sphere of the long-dead Imperium, but he knew that was the next stop on their route.

"None of this makes sense," he said aloud, tracing the careful brushwork on the map. The original had long since faded to dust, and even *his* family's archivist hadn't attempted to fully replicate the gold thread of the original chart.

The replacement gold ink had likely been expensive enough. IronHome had been the center of the universe to the var who'd originally drawn the map. Now it and the spheres around it were dead. What remained was, as the Seeker had warned him, *hunger*.

Past those void spheres was his real mission. All of this was a delay, a barrier to be overcome while hopefully not losing *too* many resources and var.

And yet…

Armand was no seer, but he trusted his instincts. Those instincts told him he was in the right place, going the right way—and that even the challenges they faced there *meant* something.

Even if it was only as a guide to a different answer.

He tapped the symbol for IronHome on the chart, then turned back toward the frustratingly sparse bookshelves.

"Now," he said aloud. "Did I pack the *Third Tome of Life Past the Last Horizon* or not?"

He was joking, sadly. He knew *exactly* which books he'd packed, and none of the books by the mage—the *necromancer*—Lakewater Wisdom had been among them.

For some reason, he'd packed books on voids and the nature of the spheres rather than books of stories of the so-called living dead.

Armand didn't know the exact details of everything in his books by heart. He had a very good idea of what was *in* each of the two hundred or so volumes he'd brought with him, but if he'd remembered all of their details, he wouldn't have needed to *bring* the books.

His library in the Great Red Forest was closer to five thousand volumes—and even *that* was only about half of the family archive. While not all of his books were from the Bluestaves Archive, his notes and will called for all of his books to be given to the Archive when he died.

That was how the Bluestaves Archive had come into existence in the first place, after all.

At that moment, as *Void Flyer* burned across the Warden of Fire, he wished he'd brought all ten thousand books with him. *Somewhere* in all of those pages had to be some kind of answer to just what they had been attacked by on Flame's Gem.

There wasn't much on undead—living "Past the Last Horizon," as Lakewater Wisdom had put it in the books that Armand had read before this journey—in his books at all. Things that died tended to *stay* dead, barring the intervention of immoral and powerful mages.

Sighing, he fell back on his most reliable, if occasionally silly, trick. Power flickered through the focus rings on his hands and spiraled up into the air. It shifted through the air, turning first to mist and then into the semi-translucent cat-sized form of an oracle spirit.

"Find me the book I need," he told it. It was its own creature, taking a steadier recurring form and personality each time he summoned the spirit, but it was *also* a being of his will and his power.

He didn't need to give it particularly clear or complete instructions. In his experience, the vaguer his instructions, the better off he was.

Oracular magic was like that.

The spirit flitted this way and that, clearly examining the books with its own senses, and Armand turned away to find a drink. A pitcher of magically chilled water rested on an end table halfway across the room, and he poured himself a mug.

He'd barely taken the first sip before the spirit trilled triumphantly. He turned back to see the winged creature struggling to lift a book off the shelf.

He *could* give the spirit enough physicality to act as a weapon or a courier; it just wasn't usually worth it. At that moment, though, he flicked the oracle enough magic for it to bring him a book as he drained the mug of water.

Armand could tell when he'd been pushing too hard and needed to refresh himself. The cool water helped clear his mind, and he looked down at the table as the oracular spirit dropped the book—more heavily than he liked!—onto the wood, half-visible claws flickering through pages before Armand could even see *which* book the little dragon had brought him.

It stopped with the book open on a clearly specific page and trilled again.

Nodding his thanks to the spirit, Armand leaned forward and read the page it indicated. Without context, he wasn't sure what he was reading... but it was quickly clear *why* he was reading it.

And in their defiance, He saw a challenge to his power. While the Sister and the Dragon argued, He sent forth warlords to bring the sphere to heel, and when steel and sail failed, he sent forth a fleet of the dead.

In a single flaring, an entire world died for their refusal to kneel. A Clan was no more, as creatures of hunger and shadow overran their defenses and the power of the Blood King consumed all.

In fear of His power, the Warlord acted. The power of all Clans was turned on those who had defied Him, and while the Sister and Dragon continued to argue, the Warlord brought three more Clans to heel to save all Clans from His Wrath...

It was... surprisingly little, and yet. Armand suspected he knew which book it was, but he lifted the cover to be certain.

A Warning on the Four, written five hundred dances earlier by Submissive Farmharvest—a gobvar who had escaped the Clan Spheres. *A Warning* wasn't *quite* a history of the Clan Spheres and the Quadrumvirate who ruled them, but it was closer than just about any other book available in Court and Kingdoms.

The Blood King was the second-oldest of the Quadrumvirate and one of its two immortal-or-near-enough members. An ancient gobvar, unaging and undying, the Blood King claimed to be the true and ultimate ruler of the Gobvar Clans.

In practice, according to *A Warning*, the Blood King left most of the day-to-day rule of the Clan Spheres to the First Crimson Sister and the Warlord, but some of the books suggested that was a balancing factor with Old Bloodscale—the *dragon* member of the Quadrumvirate that was its other immortal member.

Amidst a divinely chosen High Priestess, an immortal god-king and an unkillable ancient void wyrm, the Clan Warlord was *merely* the most powerful individual gobvar war leader of all the Clans.

Armand had expected the First Sister and the Warlord to be the main dangers to his mission. But if the Blood King had unleashed the wraiths of the Warden of Fire on his enemies...

There were questions in the void spheres Armand hadn't expected to ask and wasn't sure he was going to like the answers to.

"Captain, a moment of your time?"

Cat looked up at Crane's somewhat apologetic request. The limitations of space aboard the *Void Flyer* were resulting in odd choices, especially since her prior owners hadn't really set her up for a full crew.

That meant that Cat's office was attached to his cabin, on a level he shared with Brushfire and Streamwater's similar offices and cabins a few decks down from the control room. The other two officers and the three Masters split the rest of the level, with *rooms* instead of *suites*.

All told, six of *Flyer*'s thirty levels were dedicated to sleeping quarters for the crew—five holding fifty-odd var apiece, and two of *those* had been storage spaces for the Brothers.

Cat's people had brought their hammocks from *Star*, and so far, at least, no one had complained enough for the Captain to hear.

"Come on in," he told the ship's doctor. "The door was open."

There were officers he'd known, civilian and military, who would not only have closed the door to their office but posted a guard in the miniature lobby to keep people from bothering them. Even as a naval officer, that had not been Cat's style—though the weight of tradition was as heavy as law and regulation in the High Court Navy.

No one except his officers would have *dared* bother the Captain of a High Court ship. But even if Cat had barred the door and posted guards, his third officer would still have been among the few allowed through.

The gaunt elvar mage softly closed the door behind them and padded over to take a chair in front of Cat's desk. That bit of furniture was a typical piece of darvar art, a solidly built block of wood with intricate carvings cutting into, but never weakening, the squared-off surfaces.

It was also propped up on two even plainer slabs of wood, as darvar averaged a good hand and a half shorter than elvar. Even Cat needed an extra couple of inches of height on the desk to make it usable.

"What do you need, Officer Crane?" he asked, something in their body language suggesting the formality was needed.

"Rumor has it the archmage made foci while we were on the surface," they told him. "Alloy received one at the end, before the wraiths came."

"He did," Cat agreed. "He's been distracted with researching the wraiths since we left the Gem, but he has made several foci he can attune as personal foci, and the plan is to offer them to the officers of this ship."

He shrugged delicately.

"You are welcome to refuse, if you are unwilling to be bound closer to a halvar archmage, of course," he pointed out. "On the other hand, we will all outlive Master Bluestaves."

It was perhaps harsh to point that out, though Cat occasionally needed the reminder *himself.* The archmage was in his forties, barely older than Bogsong Smallwolf. As an archmage, he'd live long for a halvar, but that still would only give him a hundred dances.

Faith Streamwater, the oldest of the four elvar officers aboard the ship, could still reasonably expect to outlive Armand Bluestaves by fifty dances or more. Crane, who was closer to Cat's age, would likely outlive the archmage by somewhere around two *hundred* dances.

"That is not the rumor that concerned me, sir," Crane said. Their voice was oddly formal to Cat's ears, more like what he'd grown used to in the Navy than the *slightly* more relaxed tone he'd adapted to aboard theoretically civilian ships.

"Then what is your concern, Emberlight?" Cat asked softly, using the other elvar's first name to prod gently at that wall of formality.

"Rumor said he made foci for the gobvar, sir."

Cat nodded, leaning back in his chair—as undersized as the desk, it had required significant work by the gobvar carpenters to be remotely comfortable. He eyed the gaunt dark-haired elvar in front of him and considered his words carefully.

"Rumor, in this case, is wrong," he told Crane. "But only because of the attack by the wraiths. His intention was to prepare several general foci, as well as several foci linked to Hammerhead Tribe. Even without formal assessment, we have identified several members of Officer Brushfire's tribe who can be trained as mages."

He didn't bring up Fistfall's personal focus. That seemed like it would aggravate a situation he needed to calm down, *quickly*.

"But *why*?" Crane demanded. "I understand giving Brushfire a focus—we need her to lead her people, and her power is extraordinary. She was already a shaman, a magic-user. Training her as a mage is a distasteful necessity.

"But you must understand there are *reasons* we don't train gobvar as mages. Given the best of intentions, the strongest of wills, they are vulnerable to Her Crimson Sister and the other bloody-handed gods. Any gobvar we teach magic is a risk of creating a powerful new enemy!"

That... was not a tack Cat had heard before. He'd made sure, on hiring Crane, that they could work with gobvar. Gobvar subordinates, even a gobvar superior, hadn't bothered them.

But apparently, teaching gobvar *magic* was a problem?

"Emberlight, I have never heard any such thing in my life," he told them carefully. He wasn't going to call it grazer leavings, not *immediately*, but it certainly sounded like it to him. "There is no member of this crew I would not trust at my back with a battlewand and a sword.

"Equally, there is no member of this crew, of *any* var, I would not trust at my back with a focus and full command of the power of magic. Would you say differently of *any* of our var?"

There was a chilly silence.

"I would trust any of our crew," Crane allowed, grudgingly. "With a weapon, yes. But magic is more than a weapon. It is an opening to the spheres themselves, a path upon which the will of gods can walk.

"We saw the darvar Seeker in Brokenwright. Through her connection to the spheres, Her Dark Brother touched her soul and turned her into a monster. *Any* gobvar is vulnerable to the same. Her Crimson Sister hunts their souls."

"So, you expect Brushfire to turn on you at any moment?" Cat asked drily. "I know enough of how the Seeker came to be, Emberlight, to know that she was not lured through her magic. That was a *choice* on her part, one in a series of choices that began, long ago, with the decision to worship Her Dark Brother.

"That was not due to some channel in her magic. That was *her*. All her."

Terrifying as that thought was. Cat couldn't quite grasp how *anyone* would choose to worship Her Crimson Sister or Her Dark Brother—his own faith was focused on the High Court, the beings for which the High Court's floating continents were named.

He'd been born on the continent named for the Warden, a place of trees and carefully protected wildernesses infused with ancient magics. His oath to use his magic in the service of others had been sworn to the Warden and the Sage, the guardian of his birthplace and the elvar god of knowledge.

"I do not believe Brushfire will turn on us," Crane conceded. "I have touched her magic and her will. I have no fear of her. But a lesser will? One of the younger members of her tribe, less trained in the ways of mage and shaman, given power without understanding?

"The Dark Brethren will feel their weakness. Draw on it. Claim them."

Her Dark Brother and Her Crimson Sister were the best-known of that set of five siblings, one of which was completely unnamed, the *She* whose siblings the other four were. They were known best as gobvar gods, though included in the general pantheon recognized across Court and Kingdoms. Given what Cat had learned of the var's history over the last clock-days, though, he had his suspicions about the origins of *everything*.

Including the gods.

"I was an officer of the High Court Navy, Emberlight," Cat said softly. "We were taught many things about the gobvar. Much of it lies, to sharpen our wills and our blades against our most likely enemy."

And *that* was not something he could admit outside of this ship. The High Court Navy might engage in propaganda and indoctrination, but *calling* them on it would risk the Navy's reputation. Its *face*, ever so critical among elvar.

There would be swift retribution for that, if he repeated those words in public in the Court and Kingdoms.

"But nothing in all that I was taught ever suggested the gobvar were somehow inextricably bound to the Dark Brethren," he told them. "That Her Crimson Sisters controlled any Clan near the border, yes. That any child among the Gobvar Clans born with the gift was claimed and kidnapped by the Sisters, yes.

"Any mage of the Gobvar Clans is sworn to the Dark Brethren, yes," Cat conceded. "But that is not by any nature of their var. That is the fruit of centuries of violence and kidnapping inflicted upon the gobvar.

"And that same commonality will present *us* with a tool when we reach the Clan Spheres. Any gobvar mage we can send forth will be treated with respect—with *terror*, even—by the gobvar of those spheres."

He shook his head.

"We need any mages we can train from our crew, Emberlight. And I trust them. As I trust you. Do you understand?"

Cat knew perfectly well that Emberlight Crane was smart enough to pick up the warning in that statement. Armand Bluestaves had not yet, after all, attuned a focus to the other elvar.

CHAPTER

14

BRUSHFIRE HAD SPENT A GOOD THIRD OF THE FIRST CLOCK-DAY after leaving Flame's Gem asleep. From the appearance of the other three gathered in Armand's workshop-slash-library-slash-quarters, Cat appeared to have at least *rested*, and neither Alloy nor Armand had so much as stopped working.

Alloy Bellowforge, for his part, dropped what looked like an over-sized lantern on the currently clear kitchen counter in the archmage's quarters.

"Here," he said gruffly. "Based on an old smuggler's lantern design I worked on as a kid. Two panels, here and here." He tapped the panels, not opening either of the long vertical sections.

"Open them up, you get a wall of light on either side. Needs a mage to give the gem at the heart a good burst to start, but it'll run on that for a bit and can be used by anyone."

Brushfire studied the strange lantern appreciatively. She'd used up a *lot* more power than felt reasonable to her managing her orb of light. It seemed strange that Bellowforge could duplicate it in something anyone could use, but that was part of the trick of a mage-artificer.

"How can it amplify *that* much?" Cat asked—clearly having the same concern as Brushfire.

"That's what the gem is for," Bellowforge told him. "I... Well, I'd say it was an artificer's secret, but frankly, even *we* don't understand how it works.

"But certain gems, like the light crystals in some spheres, have a resonance to them." The darvar shrugged. "I can pick 'em out of a bin, but I've never met anyone who can predict what stones, even out of a single vein, will have or won't have resonance.

"But the ones that do, I can put magic into, and give them a clock-day, and they'll hand me back fifty times the magic I put in. A hundred times. So long as it's doing very specific, neatly aligned things."

He grinned.

"Fortunately, crystals that want to make light are easier to find than crystals that want to *float*, and we need enough of the latter that I can always find resonant stones."

"We're asking a lot of the light in this lantern," Brushfire said quietly. "Are you sure it will cut it?"

"I've tested it. It's of the same… nature, let's call it, as the Captain had us throwing around on Flame's Gem," Alloy said. "They might need some fine-tuning, so I'd suggest we not *rely* on them until they've had at least one encounter with the wraiths, but they should hold."

"That will be needed," Armand said calmly.

Brushfire couldn't quite put her finger on how Armand did it. None of the four var in the room lacked for presence or authority, but the moment the pudgily cute archmage spoke, everyone was looking at him.

"There will be more?" she asked him.

"I don't know what created them," he told them. "I have gone into as much as divination and the books I have can find, and it isn't much. These wraiths are…"

He gestured vaguely in the air.

"A tool of a manifestation of a leftover of a magical working unlike anything I have ever seen or ever heard of," he explained slowly. "They aren't… real, in a sense. They aren't spirits or undead, though they take on some of the form of such and draw power from the death that happened here.

"But it is more than they are creations of what *created* that death than they are creatures of that death."

Brushfire shivered and felt Cat reach over to squeeze her shoulder reassuringly. It helped a surprising amount, given that the elvar's hand didn't even *cover* her shoulder.

"But what kind of magic are we talking about?" Cat asked. "I was hoping the void spheres were a… strange but natural occurrence."

"No." The word hung in the air like a weapon. "They were *not* natural. Whatever wiped Warden of Fire clean of life is what destroyed the other void spheres as well. This route we have chosen, this 'back door' into the Clan Spheres, was created by something very powerful a long time ago.

"And when these spheres became what they are, everyone in them died."

Brushfire had put that together, but hearing it plainly laid out in Armand's "teacher" voice still sent a shiver down her spine.

"Any idea what?" she asked.

"Any idea *who*?" Cat added.

"I don't know *what* happened but I know *who*," Bluestaves warned. "In the handful of records we have on the Quadrumvirate, there is a story of the Blood King unleashing a horde of hungry wraiths on his enemies.

"It's possibly mythical—it certainly is given as part of the reason why the Warlord makes sure *nobody* truly defies the Blood King—but the descriptions align with what we fought. I don't know if they are an intentional result of whatever created the void spheres, but the Blood King commands them."

There were aspects of the mission Brushfire had taken on that she didn't like to let herself think about. Cat and Armand had treated her as an equal and a partner, providing her and her family with options and support they never would have had otherwise.

But they were also going into the Clan Spheres, where the Quadrumvirate ruled and where people like *her*, specifically, were required to be turned over to Her Crimson Sisters to be broken and reshaped into Sisters themselves.

The Blood King loomed behind Her Crimson Sisters, and the Clan Fleets, and the Warlord and all of that. Like Old Bloodscale the great dragon, he was more myth and terror than really a ruler of the gobvar in her mind.

Unlike Old Bloodscale, though, she had figured the Blood King wasn't relevant to their task. Bloodscale was almost certainly connected, one way or another, to the rise of the dragons that Armand had seen coming.

The Blood King shouldn't have been, and if they were in *his* territory, that meant she could no longer ignore the stories and horror wrapped up with that name.

"So, we're going to fight him?" she asked.

"I certainly hope not," Cat replied. "Just because these spheres are occupied by wraiths like those he commands does not mean he knows what's going on here or is going to complain about our passage.

"We're travelers, passing through. No one should expect us to come out of these spheres, and we should be safe. After all, do we even need to land on another world to make the journey?"

That question was directed at Bellowforge, who shrugged impassively.

"We've the fuel to make the trip," he observed. "We won't have much left when we enter the Clan Spheres, but enough to reach a world in Drinkstar. We'll need fuel there."

"Or another ship," Brushfire suggested. "We might not find a ninesail floating around, but there are merchant ships in the Clan Spheres. Like those in Court and Kingdoms, they'll have six masts and no weapons—but we can crew one."

"We'll see what options we have once we reach Drinkstar," Armand said. "I am nervous about where we are. This was the only way, but my divinations are not... pleasant."

"I drew the Aether Storm for a *navigation* cantrip," Cat pointed out wryly. "I have the feeling this course will be worse than we fear."

"And yet it remains the only course that would get us into the Clan Spheres," the archmage said. "We have no choice, my friends. We complete the journey into the realm of our enemy, and then we start finding ways to ask questions.

"Somewhere among the Clans is the key to the danger I foresaw. It's not the Blood King. I don't know what it is, but I'm quite certain he has nothing to do with these dragons."

"If nothing else, we know there are at least two of them that we can find and ask questions of," Cat observed, though the thought sent a shiver down Brushfire's spine.

She had seen an illusory recreation of the battle that had destroyed Cat's squadron and ended his career. Two dragons had torn apart three ninesails, and only luck and a strange type of courage had saved Cat's own ship.

Perhaps an archmage could capture the foe that had slaughtered an elvar fleet. Brushfire wasn't sure. She only knew that this was the mission she'd accepted.

"We'll find our answers," she said calmly. "It helps, of course, that we will have gobvar to ask questions of gobvar."

She smiled.

"Though I suspect it will be a strange feeling to be somewhere where the *elvar* crew has to hide!"

CHAPTER

15

VOID FLYER DIDN'T HAVE THE THREE OPEN DECK SPACES OF A REGU- lar aether ship for gatherings, but those would have been useless for Armand anyway. Of the nearly three hundred var on the void ship, only five—Armand himself and the four Bellowforges—couldn't breathe aether, which had made *Star*'s open decks, for example, useful for gatherings of more than a handful of var.

Still, the ship was thirty yards across, which gave each deck a surprising amount of space. Most of the decks were at least half-full of machinery, fuel or control crystals, but the deck the Seeker had claimed for her quarters—and which Armand's people had assigned him without asking—had less.

He had enough space, if nothing else, to lay out a meal for eight var at a midsized table. He'd needed some help to prepare the meal, but the kitchen crew were more than willing.

Now two gobvar, a darvar and four elvar sat around his table tucking into the food, and he indulged himself in a broad smile.

"Moongleam knows his work," he told his guests. "I know we don't have nearly as much to work with as anyone would like, but he has done us proud."

Moongleam Hammerhead was an elderly gobvar, who had taken Armand's instructions to create *a fancy dinner, we're celebrating* to heart.

"Moongleam is used to working with stale bread and scraps," Brushfire said drily. "Fresh grain and frozen layer breasts? He can make a feast of that."

"And he has," Alloy said, lifting his mug in salute. "Remind me to thank him in person again."

Armand chuckled, delighting in the warm familial feeling of his people. *Technically,* only Cat, Brushfire and Alloy were his people so far. Fistfall and the three officers were employees, but everyone knew what the case on the side table held.

"He wouldn't even let me bake the bread," the archmage half-jokingly complained. "Wanted to make sure it *matched the seasoning.*"

Which the lightly spiced cheese buns had done *perfectly*, of course. Armand knew when he was being overruled by an expert, after all.

"What did that cost my poor third-brother?" Brushfire asked.

"Dessert," Armand said with a smile. "We traded recipes and worked together on the pie."

"Wait, you got *Moongleam* to give up his *pie crust*?" Fistfall demanded, then flushed and tried to shrink back into himself.

It looked *very* strange on the big gobvar.

"Oh, I *tried*," Armand said with a chuckle. "No, I just got his recipe for spicing blackberry-apple jelly and made the filling. *He* made the crust."

And while the jelly recipe was impressive, mostly Armand had stood aside and let the expert work. Moongleam had put together a three-course meal from extensive, if bland, supplies on a quarter-day's notice.

Armand was impressed—and he was almost *more* impressed by the fact that Moongleam's family seemed to think this was normal.

Again and again, he was convinced he'd lucked out when he'd hired the Hammerhead Tribe. Not that *luck* had had that much to do with it. Prophecy had led him to Cat and Brushfire, and Brushfire wouldn't have gone anywhere without her family.

"Dessert will be a few minutes, regardless," he told them all. A gesture brought the case of foci floating forward and onto the table in front of him, where a pair of elvar sailors—currently lacking staves to work on—had cleared everything away a few moments earlier.

"You all know—by rumor, if someone has forgotten to tell you—why I asked you here," he continued. "While we were on Flame's Gem, I spent time working on new attunable foci for our officers—and for the strongest of the potential mages we have assessed among our crew."

He addressed that last to Fistfall with what he hoped was a reassuring nod. The gobvar might be the *biggest* var in the room, but he was also the youngest by half a dozen dances.

Which meant, of course, that he was basically the same age as Smallwolf by elvar or gobvar standards, and far older than the majority of Armand's halvar students.

"Unless I believed you would accept this, I would not have put effort into making the foci," Armand observed. "Still, I feel I must make clear that you do *not* need to take it. There are metaphysical and moral bonds that come with taking a personal focus from the hands of an archmage, and while some of these are not true personal foci, the difference on *that* front is irrelevant."

Fistfall was the first to say anything into the silence that Armand let hang.

"You came to our tribe," he said, slowly and steadily. "You *speak* of fighting for all var, protecting us from a dark future you have foreseen… but you came to our tribe and you *treated* us as equals.

"You, a halvar and an archmage, treated a family of gobvar as *equals*."

Fistfall shrugged and spread his hands.

"You say you are sworn to protect everyone," he repeated, "but it is your actions, Archmage Bluestaves, that prove the truth of your words. I'm no mage, no student of *anything* by nature.

"But if you lead, I will follow. If you teach, I will learn. I'll take your focus, Archmage, for all that may mean."

Armand held the younger var's gaze for a few moments, assessing the truth of the words. Then he rose and carried the focus—carved, as he understood it, from the leg of a chair the gobvar had assembled from glue and scraps—over to Fistfall.

"Cut your thumb and smear blood along the wand," he ordered.

Fistfall obeyed and Armand summoned the binding magic. The moment Fistfall's blood touched the focus, there was no more question of whether Fistfall was a mage. The young var's power answered the touch of the focus and of Armand's magic with an eager surge.

He was not as strong as his sister, Armand judged, but few mages *were*. He would need training, but Fistfall would do his family, his tribe and his new archmage proud.

"Cat, if you could heal Master Fistfall, please," Armand asked. "Thank you, Fistfall."

"That's it?"

"You can feel it, can't you?"

Armand knew the answer to the question. The way the focus slid into Fistfall's hand, the way he held the focus, *everything* about the var's body language told him that the link between the two had been forged.

Fistfall's awed nod answered him.

With a returning nod, Armand turned to Bogsong Smallwolf, sitting next to the big gobvar, and summoned one of the attunable foci to him. These wands, carved from wood found on Flame's Gem, would never *perfectly* match their mages the way the personal foci he'd made the other mages would.

But they would put any focus less narrowly attuned to shame.

"Well, Officer Smallwolf?" he asked the ship's youngest officer. "I suspect you know, in full detail, what taking this from my hands means."

He'd made certain that Brushfire had explained it to her brother. The three elvar officers, formally trained in academies like the one he normally taught at, would have had the full history lesson somewhere along the way.

"I'm already on this ship, heading into hostile spheres to hunt dragons for you, Archmage Bluestaves," Smallwolf said with a small giggle. "I know this binds me, but I can't think of anything *more* dangerous you might ask me to do when we're done!"

"Fate has a way of surprising us," Armand conceded, but he drew a wand from the case and handed it to her.

Smallwolf didn't need instructions. Her blood smeared along the focus, and Armand's power met hers in the center of the wand. He, at least, could *feel* the difference between the bond he'd forged for Fistfall a moment before and the bond he forged for Smallwolf now.

The elvar mage would always have a deeper well of magic to draw on than Fistfall, he judged, but with the personal focus versus the "merely" attuned focus, the gobvar would be able to call more magic *at once*.

It would be an interesting balance between the two, he judged, and one that would serve them well if they learned to work together. As

Armand figured they would. He had seen enough students pair up over the years to see the beginnings of the movement.

"And done, Bogsong Smallwolf," he said quietly. She healed herself without a word as he smiled and nodded gently to her.

Two more officers, and then he would have a tiny but terrifying legion of mages armed with personal foci at his direct command. Whatever awaited them in the rest of the void spheres was never going to know what hit it!

"Are we sure that sextant is calibrated correctly?" Cat asked, staring at the device he'd just finished updating and matching to the spheres around them. "I'm not sure I've ever seen *four* leagues a minute before."

"That's what having enough fuel gets us," Bellowforge told him. The darvar was fiddling with the second sextant, the two tools combining to give *Void Flyer*'s control room an idea of both where the void ship was and how fast it was going.

"We can go faster than any aether current could ever move your ninesail. We have more issues slowing *down* than a sailing ship would, but we can go faster, and we can go places she never could."

Cat grunted and made one more measurement. He held the numbers in his head for a moment, then smiled and took a log journal from Smallwolf with an appreciative nod.

"I'm going to go check against the charts, but I think we've got about four days left in Warden of Fire," he told Alloy. "After that... how fast *can* we go? I'm not liking the idea of being in IronHome for long."

"I wouldn't want to go much past four leagues a minute," Bellowforge admitted. "Mostly because we have no way to really refuel. *You* might start feeling comfortable hitting the straits at speed, but His Dark Brothers never did at more than a league a minute."

He snorted.

"One of the places where they actually *listened* to me," he noted. "*Void Flyer* can handle things no aether ship ever could, but my gut feel is that she's more vulnerable to the stresses of a strait than they are."

"I'll take the helm for the passage to IronHome," Cat promised. "That will give me a better feel for what I think she can take."

Cat trusted the darvar, but needing to slow down before they hit the strait would add a day to his calculations. *This* time, he would go with what Alloy said.

But *he* was *Void Flyer*'s Captain and he wanted to judge her weaknesses himself. There would come a time, after all, where he would need to push the strange metal ship to its limits.

"I know engines and metal and mechanisms, Captain," Alloy said. "I don't know ships, outside of what I learned to build the *Flyer*. I'd be *delighted* to have a second opinion."

Cat finished his math, double-checking a number with the abacus in the chart room, and sighed to himself. He *still* felt like he could find a faster route if the sphere had aether, but that was a pointless wish.

He wasn't used to his aether sense feeling *so* quiet. The complete lack of aether there was like a wound that didn't heal, a constant stitch in his side that would *never* feel right.

In some ways, he suspected it would be better if he truly couldn't feel *anything*. Instead, there were flashes of a feeling that wasn't *quite* an aether current. In a normal sphere, he could have figured he was feeling a current that was warped by something.

Or, potentially, a working of the aether to create magical effects. Those were *rare*—few other than archmagi could summon the power to manipulate enough aether to have a useful effect, and archmagi knew that doing so could cause problems for navigation across an entire sphere.

There weren't enough of those scraps of feeling for him to pin them down. Given that he'd felt *something* on Flame's Gem when the hunger wraiths had come for them, he suspected they were linked. He certainly wasn't going to seek them out—and if he *could* locate them, he'd probably plot a course around them.

Their course out of Warden of Fire was pretty fixed. They would basically drift at their current course for three more days, then use a mix of the lift crystals and rockets to rotate her to point the rockets directly at the strait.

Then, over the course of a day and a half, they would carefully reduce speed and align their course before entering the strait. Passing through the strait would take a few hours in a strange space between spheres, and they'd be in IronHome in five days.

An aether strait made sense to Cat. It was a linkage between two spheres of aether, a long channel where aether was trapped by similar forces to that which held the spheres in place. The one void strait they'd passed through at least connected an aether sphere to the void sphere, with traces of aether filling most of the channel.

But this would be a strait between void spheres, and Cat wondered if they even *needed* a strait to pass between the Warden of Fire and Iron-Home. Perhaps, if they left the sphere on a parallel path, they'd reach the same destination.

On the other hand, he'd heard *stories* about what happened to people who took aether-sailing ships too close to the limits of an outerlit sphere.

Only stories. Because the people who tried that didn't come home any more reliably than people who tried to *land* on the great crystals and embers that lit and warmed other spheres.

He wasn't going to experiment with *Void Flyer*. Not with their mission riding on her and practically everyone he cared about outside his family with him. They'd follow the straits on the old charts and make the passage through IronHome.

That thought led him to turn to the chart for the Ironhand Imperium's ancient home, their next sphere.

"If anything is going to go wrong, it'll go wrong there," he muttered to himself. Almost unconsciously, he drew the oracle deck from his belt pouch and looked down at the cards.

If the charts were accurate, there was no real need for his navigation cantrips. *Void Flyer* would enter the sphere, point herself at the exit to their next sphere—Warden of Stone—and accelerate up to four leagues a minute.

Including about two days for gaining and losing speed, they'd be in IronHome for about six days. It wasn't *quite* as vast a sphere as Warden of Fire, but it was on the larger side. If its ember still burned, the charts said that the near-eternal fire would be among the half dozen largest Cat had even *heard* of.

It wasn't going to be that simple. Even without doing a reading, he knew that. Which meant that *some* touch of the future, some piece of guidance, was needed. Armand would be better, but while Cat would follow his archmage to the ends of the void—not merely the end of the aether, because they were *past* that—he would forever rather be trapped by his own hand than led to safety by another's.

He drew the cards from the deck. One hundred and one of them, each a concept, archetype or god.

Cat shuffled them, his gaze on the chart as he focused on the sphere.

"Show me," he commanded, his hand laying out a spread of four cards. A pure future reading, it *should* warn him what was coming.

Looking down at the cards, he sighed.

The *problem* with one of your potential obstacles being a not-quite-god who'd been around for a thousand dances was that the bastard had his own oracle card. *Normally*, the Blood King meant emphasis, reinforcing the point being made by the card right after it.

Did it mean that this time? Or did it mean that the situation *did* involve the Blood King, in which case they were probably doomed?

Either way, the second card was fascinating. The Warden. The patron deity of the House of Forests, the guardian of the forests that covered the lodestone continent named for the same god.

In an oracle reading, though, the Warden spoke to a need for caution and care. But it *also* spoke to meticulous care leading to *success*.

Given *that* reading, the third card should be the success or reward for that care—and somehow Cat was unsurprised to see the Sage, the patron god of elvar mages. Care and caution would reward them with knowledge.

So, was the Blood King emphasizing that caution and care would bring them knowledge, or saying that the knowledge was *about* the Blood King?

He snorted. From everything Cat had heard about the supposed King of the gobvar, he doubted that information about the Blood King would come freely—and suspected knowing too much would draw his ire.

Flipping over the last card made him grimace. The Sword. It wasn't a soldier's sword, though, but an *executioner's* blade. It meant conflict, yes, but not necessarily a battle or a fight that couldn't be won.

More than anything, it meant… retribution or restitution. The Sword meant that there would be a price for whatever happened.

He looked at the four cards and sighed.

It was actually surprisingly clear for one of his divinations, assuming the Blood King meant what it usually did. Extra care and caution were needed, but if they did things carefully and watched for traps, they'd learn something of great value—but even that caution and care wouldn't keep them from paying a high price for it.

The Blood King added weight to *all* of the cards, suggesting greater needed care *and* greater potential rewards *and* a greater price.

"So, what happens if we just… head straight to the Warden of Stone?" he murmured, and pulled another card, tossing this one onto the chart, separate from the reading.

The card landed *on* the strait to the Warden of Stone… and he'd seen that exact card on his charts all too recently. The Aether Storm. Failure, disaster.

"I need to talk to Armand," he muttered. "My readings are *never* this clear."

Which was both useful and potentially a problem.

AN ORACULAR SPIRIT TRILLED AS THE STRANGE-SYMBOLED DICE rolled across the mat. Armand studied the pattern—both of the images showing on the faces of the eleven twelve-sided dice and of the pattern the images and dice themselves formed.

The pattern wasn't the *exact* same as the last three, but the general thrust of the message was. There was something in IronHome critical to Armand's mission, something that would either answer key questions or, possibly, just let them get through the void spheres alive.

"I should have baked a cake instead," he said aloud.

"Is that a new form of divination?" Cat's voice asked, and he looked up in surprise to see his ship Captain.

"When did you come in?" Armand replied.

"Somewhere in the middle of *baked a cake*," Cat told him, the slim-framed elvar stepping over to study the table with the dice mat. "I wonder if anyone else on the ship is beating their head against divination magic."

"Brushfire and Streamwater are teaching Fistfall first-year magic class, so presumably not them," Armand replied. "Alloy mostly uses magic to *build* things, so he might be building some sort of lens that sees the future?"

He sighed.

"What are *your* divinations showing, Captain? They led us to the fuel depot here in Warden of Fire, after all."

"No, that was Alloy," Cat corrected. "Mine simply warned that going back into the Kingdoms would end poorly."

"I wonder if we should have asked if going *forward* would end poorly," the archmage said grimly. "Because I have seen at least one path through the dice that ends in all of our deaths."

"My own divination skills are... basically limited to cantrips and an oracle-deck reading," Cat admitted. "But I pulled the Aether Storm again, for if we head straight to the Warden of Stone."

"The dice carried the same warning," Armand admitted. "There is *something* in IronHome that we need to see or our mission will fail. I don't *like* that kind of vague warning and direction, though I should be used to it after Brokenwright."

Cat was staring at the dice pattern.

"I'm not sure yours is actually that vague," he observed. "You have the chart of IronHome around here somewhere, yes?"

Armand had to cast about for a moment to find the map, but it was close to hand. He passed it over to Cat, who held it out next to the dice and glanced from one to the other.

"I don't want to touch your dice with magic," the Captain said slowly. "Can you lift them?"

Touching someone's divination tools was rude. Touching someone's divination tools with *magic* could actually break them, rendering them useless until the original diviner put a great deal of work into them again.

Armand lifted his own dice, holding their positions relative to each other as Cat slid the chart under them. The Captain studied the floating icons for a few moments, rotated the map several times to get it into a position that presumably made sense to him, then nodded for the archmage to lower the dice.

As soon as Armand laid the eleven dice—plain wooden blocks an aunt had given him as a precocious teenager, plainer and yet *more* meaningful than the hand-calligraphed gold-foil oracle cards a King had given him—down on the chart, he saw Cat's point.

Each of them had landed atop the tiny not-quite-map of a worldlet in the IronHome. It was by no means *all* of the worldlets in the sphere, but if Armand read the chart correctly, it was basically all of the *important* ones—the ones with at least a few million var or, in one case, the immense military shipyards of the Ironhand Imperium.

"Well, that tells us one place *not* to go," Cat observed, looking at the face-up skull of the die sitting atop the shipyards. "I don't believe I want to know why your scrying says we shouldn't go to the old Navy…"

He trailed off as the oracular spirit landed in the middle of the chart, about as heavily as the half-insubstantial spirits *could* land, and turned one of the dice to bring a different face to the top.

A tiny stylized castle now met Armand's gaze as he looked down at the map—and a *triumphantly* trilling cat-dragon spirit wound its way up his arm to make sure he looked. It wasn't resting on the painted icon of a worldlet. It rested on the painted icon of a floating continent, a lodeplate.

"The Home," Armand said quietly. "And according to my little friend, we're looking for a *building* on the Home. We might be able to narrow that down once we're closer, but…"

"But this says we go to the Home. And that if we go somewhere *else*, we die," Cat concluded. "I thought the void spheres were supposed to be the easy route, Armand."

"I never said they would be *easy*, Cat," Armand pointed out. "*We* concluded that the border with its fleets in service to Her Crimson Sister wasn't something we could breach. It wasn't that this was an easy or a simple trail. Voids, in any other ship, this journey is impossible."

"It's just that this is what your divinations say is the only way."

"Exactly. And now, as we grow closer, those divinations say we need to visit the capital world of the Ironhand Imperium," Armand agreed. "I was hoping to bypass all of IronHome."

"We still could," Cat offered. "Point the ship at the strait to the next Warden and fire the engines at full power. Alloy doesn't want to go over four leagues a minute, but I see no reason why the ship couldn't do double that.

"We'd clear IronHome in four days. Divination isn't an exact science. Whatever threat is in our way, we might get there ahead of it or slip around it at speed."

"It's possible. But the risk remains, and…" Armand trailed off, looking at the castle-up die.

"And you're curious," Cat said.

"And I'm curious. There is an answer in this sphere that seems to *matter* to our mission... and I have too many questions to turn down answers, Cat."

CHAPTER

18

"CAN ANYONE SEE *ANYTHING?*"

Streamwater's plaintive words made Cat smile grimly to himself. *Void Flyer* was hurtling through the void at twenty cables a minute, five cables slower than the league per minute Alloy had suggested for the transit.

Except that where an aether strait was a visible smear of light across the sky, marked by magic and aether and energy, a strait between void spheres appeared to be completely invisible.

Or wasn't where it was supposed to be.

"Turn is complete," he said aloud, not revealing his own fears to his officers. "According to the charts, we are on the entry line and should hit the strait in about ten minutes."

His second officer stood by the starboard sextant, looking more than a touch concerned. Brushfire, standing by the port sextant, didn't look *quite* as bothered.

Cat figured that had to be the gobvar successfully putting the masking skills she'd learned as a gobvar in elvar spheres to use. Brushfire might not have been a deck officer for dozens to hundreds of strait passages like Cat or Streamwater, but she *knew* what an aether strait looked like.

And there was no aether strait in front of them. Worse, the outer edge of the sphere was only a thousand leagues past their planned destination, which meant the light and heat from the spherelight was beating down on the ship.

Cat suspected that the crew was *delighting* in the fact that *Void Flyer*'s construction meant less than two dozen of the crewvar were visible to the Captain as they approached the transit. He figured that, throughout most of the rapidly heating ship, shirts had become a thing of yesterday for a large chunk of the crew.

If he could *see* that, even as a theoretically civilian Captain, he'd have to say something. *He*, after all, wore a dark blue tailcoat that barely differed from his High Court uniform beyond its lack of gold braid.

And if he was using magic to keep from melting inside said coat, well, face and image had required stupider things of him over the years.

"No one, that I know of at least, has *ever* transited between void spheres," Cat pointed out loudly. "We are the first. Our names will go down in history, thanks to Archmage Bluestaves."

"Assuming the strait is there," Streamwater countered.

And that they *survived* the archmage's mission, Cat knew. No one was going to *say* that, though. Not where he could hear them, anyway.

"Five minutes," Brushfire declared, her eye on the clock on her sextant. "We should be four leagues out from the strait."

At four leagues, an aether strait should be an easily visible bruise in the sky. To Cat or any other var with his sense of the aether, its position would have been blatantly obvious. He could have guided *Void Flyer*—or any aether ship he'd ever sailed—through an aether strait with his eyes closed.

In fact...

Cat closed his eyes. He focused for a moment on the feeling of the wood under his hands, *Void Flyer* having the same kind of tilting helm as *Star* or another aether ship. He could adjust the ship's course from there, though *big* changes would require orders to the crew.

Less so than aboard an aether ship, in truth. They'd brought all of *Star*'s crew with them, but *Flyer* really only needed a hundred var to fly her—especially since she had no storm staves.

Through the helm, though, he could guide the ship through her last approach to the strait. Despite the lack of aether around them, if he focused hard enough, he could still pick up a sense of *Flyer*'s position. Relative to his own position, anyway.

In the distance, he could feel sparks of *something*, edged with an emotion he suspected was hunger, but that wasn't what he was looking for right now. He knew what an aether strait and the currents around it felt like.

But now, for the first time in his life, he reached out through that strange magical sense and tried to find the *tension point* of the strait, without the aether that shaped around it normally. He knew the flow, but could he find the weave that *shaped* the flow...

And there it was. Cat inhaled sharply in surprise as it *clicked* into place, a warp in the weave of the universe, a gap in the fabric of the spheres.

"We're not quite right," he said aloud. "Chart's a thousand dances out of date."

And the chart was more of an equation than a map, anyway, saying where something *would be* relative to everything else. Mistranslating one number of a dozen could easily put them off by a minor angle.

Like they were. They were going to miss the strait by a full cable. But they were far enough out and slow enough...

"Alloy, I need full thrust on my mark," he said aloud. "Adjusting our line."

He didn't even remember kicking free the lock that held the wheel in place. He twisted and tilted the wheel, the magic of the lift crystals moving with him, and he felt *Void Flyer* move around him, turning in space as they swiftly approached their destination.

"Two leagues from the charted point," Brushfire said, and *Cat*, at least, picked up the nervous edge in her voice. She knew he'd caught something. If they *missed* the strait, turning around and coming back would take days.

"Alloy?"

"On your mark."

"Full thrust... *now*."

More than any other ship Cat had commanded, *Void Flyer*'s courses were a thing of calculation and maps. *This*, though, couldn't be. Calculation and maps had brought them *to* the strait, but it would take instinct and magic to get them through.

It was also going to take *full thrust*, which was something Cat had only felt the ship unleash to leave Flame's Gem behind. *Void Flyer* hurtled along the line he'd drawn in space, the pressure of her engines pushing him into the floor as he semi-locked the wheel and hung on for dear life.

The engines hammered beneath him, and he kept his eyes closed as he moved the helm against the partial lock. The line was close, but as the rocket changed course, arcing toward the strait, he knew he'd misestimated.

Lack of practice. He was used to sails, not rockets. A few minute adjustments got her on the *right* line, and he held his breath, *feeling* the course for a few critical heartbeats.

"Cut the engines," he ordered. "Streamwater, Brushfire, keep the lift crystals pulsing. Last maneuvers will be *very* tight."

Someone muttered something he couldn't hear—something it was probably good he *hadn't* heard—and the engines cut out again. Silence and heat filled the control room as Cat continued to guide the ship with his eyes closed.

"I have *no* idea how close we are now," Streamwater warned.

"Close," Cat told her. "This may be… strange. Hang on!"

He barely managed *not* to hold his breath as they entered the distortion he could feel in the weave of reality, the big cylindrical ship riding the line he'd marked in the void like it was nailed to it.

Nothing. There was no sign that they'd hit or missed it or…

"We're in," Streamwater told him, her voice very soft.

"Open your eyes, Cat," Brushfire told him. "Please."

Laughing, he did and saw why his officers were so sure they'd hit the strait. The glowing outersphere of the Warden of Fire was gone. In front of them was simply void, with a few sparks of light and dust marking the edges of the strait.

"So, let's… not move from this course," Cat said slowly. "Because I am quite certain *this* path is safe, but given that *I* can't see where the strait ends and *nothing* begins… we will wait until we are in IronHome before we touch the crystals or engines again, yes?"

"Please," Brushfire repeated. "And Cat?"

"Brushfire?" he replied.

"If you close your eyes while flying the ship again, I think poor Streamwater might actually *faint* from the stress."

CHAPTER

19

AFTER THE CLOCK TICKED PAST THE SECOND HOUR IN THE STRAIT, Brushfire started to worry. Cat seemed unbothered, but she was *all* too aware of how skilled her Captain was at concealing his feelings.

She only knew elvar culture from a distance and only knew High Court culture, especially, by reputation and rumor. But she suspected that *not* having full control of how people perceived your emotions would have been unwise for a senior High Court officer.

Even so, she'd learned to read him better than she hoped he realized. So, either he really *was* unbothered by the complete lack of a clear form to their strait or sign of an exit, or he was *very* determined to shield his concern.

"Shouldn't we see the exit by now?" Faith Streamwater asked, the second officer running out of patience first.

"We don't know," Cat said calmly. "Brushfire, how far have we traveled down the strait?"

Brushfire looked at the sextant she'd been using.

"We have no external markers, Cat," she replied. "*None.* Given our speed on entry and the time we've spent in the strait, well over a hundred leagues."

She'd worked on ships that had passed through longer straits, though she'd only *navigated* a ship through one herself. One of the straits along their journey to Brokenwright had been a hundred and sixty leagues long—but they'd had charts and had been able to see the sides and the end of that strait.

"The charts say the strait is a hundred and ten leagues long," Cat told her.

"I would say we're past that," she warned. She was surprised when he simply nodded.

"I know. But I haven't seen any sign we've left the channel, which means the channel has *changed*. Our charts are over a thousand dances out of date, Faith, Brushfire. No var has traced this course in over two elvar lifetimes.

"It's not something we commonly think of, but straits change over time. Their positions in a sphere continue to follow their orbits, but their lengths are far more variable than we imagine."

He shook his head.

"It's just that those variations take place over cycles of a hundred or more dances. A thousand dances without a chart update? *Finding* the strait was still almost guaranteed, but we couldn't be sure how long it was going to be."

Brushfire didn't *quite* shake her head. She had her own reasons to have learned to control her expressed emotions, after all. Cat was spinning a solid line—it was probably even true!—but the combination of a potentially unusually long strait and the inability to clearly see the *sides* of the strait had to be nerve-wracking.

"That should help your nerves," Alloy suddenly declared, gesturing. "I see a light."

Brushfire followed the darvar's pointing hand and let her shoulders relax as she saw what he saw. It wasn't much more than a dot at the moment, but the warm golden glow of an ember meant they could *see* the end of the strait.

"And there we go," Cat said aloud, suddenly resting his hand on Brushfire's shoulder. His touch sent a reassuring shiver through her— but she could also tell that *he* was drawing reassurance from *her*.

"If we can see IronHome's ember, then we are almost through the passage. So, let's keep her straight and clean and see where the ancient road takes us, shall we?"

The crystal "windows" surrounding the control room aboard *Void Flyer* were more magical than transparent, but they gave the crew in that space a clear view into the void around them. Thanks to that view, the exit from the strait into IronHome was clear.

One heartbeat, all they could see was the ember growing larger ahead of them. The next, they emerged from a cave-like opening in reality and the entire sphere spread out around them.

IronHome was seventy-six thousand leagues across, according to their charts, with this particular void strait emerging some twenty-six thousand leagues from the burning ember that lit the place. Of course, that diameter was based on where aether ended and void began, so Brushfire saw some awkward questions about how accurate it was now.

"Here we are," Cat announced from the helm. "Let's see if we can locate the Home itself. That's our next stop."

Brushfire pulled a telescope from the scabbard next to the sextant. Unless the charts were more wrong than they'd been in the Warden of Fire, they should have a decent idea of where to find the single lodeplate that occupied the sphere.

As she put her eye to the device and swept her vision across the sphere, though, she shivered. According to Armand, the archmage's divination had flagged eleven key places, worldlets of a few million var or the Home itself.

Those may have been *key*, but the sphere had been home to far more worlds and outposts and possibly even artificial lodeplates. It seemed like everywhere her telescope fell, as she guided it toward the big lodeplate, there was *something* reflecting the ember's light.

"This place is… something," she said aloud. "I don't think I've ever seen this many lodestone sources, rocks and worlds and floating cities…"

"The High Court is much the same," Cat told her. "We often only speak of the Sixteen, the High Court themselves, but there are about a score and ten small worldlets as well. Plus, the shipyards and other aether works."

"I haven't seen the High Court, but this place looks just as busy," Brushfire told him. Her telescope finally settled on the massive shadow of the Home. "Found the plate. About a degree up from where we calculated, but in about the right area."

Cat didn't use a telescope to follow her direction. She felt his magic take shape and took her eye away from the telescope—which used magic of its own to make a floating continent thousands of leagues away visible at all—as her Captain wove a magical illusion into place above the helm.

The illusion mirrored what her telescope had seen—it *was* a telescope, but one operating entirely from magic and giving a both more focused and broader view of the specific target.

"That… is huge," the elvar said slowly. "How far are we?"

"Just over ten thousand leagues," Brushfire confirmed.

Cat nodded and held up his hand to the illusion, measuring it with his fingers. Presumably, he was doing some kind of math she didn't understand yet.

"It's got to be two thousand leagues across," he concluded after a moment. "Only the Prime of the High Court is larger. I'd never… I'd never heard of anything like this outside the High Court itself."

"Armand says that's why your people buried the knowledge of the Ironhands," she pointed out, taking advantage of a moment to softly prod him. He needed the poking sometimes.

"We're not quite on the course to the Home," she continued. "I don't think we'll get to her without firing the engines."

"We can straighten out our course and it'll take us seven days," Alloy suggested.

"No, we'll go faster," Cat decided aloud. "Alloy, do we have the fuel to detour out to the Home at two leagues a minute?"

"Aye, but it will make our trip through the last two spheres slower and more careful," the darvar warned.

"Maybe we'll find fuel on the Home?" Brushfire asked. "It does seem like there was a lot going on there."

"Not void ships, though, and regular alcohol won't work," Alloy told her. "Only way we're going to find much more fuel for *Void Flyer* now is to settle somewhere for a bit and *make* it."

Brushfire figured they weren't doing that until they got to the Clan Spheres—if then. *Void Flyer* would take them this way, but both finding their answers and coming home were going to require more work.

"Some of our answers are on the Home," Cat said, like he'd been listening to Brushfire's thoughts. "Two leagues a minute will make it a four-day journey there, yes?"

"Agreed," Alloy said.

"Six from there to the strait to Warden of Stone," the Captain continued. "Brushfire, cast an eye around the sphere. Something about this place..."

He shook his head.

"See what you can find," he instructed. "I'm going to go talk to the archmage."

CHAPTER

20

The ember was wrong.

Armand knew he wasn't an experienced aether sailor, the type who'd walked a thousand different worldlets in a hundred different spheres. Prior to the vision that had sent him on this particular quest, he'd never actually left the Shining Kingdom.

The Shining Eye, the light source for the Kingdom and its sphere, was a light crystal. Almost a hundred leagues across, it glowed from within with a magical energy no var had ever been able to control or identify.

Most archmagi like Armand suspected that the crystals and outer-lights and embers drew from the Deep Magic that underlay all spheres. It was where their own power came from, and it made sense that the same underlying energy field that seemed to empower all reality would empower the lights that sustained all life.

But while Armand Bluestaves only knew one crystal well, he had read more books than most var would ever even see. Many had even had pictures, including drawings and illustrations of what embers and outerlit spheres and light crystals usually looked like.

None of his experiences so far had shown him anything that departed from what those drawings had shown him. Until now.

More than that, even, the papers he'd brought with him included sketches and illustrations and descriptions of what the IronHome's ember had looked like.

A flaring pale red, like iron ready to be forged, one text had described it. Other documents and imagery had matched that descriptor.

But now Armand looked through the magical crystals that turned this deck of *Void Flyer* into an observatory, and the color of the fire at the heart of IronHome did *not* match that description.

There was a red, yes, but it was a darker, *bloodier* color than he'd seen in the art. Worse, gangrene-like green and purple streaks wove through the colors.

Studying them was not *easy*, of course, as the ember burned brightly enough to hurt mortal eyes. A combination of magic and simple optical tricks allowed Armand to confirm his fear, though.

The ember of the IronHome was sick. It wasn't *dying*; he judged its illness to be something very different from that. It was an infection, one that the ember served as the anchor and main source for.

The ember wasn't dying. It was *consuming*. The magical weave that had swept these spheres in death was anchored on that ancient flame. Armand knew that in his bones, with as much certainty as if he'd cast the spell himself.

He had no idea *what* had been done or *why*, but some of the *how* was beginning to become clear. He did not know how any being could have bent the power of an *ember* to their will, but that seemed to be the core of it.

The IronHome's heart had betrayed it and the very light that had brought life to the Home, the ancient lodeplate the Ironhand Dynasty had anchored their empire upon, had brought death to half a dozen or more spheres.

"Come in, Cat," he said absently, barely aware of his Captain knocking. The elvar's presence was always reassuring, even before either of them spoke.

"We have a course for the Home," Cat told him quietly, coming up to stand next to him and examine the strange construction on the table. "What is this?"

"I am studying the ember," Armand replied. "Trying to see how much I can learn of what is wrong with it."

"*Everything* in this sphere has something wrong with it," the elvar said. "I don't know how many var lived here, but only the High Court even comes to mind as a comparison."

"This was the capital of an empire that put the High Court's…" Armand trailed off, unsure quite how to describe the High Court's influence and power in the Kingdoms. It was *impolite*, even for an archmage, to say that the High Court ruled the Kingdoms, after all. But no King or Council, not even an *elvar* King or Council, would defy the High Court.

"The High Court lacks the direct power of the Imperium," Cat finished for him. "And exerts their influence over fewer spheres. I could read the charts you showed me, Armand. The Ironhand Imperium was unlike anything we have seen since."

"And if something like it existed before, we have no history of it," the archmage concluded. "Hard enough for us to remember anything of the Ironhand, a thousand dances past."

"Yet, a thousand dances past, this entire sphere died," Cat said quietly. "I can feel it where I would normally feel aether, you know. The *hunger*. It's getting worse."

"The ember is its anchor," Armand replied before fully catching up with Cat's words. "You can *feel* it?"

He knew Cat had a sense for the aether that was unusual. It was what made the var one of the best navigators Armand knew of. Still, his understanding was that the sense was limited and one-dimensional.

Now, he wondered if that was merely an assumption he had made… and if anyone else had ever investigated the limits and abilities of what was both a rare and a *valuable* talent.

"I felt it most strongly when the wraiths came at us," Cat murmured. "Fragments of it afterward. Like sore spots against the fabric where the aether *should* be."

"What do you feel now?" Armand asked. It might be helpful. It might just sate his curiosity—they were still several days, he presumed, from the Home. Anything to keep them distracted from the dead sphere outside *Flyer's* hull.

"There are more of those spots here than there were in the Warden of Fire," Cat noted. "The ember itself... Now that you *tell* me it's a source, I can feel it. It's almost like..."

Armand waited. He was, after all, primarily a teacher. He knew how to wait out a student trying to find the right words—and he'd found the same skill useful as a researcher.

"It's like the whole sphere is a pond and the ember is floating on it," the elvar finally said. "It shifts up and down, creating ripples. And those 'ripples' feel similar to how I'd sense aether currents.

"I don't think I could sail on them, but I can definitely *feel* them."

There was just enough curiosity in Cat's voice to make Armand smile.

"I imagine that us trying to sail on the currents of the void's hunger would end poorly," he agreed. "But even if we were tempted, *Flyer* doesn't have sails."

"No, no, true enough." Now Cat sounded vaguely disappointed, and Armand chuckled.

"What else can you feel?" he asked. "Anything we should be wary of?"

He wasn't used to seeing Cat hesitate. In so many matters, the elvar Captain was utterly self-assured and determined to see things through. Armand was *beginning* to realize how much of that was a shield put up to survive the realities of High Court life, but it was still rare for him to see the Captain actually *hesitate*.

"I'm not sure I have that much... well, anything." Cat shook his head, stepping away from the counter with its boxes and pinholes to look out at the magical windows, surveying the sphere. "There are those ripples running through everything."

There was a long, silent pause.

"We are not welcome here," the Captain finally said. "I can feel it in ways I can't even describe. There is something here, not living, not dead, and it *knows* we don't belong."

"The manifestation," Armand agreed. "A vestige of a magical working, a ritual. I am aware of the theoretical concept, but to see it like this... Even an archmage shouldn't have been able to do something on this scale."

"But *why*?" Cat asked. "Our path takes us through four spheres that suffered like this. My reading of the chart puts the total at nine. What would bring someone to *do* this?"

"I don't know." Armand shook his head, following his Captain's gaze out the windows. Still thousands of leagues from anything in the sphere, all he could see were sparks where rock and wood reflected the light of the sickly ember.

"I am just barely beginning to comprehend the *what* and the *how*," he continued. "The *why*? That might be forever beyond us. A thousand dances separate us from whoever created this horror."

"There." Cat pointed outward. "I can feel a few denser spots, but somewhere along *that* line through the sphere, there is something. Something more… awake. Something hungry."

Armand followed the elvar's gesture and summoned magic to follow that line. Illusions stacked upon illusions, the archmage *always* delighted to lean into his specialty, as he made hundreds of leagues vanish through a magical survey that extended out along Cat's arm into the darkness.

He barely noticed Cat turning away to consult a chart until he found the first *thing* along that route. The floating outpost had probably been attached to *something* of value originally, but now it simply hung in the void.

It wasn't much of a structure, a cloudwood-and-iron var-made island with a tower on each of its three corners—on both sides. The six towers slowly spun through space, as if standing watch over some ancient, now meaningless, piece of void.

There was nothing *there* that spoke of threat or hunger. Just a forgotten watchpost that had drifted away from its charge over hundreds of dances.

Armand's magic swirled away from the old watchpost, compressing hundreds of more leagues until he found a site that almost certainly *did* host something.

"It's the shipyards," Cat said, at the same moment that Armand's magic conjured an illusion into full existence in his observatory living room.

Eight rocks, each a mirror to the Seventh Ward in Brokenwright, marked the corners of a massive cube in the void. Even the Ironhands hadn't gone so far as to link the fortresses for their aether-ship construction complex together, leaving each of them to rotate around the ember on its own path.

Amidst those rocks were larger versions of the watchpost, artificial two-sided islands anchored on var-made lodestone plates to host workers and their families. Intermingled with them were frames of wood, stone and iron that had once held under-construction ships.

And forever drifting between the old yards and the Wards that guarded them was the fleet.

Armand wove his magic with the skill of long dances of practice and what he privately thought was a touch of natural artistry no one could teach. The illusion expanded, but it was still a cube a hundred leagues on a side compressed into a space less than two yards across.

"Okay, *those* look roughly like ninesails," he said, gesturing to a group close to him. "But I'm not recognizing a lot of these."

Cat had turned away from the chart and was studying the illusion like a hawk looking for prey. He slowly walked over to it, circling the two-yard-wide image and studying it.

"Most of them are smaller," he observed. "Interesting design, these."

He tapped one of the illusions, drawing Armand's notice to it. It *did* have the three sail decks and nine masts of an elvar ninesail, but where a ninesail divided the sail decks from each other with stave galleries, this ship let the lower two sail decks merge directly. With only two weapon galleries, it was a five-sided shape to a ninesail's six.

"I don't know any elvar Captain who'd accept not having a lower stave gallery, but we have a few hundred dances of tradition with our current ships," Cat continued. "They get a bit bigger, and we pack a few more staves onto the galleries, but we don't *change.*"

"That's the problem with your people as a rule," Armand pointed out. "The High Court changes so slowly that to the halvar, at least? You *don't* change. At all."

Over a hundred dances? Almost certainly. But even Armand, whose link to the Source would give him half again the life of a regular halvar, wouldn't see *two* hundred dances. Cat, on the other hand, was already over a hundred dances old.

"Can you bring one of these out, make it larger?" Cat asked, still examining the five-sided ship.

Armand nodded, pulling the illusion of the vessel away from the main construct and vastly increasing its size. Now almost two-thirds of a yard long itself, it was far easier to make out details than when it had been one tiny piece of hundreds among the main illusion of the old shipyards.

"Nine sail-masts, as our ships of the line," Cat murmured. "Can't tell the size, but I'd guess a hundred yards at most. Half the size or less of a ninesail. But the galleries…"

Armand could see the bits that Cat was pointing to and speaking about, but he didn't know what they *meant*. Not really.

"She's pierced for ten staves total," the elvar Captain murmured. "Five on a gallery. Those staves are either massive or need larger safe spaces than ours. The ninesails I commanded had twelve in each gallery on a hundred and eighty yards."

Star hadn't, Armand knew, but *Star* had been an older ship, and for all the doors being an archmage opened, the Kingdom of Blueswallow simply hadn't *had* that many spare storm staves to sell.

"Twenty yards a stave?" Armand asked, doing the math.

"Measurements are impossible to really tell," Cat admitted. "Anything I could compare to is built to the same scale as the ship, whatever that is. But we use twelve yards in the Navy these dances, making sure we have ten yards between staves."

Armand mostly followed. Each stave was two yards across, with five yards on each side, which put ten yards between any two weapons. But that was for the staves the *High Court Navy* used, a thousand dances after this odd pentagonal ship had been built.

"These five-siders appear to be most of their fleet, but as you said, there are ninesails, too." Cat stepped away from the expanded illusion, looking back at the Ironhand fleet. "Have to be *thirty* ninesails alone, plus a hundred of these ten-stavers."

"That means something to you," Armand said drily. "Explain for *me*, please?"

"The High Court makes a very real effort to keep the number of ninesails in commission secret," his Captain replied. "*I* didn't know the total number. But there is what a var *knows* and what the rumor networks of a Navy share."

"I understand," Armand allowed. "So, how many?"

"About two hundred. We keep fifty ships in the High Court, standing guard over the plates. The rest are in divisions and squadrons of two to six, across the Kingdoms. We encourage the Kingdoms to hire elvar to fly sixsails, which are cheaper to crew and maintain, but there are probably another fifty ninesails, at least, across the Kingdoms."

Armand looked at the illusion of the ancient shipyards.

"And there are a hundred and fifty ships *here,*" he observed.

"There were definitely *ships* in the Warden of Fire, too," Cat noted. "We didn't spend time taking a look at them. It didn't seem relevant, but... a hundred and fifty ships, Armand. And if the five-siders are smaller than ninesails and the ninesails themselves seem smaller than ours, well... There are *these.*"

Armand switched the five-sider for the ship Cat indicated without much thought—which meant he inhaled sharply as he took in the sheer size of the monster of the aether the Ironhands had commanded.

Scale was still hard to tell, but it was definitely bigger than the five-sided aether ship. Five sail decks, each with four sail-masts, were divided by five stave galleries.

And each of *those* galleries, Armand counted, was pierced by openings for *twenty-four* staves.

"How big is she, Cat?" he asked slowly.

"She has to have multiple keels," his Captain said instead. "The High Court is only up to forging a single lodestone keel a cable long. *Plates* are a bit easier, but that's because we don't really *forge* those so much as just hack them to shape.

"And the Ironhand ninesails *are* smaller, so... she has to have at least two keels. Maybe three, overlapping?"

"Cat," Armand prodded.

Cat nodded and exhaled.

"At least two cables long and broader in the stays than any ninesail I've ever served on," he admitted. "Twenty masts, a hundred and twenty staves. She's a monster."

Armand studied the ship with a careful eye. He couldn't judge her as clearly as Cat could, but he knew a massive, impressive piece of artisanry when he saw it. And he *did* know that the largest ninesails he'd ever heard of had been roughly *one* cable—two hundred yards—long and mounted less than forty storm staves.

"That ship could fight an entire High Court Navy squadron, couldn't it?" he asked.

Cat shrugged slowly.

"I *think* I see ways her size weakens her, and I couldn't say for sure until I see her sail, but maybe," he conceded. "A full six-ship squadron would take her, but a four-ship squadron would be an even fight."

A four-ship squadron like the one Cat had served in most recently, until he'd been forced to abandon three other ships to their fates to warn the High Court about dragons. That the dragons appeared to have *disappeared* afterward hadn't reduced the courage necessary to do that.

Under elvar law, after all, Cat could have been executed along with every tenth member of his crew for retreating. The latter part, the decimation, *probably* wouldn't have been implemented—Armand suspected that he would have heard if it had *ever* been used—but it was definitely in elvar law!

"Tow that home and the High Court might give you your commission back?" Armand asked. It wasn't something they could really do, he thought, but it was an amusing thought.

"If we brought one of those monsters back to the High Court, Armand, they'd give *Brushfire* a commission," Cat said grimly. "And we aren't going anywhere near them. Because while I don't think it's the *ships* that I can feel from here, the hunger I spoke of?

"It's in the shipyards. And while we have beaten the manifestation's wraiths on the ground, with wand and light and courage... *Void Flyer* has no weapons. We couldn't install them."

"I didn't think to ask," Armand admitted.

"Believe me, my archmage, *I did*," Cat told him. "There were a few places where we could open up panels to open room to mount a stave, but we couldn't create a space that was open to the void *and* had air or aether to breathe."

"So, we're defenseless, even once we reach the Clan Spheres," Armand murmured.

"I didn't say *that*." Cat chuckled grimly, still staring at the aether battleships that had anchored the IronHome's defense fleet. "We *did* bring some of the storm staves over from *Star*. We just can't do anything *useful* with them until we're back in aether.

"So long as we're in the void spheres, those staves are just weight."

"Thankfully, the wraiths seem as bound by lodestone pull and the void as anything else," Armand told him. "We may encounter difficulties on the Home, Cat."

"I am quite certain we *will* encounter wraiths on the Home," Cat agreed. "Or something worse. But we'll bring Alloy's lamps, and with Fist-fall trained and the officers up to speed with their new foci, we'll be ready."

"Even for something worse?"

"We can't be ready for what we can't predict, I admit," the Captain said. "Only as ready as we can be for whatever comes. With this crew, these officers and the tools *you* have given us, Armand, I believe that we *will* face whatever is waiting for us on the Home.

"I cannot guarantee we will overcome it. I cannot guarantee we will not lose var. Only that we will face it and that no one else would have made it this far. Thanks to you."

Armand flushed. He knew he'd spent money like water and handed out personal foci in a manner that even other archmagi might question, but all *he* had done was enable others.

"I would not have made it off of Blueswallow on my own," he pointed out. "With another Captain, I would have died at Brokenwright. You and Brushfire are what has carried this mission this far."

"*Captain and Shaman; Shaman and Archmage*," Cat quoted back at him, the capitals clear as he repeated the prophetic words that had driven him to Armand's service. "We make a trio, don't we?"

"Lucky us," Armand murmured. And he meant it. Drawing strength and warmth from Cat's presence even as he dismissed the illusion of the ancient shipyard, he knew he would be lost without the other two now.

He hoped they didn't feel *quite* as needy as he did... but he had to admit he *also* didn't want either of them to go anywhere else!

"First-sister, can we talk?"

Brushfire looked up at her little brother and chuckled at Fistfall.

"We are over a day's flight from the void strait and still three days' flight from the Home," she pointed out. "There is, so far as we can tell, nothing alive in the entire sphere of IronHome, and none of the things that *aren't* alive but can still move are anywhere near us.

"While I am hardly *bored*, I can certainly spare time for my first-brother. What is bothering you, Fistfall?"

The big gobvar stepped into her office carefully. He, like Brushfire, was *definitely* too big for a ship built for darvar. While Alloy's design had clearly considered the possibility of having other var aboard, gobvar were the tallest of the four var.

And the least likely to be aboard a unique and valuable ship in most situations. She could understand, if not necessarily accept, why allowing for two-plus yards of var and more in horns hadn't really been factored into the design process.

Brushfire could at least walk the decks without hitting her horns; she just had to be careful with doors. From the way Fistfall crossed the office in her quarters, he needed to be conscious about how he walked *everywhere*.

"The ship is wearing on you?" she asked, realizing he hadn't spoken.

"I'm getting used to it. My neck hurts almost as much as Windheart complains about his," Fistfall said with a clearly forced smile. "Couple of the others are having more trouble getting the gait right. Been a few bruises."

Once, Brushfire would have been the one to know all of that. Now, she was not only taking care of the hundred-ish survivors of her tribe but another hundred gobvar and a hundred elvar.

Plus one halvar and four darvar, not that Armand or the Bellowforges had needed much managing.

Like walking around the ship, it was taking practice and learning.

"And the focus?" she asked, gesturing to the wand her brother wore.

Fistfall's wand hung along the bottom third of a bandolier designed to hold battlewands and throwing knives. Brushfire wasn't sure where he'd *got* it, but it was clearly a sized-up version of the two Hunter Paintrock wore.

Of course, with the focus, Fistfall didn't need battlewands anymore. But he'd kept the bandolier.

"That's the weird one," he admitted. "I... I don't think I'm a quick student, not like you, 'cording to the second officer. But she isn't complaining, either."

"No," Brushfire agreed. She had been told that her ability to watch a piece of magic be done and duplicate it almost automatically was as unusual as her Captain's ability to sense aether currents across several thousand leagues. And while her own lack of training had kept her from helping with Fistfall's magical education, she'd kept her ears open.

If Streamwater and Smallwolf had any complaints about Fistfall's speed of learning, she hadn't heard a peep.

"The thought of me as a mage is strange enough," Fistfall said. "But I have listened and learned, as you told me to. It's real."

"It is," she confirmed. "There are others in our tribe, Captain Greentrees tells me. We don't have foci for them, but time will tell. Once we're clear of the void, the archmage may take time to fix that."

"We'll be among the Clans then," Fistfall noted. "Our var."

"Our var," Brushfire agreed. "Strange to think it, but it may end up being you and I who speak for the ship the most. I'm *told* mages among the Clans are given a certain deference."

"Fear," her brother whispered. "Mages among the Clans are taken by Her Sisters, 'cording to Axfall and Windheart. The other Elders. They..."

"Are they causing you trouble?" Brushfire asked. She doubted it of Axfall and Windheart, but there were a handful of other Hammerheads who'd made the flight from the Clan Spheres.

"They are afraid, first-sister," Fistfall told her. "Not of me, not really. But of what happens when the Sisters find mages among us. They think the Sisters will know."

"They might," Brushfire conceded. "Cat knew you were a mage as soon as he took the time to really *look*. The Sisters might be able to tell *they* didn't train you. But I'm betting"—they were all betting, really—"that no one else can. And that *fear*, whether we like it or not, will help keep us all safe."

"I dunno if I like the thought of more folk being afraid of me," Fistfall said. He grimaced. "Never liked. Might have helped avoid some fights, I s'pose, but I didn't *want* folks afraid of me."

"You always had too kind a heart, my brother," she told him. "I love you dearly for it, but I am afraid *for* you sometimes."

He chuckled and laid his hands on the desk. Like the rest of the ship, it was darvar workvarship and *definitely* not sized for their kind.

"Plenty reason to be," he told her. "I ain't the brightest, but I try."

"You aren't as foolish as you like us to believe, either," she argued. "And you're bothered by something, little brother. Talk to me?"

He sighed, rolling his shoulders and, even seated, nearly brushing his horns against the ceiling before he ducked his head down a moment.

"It's Petal," he said quietly. "And... it's Petal."

Brushfire chose not to interrogate his pause, just gesturing for him to speak about his dead lover.

"Everyone always seemed to think we were going to get together," Fistfall murmured. "And I... I..." He trailed off. "She was never to me what I was to her. You understand? She loved me and I..."

He shook his head, a guilty look crossing his face.

"I went along *because* she loved me, and she was sweet, and it could be fun," he admitted. "And everyone else encouraged it, but it never felt *right*. And sometimes it felt *real* wrong. And it was feeling real wrong when we came to Brokenwright, but..."

"Thought you two were together," Brushfire said, slowly wrapping her mind around his words. She had a spike of her own guilt—she'd been there with everyone else on thinking Fistfall and Petal were adorable and just a question of him getting his head on straight.

And never realized that maybe he'd had his head on *straightest* when he'd walked away.

"At the end, yeah," Fistfall said quietly. "Things were busy, worrying. She needed a shoulder, and I couldn't *be* her shoulder without being that, so I let it be. And then she died.

"Died thinking I loved her because I lied to her."

Brushfire sighed. Even with both of them seated, she was looking up at her brother—but she'd been doing that for a dozen dances at least.

"Did you, though?" she asked. She *knew* her little brother.

Fistfall looked down at his hands.

"Sure as void let her *think* I did," he muttered. "Let her drag me to bed and all that."

"She needed you to be something you weren't, but you did the best you could," Brushfire told him. "Would you *rather* she'd died miserable, thinking you hated her because you'd just had an ugly breakup? You cared about her; I know that."

"She was tribe. And she was a friend, and she was sweet." He sighed. "Yes, I cared *about* her, but not the way she wanted."

"But she died thinking she had you," Brushfire reminded him. "And cold as it sounds, that meant she died happier than she would have if you'd told her the truth."

And Petal had died quickly, if that mattered. A storm stave in the hands of His Dark Brothers had torn through the section of the ship where she'd been helping carry supplies. She and the two elvar with her had died instantly.

"I suppose. Still feel guilty, though," he admitted, still staring at his hands. "Like I took advantage of her."

"I could argue that she took advantage of the rest of us being fools to pressure you into giving in," Brushfire told him. "That *she* took advantage of *you*. But I know you both better than that."

Fistfall might never have seen a future with himself and Petal, but he also wasn't the type to just use someone for sex. If he *had* been, the tribal elders like Axfall and Windheart would have found ways to gently keep him away from members of the tribe.

Instead, everyone had seen the pair as adorable, a likely source of a next generation of Hammerheads—always a concern, with a tribe of barely a hundred. Especially one that had rarely stopped anywhere for long enough for its half dozen younger var to find partners who *weren't* their fifth-siblings at best.

"I won't say I *don't* listen to the rest of the tribe," Fistfall said slowly, "but no one was taking advantage of *me*."

"I didn't think so," Brushfire said with a smile. "You did what you thought was right. And maybe things didn't end as *honestly* as you'd like, but she didn't leave us angry at you or herself. And that's worth a *lot*, little brother."

"Aye." He exhaled and nodded, lifting his gaze away from his hands. "That helps a bit. Thank you."

Brushfire held his gaze for a heartbeat, then a horrible thought struck her about her *own* discussions with Fistfall.

"Brother, I need you to be honest with me," she told him. "The wand. The becoming a mage. All of that... I know there's a lot of pressure there, to take that on and to 'step up' to be what the crew needs."

She wasn't entirely sure what that was going to *be*, beyond "another mage," but she knew they needed him.

"I don't want you to do anything in these spheres that you don't want to do. That terrifies you. If we pushed too hard, with the magic, as we did with Petal... I need you to tell me."

Fistfall's resounding belly laugh surprised her, and she met his gaze as he calmed from his own surprise.

"No, first-sister, you didn't pressure me into *this*"—he tapped the wand on his bandolier—"any more than Hunter pressured me into learning battlewands and swordplay and stavework from him.

"I *want* this," he told her, his tone fierce and urgent. "I *want* every trick, every tool, every skill I can learn to protect our people, first-sister. You and the Elders have carried that burden as long as I can remember, and I've added to it more than I should.

"Been time for a while that I stepped up and helped *carry* burdens rather than *create* them."

Brushfire eyed her brother. She *knew* him, and this was… less of a surprise than she would have expected. Of course, there were sources for it that could be just as much trouble as any drunken foolishness he'd ever engaged in.

"You know cursed well none of this was your fault," she said softly. He'd been one of several var in the fight that had seen the tribe kicked off their last ship—but she'd known, even *before* talking to everyone involved, that her people hadn't started the fight and that Fistfall had tried to calm it.

He hadn't created nearly as many burdens as he might think.

"I do," he agreed—and while Brushfire wasn't *entirely* sure she believed him, she let it ride. "But that doesn't change that our Elders are… getting older. And everyone looks to *you* as our shaman, but there's *nobody* else coming after. Faithful can't lead—even *she* says that—and odds and spheres say Axfall will outlive her anyway.

"But after Windheart and Axfall, there's no one in that generation who's stepping up. And 'cause we *have* our two Masters, we miss that. Someone has to be ready to stand at your side when their times come.

"And, for all that I don't know why some days and dances, you *trust* me. So, *this*"—he tapped the bandolier as much as the wand this time, drawing attention to both the magic he was learning now and the other skills he'd learned from Paintrock—"is a step in that direction."

Of course, teaching a *gobvar* magic in the Court and Kingdoms was… so frowned upon, no one had *needed* to make it illegal. Teaching them to use *storm staves,* a skill Brushfire knew her brother had acquired under Paintrock's tutelage, *was.*

"So long as you wear the blue sash of an archmage's staff, you're shielded from a lot of things," Brushfire murmured. "But carrying a focus back in the Kingdoms will draw eyes."

"Then we draw those eyes, first-sister, and we show them that we *can* be trusted," Fistfall said calmly. "Not easy. Not simple. Shouldn't be necessary. But we carry the burden so that those who come after us carry a smaller one.

"Isn't that right?"

Brushfire almost choked on air as she swallowed.

That wasn't a phrase she'd heard since their mother had passed thirty-some dances earlier.

We carry the burden so that those who come after us carry a smaller one.

Her mother had found Brushfire her first shaman teacher when she'd shown the tiny signs of magic that had allowed her to be identified. Finding shamans was difficult among gobvar. The signs they looked for, Brushfire now realized, spoke to either extraordinary power or to unusual forms of it.

More of the latter, she guessed, for shamans to be as common among gobvar as they were. There had to be *enough* gobvar shamans for the traditions to continue, after all, and magic as the other var judged it was rarely visible without training.

"There are days, Fistfall, I think that you would have made a better shaman than I," she told him. "I don't know what the Clan Spheres will hold for our crew and our tribe. I know I'm not planning on *staying* there."

"Gods, no," Fistfall agreed. "Smallvar are *annoying*, at times, but I can't even *think* of living solely among our kind.

"Just want a world where everyone can be themselves. All var, all folk, one big happy Clan."

There were days Brushfire thought her brother would be a better shaman than her. And then he would say something like *that*.

CHAPTER

22

"AND... *NOW*."

Magic snapped across the far-too-small storage room they'd set aside for the training. A ball of seemingly harmless light had been bobbing through the space, with Armand giving careful direction to his attentive students.

Now Bogsong Smallwolf went into the *second* piece of the spell the archmage was teaching, and the will-o'-the-wisp *exploded*. What had been a single point of light, perhaps the size of a fist and serving as a flying lantern *just* smart enough to follow its caster, burst into a brilliant blaze of magical power.

Armand's own shields protected the three var in the room, though *this* wisp was "merely" conjuring a blaze of the light they'd used to push back the wraiths. On the other hand, it was the first time Smallwolf had worked with any active constructs in her *life*, and he'd figured she'd get something wrong.

And, as expected, her power hammered into his shields with far more than mere light. He held up a hand, palm up, and snapped it closed into a fist.

Shields closed and the spell was silenced. He smiled at the young elvar—and *him* calling Smallwolf *young* was rich, he knew, as he wasn't entirely sure she wasn't *older* than him.

"Well done," he told her. "Power balance was off from the plan, but that's why you have a teacher shielding when you're experimenting with something like this. Setting up the construct to self-sustain and to release its charge on command? That is significantly more difficult than making sure you have the *right* charge."

And if Armand could summon about sixty wisps in a single breath, well, there were *reasons* he was an archmage. Smallwolf could learn many of the tricks inherent in that, but she might never have the strength to hold that many constructs.

"Did it work?" she asked. "I thought I was losing control at the end."

"The opposite, I'm afraid," he corrected gently. "Where you risked collapsing the matrix was when you *didn't* let go. The entire purpose of a self-contained construct is that it has a pattern and orders and will follow them even without you holding an active link.

"Completing the spell created and empowered the construct, but you didn't quite let it go. And the construct, as we structured the spell, didn't quite have the pattern for an enduring link."

The third occupant in the room, both student and senior officer, was Brushfire. She was listening attentively, clearly absorbing every word Armand said in a manner that he found surprisingly flattering.

Bogsong was as attentive a student as any teacher could ask for. Brushfire was… something else, which Armand's mind shied away from as he considered it.

"Officer Brushfire, would you like to give it a try?" he asked her, expanding his shields to protect both his tiny class and *Void Flyer* herself.

"Of course," Brushfire agreed. She grinned down at Smallwolf. "I think my going second might be cheating, Fourth Officer," she told the elvar. "I now know what you did wrong."

"Learning from each other's mistakes is a key part of this process," Armand told them both. "As much as possible, I am trying to enable you to learn from the mistakes *I* made, dances upon dances ago."

"Oh? And how messy was your first construct?" Smallwolf asked, stepping back to give Brushfire room to work.

"My first *attempt* at a construct was a complete failure," Armand admitted. "I had misread a key portion of the notes my instructor gave me and inverted several steps of the process. I overcharged the spell, knocked myself unconscious and failed to create any form of construct at all. Nearly blew the roof off the training center along the way."

That earned him the chuckles he was aiming for from both var. It helped that the story was *true*—and if anything, he understated how badly he'd misunderstood his lectures on the topic. The time he'd knocked himself unconscious and nearly blown up a building had been the *third* attempt.

After failing to generate anything the first two times, he'd overdone it and, well, he'd already been an archmage candidate by then. This wasn't a *common* form of magic, after all.

Smallwolf had graduated from a well-respected academy in the Kingdoms. Her training was likely inferior to, say, Cat's—who had graduated from the *Navy* academy in the High Court—but she had a complete and competent education.

That education had never touched on self-sufficient pre-patterned constructs.

Armand smiled to himself as he saw Brushfire's focus glow softly with power. The pieces fell into place slowly—this was the first time she'd done anything like this, after all—but fall into place they did.

And a *show-me-once* student was as capable of learning from others' mistakes as she was of learning from seeing it done right. Brushfire took her time, but the will-o'-the-wisp construct was perfect, flitting to and fro about the shielded space while the three var watched it.

"Now."

Armand half-whispered the word, knowing that Brushfire was waiting for it. Even *expecting* the next step and shielding against it, he still found himself blinking away afterimages once the brilliant blaze of light filled the room.

"I'm not the teacher, but that seemed closer," Smallwolf said drily. "Or so I will guess, once I can *see* again."

"The shield would prevent more than a moment of confusion, Officer Smallwolf," Armand noted, his own vision returning to normal. "And yes, that was roughly what we're after. A light source as we move and a first defense if the wraiths strike.

"Alloy's lanterns are one thing, but they *do* require a touch more than a thought and a gesture. Any group with our mages *should* be fine, but the readier we are…"

"The safer our people are," Smallwolf finished, which brought a smile to Armand's face.

He'd expected that response from one of them, but he was a touch surprised the elvar had got it out first.

"Exactly," he told her. "If we have these long stretches of time in the void, without even work on the engines to distract us all, then training may serve us well once we reach the Home."

"Letting the crewvar get bored is a *bad* idea," Brushfire rumbled. "But the ship's Masters are on that. Letting *us* get bored, well."

She chuckled.

"There is always *something* for a ship's officers to be doing, but training is on that list. And, as Smallwolf notes, it falls to us as the mages aboard to do all we can to protect our crew."

And vice versa, as Armand understood it. There were also, he suspected, officers who focused on the crew-protecting-them aspect of the deal… but he *also* suspected that Cat Greentrees would never have hired an officer like that.

The entire concept would probably offend Armand's Captain, and *that*, the archmage knew, was why his people would follow Cat to the ends of the spheres.

He just wished, some days, that he didn't need Cat to lead them there.

Unlike a worldlet or a rock, a lodeplate didn't rotate around any kind of axis. A worldlet in a sphere lit by a crystal or an ember had a definite day and night. Only in outerlit spheres, where light came in from every side, did worldlets approach the eternal day of a lodeplate's upper side.

The *lower* side of a lodeplate was a different story, and Cat stared bleakly at the rocky and lifeless underside of the Home. Leagues upon leagues of stone drifted away as far as the eye could see as they approached the lodeplate, but while few plants and animals thrived on the underside of a plate, the hands of var had been at work beneath the Home.

The High Court was the same, with towers and fortresses and man-ufactories rising from places no one would seek to live. So long as a significant population of aethervar—those who could breathe aether—was available, the underside of a plate was a fantastic place to put any industry that would create sights or smells no one wanted.

That was part of how the High Court's lodeplates remained pristine, with even the most developed having dozens or hundreds of leagues of nearly untouched wilderness.

The Home, however, seemed to concentrate as much industry onto its underside as *all sixteen* of the High Court's plates managed. There were few natural tors or mountains in what he could see. *Everything* looked like it had suffered the touch of pickax and explosive.

Massive plateaus and clear fields had been forged by mortal hands, open spaces swiftly consumed by buildings of a thousand types. Massive chimneys marked foundries and other industrial sites—and Cat knew to look for the sites where long-gone balloons had marked the deliveries of air from the other side.

The *var* could breathe aether and work in it, but many of the processes necessary to work metal and lodestone itself still required air. The chimneys would sweep the byproducts up in the air and spew it out into the aether, well away from the plate.

"We're coming up on the horizon," he warned the other var in the control room. Cat knew that not only had none of his officers seen the High Court, none of his *crew* had.

He was the only person aboard *Void Flyer* with any existing experience of the vagaries of a lodeplate. He kept his hands on the wheel as the ship headed toward the edge.

They were moving *relatively* slowly, a sedate league every two minutes, but the edge of the plate was coming up quickly. It was hard for an unpracticed eye to see, too, with the light from the ember at the heart of the sphere blazing around its rim.

"I make it less than a league," Streamwater confirmed, the second officer keeping her hands on the sextant. "Can't see much of the underside anymore."

The Ironhands had left—or *created*; he wasn't entirely sure—a perimeter of raw rock and mountains on the lip of the lodeplate. From a league beneath the plate, they could easily see past it into the vast fields of factories.

As they approached the horizon, more and more of the undersettlement became invisible behind that semi-natural barrier. Then that barrier was all he could see—and it was blending into and lost against the league-and-a-half-thick presence of the Home itself, a continent floating in the open void.

As they rose past the lodeplate, the haloing effect of looking at the ember *past* the continent reduced, and Cat could turn his focus to the world they were now above.

"Give me a ten-second burn on the engines on my command," he told Streamwater. The helm answered easily to his hands, practiced now at maneuvering the strange ship, and he sent a trickle of power to the lift crystals to align her.

"Burn... *now*," he ordered.

The burn shed much of their remaining speed, now away from their destination, and sent them drifting across the vast plain of the Home.

As he'd expected, the surface looked like it *had* been quite different from the underside. Since then, of course, everything in IronHome had died.

The Home hadn't been left as untouched as the High Court plates were, Cat observed. Where he could see open spaces, it felt clear that they'd been farms rather than parks.

As they rose farther above the IronHome capital, he noted three key things.

The first was that it very much felt like *every* part of the lodeplate had been given a specific purpose and built to it. In hindsight, he'd seen the districting pattern on the underside, but the underplate was an industrial zone.

The surface was an entire nation. He could see half a dozen cities already, and he didn't have the angle to see clearly across the entire plate. But if there had been old roads or buildings shaped by the wandering of grazers, at some point in the past they'd been overwritten with a perfect grid, with everything from farms to residential streets clearly shaped to it.

The second thing he noted was the fortifications. Some of them were subtler than others, but it was far beyond the defenses around the rim of the plate that he'd expected. Four floating fortresses, smaller versions of the Seventh Ward in Brokenwright, hung in the skies above the Home. Forts and towers littered the outside of the plate.

Even *beyond* those, though, were the small and medium fortifications woven through the grid. Patrol stations. Watchtowers. Midsized forts anchoring small villages. It was quite unlike the High Court, where the Navy was a source of pride—and the Guard were rarely mentioned and almost never seen.

There were watch stations and exterior forts on the High Court plates, he was sure, but they would never have been *this* obvious, *this* integrated into everything. Not only had the people of the Home always had soldiers within a few hours' march at worst, they had *known* it.

With those people long dead, he couldn't ask if any of them had found that reassuring—or if they'd found the *third* thing he'd noticed reassuring, either.

At the center of the lodeplate rose a single stark white mountain. The *mountain* was probably natural, he figured, but the *color* was likely the result of immense magic. No natural structure of that size was just one color—unless someone with a great deal of power had decided that it was going to be.

An immense city sprawled around the foot of that mountain, all of it either built from white stone or whitewashed, and he could see several spots on the mountain he figured were airship docks.

"I don't think we even need to consult the cards," he said aloud. "Unless the archmage finds some good reason we *shouldn't* be going there, I think that mountain is the destination."

Because if that mountain wasn't the heart of the Home and the Imperium, the capital and center of everything the Ironhand Dynasty had done and been, he'd eat the damn thing.

The presence of air made the flight across the continent more complicated than it might have been. Cat *could* have just tilted the rocket and sped up, crossing five hundred leagues in a couple of hours.

The need to get above the air envelope and safely descend through it meant that the thousand-league journey would take them over a clock-day. Somehow, Cat didn't find the fact that nothing *changed* in that time particularly reassuring.

"No life," Brushfire said quietly, standing at his shoulder as they finally descended toward the mountain. "Barely any *wind*, even, from what I can see. I know we keep asking this, but what *happened* here?"

"Nothing good," Cat murmured. He glanced away from the mountain, back toward the ember lighting it. "Armand says there is something *wrong* with the ember, and he's right. Every part of this sphere is wrong."

"Something *ate* the aether and the life here," his first officer said. "Yeah. *Wrong* fits."

He shook his head, surveying the city sweeping out beneath them.

"There," he said. "You see it?"

"The big plaza someone *cut* into the mountain?" Brushfire asked.

It *might* have been natural, but Cat doubted it. Easily a cable across and twice that deep, the cut was a sharp-sided flat area near the base of the white mountain. It aligned perfectly with the grid elements that defined the entire plate, with a major thoroughfare connecting directly to it.

Someone had decided it was a show of power and wealth to just have a two-hundred-yard-wide open space they'd carved out of the mountain. It was flat and open, smooth and polished on all sides, but with nothing in the middle to complicate their landing.

"The plaza is hard to miss, and it's the right size and place. If we want to just... land in the front yard of this place, anyway."

"We are flying a two-hundred-yard-high vessel that moves by literally lighting hundreds of gallons of alcohol on fire and blasting the result out a narrow hole," Cat pointed out. "Even in *aether*, we can be heard from leagues away."

"Coming into a city with an air envelope?" He shook his head. "I don't think it will matter if we land in the plaza or on the outskirts of the city. Anybody in the mountain is going to know we're here."

"Fair. Then we land in the plaza and see what we find," she told him. "What happens if it's more wraiths?"

He grimaced as she put his own fears into words.

"Everyone on this ship who *can* do a divination says there are answers here we need," he noted. "That level of consistency and guidance is... concerning in itself, but it's very clear.

"If we haven't found any answers and the wraiths show up here, then we secure the ship and find a way to push through them." He shook his head. "It won't be easy, but I think we can do it."

"What if..." Brushfire trailed off, and he turned to look at her when she didn't complete her thought.

"Brushfire, you're my first officer for a lot of reasons," he murmured softly, so only she could hear him. "And *one* of those reasons is that you have a different background from the rest of my officers. Tell me what you're thinking."

"I don't know enough about the divinations we're using to know, but is it possible that all of our divinations are being guided somehow?" Brushfire asked. "That the reason every divination we do says we have to come here, have to learn *something* here... is because someone wants us to be here? In this mountain?

"Because it's a trap?"

Cat paused on his initial response to her first question as she continued her reasoning, then swallowed everything he'd been thinking. Many things were supposed to be impossible, but...

"Divinations can be blocked," he noted slowly. "I've never heard of them being guided like that—and I would *assume* that no one could so influence the workings of an archmage.

"Yet... I have also never heard of magic that could tear all life and aether from an entire sphere, let alone four. I didn't think of that chance—even the dangers here seem unthinking."

"*Unthinking*, maybe, but so are the constructs Armand is teaching us to conjure," Brushfire reminded him. "And I wonder if that's... almost what we're looking at? Armand said it was a manifestation of the spell that created this place, but it has *become* some kind of self-sustaining construct.

"And we can teach those constructs patterns, actions and responses that can almost fool someone into thinking they're alive."

"I *want* to say that no construct could weave a deception of that scale," Cat said slowly. He wanted to be skeptical of Brushfire's fears, but his paranoia had picked up her cause.

"But I can also see a trap like that being laid and a construct simply being part of it," he continued. "Those same divinations, though, told us going forward without learning what was hidden here would doom us.

"That, too, may be a lie—but we must seek the answers nonetheless." He held out his hand to her and grinned as she clasped his forearm.

"But we can make very sure we're *ready* for a trap, can't we?"

What she was suggesting was beyond anything he had ever known of magic.

But so were the void spheres themselves!

CHAPTER 24

THE PLAZA WAS SPECTACULAR. BRUSHFIRE WASN'T, AS A RULE, particularly interested in anything that wasn't practical, but she had to admit to the austere grandeur of the place.

At its deepest point, the plaza cut into over a hundred yards of stone, the walls as sharp and straight as any blade she'd ever seen. On the outside, the lower slopes of the mountain rose up toward it, with a paved roadway leading through the town right to it.

The ground had been covered in perfectly fitted white stones, placed so close together that it was easy to miss that no stone was the same size as the ones surrounding it. Each stone had been placed and shaped by hand, even as powerful magic had cut away the mountain itself to create the space for it.

And there was *nothing* in the plaza. *Void Flyer* had landed near the entrance to the cut, giving the crew a clear view out over the long-dead city. Looking toward the mountain, there was simply the expanse of white stone, still gleaming somehow after a thousand dances like it had been polished yesterday.

"If there was nothing else blatantly wrong about all of this, the fact that everything is still perfectly clean makes no cursed sense," Paintrock said loudly. The elvar was standing with Fistfall and Smallwolf, the trio hanging just behind Brushfire in case something tried to jump the first officer on a dead lodeplate.

"Guess everything that would make it dirty is also dead?" Smallwolf asked. "That seems..."

"Thorough," Brushfire said quietly. She surveyed the crew. Most were going to stay with the ship and were setting up Bellowforge's lanterns and similar defenses.

"What killed everything here was *very* thorough," she repeated, "but I'd expect that wind alone would leave some dirt on all this white."

As if to prove her point, a chill breeze cut in from the city and sent a shiver down her spine. There was less dust on it than there should be—Paintrock *definitely* had a point—but it wasn't just air, either.

"There is magic bound into these stones," Armand told her, the archmage stepping up to join her. "It's faint, long worn away, but what's left may still be enough to repel dirt."

"Does this whole affair seem as over the top to you as it does to me?" she asked the archmage.

The chubby halvar looked over to meet her gaze and shrugged, his expression somewhat embarrassed.

"I helped *build* something about as outrageous for the Shining King as one of my first contracts after my Trial," he admitted. "And the Shining King only rules one sphere. A wealthy, powerful and independent sphere, but just one.

"The Ironhand Dynasty may have ruled more than we still know exists. So, *yes*, this is grand and pointless and a waste of space in many ways... but it served a purpose, and I have seen almost as foolish created by those with less to support it."

"The High Court has similar places," Cat added. The Captain was trailed by half a dozen var with halberd-wands as he joined them. The var were a mix of the two races aboard *Flyer*—which was the point of the halberds, to allow a group of mixed var to have comparable reach and armament.

"I don't think we often magically transmute the mountains to white marble, but I cannot be certain we have *never* done it," he admitted with a wry tilt to his smile.

"So, these people might have been *more* arrogant than halvar kings and the elvar High Court?" Brushfire asked. "That doesn't make me want to like them much."

Cat had pointed out the array of fortifications woven across the plate. Brushfire was far more aware of the underside of the Court and

Kingdoms than her Captain, which meant she knew *exactly* why the Ironhands had kept soldiers on hand everywhere.

They hadn't trusted their people. Even there, at the heart of their Imperium, they'd had soldiers and, presumably, spies in place to watch over their subjects.

"I doubt any of us would have liked the Ironhands much," Armand agreed. "The best any of the old records and books I have says about them is that they brought *order.*"

Brushfire chewed on that mentally, but it was Cat who spoke.

"Not peace. Not prosperity. Not even *safety*. Order."

"Yeah."

Brushfire shook herself, turning away from the city and looking past *Void Flyer* to the other end of the plaza, over three hundred yards away. Six massive statues of unfamiliar, presumably mythical, creatures had been carved into the native stone wall. Like the rest of the plaza, they *gleamed* in the light of IronHome's ember.

And in the middle of the central pair was a set of doors thirty yards high.

"Are we looking in the dead city or poking at the giant creepy doors?" Brushfire asked.

Armand held out his hand and conjured one of his flying cat-dragons. The spirit flittered around his arm and head for a few heartbeats before settling on the archmage's shoulder and very clearly pointing its nose toward the mountain.

"Into the mountain, I think," Armand said.

"Don't suppose that friend of yours knows *what* we're looking for?" Paintrock asked.

"No. It doesn't work that way—all it can do is give me a direction or a yes/no answer," Armand told the Master of Staves.

"Are we ready, Hunter?" Cat asked.

"We've a dozen var and half our officers ready to go, Captain. On your order."

Brushfire fell in beside Cat and Armand as they strode toward the immense doors. Her brother and Smallwolf took up the wings of the formation, with Hunter at the center directing his dozen halberdiers.

Behind them, the rest of the crew would protect the ship and keep an eye on things. Nobody knew what to expect of this plate, only that they were looking for *something* there. Something that would make their passage through the rest of the void spheres safer.

In theory. If the whole thing wasn't a trap.

Walking up to the hundred-plus-yard-high cliff at the inner end of the courtyard, she couldn't help but be afraid. The doors towered ten times the height of even gobvar, and the statues around them were of creatures completely unknown to her.

To the immediate left of the door was an immense bird, its wings wrapped around itself to both keep it inside the same size as the other statues *and* to create a very clear impression of fire. If it had been painted, she would have expected it to appear to be *made* of fire from the shape of the stone.

Instead, of course, it was stark white like everything *else* in the plaza. White or red, the firebird was unknown to her, missing from any myths or stories *she'd* heard of.

To the right of the door was a similar creature, a sinuous snake coiling through the air to rise to the same height as the other statues. Feathers and wings had been added along the snake's body, creating an impression of grace and motion, speed and flight.

Whoever had designed the statues had been an *incredible* artist. The other four were similar, one for earth, void, water, and aether.

"Six elements and six elementals," Armand noted, surveying the statues himself. His gaze, Brushfire noted, lingered on the inverse statue that fit the void in her head.

It had roughly the form of a var, but where the other five statues had the stone carved away around them to create their forms, the *void* statue had the stone carved away to create an *emptiness* that made up its form.

It wasn't a style Brushfire had seen before, and something about it and its shadows made her shift closer to her Captain and her archmage.

"I'm not familiar with that structure," Cat said—his admission making Brushfire feel better. She'd assumed she'd just missed that part of her lessons.

"It's…" The archmage paused, considering his words as he stopped their advance to look at the six sculptures. "It's very old," he finally said. "By which I mean it was old when the Ironhands ruled here. Earth and water, fire and air, void and aether.

"Some of the documents I have seen from the Ironhand era reference it; the Six were something of an emblem for the Dynasty. Even in those documents, it's treated as an archaic throwback, an affectation of the Dynasts without any actual religious meaning."

"It's *intimidating*," Paintrock said from behind them. "And *I* saw the hole in the Seventh Ward."

Brushfire shivered at the memory. At the center of the darvar asteroid monastery in Brokenwright—once the Ironhand Imperium's Seventh Ward, one of the protective shields of their inner empire—there had been a void. That void had been part of an ancient defense that could seal the void strait to the Warden of Fire—and in the hands of the Seeker of Her Dark Brother, it had turned into a weapon.

It had also been terrifying to stand above, with only a thick glass pane between her and a fall into the void itself.

The statues were a different kind of intimidation, an intentional statement of the grandeur and power of the Ironhand Imperium.

"The statue's message rings hollow when everyone here is dead," Brushfire pointed out. "The heart of the Ward still had real power. These are just… decoration."

"The doors are a bit more," Cat said, stepping forward again and eyeing the massive portals. "I presume there's a mechanism to move them, but I wonder if *that* still works after all this time."

Brushfire chuckled—and caught the edge of Paintrock hiding a laugh at what she suspected was the same thought.

"Cat, my Captain, you are too used to going in the front door of places," she told him. "*I* have never been invited through the front door of anywhere important in my life. So, I can assure you there is a service access, intended for when the mechanism fails, near the doors."

She surveyed the wall of stone as they walked up to the immense closed doors, then pointed at the base of the firebird statue. There was a gap between the plinth of the statue and the stone wall, easily missed with the angles and the sheer scale of the fifty-yard-high sculpture.

"There, I think."

Brushfire got about four steps toward the gap before Paintrock managed to get ahead of her, the elvar managing a turn of speed that countered her longer legs.

"First officers only go first when the other option is the Captain," Paintrock said brightly. "Trueshield, Moongleam, on me."

A pair of var, a matched set of elvar and a Hammerhead gobvar, stepped up to flank the Master of Staves. Moongleam was a third-brother, which gave him enough familiarity to give Brushfire a reproving look.

Cat, she noted, had waited for the crew to take the lead. He wasn't very far *behind* Paintrock's picked pair of halberdiers, but he was clearly used to someone else leading.

She wondered how much doing so bothered him. She knew him well enough to know that he'd had a number of practices drilled into him in the High Court Navy that he neither thought much about nor actually *liked*.

In this case, though, Paintrock was right.

"Lead the way, Master Paintrock," she said. She drew her wand as the three var approached the concealed entrance.

If there were any traps or surprises in this dead place, the entrance was the first place they would encounter them.

The dark alcove was the first place Brushfire found a use for the attack light-wisp she'd been learning. It hung overhead as Paintrock examined the door, everyone else outside the alcove.

"Everyone move back a bit," Cat ordered. "If someone *was* being clever with nastiness, they'd trap out here, too."

Brushfire stayed in her place, keeping a mental link to the light as the rest of the landing party spread out a bit.

"I don't *think* there's any traps," Paintrock reported. "Can you get the light down... Oh."

The light was smart enough to follow Paintrock's gesture without any action on Brushfire's part, flitting down to highlight the section he was pointing at before he finished speaking. The Master of Staves' blue skin gleamed almost as much as the marble with the light that close, and Brushfire couldn't see what he was doing.

"Well, thankfully, locks seem to be much the same everywhere and over all time," he observed. He stepped back, the light moving with him as he pulled the door open.

The other side of the door was even darker than the alcove he stood in. Brushfire couldn't see *anything* through it but the pure black of a space with neither lights nor windows.

"Forward," she whispered to the light-wisp, which ducked through the portal and illuminated the room beyond.

Moongleam was there before Paintrock was, the gobvar delicately and politely blocking the Master—not *technically* an officer, but still one of the most important var on *Void Flyer*—from taking the lead himself.

A few moments of not-quite-confusion followed, but Brushfire and Cat were in the middle of the small group that entered the mechanism spaces of the mountain's immense doors.

The space they'd found was as tall as the statue outside, allowing the lowest level to be clear of anything except the ladders leading up. Brushfire's light-wisp gave her only the vaguest impression of vast masses of machinery above her head, and she sent the construct up into the works.

"Void."

Brushfire wasn't sure who had cursed, but she understood the instinct as she followed the wisp toward the top of the room. Immense cogwheels hung overhead, cast from iron and still, somehow, gleaming with lubricating oil.

Spaced equally through the machinery were eight great iron beams, presumably the rods that would pull the ancient stone doors open.

"That looks like it might still be in working order," Cat said softly. "That makes no *sense*. Something has to be cleaning and oiling those cogs, or the iron would rust. They don't need anything *living* to rust."

"This may be machinery, but there is magic at play here," Armand reminded softly.. "We need to find a way forward, into the mountain itself. Can we activate the doors?"

"No need," Brushfire told him. "And probably a bad idea—even if this does still work, it will make noise and draw the attention of anything that *is* here. If it somehow missed the landing," she conceded with a chuckle. "But there's a door farther in over there."

The door wasn't concealed, but they'd been distracted by the heavy machinery hanging above them. At her gesture, Paintrock moved over to examine the door, and he sniffed derisively.

"The outer door lock was mediocre and this one is worse," he observed. "Not the security I would have expected."

"There would have been guards on each of these doors, I suspect," Armand pointed out. "The Ironhands would not have trusted a mechanism to secure their mountain palace.

"Can you get us in?"

"Door wasn't actually locked from this side," Paintrock admitted, pulling it open. Something blocked their view out the door and he eyed it grimly.

"What *is* that?" he asked.

"It's called a *tapestry*, Master Paintrock," Cat said wryly. "The door is behind a hanging of some kind, to hide it. Unless I have missed my guess as to where we are, appearances would be everything in that hall.

"Be careful," the Captain continued, looking back at Brushfire. She nodded her assurances to him. "We may be here for answers, but we've already learned how *awake* some of the dead things in the void can be."

ARMAND BLUESTAVES HAD STUDIED THE IRONHAND IMPERIUM, ON and off, his entire life. The Dynasty's existence was, after all, a significant portion of the reason why the Bluestaves Archive *existed*. His family had decided to make sure that the history of the time before the High Court was in charge wasn't forgotten.

He *knew* they'd lost more than they'd kept, the handful of halvar, darvar and even elvar families that had tried to preserve knowledge and documents from the Imperium. So much had been lost that Armand figured the High Court had *forgotten* they were even suppressing anything.

Even with two var that lived five to six hundred dances, a thousand dances was enough time for a lot to be lost even without anyone burying things. With the elvar High Court pushing for all memory of a unified imperial state to be lost, only fragments of myth and legend survived.

Many of those fragments had survived in places like the Bluestaves Archive, and Armand had loved learning and books from a very young age. He hadn't *specifically* studied the Ironhands until he'd turned to their charts to find a way around the border spheres, but they'd loomed large through the old books his family had kept.

And now he stood in a place that had been mentioned in those books. The Hall of Spheres, the texts had named it. While only half the size of the plaza outside, the Hall was entirely inside the mountain, one of the key formal entries to the Ironhands' palace.

It was a cable long and half a cable wide, with a vaulted ceiling rising at least a hundred yards above them. And along those hundred-yard-high walls hung hundreds of banners. None of the symbols and flags were familiar to Armand, though he thought he'd seen *some* of them on the charts.

"Banners of subject kingdoms," Cat said, before Armand could say a word. "You'd come here to pay fealty, I suppose, and you'd look to see your banner on the wall. Proof that you were valued. Proof that you were subordinate."

"I don't recognize any of them," Armand admitted, glancing at his Captain. "Do you?"

"A handful. They're archaic symbols, but they still show up from time to time." Cat gestured to the one they'd just come through. "That one, though, was on the charts. It's the flag for the Warden of Fire."

Armand looked back at the hanging and nodded slowly. The symbols and iconography of the old charts still lost him occasionally, so he hadn't realized that they'd *integrated* the stylized fort marking the Warden of Fire's defenses into an emblem of the sphere itself.

Part of the symbol had been lost on the chart too, he judged. The hanging behind them had the stylized fort flanked by arcs of flame that rose to encircle it—but on the chart, a copy of a copy of a copy, the right-hand flame had been missed in one of the transcriptions.

It was still recognizable, confirming Cat's point.

"I don't see anything in this room that would give me an answer to… well, anything," Armand murmured. He shifted his shoulder, urging the oracular spirit down onto his hand and looked down at the creature.

The spirit was a shortcut, allowing him *some* of the value of a more-complete divination without pulling out cards or dice—or the orreries and strange observers hidden in his tower back home. Like most shortcuts, though, it lacked the effectiveness of the full process.

Still…

"Anything here for us?" he asked it, lifting his arm like a falconer sending a bird off to the hunt.

The translucent cat-dragon rose into the air, circling above the party of crew and their limited pool of light. For a few moments, he thought circling was all it was going to do, and then the dragon flitted away into the darkness.

"All right," Armand breathed. "I think we need more light."

"Bogsong," Cat said calmly. "With me."

The two elvar raised their wands, conjuring more light-wisps like the one already hovering over their head. Smallwolf conjured a single wisp that joined Brushfire's, expanding the pool of light around them.

Cat drew three more wisps out of the air, sending them up higher and brighter than his subordinates'. Armand wasn't surprised Cat knew a version of the trick he'd been teaching the crew. Self-sustaining constructs were far too handy for an elvar Captain not to be trained in them.

Smiling, Armand set a trio of his own sparks into the air. His were physically smaller but just as bright and probably held a greater level of destructive power if he needed them to.

Eight lights spread out around the Hall, illuminating banner after banner, picking out colors and metallic threads that had no right to be as clear and vibrant as they were after a thousand dances of neglect.

It wasn't until the lights were near the top of the Hall that the mural became visible. It was like a switch was flicked as one of the wisps rose high enough to cast light onto the concealed mirrors, turning the darkened ceiling into a sudden blaze of light.

Each of the pockets of the vaulted ceilings contained enough mirrors to light the entire roof of the hall, lighting up ancient paint and revealing the sphere chart emblazoned across the ceiling of the Hall of Spheres.

The hangings on the wall told the visitor *who* the spheres of the Ironhand Imperium were. The map on the roof told the visitor *where* the spheres of the Imperium were. Looking up at the mural, Armand could see that the charts his family had kept were a pale copy of the maps the Ironhand used themselves.

"Well... that's something," Cat said softly. "It would take us days to copy that onto a chart we could use, but I'd *love* to compare it to the copies you brought."

"Me too," Armand admitted. Not only was the mural immense—two hundred yards by a hundred—it was gorgeous, a work of art created for the glory of Dynasty, Imperium and the gods themselves.

It was not, he realized, where his dragon was headed. The oracular creature had stopped at one of the hangings, toward the inner end of the Hall and only three rows and twenty yards from the ground.

Armand set off to follow it, pausing for a moment to let one of Brushfire's tribe go in front of him. He suspected that any traps there would be forged of magic, not mechanisms, and he didn't have any sense of that.

There was *something* there, magic woven deeply into the white-hued stone, but it wasn't a trap. It was different from the manifestation of the death of the void spheres, too. Lesser, more concentrated.

More intentional, perhaps… but he didn't think it was a trap.

"What is it looking at?" Brushfire asked behind him, looking up at the oracle spirit. "What is that banner?"

Armand didn't know. It was the same size and shape as the rest—an unbalanced hexagon, square for much of its length with a three-sided bottom—though it was a bright white shock of cloth amidst a section of black and blue banners.

Six symbols formed a circle in the center of the white banner, each a set of three black lines taking different shapes and trying to convey a different message.

"I'm not sure what I'm looking at," he admitted.

"Um." Fistfall swallowed, and Armand turned a gaze back on his newest and most junior student.

"Fistfall?" he asked.

"I've seen those symbols, though I don't know what they mean *here*," he noted. "There aren't many books in the tribe, and only one that came from the old Spheres of Our Clans. Axfall insisted I read it, and those symbols showed up a few times.

"Earth. Air. Fire. Water. Void. Aether." The big gobvar indicated a symbol on the circle as he spoke, and Armand saw the connections.

Earth was three horizontal lines. Perfectly flat and level, representing the solidity of dirt and stone and the worldlets built of them.

Air was three curving lines at the top of the circle, with four "waves" in the line.

Fire was three curving *vertical* lines, marking the rising sparks and smoke of a flame.

Water was three curving lines at the bottom of the circle, with three "waves" in the line to distinguish it from air—and to mark that while water flowed, air was even *more* fluid.

Aether was the three lines forming a triangle, as aether marked the boundaries of the sphere.

Void was the oddest. One line, straight up, had the other two lines attached to it at angles. More than anything, the symbol for *void* looked like a *person* to Armand.

"Gobvar symbols," Armand guessed.

"Yes," Fistfall confirmed. "Old symbols with old power. That circle usually ties to the Great Fire, though. The home sphere."

Armand studied the banner in silence for several more heartbeats. The Great Fire was the largest known ember, the central sphere of gobvar culture and as close as the Clan Spheres had to a capital or equivalent to the High Court.

But what did *that* have to do with their mission? Unless…

"Is that where we'll find the dragons?" he asked.

The oracular spirit trilled uncertainly, dropping from the banner back to his shoulder. It couldn't tell him *why* that banner was important. It could say that it *was*, but more than that was beyond the magic stored in the little spirit.

"Well, that might be useful, but I hope that's not the information we came all this way to find," Cat said. "Because I was expecting to end up sneaking around the Great Fire before this was all done already."

"I was very much hoping not to," Armand said. "That hope, it appears, was a false one. Come, little one." The spirit descended back onto his arm, snuggling into him in a manner that suggested both more weight and more affection than the creature should have.

"Is there anything else here?" he asked it. It didn't move, which was an answer in itself, he supposed. And if he was honest, he already knew that. Something about the Great Fire and the elemental symbols was important, but anything else in the Hall of Spheres was so old and obsolete as to be worthless.

"I know you said there was magic in this place to preserve things, but all of this seems like it should show *some* impact of the passing dances," Brushfire said. "What are we missing?"

"I don't know," Armand admitted. "I think… something has to be cleaning this place, beyond the protective magics."

"You said yourself there's nothing alive here," Paintrock noted, the Master of Staves suddenly looking even more nervous. "What *could* be cleaning this place?"

"I'm not certain," Armand admitted again. "As Officer Brushfire said, I think we're missing something. Some aspect to the magic or the nature of this place that would keep it clean. I've seen no sign of constructs, but that seems more likely than staff."

"Or maybe the wraiths just clean up around the place and repair tapestries when there's no one around to eat?" Smallwolf suggested, the young elvar's voice trembling to undermine her joking words.

"Perhaps. There is only one way to learn what we are here for, though," Armand said, gesturing to the still-large but thankfully more-var-sized doors leading deeper into the mountain. "Some of the books I read said there are three Halls to pass through to enter the main palace in the mountain.

"I'm surprised *anything* of the records of this place survived in the books we have now, and I am not sure how far we could trust it. But if the old logbooks say the Ironhands set up the palace so guests passed through three Halls to be seen, I imagine there's at least one more!"

The next Hall was the first part of the palace they'd been to that *didn't* have perfectly clear floors. Where the plaza and the Hall of Spheres had nothing marring their smooth marble surfaces, the next space held statues.

The gleaming white statues were organized in neat rows and columns, with a distinct order to them. Each was placed on a plinth of stone a yard high and wide, with an iron plaque—as rust-free as everything else on the Home—embedded in the face.

Armand made no bones of his focuses and priorities, and stepped forward to read a plaque without really examining the statue above it.

The statue there, right at the entrance, spoke of a general pledged to the service of the Ironhands, a critical servant whose sword and martial skill had helped unify the early spheres of the Imperium.

Armand didn't recognize the dating system. Uncertain of the time frame of the general's life, he looked up at the statue, considering the elvar woman with a measuring eye. The artist's skill was clear, though he had no idea if the elvar looked as she had in life.

"Armand, Cat… I need you to look at something," Brushfire called them over. She was standing at another statue early in the path, probably in the first four or five any visitors would see.

Armand stepped over to join her and look down at the plaque. Still iron, this one had seen its text filled with gold—a sign of what he was looking at before he even read the text.

There was no first name given for the Iron Hand, the var who had unified IronHome over what sounded like a few dozen dances, then moved on to unify the core spheres of the Imperium. The Iron Hand had founded an empire, shaping the course of the spheres for hundreds of dances after their life.

"Look at the statue, Armand," Brushfire told him.

He blinked as he realized he'd barely registered it beyond *Yes, var* before focusing on the plaque declaring it to the founder of the Imperium. Now he stepped back and looked up.

And up. And then up some more. The statue was life-size, he suspected, but the Iron Hand had stood easily two and a half yards high with his horns, rivaling Fistfall as one of the largest gobvar Armand had ever seen.

There was no question from the statue, and Armand finally looked at the *statues* instead of just the layout and the plaques and all of the artistic nature of a museum as opposed to the museum's contents.

There were elvar in the room. There were even halvar and darvar, through the two non-aether-breathing var were underrepresented.

But at least two-thirds of the var immortalized in the statuary at the heart of the Ironhand Imperium were gobvar.

"Huh," Armand murmured. "I…" He swallowed. "You know, it never even *occurred* to me that the Ironhands weren't elvar. They had aether ships, they ruled a vast empire… I *assumed* they were the same var as the High Court."

"They were gobvar," Brushfire said. "But if the Ironhands were gobvar, why are the Clans the way they are? What went wrong?"

Cat put his hand on Brushfire's shoulder as Armand tried to find words.

"The Kingdoms are no more unified than the Clans," he reminded her. "A lot went wrong."

"And I must counsel against regarding the Ironhand Imperium as things going *right*," Armand finally said. "They ruled, but nothing in the books I have read says it was an easy rule. *Order*, not peace. *Security*, not prosperity.

"But they went from all-powerful to broken in a few dances at most," he said. "Even in the archives gathered by my family and others, we don't know why. But the fact that we are standing in their core spheres and *everything* is dead suggests part of what happened."

"And... I hate to say it, but we *know* why the Clans are the way they are," Paintrock said quietly, the Master of Staves surveying the entire Hall with dark eyes. "Her Crimson Sister. I've known too many gobvar, even before signing on with you lot, to think the gobvar are lost to madness and violence.

"It's the Sisters and their control that hurt the Clans—and, from there, hurt the gobvar in Court and Kingdoms. Do not blame your var for the way a handful of fanatics have distorted your people, Officer Brushfire."

Brushfire nodded slowly, seeming to find some level of calm from Cat's touch as much as from anyone's words.

"There is a path to this, isn't there?" she asked. "I think? We're standing among the people from the beginning of the Imperium."

"We are," Armand confirmed. He suspected he was the only person present who knew how a museum was supposed to be laid out. "And if there are answers here, I think they are at the end, not the beginning."

He considered the layout of the statues and assessed where the last piece of the path would be. The statues were all separate enough to allow him to cut across the pattern laid out on the floor, and he didn't need to go through *every* important var in about eight hundred dances of Ironhand rule.

CHAPTER

26

T**HE ANSWER, WHEN** C**AT FOUND IT, WAS SHOCKINGLY OBVIOUS.**

At the end of the weaving path that Armand cut across were six statues clearly carved by the same sculptor. While he couldn't read the dates on the plaques—and he didn't have the impression Armand could either—he could tell that they had all been born within twenty dances of each other.

Six Ironhand dynasts, four siblings and two cousins. He presumed they were the last generation of the dynasty.

The problem was the one he recognized. He stared at the statue—of the second-youngest gobvar of the last core generation of the Ironhands, if he read it correctly—and remembered an oracle card.

"Did anyone bring an oracle deck down here?" he asked.

"What, why?" Armand asked, the archmage turning to look at him. "I have my spirit but... Oh."

Smallwolf saw the statue as she joined them and she looked at it quizzically, as if she *almost* recognized it. Brushfire and Fistfall and the crewvar clearly didn't, but Cat wasn't entirely surprised by that.

"What am I looking at?" Brushfire asked, stepping over to join them.

"Smallwolf probably studied this in passing," Cat noted, his gaze on the statue of the tall but unusually thin-for-his-var gobvar. "I have seen art and sketches and such repeatedly, both in school and in discussions in the Navy since. And I think Armand has some idea too."

"Cat," his first officer said sharply. "What is it?"

"That's the Blood King," Cat said flatly, pointing at the statue. "If I'm reading the plaques right, Oathheld Ironhand, third child of the last Ironhand Emperor. An archmage."

"A monster," Armand said, his words heavy. "I have never met anyone who understood how the Blood King was immortal, only that he was. That he had lived a thousand dances and endured every attack anyone could throw at him.

"But command of the wraiths? A statue of him here?" The archmage shook his head. "I can *guess*."

"The Blood King of the Gobvar," Brushfire echoed slowly, examining the statue. "Immortal, unstoppable, power-hungry. I have never heard any story of him commanding *loyalty*, only fear. Obedience, not fealty."

There was something about the Blood King that Cat had been warned of over his career, something the elvar made very sure their officers were aware of when it came to the immortal mage who ruled their enemy.

"He's not the Blood King *of the Gobvar*," Cat told Brushfire. "*We* hung that modifier on it because he only rules in the Clans. But according to him and the Clans who serve him, he is simply the Blood King.

"Not ruling *one* var. Ruling all of them."

"As the Ironhands once did," Armand added. "Deities preserve us. The spell. The deaths of everyone here. The destruction. All of this was… him. He *consumed* millions of his own people to become immortal."

"And to become King," Cat finished, a horrifying vision sinking into his head. The High Court worked *hard* to avoid situations where a second or third child felt that they would never claim anything of value—not helped by parents living hundreds of dances, rendering even *firstborn* children unlikely to inherit at a useful time.

But he had seen and heard of times where second and third children had maneuvered against their elders—even against their parents!—to claim what they thought was their rightful place.

Nothing like this… and yet he could *see* how the path could have started. He just didn't understand how a var ended up where Oathheld Ironhand had ended.

Cat stepped back, almost ignoring his friends and crew as he looked up to meet the gaze of a var who, unlike every other person represented in the room's statues, was unquestionably *still alive.*

There was no question that the sculptor had seen the same var, the same face, that was in so much artwork and so many texts. A hundred thousand artists had represented the Blood King in a hundred thousand ways, but enough of them over the last thousand dances had *seen* the gobvar to allow for recognizability between the portrayals.

For all that, the statue felt like a gentler portrayal of the var than any other art of him Cat had seen. The sculptor had immortalized a wry smile and a lift to his eyes that suggested a warm sense of humor, as if he'd caught the Oathheld in mid-chuckle.

It was still clearly the same var, but Cat was more used to portrayals of the Blood King as an angry and demanding demigod. There was no *humor* in the images of the var now, only power and arrogance.

"It is the same var," Armand said, studying the statue beside him. "There is no question—both of us saw the resemblance."

"And yet the feel is entirely different. The sculptor saw a very different var than any of the art *I've* ever seen of the Blood King."

"Is this what we came here for?" Brushfire asked. She was still close to the statue, looking up at it from beside the plinth.

"I don't know," Cat said. He glanced over at the archmage—and more specifically, to the oracular spirit wrapped around his arm. "Any thoughts? Yours or the little one's?"

Armand was still staring at the statue of Oathheld Ironhand, but he shook himself as Cat asked and shivered. He looked down at the oracular spirit, presumably communicating with it in some ineffable way, then lifted his arm into the air to give it a launching platform.

The lizard-spirit winged its way up, circling overhead in the light of the wisps around them, then trilled a sharp sound that Cat *knew* was a warning.

"To arms!" he snapped at the crew, stepping to put Armand between himself and Brushfire as he drew his sword and focus.

Paintrock and the halberdiers moved without further orders, spreading out to form a perimeter. Smallwolf and Fistfall fell into formation with Cat and Brushfire, forming an inner barrier around Armand.

The spirit dove to suggest a direction, and Cat turned—and as he did, the first impossible and impossibly *heavy* footfall rang through the statues.

A second footstep sounded a moment later, a slow and ponderous pace that echoed through the space. Slowly, loudly and *heavily*, the source of the noise approached from the midpoint of the hall.

"There!" Paintrock barked—but his certainty faded halfway through the word as he stared at the oncoming stranger.

It was a statue. A more-simply carved one than the hundreds surrounding them, but still a stone var-shape cut from the white stone of the mountain. Unlike the statues around them, it lacked a plinth, standing directly on the floor.

Walking directly on the floor, a stone foot moving forward and *thudding* into the stone surface like a var at one-third speed. It continued to approach them, moving slowly as Cat's people readied their weapons at the impossible creature.

"Stop," Cat shouted, feeling foolish giving orders to a statue. "Stop or we will strike!"

"You are strangers here in the Halls." There was no source to the voice. The statue's face didn't change—but nor did its slow advance pause. "This is not your proper place.

"You are unknown, unwelcome. But strange seasons consume us. None walk these hallowed Halls. None speak the passage phrases. None honor King and Dynasty. This one did not know any could still sail the sacred skies to land here.

"Who are you, who have braved dark days and darker depths to stand in the Halls of the Ironhands and the White Mountain?"

"I am Cat Greentrees of the High Court," Cat said firmly, stepping forward to place the other mages behind him. He'd have stepped out in front of the crewvar as well, but Paintrock was half a step ahead of him.

"We are travelers, seeking stories of ages past," he continued. "We meant no disrespect. I did not believe there was anyone here to intrude upon."

"These hallowed Halls are now forever fallen. Silent emptiness where once throngs trampled. You have done no dishonest harm, no theft or violence. The Palace is not open to you, but these Halls were always open to all learned learners."

Cat… wasn't clear on what the difference between the *Halls* and the *Palace* was. But if he wasn't going to have to fight an army of animated statues to get out of the mountain, he'd take that as a win!

The statue confirmed its apparent change of mind by coming to a halt two yards ahead of him. He sheathed his sword—little good the thin-bladed stabbing weapon would do him against *stone*—but held his wand against his side.

"You are part of the Hall of Statues?" he asked the strange creature, now immobile just out of reach.

"This one is the continual caretaker of these halls," the statue replied, its head shifting slightly to appear to look at him before freezing into stone again. "This one maintains. This one watches. Once, this one answered questions, but those earnest eras are behind this one."

"Can you answer *our* questions?" Armand asked, stepping up beside Cat.

Cat had to resist the urge to push the archmage behind him. The statue caretaker *said* they were fine in the Halls, but he wasn't sure he trusted it, and he *really* didn't want to see what happened when stone fists met flesh.

"It has not been this one's daily duty since the apotheotic ascension of the Last Ironhand, but it is not a duty denied to this one. If this one can, this one will answer."

"The Last Ironhand," Armand echoed. "Who is that?"

"Oathheld Ironhand, the one true Eternal Emperor of the Ironhand Imperium, the last of the dutiful dynasty that spanned all spheres," the statue told him. "He ascended into godhood and became the last and ultimate expression of all that the Ironhand are."

"If Oathheld is the emperor, where is the empire?" Armand asked. "Everything in IronHome is dead."

"A sacred sacrifice for the difficult duty of the apotheotic ascension," the statue said crisply. "All that was Ironhand is now in Oathheld. The dynasty made one, the empire vested in a singular soul. A ritual was crafted, by some of the most mighty magicians of the realm.

"The IronHome was the heart of the fire. The Wardens were the constant chosen, the forever fuel to sustain a weft in the weave of the spheres. Some other spheres were touched, unavoidably altered.

"A price was paid. A god was born. And so, the Ironhand became eternal."

Cat had guessed the form of what had happened, but to hear the ancient construct lay it out as a *victory* rather than a *mass murder* somehow hurt.

"And the rest of the dynasty died," he growled before he could stop himself.

"The dynasty became one," the statue told him. "Past, present, future, all invested into the single and singular soul of the Last Ironhand, the Eternal Emperor."

"The Blood King."

Brushfire's use of the new title felt like half a statement, half a *challenge* to the servitor.

"This one is aware of that name," the statue allowed. "It is an accurate allusion, though not his true title."

Cat swallowed his retort and reached over to touch Brushfire, hoping to calm the spike of anger he could *feel* radiating off her. She wasn't any angrier than he was, but he doubted that attacking the statue was going to do them any good.

"What do you know about dragons and the Ironhand Imperium?" Armand asked, somehow stepping around Cat and Brushfire and even *Paintrock* to face the statue alone.

Cat cursed mentally, but he had to admit that if they had to destroy the statue, Armand was probably the most capable of it. It would just be a lot harder for the archmage to *do* that if the servitor crushed him.

"There are dutiful dragons immortalized in these hallowed halls, as there are various var," the statue told him. "Some of the brilliant beasts stood at the side of the first founder, a flying force to augment his forceful fleets.

"The alliance failed over time. By the day of the ascension, the potent pact between Ironhand and aether drake was broken."

That might actually be useful, Cat suspected, and he stepped up next to Armand. He felt as much as saw Brushfire do the same, the two of them now flanking the archmage.

"Do you know why?" Brushfire asked. "What happened between the Ironhands and the dragons?"

"Lost legends and broken bonds," the statue said. "Var forgot. Dragons forgot. Pacts bound, but only *remembered* promises were kept."

"What was forgotten?" Cat's first officer asked, pushing.

"The Ironhands did not know," the statue repeated, but Cat picked up what Brushfire was aiming for.

"Did you?" he asked softly.

"This one endures. This one remembers everything."

That... was terrifying, Cat realized. And suggested that there was a lot more to the construct than what they could see.

"You are more than this statue," he guessed. "More than the caretaker of these Halls."

The statue didn't answer him.

"You *are* the White Mountain," Cat continued. "And you remember the promise that was broken, don't you? *Can you tell us?*"

"The Mountain remembers."

There was a new tone to the voice now, and it wasn't just coming from the statue. It wasn't any *louder*, but it felt like it came from all around them, a *presence* as much as a *sound* as the construct that ran the entire Ironhand Palace, the White Mountain itself, stopped pretending.

"The Mountain endures. But the Mountain *obeys.*"

"You keep the Ironhands' secrets," Cat agreed carefully, realizing he might have just stepped in something dangerous. "But you said they *forgot.* Were you *ordered* not to speak of the Pact?"

"The Pact was always secret. That is why it was forgotten."

"They didn't ask you?" Armand asked, his touch on Cat's shoulder a warm and welcome reassurance.

"The Mountain obeys. The Mountain does not offer. The Mountain *can*not offer."

Cat wasn't an archmage, and there were aspects of magic that were closed to him. His sense of the aether often allowed him to feel some of the power around him, more than others, but not everything.

Armand had warned them that there was magic in the walls. But now it weighed down on them as the White Mountain focused its attention on them. Whatever magic was woven through those ancient white stones was powerful beyond most of his experience. He had never even *heard* of a construct of this scale—though the High Court mages frowned on binding constructs into physical structures.

"We need to know," he told the ancient spirit softly. "The fate of every sphere in that Hall behind us rests on it. The dragons are active in a way they haven't been in a thousand or more dances. That pact, that promise, may save thousands. Millions.

"Do you owe the var of the Imperium nothing?"

The pressure grew heavier, like a massive blanket of steel had descended on Cat from every side. He could see the others feeling it too. The attention of the genius loci they stood inside was *painful*.

"The Pact was broken," the Mountain said. "The secrecy was bound to the Pact. The Mountain obeys, but a forgotten command weighs on no mind lesser than the Mountain's.

"Understand: the Mountain no longer has clocks. *Time* is lost to the Mountain now. The Mountain endures and the Mountain serves, but the Mountain has not answered questions since the ascension."

Translation: the spirit could tell them what happened but not *when*. That was... a problem, but one Cat could work with.

"Tell us of the Pact," he asked. "Please."

ARMAND WAS IMPRESSED AT HOW WELL THE WHITE MOUNTAIN HAD concealed its nature from him. The closest thing he'd ever encountered to the genius loci was the diamond observer in his tower in the Red Forest. *That* artifact of magic didn't have a living spirit in it—the Towers of the Great Red Forest agreed with the High Court Academies on binding constructs to structures—but its powerful magic lent itself to certain... *attitudes*, for lack of a better word.

His own oracular spirits were a more-standard type of construct, more an illusion given a portion of his own divinatory power and a *tiny* spark of enduring memory from iteration to iteration. They couldn't exist for long even with him sustaining them—and would vanish in moments if he died.

But he could *sense* magic, had always been able to, even before becoming an archmage. He had felt magic all around them, but all he had felt had been small. Cleaning magics, not even strong enough to explain *how* clean the palace was.

And that was because they weren't all that kept the stone clean. The statue there was a guide, intended to answer questions and provide tours of the Halls, but it was merely one of *many* tools available to the Mountain. There were probably lighter and more maneuverable physical forms hidden in the Halls for maintenance.

The statue, which had faked being an independent construct well enough to fool all of them until Cat had challenged it, was meant to *appear* alone.

But Cat had seen the pieces even as Armand had wondered at the history in the Hall of Statues. He'd challenged the White Mountain and in so doing had drawn the full attention of a being that had been old when the High Court had taken that name.

Armand's Captain had found the key and pushed forward. He held Cat's shoulder, drawing strength from the elvar even as he hoped to support the Captain, and he endured the pressure of the Mountain's attention as it finally answered the question.

"There were once three spheres where the dragons could hatch their young," the Mountain told them. The alliteration, it seemed, had been a ploy to throw them off, a toy of a bored and powerful mind perhaps intended to make them think less of the mind they spoke to.

"The Ironhand Imperium never knew of the first. It was destroyed by other enemies, and the three Grand Dragons came to the Mountain to negotiate for protection for the remaining two.

"In exchange for draconic warriors to fight with the Imperium, fleets were positioned to guard the entryways to the Grand Dragons' nests. A war was fought against the Shadowed Spheres, worshippers of the Dark Brethren, to avenge the Grand Dragons' murdered hatchlings.

"The shadows were broken. The worshippers of the Brethren were driven into retreat, their spheres claimed by the Ironhands. Victory sealed the Pact, the sphere of Greenrise and the Radiant Realms forever to be guarded by the Imperium."

The Grand Dragons. That was a fascinating term—Armand had never heard it as a *plural* before. Like the other members of the Quadrumvirate, though, Old Bloodscale had more than one title. While the great wyrm that helped rule the Gobvar Clans went almost entirely by his *name*, there were other titles.

Including simply *the Grand Dragon*. Singular. Not one of three. Which said a lot about just *what* had broken the Ironhands' pact with the dragons.

"The Mountain does not know how long the Pact endured. Other duties drew away Ironhand ships. The dragons did not insist, as they too were busy. Fate and war stole key leaders from the Dynasty before orders and secrets could be passed on.

"*Why* certain spheres were to be guarded was forgotten. The dragons honored the Pact but sent fewer and fewer young warriors out as circuits of the Home passed.

"What happened in Greenrise was not malice, in the end," the Mountain intoned. "An accident. The Mountain—the *Ironhands*—never knew what it was. Perhaps no hand of the Imperium could have saved the Greenrise hatchery.

"But no hand of the Imperium was in place to try. The Grand Dragons descended upon the Mountain to proclaim the breach of the Pact. There was… conflict."

A single word shouldn't have carried quite so much weight, but with the Mountain's attention fully on Armand and his party, it did. Armand drew a sense of more than mere *conflict*. Images flashed through his mind—he wasn't sure if they were guesses or imagination or something from the Mountain itself—of the city outside burning. Of ninesails dueling dragons that *dwarfed* them.

"The Grand Dragons died. The Pact was broken. The Radiant Realms were closed to all var on pain of death, and the Dynasty, in their wisdom, agreed."

The statue moved again, slipping several steps away as it seemed to study the *Void Flyer* crew.

"The promise was that the Ironhands would forever guard the hatcheries of the Grand Dragons," the Mountain told them. "The Ironhands forgot and failed, and one of the hatcheries was destroyed. The greatest and oldest dragons died upon the Mountain. Even this would be forgotten as the Home turned.

"You are the first to ask of this in these Halls since long before the ascension," the construct said softly. "May it be the answers you seek."

Armand looked at Cat and Brushfire, realizing he'd left his hand on Cat's shoulder for the entire explanation from the genius loci. Neither he nor Cat had minded.

"I think it helps," he told the Mountain. "We should be going."

He didn't know *why*, but he suspected that was exactly what they'd needed to know. A piece of the puzzle they could have found nowhere else, in the mind of an abandoned fortress on a dead world in the center of the void spheres.

"You are not permitted in the Palace, but there are guest rooms else-where in these Halls," the Mountain told them. "There is no food, but there are beds and water. You may rest in the guest halls if you wish."

That... wasn't right. Armand knew that immediately, without even consulting with his people. The genius loci had tried to drive them out, but now it wanted them to stay?

"Why do you want us to stay now?" Cat asked, half a breath before Armand could.

There was a surprisingly long pause.

"The Mountain may not lie. But the Mountain does not need to answer your questions."

Which, Armand suspected, would work better if it didn't *tell* them there was a problem by saying that.

"Why *would* you lie?" Armand asked.

"Because the Mountain obeys."

He exhaled sharply as pieces fell into place, but it was Brushfire who stepped forward and spoke.

"You are receiving commands *now*?" she asked. "From him?"

She pointed at the statue of Oathheld Ironhand, and Armand shivered as he half-consciously funneled power through his ring foci, pushing back the mental pressure of the White Mountain's presence.

"The White Mountain speaks," the genius loci replied. "The Last Ironhand hears. The Last Ironhand commands. The White Mountain obeys. He would have you remain until he arrives."

"We need to go," Cat said instantly. "We need to go *now*."

"The Mountain has not been ordered to hold you. Go. The Mountain *cannot* hold you. But there are others. The ascension is long since complete.

"The Last Ironhand has ways to protect what is his."

Armand had a *thousand* more questions, but Cat and the others were moving already. Before the Mountain's warning was complete, Brushfire and Cat were each taking one of Armand's shoulders like they'd planned it, nearly lifting him off his feet as they urged him back toward the exit.

Any pretense at being asleep on the part of the Mountain was fading now. The white stone walls themselves were beginning to *glow*, rendering the light-wisps unnecessary. A grinding sound announced that the main doors—at the far end of the Hall of Spheres—were beginning to open.

Or, at least, that's what Armand *hoped* that sound meant. The statue the White Mountain had used as its vessel remained in place, staring after them as if forlorn at its failure to restrain them.

Armand suspected that the Blood King would be furious at how blithely the ancient construct had warned them and released them—but even Armand couldn't conceive of any way the Mountain could actually be *injured*.

If it had survived this long, a thousand dances since anyone had been regularly maintaining it, he doubted the genius loci actually required outside power anymore. It might be drawing energy from the same manifestation of the Blood King's ritual that empowered the wraiths, but it also might have simply lasted so long to simply... *be*.

"It said it can't stop us, but I don't buy that," Cat told the others as he and Brushfire continued to carry at least half of Armand's weight.

Armand shook off the supportive arms with a wry smile, making sure to keep pace with everyone as they eyed him.

"I *can* run," he noted. "And no, I don't trust the Mountain that far. The Ironhands *might* have decided that it didn't need weapons or defenses."

They might have decided that they didn't *want* a non-var magical intelligence to command weapons and defenses on its own. The statue the Mountain had used to talk to them would have made a highly effective defender if needed, though it thankfully would be terrible at pursuit.

"It opened the door for us," Brushfire noted, gesturing ahead as emberlight streamed into the massive space—adding to but still mostly overwhelmed by the magical light the Mountain had awoken around them. "That's being *helpful*, I suppose."

"We seem to have touched a soft spot on the construct, but it *serves* the Blood King," Armand warned grimly. "Cat's right. We can't trust it and we need to be as far away from here as possible."

"We did learn something, though, didn't we?" Fistfall asked. "I don't know much about much, but that whole bit on dragons sounded important."

"It is. But I need time with books and my divination tools to make use of it," Armand told him.

"If nothing else, I've never heard of the Radiant Realms," Cat said. "And *just* as important, if we don't escape whatever trap the Blood King has set into motion, it won't matter."

That was about all the conversation *Armand* had breath for, so he let it stand at that as he hustled toward the door. His mages and halberdiers spread out around him in a flying wedge, between him and any possible threat—and he had his *own* magic wrapping around all of them, a not-quite-solid shield that would snap into reality to protect against any attack.

All the Mountain needed to do to slow them down was *close* the big doors. They could still get out, back the way they'd come, but Armand wasn't entirely sure that space would be *safe* while the doors were moving. It had looked like all of the machinery was high enough up to allow access, but there had been a lot of moving parts, and Armand didn't know machinery well.

Alloy might have been able to tell them, but they'd left Alloy with the ship.

Each step was a greater burden on Armand. He wasn't as physically unfit as his circumference might suggest to a stranger, but hustling for multiple cables was still pushing the limits of his endurance.

No one around him was showing any sign of fatigue as they reached the massive doors, and he focused on putting one foot in front of the other at the best speed he could manage—and on the fact that the doors had not, thankfully, started closing.

They were out in the massive outdoor plaza, and there was nothing between them and the ship. Armand had *fully* agreed with Cat and hadn't actually expected to make it this far—both the emberlight sweeping over the cut in the side of the mountain and the sight of *Void Flyer* itself in the distance were a relief.

"We're clear," Brushfire said aloud, her tone sounding as surprised as Armand felt. "To the ship? Get out of here?"

"Exactly," Cat replied. "This isn't the end, not by a long shot."

"No," Armand agreed, doing his best not to sound out of breath. "If the Mountain can't hold us, then the Blood King will most definitely have a plan for something that *will*."

V*OID FLYER* WAS A STRANGE SHIP, BUT AT THAT MOMENT, FOR Brush-fire it was safety and the closest thing available to home. She split off from the rest of the troop they'd taken into the Mountain and gestured for the other two Masters to meet her.

Axfall and Windheart had no magic of their own, but it was clear they'd realized something was wrong. There were fewer crewvar out on the stones of the plaza than she'd expected, though there was still a decent array of Alloy's special lanterns to protect them from wraiths rising from the city.

"Brushfire," Windheart greeted her. "What's going on?"

"Long story," she told her mother's first-brother grimly. "But we appear to have pissed off the Blood King. *Directly and specifically.*"

Windheart was the oldest member of her tribe, one of the oldest gobvar she'd ever known. He'd been the eldest of her mother's siblings, and Brushfire's mother hadn't been young when Brushfire had been born—let alone when she'd died birthing Fistfall.

That meant that Windheart and Axfall were the *only* living members of the Hammerhead Tribe who had lived in the Clan Spheres—and Axfall, sixty dances his lover's junior, had seen barely twenty dances when they'd fled.

Windheart's face went as pale as his shock-white hair and she *saw* him swallow in fear. Never in all of her own dances had she seen him *that* afraid.

"You don't joke about such things," he said. It was an observation, not a warning. He *knew* her. "What do we do?"

"For now, get everyone back aboard ship as quickly as possible," Brushfire told him. "We are leaving."

She looked at the stuff they'd taken off ship. Eight lanterns, representing easily two clock-days of their sole mage-artificer's time and materials that couldn't be replaced. A few wooden barricades, crudely assembled from wood mostly stolen from Flame's Gem, she judged.

"Grab the lanterns if it's easy, leave everything else," she continued. "Var over material. Move."

They would leave no *one* behind. Gear—even priceless gear that existed nowhere else—was expendable.

Brushfire had given the orders to her tribe elders—with her being the shaman of her tribe, they'd looked to her for instruction even *before* she'd become the official first officer of their ship—but she was the one standing on the ramp, watching the last trio of trailing elvar run toward the ship.

Treevoice and Grainflow had set up to watch the approach from the city, moving to higher ground a distance from the void ship. In hindsight, *too* far from the ship, but no one had known that—and Sky had set off after their sister as soon as the shout to return to the ship had gone up.

Now the three crew were crossing the plaza as fast as they could, and Brushfire struggled with a sense of impending doom. She didn't *see* any of the wraiths they'd seen before, and if the Mountain had defenses, it would have moved to stop them already.

But her focus was in her hand as she waved the three elvar forward. Grainflow shared the same blue hue as Hunter Paintrock, she noted absently, while the two siblings were a more bronze tone.

And the shadow that fell over them washed all color from the trio. Brushfire cursed and looked *up*. She'd expected a threat from the city— *not* from the sky.

She should have known better. The skiff descending toward the lodeplate was a small thing, designed to defend the city against attacks from above, but it was still an armed airship—built of cloudwood and lift crystals and not much else.

"Look out!" Brushfire bellowed, dances of working on an aether ship giving her enough projection to be sure they heard her *probably* redundant warning.

Her crew scattered, spreading in three different directions as Brushfire threw her magic out in a desperate attempt to shield them from *far* too far away. Ancient mechanisms aboard the skiff activated with no hands to move them, and a spray of crossbow bolts crashed down where the elvar had been standing.

Sky hadn't moved fast enough, and several of the bolts caught them in their legs and lower back. Brushfire's shield hadn't reached far enough, and fear and anger tore through her at her failure. She yanked her power back from the shield and turned it back toward the first trick she'd learned.

Brushfire was still learning complicated magics, but she'd seen the arcane devices central to a ship used a thousand times now. She was less familiar with storm staves than other weapons, but she'd seen *Cat* duplicate their strike.

And now she did the same. Lightning *cracked* in the stark white plaza cut into the mountain, and the skiff dodged backward with a grace no ship should have managed.

Still, the dodge forced its second salvo of bolts to miss completely, even as Treevoice turned back to grab her sibling. Grainflow only hesitated for a few more moments before turning back to rejoin the other elvar, and Brushfire swallowed a curse.

She couldn't shield them from that far away, and the skiff's complete lack of crew didn't seem to be slowing the reload of its cluster-bows.

Lightning cracked again as she tried to drive the airship back, descending the ramp herself and half-charging in the direction of the attacking vessel. It dodged her again, and this time she got a good look at the deck of the ship.

It was a thin, flat triangle with a single sail, intended to maneuver along the edge of the air envelope via a mix of wind, aether currents and lift crystals. A single storm stave pointed upward parallel to the mast, and a pneumatically fired cluster-crossbow was mounted on each of its three edges.

There was no crew, but a translucent green mist filled the entire deck. It wasn't quite the wraiths they'd seen before, but it shared the same essence. *This* version, though, had the will and wit to maneuver a complicated airship and reload the ancient mechanical weapons.

Not enough wit, perhaps thankfully, to turn its focus from the three var on foot to the ship they were running toward—and Brushfire conjured a pair of light-wisps as she sent a third lightning bolt crashing across the open plaza.

Her focus with the storm bolts now was to keep the skiff moving and dodging, pushing it away from the crew now running as a group back toward the ship. They weren't in reach for her to directly protect them yet, so driving the airship back with blast after blast of lightning was all she could do.

Brushfire doubted the skiff had been this maneuverable with a living crew. The mist filling its sails and operating its weapons had no need to worry about coordinating the actions of multiple crew or even such minor things as *falling off*.

But because it *could* dodge her blasts, it *did*—which meant it missed its next salvo of bolts entirely, the ancient shafts smashing harmlessly into the stone of the plaza.

And then Brushfire's wisps were there, flitting across the sky with just as much maneuverability as the skiff and just a *touch* more speed. Enough more speed for the two fist-sized orbs of light to dive *into* the mist.

"*Now*," she whispered, the order more mental than verbal. Both wisps detonated as one.

Neither had the force and power of a storm-stave blast on their own. Even combined, they might have failed to do real damage to a ninesail or even a *six*sail.

But the skiff was far more fragilely built than *any* true aether ship, and the wisps were *inside* her when they burst. Bits of wood and machinery flew in every direction, debris scattering across the White Mountain's entrance plaza.

As the wreckage crashed down, thankfully clear of her people, Brushfire reached them. Sky... looked bad. *Really* bad. They'd taken at least four bolts, one of which was still embedded in their guts in a way that made Brushfire hurt just *looking* at them.

"Carry them," she ordered the other two, looking up to scan the sky with her wand in hand. She'd have carried Sky herself, but neither of the other var outside the ship were mages. Only she could shield them, and the warning in the back of her mind was...

There.

A city like the one around the White Mountain wouldn't have had just *one* skiff for air defense and security. Especially not a city belonging to as militarized and defensive a state as the Ironhand Imperium. The wraiths had sent the closest skiff in to delay them, but there were *squadrons* of the ships available to them.

She'd taken down one, but now she could *see* a dozen of the little airships sailing briskly toward them. Brushfire figured she could protect the trio with her for a bit, but they couldn't move quickly without making Sky's injuries *worse*.

"Move," she instructed. "*Carefully*. I will protect us."

The shield she wove above them now would stop a storm stave's blast, though she didn't *think* the skiffs could manage to fire their staves at the ground. The wraiths were not going to get to *her* crew.

But this time, they weren't coming alone. Four skiffs led the way, at least a cable ahead of the other eight, and she had no hope that a thousand dances had rendered their cluster-bows nonfunctional.

They were still a hundred yards short of the ship, and Brushfire figured all twelve of the skiffs were going to get a salvo in before they reached the shelter of *Void Flyer*'s metal hull.

Of course, *Brushfire* wasn't the only mage on the *Flyer*'s crew. Her fight with the first skiff had bought time for Cat and Armand to reach the top of the ship—the control room with its magically transparent walls and ceiling.

Four skiffs dove toward her and her charges, and she stiffened behind her magical shield. Then thunder rolled in the clear emberlit skies, and the lead skiff simply exploded. Lightning struck from nowhere, and the second skiff dodged—only for something else, something Brushfire couldn't even *see*, to meet it as it dodged and cleave it in two.

More thunder rumbled across the white stone plaza, and the power of an archmage spoke in the eternal day. Lightning cracked through the air like shattering glass, and there was no escape for the wraith-crewed airships.

The second pair of the lead group burst into flame in the same moment as Armand's power tore their sails from their masts and sent burning pieces flying in every direction.

A chunk of debris—a few square yards of wood anchored on a still-glowing lift crystal—smashed into Brushfire's shield. She threw it aside with a thought and a gesture, urging her trio of lost grazers back toward the ship with her other hand.

Armand had broken the first wave, but eight more skiffs were behind them, and Brushfire had a grim suspicion about where the wraiths from the first ships were going. They hadn't unleashed the brilliant light that seemed to actually damage the creatures yet, after all.

The mist that had filled the skiffs' sails was still around there somewhere. But her wounded sailor was only twenty yards from the ramp. Brushfire turned on her heel, gesturing for the crew to keep going as she slowed and began to walk backward, her shield wide and her wand at the ready.

Eight more airships were stooping into the cut, diving toward the *Void Flyer* and her crew with lethal intent—but Brushfire wasn't looking for them. She was looking for the mist-like spirits from the first five ships, the ones that she and her archmage had broken.

They burst out of the stones in front of her even as Armand's power cracked through the sky once more. Why they didn't come closer underground, she didn't know. Maybe they couldn't embed themselves in a solid surface for long? She didn't know what rules these creatures played by.

Only that a strange wall of thick green mist, with the vague shapes of var visible woven through it, was now charging toward her and her ship.

"No."

Brushfire wasn't sure what impulse drove her to speak. It wasn't like the mists or the strange manifestation behind them could *understand* her even if it somehow heard her. But for her own will, her own sake, she had to defy them aloud.

With the skies clear for a moment and the wounded Sky already halfway up the ramp, she dropped her shield and refocused her power. The mists swirled toward her at a speed no natural fog could ever have matched and her power rose to meet them.

Light burst from her wand. Her arms. Her eyes. As she stared down the mists that had consumed a dozen spheres, her power spilled from every fiber of her being in brilliant, blinding light. For a few draining heartbeats, *she* was an ember, and the light she sent forth flung the mists back, driving the creatures before her will like dust before the windstorm.

Brushfire barely even noticed the first lantern lighting behind her. As her power wavered, though, she sensed their presence. Half a dozen of Alloy's lanterns now gleamed behind her, their wall-like beams reaching out to reinforce, complete and then *replace* her own glow.

"Get up here, eldest sister," Fistfall shouted from the top of the ramp. "We need to launch!"

The wraiths fell back faster than she did, a sense of frustration rippling off them, and Brushfire strode up the ramp to *Void Flyer* like a conquering queen—waiting and praying for the moment the hatches sealed and the mighty rockets finally fired!

Launching from a worldlet or lodestone plate into the void was far from pleasant, attached to a feeling of immense pressure and weight that had nothing to do with the lodestone plates in the base of the void ship, but right *then*, it was the warm hug of her friends and family.

It meant at least a momentary safety.

CHAPTER

29

THE TREMENDOUS POWER OF AN ARCHMAGE DIDN'T EXACTLY GROW boring on repeated exposure. More than anything, Cat was becoming aware of just what Armand was and *wasn't* capable of—and the price Armand had to pay for his more incredible stunts.

Armand could conjure more power at once than Cat could, as demonstrated by the lightning storm he'd unleashed over the skies of the White Mountain. Cat could have summoned a handful of lightning bolts, but the sustained sheets of lightning that had struck down the wraith skiffs would have been beyond him.

From what Cat could tell, Armand's "maximum output" was well above his own, but the archmage could only truly sustain his power for about the same amount of time as Cat. Except that when *Cat* hit that limit, he paid for it in locked-up muscles and crushing fatigue immediately.

Armand could *borrow* energy from somewhere to keep going, allowing him to not only wield greater magical power than a non-archmage but to do so for longer than a regular mage could wield their lesser power.

But it was a *loan*, and Cat had seen Armand sleep for a full day after the battle at the Seventh Ward. To wield the full power of an archmage for any significant length of time accrued an energy debt, and Cat wasn't sure what the long-term costs of that debt would be for his archmage.

As they blasted clear of the Home on a pillar of fire, though, he needed to let Armand make his own assessment of his limits. The lightning storm slowly faded beneath them, the first dozen-odd defense skiffs having been reduced to scattered wreckage but others now clearly visible as they rose higher.

"Can they chase us?" Armand asked.

"They don't have the sails or the control for distant travel," Cat replied. "Without aether, they *should* be limited to the air envelope, too.

"No, once we're clear of the Home, those skiffs are no threat."

"And if the wraiths have different rules in play?"

Cat grimaced and sighed.

"I don't know," he admitted. He kept one hand on the wheel and glanced over at Streamwater where his second officer was operating the port sextant.

"Faith, I need a course for the Warden of Stone," he told her. "Can you work it up? I've a sense I shouldn't leave the wheel, and Brushfire is still working her way up the ship."

Crane would be in the sickbay, waiting for the wounded. Thanks to Brushfire, they *had* a wounded sailor instead of three dead ones—a point he'd make gratefully to her later.

"I'm on it," Streamwater replied, saluting and gesturing a gobvar crewvar over to watch the sextant. She disappeared into the ladder down to the chart room, and Cat grimaced as he looked back over the lodeplate.

"Did we learn something worth this detour?" he asked Armand.

"I think so," the archmage replied. "Not least, though… some of the reason behind the detour was a lie."

"A lie? We *did* find useful information, and the Mountain's warning may let us evade the King."

Armand shook his head.

"I don't think the Blood King knew we were in the void spheres until the Mountain told him," the archmage admitted. "But some effect he wove over these spheres tells everyone they have to go to the Mountain. It *was* a trap, Cat, and we triggered it."

Cat had worried about a trap, but the Mountain's answers had actually convinced him their divinations were right.

"But knowing about the Grand Dragons and their pact with the Iron-hands answers something, doesn't it?" he prodded.

"Yes. I need to check my books and do some divination to be sure, but that gives me an idea of what *might* be happening," Armand said. "I don't believe the White Mountain lied to us, strangely, but it had very different priorities from what a living var might."

"I'd never even heard or conceived of anything like it," Cat said. He looked out the side windows as a shiver ran through the ship. They were clear of the lodeplate's air envelope, which should give them some protection from the wraith skiffs.

"I have heard of *smaller* fixed constructs," Armand observed. "We anchor many magics to physical objects; there is no reason we can't anchor a construct to one. Tradition says we don't, and what I have read of involved forms that needed to be able to move on their own—more marionettes than statues, and limited for it.

"But, I suppose, knowing what we *thought* the limits of a fixed construct were is why it didn't occur to *me* that that was what we were facing. Well done, my Captain."

Armand's words sent a surprisingly warm shiver through Cat. He didn't think a small compliment was *that* big a deal—though, to be fair, he *would* have expected the archmage to see through the nature of an arcane thing before he did.

The skiffs, he noted, were no longer rising. Whatever strange essence empowered them, it wasn't enough to break the basic limits of the airship.

Without aether, they could not pursue his people, and he sighed in relief.

"Do you know where this Greenrise or the Radiant Realms *are*?" he asked Armand.

"No. They are not names I am familiar with," his archmage told him. "You?"

"Never heard of them. I imagine, though, that if the Radiant Realms are the last dragon hatchery and our problem is dragons coming out of the Clan Spheres, the Realms are in gobvar territory."

"Where we were heading anyway," Armand agreed. "And I *hope* that the Blood King is as powerful, arrogant and focused as I believe he is."

Even the High Court Navy briefings on the Quadrumvirate treated the Blood King as more a myth or legend than an actual political leader, which didn't lend itself to accurate assessments. Or ones that were wrapped in anything other than fear.

"I am not sure how him being as powerful as we fear helps us," Cat murmured.

"Because if the Blood King is all that I believe him to be, he will not tell the others of the Quadrumvirate that his sanctuary has been breached," Armand said. "He will not admit, even, that there *is* a passage through the void around the borders guarded by Her Crimson Sisters.

"He will come for us himself, which is bad enough, yes, but if we can sneak past him in a ship unlike what he expects, then there will be no one else to bar our way," the archmage concluded. "We have escaped the Home. There is nothing in this sphere to challenge us, so the Blood King himself is the barrier between us and our destination."

Cat swallowed his initial reaction, recognizing that admitting *his* fear would only aggravate that of the handful of var in the control room.

"Perhaps," he said quietly. "Alloy, can you take over the wheel? Our course should be straight enough now."

He'd told Streamwater, *accurately*, that he felt the need to have his hands on the wheel. He still did. But sometimes, other things had to take priority—and while he wasn't going to put his *hands* on his archmage, there needed to be a conversation that rumor wouldn't carry through the entire ship.

"Join me in the chart room, Lord Bluestaves?" he asked calmly—well aware that he *didn't* address Armand that way very often.

Hopefully, that would get the message across.

Streamwater was confused to have Cat and Armand enter the chart room as she was working away, but disappeared back up to the control room without even a peep of pushback. If anyone could read the mood of an elvar noble despite his masks, it would be an elvar officer with two hundred dances of experience!

With just the two of them alone in the room, Cat crossed to study the chart where Streamwater had been working. She'd worked up the basics of the course already, though it would be a few clock-hours before they would need to change anything.

Clock-days after that, of course, before they reached the straits. Seventeen thousand leagues would take six days at three leagues a minute, the most they could expend the fuel for.

Except that even *that* speed would leave them low on fuel, unable to go any faster in Warden of Stone or Stormfall. Their journey to Home had left them able to make it to the Clan Spheres, but they would have little fuel left once they were there.

They would need a new ship at that point, and Cat didn't like the options he could think of. Still, even that hour of potential piracy was long days away and required them to make it that far, and he finally turned his attention back to the archmage waiting patiently for him to speak.

"Do you have a *plan*, Armand?" he demanded. "The Blood King is effectively a *god*. Immortal. Indestructible. More powerful than any mortal var mage or archmage. We can't fight him. We can't outrun him. We can't hide from him."

"Hiding was my plan, I admit," Armand told him. "This ship is new, unlike anything he could be expecting. My understanding is that if we aren't firing the rockets, we should just drift by unnoticed."

Cat grimaced, closing his eyes and rubbing his temples—a weakness he would show no one else.

"He already knows, Armand," he told his archmage. "I suspect the White Mountain told him the entirety of our conversations. He knows our names. He knows our *faces*. He *cursed well* knows our ship.

"More than that, though, can't you feel it?"

Armand looked at him and raised an eyebrow.

"The wraiths are different now," Cat said. "I can feel the vibration where there should be aether. They are *made* of hunger and I feel that hunger, but there is a *will* to them now that there wasn't before. Some of that is that IronHome is the center of the ritual and so there is more of the manifestation here... but most, I think, is that the Blood King is paying attention now."

"You think he controlled the skiffs that attacked us?" Armand asked.

"Not directly, I don't think, but he saw through them and commanded them," Cat confirmed. "These wraiths may be a side effect of the ritual. They may, honestly, have been something he created afterward to guard these spheres from potential interference.

"There is a *hunger* to the void here that eats at my very bones, but I can feel his will in it now, and I couldn't before." He shook his head. "The Blood King knows we're coming, Armand. We can't sneak past him. I can feel the hunger of these spheres all around me—and that hunger is *his* to command."

The chart room was silently chilly now as Armand finally began to understand Cat's fear.

"What do we do?" his archmage asked.

"I was hoping you had an idea, my lord archmage," Cat said drily. "Because *hiding* isn't going to work. This ship needs fuel in a way nothing I've ever commanded did, which limits our ability to outrun or outfly him—and *Void Flyer* mounts no weapons."

"This is not my battlefield," Armand told him, reaching over to place his hand on Cat's forearm. "It's *yours*, Cat. My power is at your disposal, my skills and knowledge too. But I can't plot or plan a battle in the void.

"You can. I have faith in *your* skill."

"*Go kill a god. I have faith in you*," Cat quoted back to him. "That's not a small ask, my archmage."

"My power and your skill, Cat Greentrees, can match many foes that think themselves invincible," Armand said. "And the Blood King, for all his power, is *not* a god. A var made immortal by mass murder, yes, but not a god."

Cat snorted, but nodded as he turned to study the chart of the sphere once more. Something plucked at the warning strings in the back of his mind. A sharper sense of the hunger he'd felt through the entire sphere for a while.

"If he's immortal, what happens if we blow him to pieces?" he asked.

"I suspect the pieces will eventually reassemble," Armand admitted. "But that would render him incapable for some time." The archmage paused, clearly realizing that Cat was distracted, and stepped forward to squeeze his shoulder.

"What is it?"

Cat closed his eyes, turning in place as he tried to follow the twang on his mental senses.

"Something woke up," he said softly, the words only making sense as he spoke them. He stabbed a finger into the air. "Over there."

He opened his eyes and measured the angle by the ease of long practice. The charts gave him the answer he needed.

The answer he feared.

"There is a nexus of power in this sphere that wasn't there an hour ago," he told Armand. "At the shipyards."

"That… is bad, isn't it?"

"Probably."

"Guide me to where," Armand instructed, his power taking shape in the air. He held his hand out to Cat, expecting Cat to understand what he needed.

And somehow Cat did. He took Armand's hand and leaned into the other var's power. His own sense of the strange nexus of power gave him a direction, and his own view of the charts gave him a distance.

His illusory telescope needed to be able to directly draw light and would be useless inside the sealed chart room. *Armand's* conjured illusions of a far-distant chunk of space had fewer limits.

The shipyards they'd studied before appeared in the middle of the room, details flickering past as Cat's guidance and Armand's power drilled in toward the source of the threat ringing through Cat's mind.

Somehow, he was unsurprised to see the twentysailed leviathan moving. Green mist swathed the monster's decks and trailed up her rigging, but it was something *else* that filled her sails. Not the wraiths of the sphere's hunger.

"What… What *is* that?" Armand whispered.

"The last flagship of the Ironhand Imperium," Cat told him. "Her decks crewed by the damned… and her sails filled by the Blood King's rage."

CHAPTER

30

Brushfire was intercepted before she reached the control room by Alloy, the darvar artificer looking concerned as he waved her down.

"Greentrees just called me down from the controls," he told her. "The runner didn't seem to know what for, but I figure if he's asking for *me*, he definitely wants *you*."

Brushfire wasn't quite sure she followed Alloy's logic, but she fell in beside the darvar as he approached the chart room. The *second* clue was that the chart room was closed and magically sealed. Not heavily, but enough to discourage anyone casually wandering in.

Alloy knocked before Brushfire could and the seal released, the same magic opening the door.

"Come in," Cat ordered. "We have a problem. Oh, Brushfire—thank the gods; I sent a runner looking for you, but I had no idea where you were."

"Crane's infirmary," Brushfire said as she entered the room. "We got Sky into their care in time. They'll live, but Crane still wasn't sure if they'd be able to save both of their legs."

Fortunately, while missing a leg would be a problem for Sky, Brushfire was certain there were a dozen and one tasks they could still use the elvar sailor for aboard *Void Flyer*. Taking care of the chart room they were standing in, for example, was currently a rotating duty but could easily absorb one less-mobile sailor's entire time.

Brushfire wasn't as skilled at navigating as a first officer should be, let alone as skilled as she'd *like* to be. She could read the charts around the room and make sense of them, but it only took her a few moments to realize that Cat and Armand—what was the archmage doing in the chart room?—were looking at something entirely different.

"What am I looking at?" Alloy asked, having joined the other two men while Brushfire was taking in the whole scene.

"The Ironhand shipyards and their old home fleet," Cat said calmly as Brushfire joined them. He then reached out to tap the illusion of one of the handful of massive twentysail behemoths.

"And that."

Brushfire hadn't realized it was moving. That was *impossible.*

"That is an aether ship," she said softly. "How is it moving?"

"From what I can tell," Armand told her, "it moves because the Blood King wishes it to move. The sails and arms are crewed by the same hunger wraiths we have encountered again and again across the void spheres, but I do not believe that hunger could fill the sails of an aether ship here."

"But the Blood King isn't even *here*," Brushfire told them. More a hope, she supposed, than an absolute certainty.

"No, he's not," Armand agreed. "We have drawn his attention, though, and it seems he has some power over the remaining manifestations of his ritual. In these spheres, I am afraid, the Blood King may as well *be* a full god."

"Depending on how confident he is in this trick, he may well be on his way to bar our exit into the Clan Spheres as we speak," Cat said quietly, a heavier undertone to his voice than Brushfire had ever heard before. "Or he might believe that the largest warship I have ever seen, with a crew that cannot die, is more than sufficient to deal with a single void ship that can't fight back."

Brushfire reached over to squeeze Cat's arm, hoping her support helped. She'd never seen him like this—and she didn't like it.

"I haven't read the same books you have," she warned the others. "But my Elders have their own stories of the Blood King. He never struck me as a creature to trust in *one* tool when he could use three."

"Agreed." Cat sounded exhausted. "He's coming. I don't know if we can get away from this ship, and I don't think we can hide from the *Blood King*."

"Can we fight the twentysail?" Armand asked. "It may be big, but it doesn't have an actual crew, and it's been sitting untouched for a thousand dances."

"There are twelve storm staves in our storage decks," Brushfire said slowly. "But we have only *four* void suits aboard... and they're sized for darvar. I don't think Alloy's daughters are trained to set up and fire a storm stave!"

"If I thought it would help, I might ask them anyway," Alloy noted grimly. "But none of the four of us have a clue with a storm stave. I could work it out, I'm sure, but in a clumsy void suit while under pursuit?"

"We have no other options?" Armand asked. "Cat, you never learned *any* magic to fight without staves?"

Brushfire squeezed her Captain's forearm again. There had to be an answer, and she was with Armand. The rest of them had the *power* to contribute, but it was Cat who might have the *skill* to know what to do.

Cat was silent for longer than she liked, then turned away from the illusion of their pursuer to look at the chart of IronHome.

"There are a few tricks," he conceded. "As Brushfire showed me, any mage can duplicate a storm stave. Doing so from the outside of the ship while we're inside? Harder. There are other options, but they are... tools of desperation.

"They are *traps* more than weapons, requiring an enemy lured well within a league. These..." He sighed. "The wraiths are not being sent to capture us, my friends. They will destroy us. We *must* outrun them."

"How fast can they move?" Brushfire asked.

"Faster than you might think," Cat told her. "But they are limited by what those sails can take. I don't *care* what magic fills them; a mast and her sails can only carry so much force. No ninesail I've ever commanded could make more than perhaps five leagues a minute, even with the most favorable currents and crew.

"I don't know what *her* masts are made of, but a thousand dances— even in the void—must have weakened them. Five leagues would be my guess, but we'll see soon enough."

"We can go that fast," Alloy pointed out. "There's… no real limit to how fast *Flyer* can go except for fuel. It's just that… well, basically, we store about fifty leagues per minute's worth of fuel when full. Getting out of a lodestone's effect costs us about three. And it costs us the same fuel to slow down as to speed up.

"Our plan was to head for Warden of Stone at three leagues a minute, and we'd burned about two-fifths of our fuel getting from Flame's Gem to the Home and back into the void. Whatever speed we gain, we need to lose most of before we enter the strait—and then we need to accelerate again in both the strait and each sphere."

Brushfire understood the *basic* concept of their fuel translating into speed—and that the plan called for them to enter the Clan Spheres with less than a third of their fuel remaining.

"Every bit of fuel we burn is speed we cannot gain or lose later," Alloy warned. "But we *can* get up to six, maybe seven leagues a minute while still having *some* fuel when we reach the Clan Spheres."

The darvar paused, clearly doing math in his head.

"Enough to transit maybe two spheres, if we're slow and careful."

"Slow and careful later beats dead today," Armand pointed out. "Cat?"

The Captain was studying the charts in silence, though Brushfire was quite sure he'd been listening.

"Everything about maneuvering in the void bothers me," Cat finally said. "There are no tricks, no currents, nowhere I can find a better way. They will follow a straight line, likely aiming for the passage to Warden of Stone to intercept us.

"All of these maneuvers are mechanical and mathematical. We cannot change them," he said grimly. "Seventeen thousand leagues for us from here. Thirty-five thousand for them. They'll reach the strait in five days—less, really."

"If they can manage that speed," Brushfire noted. "They may be slower."

"They may be faster," Alloy pointed out. "Captain…"

"If we double our speed, four leagues a minute, we should beat them to the strait by two full days," Cat said swiftly. "That still leaves us with a fifth of our fuel once we pass out of Stormfall and back into aether.

"Whatever power propels them will have a harder time in regular spheres, I think," he continued. "Though I fear we will meet the Blood King before we make it out of the void."

Brushfire shivered. The Blood King was… a myth, a scary story used to warn children and tell tales around the campfire. The thought of him as a *real* being, one who was coming to catch them, made no sense.

"Alloy and I will see to the course on the bridge," Cat continued. "Brushfire, Armand… keep an eye on those ships. It will be half a day or more before we can really measure their speed, but it's possible there are other magics and other tricks at the Blood King's command."

"We'll watch," Brushfire promised.

"We'll get the ship moving," Cat confirmed. "And then I'll check in on Sky. Thank you for getting them to the ship safely, Brushfire."

He smiled thinly.

"This has grown more difficult than even my worst fears, but I won't lose one var I don't have to."

The Captain and the artificer left the chart room, headed up to the control room, and Brushfire stood at her archmage's side as she studied the ancient ship sailing grimly toward them.

She could *feel* Armand's tension and reached over to gently touch his shoulder.

"Armand?" she asked softly.

"I…" Armand trailed off, covering her hand with his for a moment before exhaling a deep sigh and stepping forward to study the model of the aether ship more closely.

"I have made a mistake," the archmage finally finished. "Sneaking an aether ship through the border spheres is difficult. Impossible, they tell me. Except it clearly *has* been done. Your tribe came to the Kingdoms, after all, and others have come more recently.

"While the questions and funds of an archmage did not open doors, those doors *had* to exist. I found the answer of this side route, and I stopped looking for other ways," he admitted. "I have led you, Cat, your tribe… the rest of the crew… I have led you all here, into these spheres I thought would be safer. Easier.

"And now it appears that the closest thing I know of to a *living god* bars our way."

He wasn't looking at the ship he was studying, Brushfire could tell.

"We were looking for dragons," he noted. "Dangerous creatures, yes. Smarter and more magically powerful than any var. The attack on Cat's squadron was a *test*, one that no one except the Clans involved should have known about.

"After all, the High Court Navy *does not run*. Cat's retreat saved his ship and crew, but it cost him *everything*. The dragons could not have predicted that an elvar Captain would make that sacrifice.

"But compared to the Blood King, what is a dragon? The ones Cat saw were youths, their scales not even closed up to fully guard their flesh. My scryings showed older ones but no *old* dragons. I didn't see Bloodscale, for that matter.

"I certainly didn't see any *other* member of the Quadrumvirate. The Blood King had nothing to do with what I foresaw. But compared to him, is the threat we seek even worth mentioning? I put together a crew to find answers.

"Not to fight a god."

Brushfire hesitated for a moment, then gave into her impulse and pulled Armand into a fierce embrace. He stiffened for a heartbeat, maybe two, then seemed to melt against her, drawing strength from her height and muscles and warmth—and wrapped his arms around her in turn.

"My foolish archmage," she murmured to him. "There are clock-days I feel I know nothing compared to what you and Cat know, but there are things I know that you clearly don't.

"My tribe left the Spheres of Our Clans two hundred dances ago. *Two hundred.* Things have changed. Once, ships could go both ways so long as they were discreet. Then, even once the Crimson Sisters wholly closed the border on the Clans' side, the High Court Navy was perfectly willing to turn a blind eye to single ships that carried no arms."

She chuckled.

"I would never say such to Cat," she admitted, "but the High Court Navy exists to *support trade.* Specifically, the trade of the elvar ships who pay fees to the High Court, but they need a reason to block even smuggling without orders.

"But those orders eventually came. And the Crimson Sisters locked down more harshly on their side. Fifty dances ago, you could have smuggled a family from the Clans into the Kingdoms, but not a tribe. You could not have gone the other way.

"These dances?" She shook her head before resting her chin on the top of his head. "No, Armand. There was no other way, not that wouldn't have ended in death at the storm staves of a dozen galleons. No smuggler ship could sneak past by stealth, and it would take fleets upon fleets to breach the border by force."

"And yet this way appears to end in disaster," he whispered. "I look to Cat for answers. I have *power*, but I don't know if my power can change this. Even against this wraith ship, I don't know if we have the tools, the skills and the strength to beat them.

"We can outrun them for now, but how far will they pursue?"

Brushfire sighed. She'd noted that gap in the discussions too. The plan to push to four leagues a minute to get out of IronHome didn't account for any pursuit in the Warden of Stone... or what to do when they met the Blood King.

"I don't know," she admitted. "We need to have fuel once we enter the Clan Spheres. We can't enter a strait at more than a league a minute, I don't think—not when they're basically invisible and Cat is the only one who can guide us in.

"So, every bit of speed we add, we have to take away later. All of which costs fuel. I don't know what happens if they chase us."

"They will," Armand said, his voice very soft and tired. "The manifestation of the Blood King's ritual is *more* present here, yes, but it was present even in the Warden of Fire. I suspect that the wraiths of one sphere may have difficulty transiting to another, but that ship has the Blood King's direct attention.

"It will follow us. And we *will* have to fight it."

"Then you will need to find a way, my archmage," Brushfire told him, squeezing gently before releasing him. "I have faith in you. And Cat. And our crew, for that matter.

"If it can be done, this ship and these var will do it. And if there is an answer, I believe *you* will find it."

She smiled down at him and hoped that her belief lifted him up rather than dragging him down.

"You've got us this far, haven't you?" she asked.

"We all have got us this far," Armand countered. "You, Cat, Alloy. I've had my part, but it wasn't *just* me."

"Then maybe the answer isn't just you, either?"

He paused, staring blankly off into space.

"Maybe," he said slowly. "Maybe… I need to research something. I just hope I have the right books…"

CHAPTER
31

ARMAND HAD SELECTED THE BOOKS HE'D BROUGHT WITH HIM ON this journey carefully. Most were directly relevant, picked because they either spoke to the void, the Ironhand Imperium and the charts he'd acquired, or the Clan Spheres. Some, though, he'd thrown in on an impulse he *knew* was part instinct, part divination.

One of those books now lay open on the desk in front of him, next to a half-eaten pastry as he stared at the text. Every book he had with him was a copy, many printed on presses in the Shining Spheres, and others carefully recreated by highly paid scribes at the Towers of the Great Red Forest.

This was one of the latter, and he honestly didn't *remember* packing it. He'd brought books on navigation and aether ships and history. He had a few standard texts on magical theory that he liked to reference, and those had come with him. This was closer to the latter than the former, but it wasn't a book he normally kept with him.

He'd *read* it, of course. He'd read every one of the two thousand–odd texts in his tower library. But the slim tome, bound in red-dyed wood panels, was only vaguely familiar to him. A text on *interlinking* the magic of multiple mages, it wasn't a text that an *archmage* would have spent much thought on.

An archmage, after all, had all of the power they could ever need. An archmage was a master of the mystic arts and would rarely lack the skills they needed, either, at least when it came to magic.

But Armand only knew the most basic levels of how conflict in the aether worked. He also knew the *void* was different. Cat, on the other hand, *did* know how conflict worked in the aether and had hopefully learned enough of the void by now to master the differences.

Cat didn't have the power to fight a warship at a hundred leagues. Armand didn't have the skills and spells to fight a warship at *any* distance.

The strange melding nexus of minds and powers the book contained might be an answer. But it was, of course, neither safe nor easy.

The meld could allow two—or more, though the author had apparently only tested with three and didn't even recommend *that*—mages to merge their powers. More than their powers. Their minds. Their wills. Their *selves*.

After testing and measuring the risks, it becomes clear that this spell should only be utilized for the most short-term of endeavors, the page read. *By preference, with another mage present who is capable of severing the ritual.*

Even a single spell, combining the power and knowledge of two mages, will have a greater impact than either mage on their own. However, it must be understood that there are no *boundaries between the members of the meld. No secrets.*

Every archmage had their secrets. Armand wasn't sure if he had any, at that particular moment, that he was concerned about Cat Greentrees knowing—many of the ones he'd sworn to keep to his grave were related to the Bluestaves Archive, and he'd *used* the Archive's knowledge to get this far.

Of course, Cat had his own secrets. Armand knew that. He had seen enough in the court of the Shining King to know that nobles and rulers were a treacherous and shadowy lot. And the High Court was *worse* in every way.

Cat *probably* wasn't high enough up in his House or the High Court Navy to carry the kinds of secrets where death was preferable to revealing them. Armand certainly had no secrets he would keep from Cat—not least because until he released the other var, Cat was his sworn servant.

As such, Cat was already sworn to keep Armand's secrets. Even of the handful of var sworn directly to Armand aboard *Void Flyer*, Armand would trust Cat above all others.

There were more risks than the loss of secrets, though. The author was specific in that they'd *never* included an archmage in the meld and couldn't predict what would happen.

It was a strange magic, one requiring more subtlety than power. But while Armand had plenty of *power*, he also figured he could manage complexity and subtlety of magic, too.

Especially when he was starting to suspect that his failure to work through the complexity and subtleties of *why* the spheres they needed to cross were gone might be about to kill them all. He should have *known* the spheres of the Imperium hadn't been lost to the void by random fate.

But as Brushfire had reminded him, his research and his divinations had agreed. There was no other option. If he wanted to learn what was going on with dragons taking control of the gobvar, he needed to go to the Clan Spheres.

And that journey was possible in only two ways: with the fleets no one would give even an archmage without evidence or by an end run through these cursed spheres.

Armand's research was interrupted by a runner, who brought him back up to the control room. The archmage entered the clear-roofed space and looked around carefully. The hands on the sextants and other equipment had changed—it had been half a day, so that was expected.

Of his sworn servants, only Cat was present. Smallwolf, the most junior of the officers, stood with the Captain as the elvar held the ship's control wheel, studying the skies above him.

"Captain, you asked for me?" Armand said, stepping up to the central dais.

"Aye. We have a speed on the wraith ship and it's… not good." Cat wasn't looking at him, his focus still on the void around them.

"Six leagues a minute," Smallwolf reported briskly. "We'll still beat her to the strait by a full day unless she finds more speed somewhere."

"Unlikely," Armand noted. "If she's propelled by what we think, he would push her as fast as she could possibly go."

"I suspect this may be faster than she can go," Cat told him. "But the sails and masts *may* endure it for a few days. And it's not like the Blood King cares if he wrecks the ship, either."

"No," Armand agreed. "Does this change anything?"

"Not yet." The Captain finally looked down from the crystal paneling above them to meet Armand's gaze. "But I question what happens when we reach the Warden of Stone."

His voice was quiet enough and there were few enough others in the control room to keep the conversation between the two of them and Smallwolf, who presumably needed to know what was going on.

Armand would freely admit he wasn't entirely sure on what the officers did or didn't need to know, and would err toward telling them everything.

"They will pursue into the strait," he told Cat. "I… *suspect* they will be at their weakest there. This journey has proven much of what is 'known' about the links between aether spheres wrong, I think.

"I believe that the hunger wraiths will be weakened when they aren't in a sphere holding a fragment of the Blood King's ritual," he concluded. "They will pass through the strait with difficulty… but once they emerge in the Warden of Stone, they will likely be fully empowered by the Blood King and the hunger of these spheres once more."

"That was my fear," Cat said calmly. "But IronHome is very clearly the center of the ritual, right?"

"Yes," Armand confirmed, wondering where Cat was going.

"I don't think we can fight them here," the Captain told him. "But in the Warden of Stone… they will be weaker."

"I'm not sure how *much* weaker," Armand warned. "If we could fight them in the strait…"

Cat grimaced.

"I thought about it," he admitted. "But without the aether to mark the edge of the strait, we are so blind as to our own course… If we change course, if we even *maneuver*, we will be lost between spheres forever."

They would survive that longer in *Void Flyer* than any other ship, Armand supposed, but that still didn't mean they would *survive*.

"So, in the Warden, then," he murmured. "We could keep running."

"Right now, if we follow our planned course from here to the Clan Spheres—our entry point is called Drinkstar, of all things—we will arrive there with one-quarter of our fuel remaining. Enough to travel through perhaps two spheres.

"Certainly not enough to deal with any threats or allow anything particularly *clever*." Cat snorted. "Thankfully, Drinkstar has several occupied worldlets. And none of them are Ironhand Wards, either—the Eleventh Ward is in Stormfall."

The Seventh Ward had been the var-shaped asteroid His Dark Brothers had turned into their monastery on Brokenwright. Its purpose had been to serve as an anchor for an arcane device to separate the core of the Ironhand empire from the rest of the universe. The *Eleventh* Ward was the one that could, in theory, block their escape entirely.

Armand hoped they either got to Stormfall in time to prevent that or that the Blood King was *so* angry at their intrusion, he wouldn't block them like that. He was grimly certain that the King was quite likely to be that angry, which helped.

Sort of.

"So, we can find a ship in Drinkstar, if we burn all of our fuel getting there."

"Assuming we have the fuel left to approach and safely land on one of those worldlets," Cat said. "And that we have some way to *get* a ship."

"I have options," Armand told him. Money might not trade between the Clans and the Kingdoms, but gold and silver did. There were chests stuffed with both in the storage decks, enough money to buy a ship wherever he went.

He also suspected that producing foci would be just as lucrative for his purposes there.

"But we can't get up to six leagues a day in the Warden of Stone *and* Stormfall and have any fuel left in Drinkstar," Cat warned. "We *have* to fight her.

"I just don't know *how*."

"I... have the beginnings of an idea," Armand told his friend and sworn servant. "Or, at the very least, the potential to create *options*."

CHAPTER

32

Armand's explanation of the strange magic he was planning still hung in Cat's ears and mind as he guided *Void Flyer* toward the strait out of IronHome.

"Eighty-five hundred leagues," Smallwolf reported from the left sextant. Between the telescopes and the sextant's mix of arcane and mechanical devices, she no longer needed the illusion from Armand to track the wraith ship.

"She's gaining on us."

Which wasn't helped by Cat slowing *Void Flyer* to make an entrance to the strait. The twentysail would need to do the same, but the wraiths were still a day away from making that adjustment.

"I still have no eyes on the strait," Brushfire said, standing by the right-hand sextant. "Streamwater and I refined the chart estimates based on where we found the one in the Warden of Fire, but I *still* can't see anything."

"We couldn't see the one in the Warden of Fire, either," Cat pointed out. He closed his eyes, focusing on the aether around them. There *was* no aether, not really, but the same sense that allowed him to feel the normal fabric of the spheres let him find the gaps where the fabric broke.

Even from over eight thousand leagues away, the first thing he felt was the ship. He wasn't sure if the ship was a denser source of power than any of the previous encounters they'd had with the wraiths or if he was getting more sensitive. Either way, the hunger and rage billowing off the old warship loomed large in the emptiness of the IronHome.

Pushing past that bloom of power, he focused his attention ahead of them. *There.*

"We're almost on the course," he said aloud, adjusting the wheel slightly. The engines were offline, but lift crystals would suffice for this. They had little to push against there, the lack of aether impacting them too, but they still had enough to turn the ship.

If they hadn't, he suspected Alloy would have fixed that long before they'd taken the ship. The mage-artificer knew his work. Cat was almost as confident in the darvar as he was in his original crew and officers—and that was high praise.

"On the line. Mostly," he told everyone, opening his eyes. There was *nothing* to mark the spot in the void he'd pointed the rocket at. He considered what he could see, what he could feel—and what the instruments Brushfire and Smallwolf were constantly updating told him.

"We're going to need the rocket," he said. "I don't think we can stay on the line with the crystals. Ready?"

"We are ready," Alloy told him, the darvar seated next to another panel of instruments. There were more instruments in *Void Flyer*'s control room than had been on the bridge of any ship Cat had ever commanded.

Probably more than had been on every bridge combined. Ninesails were navigated by a sextant, a chart and a will. Not much more was needed.

Void Flyer was a strange ship, with many mechanisms and magics that needed to be watched to make sure everything worked properly. Cat was comfortable enough with the instruments now that he could fly the ship without Alloy, but he didn't pretend to fully understand them yet.

There were probably a dozen var from the crew, including Smallwolf but *not* the other officers, that he would trust to manage the instruments of the control room around him. He'd trust Brushfire to *fly* the ship, so long as either Smallwolf or Alloy was present, but he knew she hadn't mastered the strange instruments to the level she'd need.

One of the reasons he'd trust Brushfire above all others, possibly even Armand, was that he knew *she* knew that. And she wouldn't even attempt flying the ship without the right support.

"Five ticks, no more," Cat told Alloy. "Burn."

The ship trembled underneath him as the rockets flared. Irreplaceable fuel blazed fire into the void, and the ship's course changed.

"*Now* we're on the line," he concluded with satisfaction. "About five leagues out."

"No change to their course or standings, Captain," Smallwolf told him. "She's coming right at the strait."

"She's not bound to this sphere any more than we are," Cat conceded with a sigh. "Or she may still be and they're just hoping to bluff us. It's not like they can *hit* us from here."

If they'd been even half the distance from the wraith ship, he might have hesitated to be so certain about that. No storm stave *he'd* known could hit ships thousands of leagues distant—but the ship chasing them wasn't bound by the rules he'd known.

"And when we're in the Warden of Stone?" Brushfire asked. "Do we have the fuel to outrun her, Cat?"

He barely looked at Alloy before shaking his head.

"If we went up to six leagues a minute in the Warden of Stone and then again in Stormfall, we'd stay a day ahead of them... and enter the Clan Spheres without a drop of fuel aboard. We cannot leave the void spheres in a ship than cannot maneuver, cannot fly."

Void Flyer was unlikely to get them far past Drinkstar, the first Clan Sphere, but Cat admitted he should probably stop worrying about what they would encounter past the void.

But to outrun the wraith ship wouldn't leave them without enough fuel to *get* out of the void.

"We need fuel left to maneuver around the *next* threat," he told his officers. "But passing through the strait means they will be blind to what happens in the Warden of Stone. And they *are* a day behind us."

The control room was silent as he met Brushfire's gaze. He knew she could see through him by now, in a way no elvar subordinate would have *dared* to learn. Still, he met her eyes and projected confidence.

"We, after all, have a force that no other ship would carry," he reminded them. "Let the wraiths come. They have an ancient ship of the damned.

"*We* have an archmage."

They broke free of the strait into the Warden of Stone, and Cat let his senses reach out as his people took a more-conventional view around the sphere. He could feel the strait behind him. He could feel a vague thrumming sense of *hunger* coming from the crystal at the heart of the sphere.

Nothing else. Like the last two spheres they'd passed through, there was no aether there. Only the void. He opened his eyes and looked with more ordinary senses.

"What do the charts say about this place?" he asked.

"Four inhabited worlds, none more than two thousand leagues across," Smallwolf said instantly. "I've taken a look at two of them so far. Not much to see at this range, but I'd say they're just as dead as the Warden of Fire or IronHome."

"And no strange divinations saying we should do anything other than run for Stormfall, right?" Cat asked wryly. He addressed that question to Brushfire, but all three of his junior mages shook their heads.

"Just the usual frustrating vagueness," Smallwolf told him. "I've never had particularly clear divinations. Except in IronHome."

"And that, Officer Smallwolf, is the same experience as almost every officer and mage I have ever known," Cat reassured her. "The High Court Navy seeks out seers specifically, and they are given leeway few other var are given in the High Court Navy."

The prophecy that had led him to him retreating from the dragon attack had been given to him *on top of the mainmast* of his ship. Seers in the Navy were a very special breed—and Cat's experience with the type *outside* the Navy suggested that the Navy's seers were, if anything, *saner* than most of their kind.

Any mage could do some divination. It took a strange mind to truly predict the future. The prophecy Armand was seeking to prevent had been the result of what Cat was told was a dangerous and powerful tool concealed somewhere in the Shining Eye Sphere.

The exact location and nature of that tool was one of the few secrets his archmage had kept from him, which reminded him of the warning

Armand had given him about the *meld nexus* that seemed their best chance against the wraith ship.

Cat knew he *did* have secrets he shouldn't tell a halvar archmage. Stories and places and treasures of the House of Forests or even of the Greentrees family, things he'd sworn to keep secret even from the Navy or potential future spouses.

But those were hardly secrets he was sworn to keep with his *life*— and he would question his own honor and integrity if he chose minor secrets of his House over the lives of his *crew*.

"Bring us about," he ordered aloud. "Alloy, we'll want to shed all of our speed and head back to put ourselves above the exit from the passage."

"Sir, we have no weapons," Smallwolf said quietly, her voice stiff.

"We have an archmage," he repeated. "And we have me. Lord Bluestaves and I have a plan, Bogsong. Have faith."

He was surprised by how much that seemed to reassure her. Smallwolf gave him a small nod, turning her attention back to her sextant as Cat began to maneuver the ship.

"Cat." Brushfire's voice was very quiet, and he realized she'd left her sextant behind to practically whisper in his ear. "I *have* faith in both of you. But against this enemy, I am wondering if we need a backup plan."

"What did you have in mind?" Cat replied, his own voice pitched to match hers so no one else could hear. "I'm already planning on getting a *lot* closer than I want."

"I *think* most of the mages can generate enough of a bubble to step outside the hull without the void suits," she told him.

"Which will consume *all* of a mage's focus and power," he pointed out. He'd considered the option. "Just to be able to breathe on their own."

"Yes. But if that mage was trained to use a *storm stave…*"

Cat was about to point out that *none* of them were actually trained in that, then trailed off as he remembered that wasn't actually correct.

"That's one voids-cursed risk for him to take on," Cat murmured. "With help from the others, we might be able to mount two, even three storm staves on the hull, but he's the only one who can discharge them—and without aether to draw on, they won't have a second shot."

"I'll ask him, but to protect this crew? We know Fistfall will do it," Brushfire told him. "Any of us would."

CHAPTER 33

"YOU NEEDED TO SEE ME, ELDEST SISTER?"

Brushfire gave Fistfall a long-suffering *look* and the big gobvar chuckled. The focus at his side and all that it represented seemed to be bringing out a new side of her brother. It was still a hesitant and fledgling thing, but she could begin to see the mage and leader he would become.

She wasn't sure if *he* saw it yet, but he was more ready to tease her than he had once been. And *that*, she figured, was a good sign.

"Grab a seat, Fistfall," she told him. The "office" of her quarters was also the sitting area—but even as first officer on *Star*, she hadn't had *two* rooms to her own name. An entire deck, thirty yards across, had been put aside for the ship's leadership, and Brushfire figured that was probably excessive.

She didn't want to get used to it, anyway. There was no real plan for how they were getting around the Clan Spheres, but she doubted it was going to be aboard *Void Flyer*—if only because of the very problem she needed Fistfall to help fix.

"We don't have a lot of time," she reminded him. *Flyer* was now in the position Cat had wanted, ready to ambush the much larger and much more dangerous ship pursuing them—but that had taken a sixth of a clock-day to manage.

"The Captain has a plan for when the twentysail arrives, right?" Fistfall asked. "You need me to do something."

He didn't ask more and he didn't say he was volunteering. He *knew* she understood what he meant.

"You've been learning magic since we left Flame's Gem," Brushfire said. "I *know* you haven't learned enough to stand against a fully trained mage or anything like that yet, but with that personal focus, you have the *power* and the *potential* to do so."

"So you and the others tell me," he agreed cautiously. "Mostly feel like a child playing with my first-uncle's tools again." He smiled. "But then, borrowing Windheart's tools was how I started learning carpentry."

"I don't think Windheart called it *borrowing*," she reminded him with a smile. "But I agree with you. You're still learning, and *play* is a good way to learn. We've got time and distance to get you to where the archmage wants you.

"But today, I need you to be a mage," she told him, her smile fading. "I believe Streamwater taught you the air-bubble spell?"

"She did," Fistfall confirmed. "Just in case I was the only one close enough to save one of the non-aethervar on the crew. Or anyone on the crew while we're in the void!"

"It's a useful spell, a critical tool," she said. "Being in the void, all of the mages aboard need to know it, and Streamwater made sure everyone was refreshed on it. Now... Now it may be the key to surviving the next clock-day."

She rubbed her horns, her fingers touching the inlay marking her old training as a shaman. The *plan* had been for her to teach Cat and possibly even Armand some of the more subtle and physically focused magic she'd learned as a shaman, but they'd never really had the time.

It had always felt more important to train her as a mage, to use that larger and more external magic. Brushfire had drawn on her shaman training to endure when she summoned too much magic, though, and suspected that was part of what allowed her to keep going when even Cat felt the strain.

"We have storm staves on the storage decks," she reminded Fistfall. "But no one who can get out on the hull has a clue how to use them. Except that even though Hunter hasn't *told* any of the officers, I am absolutely certain he trained a number of the gobvar crew on the staves."

Fistfall stiffened, staring past her.

"He did," her brother admitted levelly. "He told us that he didn't much care for laws, so long as it helped protect his crew and his Captain. But he worried that was a step too far for Cat... and by the time I think he realized better, we'd left *Star* behind."

"But no one can go out into the void..."

"Except the mages," Brushfire finished as he trailed off. "Because that bubble *will* allow you to talk into the void and breathe for a while. It takes enough power that you can't use any other magic—and, to be clear, I'm not sure *Armand* could use any other magic; that's not a slight on you, brother."

"And I have some idea of what to do with a storm stave," Fistfall said. "I... I'm not very *good* with them, sister. I can aim and discharge, but I'm not a great shot, and I don't know much of the subtleties of recharging one."

"The good news, I suppose, is that they *can't* recharge in the void spheres," she told him grimly. "Hunter is checking the staves as we speak. I'm *hoping* that out of a dozen, we'll have half that still have enough power to be released.

"I and Smallwolf will help you move as many as we can fit onto the hull outside," she continued. The thought of walking out into the void, with only her magic allowing her to *breathe*, was terrifying. But to protect the crew, she would do it.

"But I'll need to be in the control room when they arrive. I need you to remain on the hull and aim the staves. No one else who can be out there knows how to use them properly. The Captain has a plan... but if it fails, it may *all* come down on you."

Fistfall swallowed visibly, her little brother and biggest member of her tribe clearly recognizing the weight of what she was asking... but all he did was nod.

"When do we get started?"

Brushfire had absolutely, unquestionably, utterly underestimated how terrifying stepping out into the void shielded only by a frail bubble of air would be. She focused on the arcane weapon she was holding one side of and tried to breathe normally.

"Door's open," Fistfall noted. "Forward?"

"Forward," she agreed. There might not be void suits to fit the gobvar, but they at least had harnesses that could pull them back into the two-doored chamber that protected *Void Flyer*'s interior from the emptiness outside.

Maneuvering the storm stave out the side of the ship was an exercise in frustration, not helped by the fact that the pull of *Flyer*'s lodestone plate began to angle once they were no longer directly above it.

More ropes and hooks came into play, and Brushfire wished she could pull magic in to help her footing. It was taking a ridiculous amount of focus to keep the air intact around her and *move*, though. Adding more magic would be too much.

Thankfully, Fistfall's air bubble was merging with hers. From some of the dire warnings they'd received, they might not be able to *talk* to each other if the bubbles separated.

The void was not the aether. Both of them had climbed masts in the aether, with only ropes and a too-distant lodestone keel to keep them in place. In the aether, though, a gobvar could breathe. If they drifted away or lost concentration on their magic, Brushfire wasn't sure how long either of them would survive in the void.

She wasn't planning on finding out.

The pair finally got the storm stave onto the outer hull and strapped with its own ropes. She finally took a moment to look "up" and away from the cylindrical rocket.

"You know, it doesn't look any different from out here than in the control room," she admitted. "It's just... *knowing* that bubble is the only thing keeping me alive."

"I have more faith in your magic than mine, Brushfire," Fistfall pointed out. "But if we want to get the best use of this stave, we want it about twelve yards up there."

He gestured.

"We can put three staves on the hull, each ten yards apart," he continued. "I can only aim one at a time, but that gives us three shots, right?"

"It will," she confirmed. "Maybe you should mark the spots while I keep an eye on this stave? Smallwolf and Streamwater won't be long with the second stave."

He nodded and set out, carefully moving from clip to clip, and leaving Brushfire *very* aware that the outside of the ship didn't have nearly as many loops for clipping on to as she'd like. It took him a few minutes to make the marks where the three storm staves would go, measuring the gaps by eye and step.

Brushfire wasn't sure *how* he was judging the gap he would need, but she trusted him. Hopefully, Hunter Paintrock had put in his own few silvers on that topic. She wasn't sure she necessarily *trusted* the blue elvar, but she had faith in his *competence.*

Relying on the bubble wore on her nerves, but she also grew more used to it, more stable in sustaining the spell. She still wouldn't have wanted to be doing any *other* magic, and the strange silence left her feeling utterly alone on the hull.

She'd spent her entire life in an extended-family clan of a hundred var. *Alone* wasn't something she experienced much, and she wasn't sure she liked it.

It was a relief when the hatch popped open and the edges of two more bubbles of magic announced the arrival of the other pair of mages with the second storm stave. Fistfall was working his way back, and the bubbles of air merged to allow the four of them to talk.

"Okay," her little brother said, a new confidence in his voice. "I've got marks on where we want the three staves. Ten yards apart should give them enough clearance to fire—but we need to mount them *solidly* to get the amount of flex I'll need for proper aiming."

"If we get this wrong, we might as well not go through the effort," Brushfire pointed out to the two elvar. "So, let's do them one at a time and see what we think of the first one, shall we?"

And then, much as she loved and trusted her brother, she was going to hope that Armand's plan worked. Because *she* certainly didn't think three staves, laid in by hand and operated by a single var, were going to win against a ship with over a *hundred* of the same weapon...

IF ASKED, ARMAND WOULD HAVE FREELY ADMITTED THAT HE COULD barely tell one *worldlet* from another, let alone any given piece of aether or void from another.

Standing in the control room aboard *Void Flyer*, watching the clear panes of crystal above and around him as Cat and the other officers worked through their preparations, though, he realized that wasn't quite true.

Not anymore, at least. He'd passed through more spheres since leaving the Great Red Forest in pursuit of his vision of catastrophe than he had *ever* expected to travel. Now, he could tell that the Warden of Stone was a crystal-lit sphere without even looking at the great crystal glowing fifteen thousand leagues away.

He could also tell that there was something *wrong* with the crystal. It had just been a vague sense in IronHome, that there was almost an *infection* in the ember there, but the ember had still burned clear and red.

The crystal in the Warden of Stone was both less *infected* and more *affected.* Any crystal sent off sharper light than an ember or an outer-sphere, though Armand would have been hard pressed to explain quite what that meant.

Only that it was very obvious, having passed through each type in the last few clock-days. The void spheres had a sharper edge to light overall, he'd noticed. He was quite certain it was due to the lack of aether, but it also made the *wrongness* of the Warden of Stone's light crystal clearer.

The light—even the crystal itself when he took careful looks at it—was *bruised*. The soft white-green that he believed was the true underlying color still came through clearly, but there were streaks of darker greens and purples, plus reds and even, somehow, *blacks* woven through the light.

The crystal and its light showed the infection more clearly than the ember and outersphere had, but Armand was certain it had been present throughout all three void spheres. Whatever the Last Ironhand had done to his people's core spheres, it endured in ways that Armand suspected the Blood King had never expected.

And it was dangerous, both in the ways they'd already seen and in ways they had yet to even *begin* to comprehend. The kind of magic Oathheld Ironhand has unleashed was powerful beyond dreams and nightmares, but it was also only so controllable.

Armand wondered if the Blood King believed he controlled it. Certainly, the power the demigod wielded there was unimaginable, but the archmage could *feel* the power around them. The Blood King's will was guiding it, channeling it toward resisting their passage and empowering the wraith ship that pursued them, but he didn't think the King was actually in control.

He didn't think anyone could *comprehend* the full scope of what had been created in these spheres, let alone control it. That was, perhaps, something they could use.

Assuming neither the manifestations of the ascension ritual nor the Blood King himself killed them all.

"I make it about five minutes," Brushfire announced, examining a clock that Armand had been studiously ignoring. "If they were coming through the strait any faster than we did, we'd have seen them by now."

"I'm surprised they slowed down that much," Streamwater said. "*I* expected them half a day ago, to have pushed through at the same half a dozen leagues a minute."

"The strait, despite the name, is not *straight*," Cat pointed out, in a tone that suggested everyone in the control room *should* know that but he was explaining it anyway to be generous.

Armand, on the other hand, *hadn't* known that.

"If they tried to push the passage at that speed, I don't care what semi-divine hand guides them. They *would* breach the strait," he said. "And if they *have* breached the strait, we won't be seeing them in any of our lifetimes."

Armand wasn't so sure of that, but he believed Cat when his Captain said that the wraiths couldn't make the passage at speed. For the moment, he stepped up next to the main wheel and gently pressed his shoulder into Cat's.

"Should we be ready?" he asked. "We can't sustain the meld safely for long—a few minutes at most."

"Then we should be ready but hold off for a touch more," Cat replied. "How long will the meld take?"

"Moments," Armand said. "I've prepared much of the magic already."

And sat on most of his fears and anxiety over it, too. It would never do to show the crew and his sworn servants that the *archmage* wasn't sure of his solution. The enemy was coming. If his plan failed, well... Armand was aware of the backup plan.

It might even work. But while he knew *nothing* of war in the aether, the cold math of three storm staves versus one hundred and twenty seemed obvious enough to him.

The void above his head was less clear to Armand than he hoped it was to everyone else in the control room. He knew every var working the instruments, beyond even the officers, for all that he still spent most of his time in his quarters.

At least aboard *Star*, he'd learned how to link his magic into the crystal lattices woven through the aether ship so he could keep an eye on things going on outside his small bubble of air. Aboard *Void Flyer*, he was more capable of walking the decks and talking to people, though he still kept to himself.

He was a teacher and a scholar, but he wasn't, he would freely admit, much of a people person. His best idea for making friends was and always had been feeding them fresh-baked pastries.

Which had always *worked*, so why would he try anything else?

Armand was splitting his attention between the void, the crew, Cat and Brushfire—which meant he actually saw *Brushfire* reacting to Cat's sudden tension before he saw the Captain tense up himself.

"Cat?" Brushfire asked.

"I can *feel* them," Cat half-whispered, half-snarled. "Their hunger. Their anger. They're almost here."

He turned to Armand.

"It's time. What do I need to do?"

Armand had the answer hanging from his wrist on a cord and pulled it up into his hand. He was no artificer, but just as any archmage could fill in for a seer in their absence, he was capable of enough arcane construction to manage this.

"Hold your wand in your right hand," he instructed. "And take my hand with your left. Hold the charm between us—as much as I could create of the spell in advance is on it."

Cat obeyed and Armand reached out to take hold of the elvar's focus. One of the secrets archmagi didn't admit was that even a *personal* focus would still respond to the archmage who'd made it. Even the most attuned focus could still be used by the var who'd made it.

That wasn't *required* for this—the original spell had never been used with an archmage, after all—but Armand knew it would make things easier. Both of his hands now touched Cat, his left palm holding the other var's focus next to him, his right crushing the tiny parchment charm against Cat's left hand.

Power shimmered through him and he focused on the charm and the foci—Cat's wand in his left hand and the focus rings Armand wore on his own right hand.

The charm flickered in his senses, then *burst* as it released its magic and its half-formed spell. Armand saw Cat exhale as the energy flickered out through them both, but his own focus was on completing the matrix, tying both of them into the nexus.

He wasn't sure at which point *he* became *them* and *his* focus became *their* focus.

They opened their eyes. Cat was Armand, looking at Cat—and Armand was Cat, looking at Armand. A shiver of *something* ran down both their spines, and Armand focused on a *touch* of separation.

He failed. The meld nexus pulled him back in and he saw himself as Cat Greentrees did—nebbish, terrifying, soft, powerful, weirdly cute, strangely attractive. There were emotions and impressions in the nexus that Armand realized even *Cat* hadn't interrogated.

And his *own* emotions and impressions. They weren't certain at what point Armand's respect and fascination with Cat had become something *more*, any more than they were certain when Cat's amused fascination, gratitude and loyalty had.

In the meld, there were no secrets. Not from each other. Not from *themselves*, which was not a consequence they had predicted.

There was no conscious discussion. None was needed. The moment of realization and emotional surge had to be put aside, not examined. Not dealt with—not in front of the crew, at least, which they *knew* was the Cat part of the meld thinking.

The other thing the Cat part of the meld provided was the sense of the aether and its turbulences, the tremor in the fabric of the universe that marked the approach of the wraith ship. *Armand* provided a sense of magic, to track power with a discernment and range Cat had never possessed.

They could *feel* the oncoming wraith ship. It hadn't entered the Warden of Stone yet, but it was only moments away, and they considered their options.

Three heartbeats pulsed in the meld. Cat's, Armand's, and the heartbeat of the universe through Armand's link to the Source, the Weft. The Deep Magic.

That link would give them the power, but it was Cat's training that would give them the weapon.

They realized that Cat had spent time mentally reviewing the magic he'd learned for this kind of situation. All of it was intended as a desperation tactic, the kind of skill that was learned and hopefully never used. Certainly almost never practiced.

With the knowledge of both the archmage and the Captain, they ran through the options. Most, even with the link to the Source, were simply too short-ranged. Cat had positioned *Void Flyer* as close to the strait as they could possibly be, but they were still half a dozen leagues from where they expected the wraith ship to emerge.

Even with Armand's power fueling the meld, they couldn't reach that far. *Some* of the magic might work if they had clear line of sight, but that would have required them to be out on the hull with Fistfall.

There was one spell. It didn't have the longest reach of the spells Cat had learned, but it was the only one the meld saw that didn't need to launch from their own hands.

They rolled the concept back and forth in the meld, not *quite* a discussion but still an exchange between the two var in the matrix. Neither of them saw another option, but the range was still a stretch.

What else could they do? They'd already placed themselves in a position where they had to destroy the wraith ship or die themselves. The meld saw that more clearly than Armand had. The math of fuel and distance and spheres had mostly gone over the archmage's head, but *Cat* understood it to his bones.

To outrun the wraiths, they would have left themselves utterly unable to evade the Blood King and only *barely, maybe,* able to even land on a worldlet in the Clan Spheres. From the moment the twentysail had revealed its full speed, escape hadn't been an option.

But only now, in the meld, did Armand realize that Cat had been running on determination and momentum, not hope. He hadn't *let* himself give into fear or despair, but he hadn't seen a path to victory.

"Here they come."

Both of them spoke, the words blending together inside and outside their heads. From there, the strait was even less visible than it was from in front. There was no sign that the ship was coming, only the growing sensation they recognized as the enemy ship approaching.

Until it was *there*, bursting through a gateway in reality like a bubble popping. Illusions from a distance hadn't given the full weight of the ship's scale. Cat had known... but he hadn't *known*, in his bones, just how immense the ship was.

Armand hadn't even begun to understand. But now they understood. Over four hundred yards long, the ancient Ironhand ship *dwarfed* the *Void Flyer* and any other ship either of them had ever seen.

It had a size and a weight to it that Cat associated with *fortresses*, the rocks hacked into shape by magic and picks and maneuvered into place above worldlets and lodeplates to stand guard. No sails and few magics could move those floating bastions, and none of them could move one at *speed*.

But even as the twentysail breached the Warden of Stone's void, her sails were spreading and she was gaining speed—presumably searching for her prey through some senses neither of them understood.

There was no time. Hands clenching on each other's, they drew power from the Source, merging it with their own strength, and then reached out to strike.

Fire erupted in the dark, a minuscule fraction of the size and power of an ember but mirroring the life-giving flames with their ability to burn even in the aether. The ball of flame erupted just in front of the wraith ship, and her own speed plunged the wraith-crewed vessel into its heat.

Any smaller ship would have been devastated. Armand might have known that, but Cat *definitely* did. Backed by the Source, a spell intended as much to distract an approaching enemy as anything else turned into a roaring inferno.

But fire could not burn in the aether. Many of the permanent magical systems aboard *Void Flyer* were dedicated to generating air, not just to allow the crew to breathe but to let her rockets burn.

The fireball faded and the wraith ship emerged. Her prow was gone— cloudwood, metal and crystal alike reduced to twisted and charred wreckage—but over two-thirds of the ship remained, and she began to turn toward them.

The first storm stave fired while they were still assessing the damage. Fistfall was, they assessed with the ease of Cat's experience, a mediocre shot at best. But the twentysail's course was clear enough that his not-quite-miss burned away an entire mast, sails and all.

Again.

They weren't sure if they'd said it aloud or just thought it to each other, but they channeled power again. The twentysail—missing her forward half dozen masts now!—was slow to turn, which *Cat* had expected but Armand hadn't, and that gave them a chance.

Another fireball burst in the *center* of the ship now, her slowing to turn making aiming even easier. Sails vanished in the inferno and masts went up like kindling. Crystal lattices exploded in bursts of blue-green fury visible from *Flyer*'s control room, and Cat's training and experience filled in the scything of debris across the wraith ship's decks for Armand.

But *still* the ship continued to turn. Over half of her staves had to be gone now and *more* than half of her masts, but *Void Flyer* couldn't dodge if she got the broadside aligned.

A second storm-stave blast shot out from their ship, and Fistfall's aim was truer this time. The bolt hammered home into the gaping hole the meld had just torn into the center of the aether ship and hit *something*.

The explosion of energy felt like an arcane mechanism breaching—and the second hit where the meld had struck with fire achieved something Cat hadn't expected to be possible.

The lodestone keel broke. The Ironhands had clearly been at least *somewhat* more able to build long keels of lodestone, but they'd settled on linking at least two long beams of lodestone together to forge the twentysail's two-cable-long keel.

And Fistfall's stave bolt snapped that connection. Combined with the damage already done, the massive ship broke in half. One half kept spinning, far too quickly to aim at anything. The back half still stayed under some level of control, still turning to bring whatever staves it had left to bear.

Even a quarter of one of the ship's original galleries might still wreck *Void Flyer*. The void ship wasn't built for battle. A *single* stave bolt could ruin everything, and the galleries coming to bear still had half a dozen each.

Fire erupted *inside* the gallery as action followed thought and fear. The momentary ember tore wood and crystal apart with equal ferocity, and the storm staves had been fully charged. All six staves backfired, converting the energy that would project lightning across dozens of leagues into blue-white explosions.

The back half of the wraith ship disintegrated. Debris scattered in a thousand directions, and both halves of the meld breathed a sigh of relief.

Only to remember that the front half of the enemy ship still existed. It had taken less time to stabilize than Cat's experience had expected, the wraiths clearly suffering less from shock and dismay than a mortal crew.

There was no time. There were fewer staves left on the remaining chunk of ship, but it would only take *one* to wreck the *Flyer*. Lightning *crashed* in the dark… and *Flyer's* rockets flared under their feet as someone—Alloy or Brushfire, they couldn't tell—made a call.

The sudden motion threw off Fistfall's last shot, the storm bolt passing in front of the mostly wrecked enemy ship, but it forced *most* of the enemy broadside to miss.

Not all. Both Cat and Armand *felt* the ship lurch under their feet as something struck home—but *Cat's* memories told them that it was a glancing hit. They'd dodged the worst of it.

The meld was fragmenting. They were two linked minds now, not just one, but Armand thought he understood the spell. Enough, at least.

He lost Cat, the elvar dropping from the matrix as their ship screamed beneath them, but he still managed enough focus and power to slam a final fireball into the terrifyingly functional fragment of a ship assaulting them.

The wreck was turning, rotating to present another broadside of storm staves, and Armand hammered the fireball *into* the stave gallery. Blue-white fire erupted again and the last fragment of the wraith warship vanished.

Then the last of the meld collapsed, leaving Armand sagging backward, falling to his thankfully padded butt on the hard floor as he stared up at the ceiling.

Cat looked imperturbable as ever, the elvar a statue carved by a sculptor told to create the perfect Captain. He spared a glance back at Armand, checking that the archmage was okay, and the moment of locked gazes told Armand that Cat had gone through the same realizations at the start of the meld.

That was a problem for later.

"Are we clear?" Armand asked, slowly making himself more comfortable on the floor.

"It's gone," Cat said calmly. "Thank you, Archmage. Bogsong?"

"Fistfall got good shots in, Captain, but it was those fire blasts that did it," the young elvar confirmed—sounding more impressed with Fistfall's stunt than the dangerous piece of magic Armand and Cat had just managed.

Which Armand figured he was fine with. His pride was almost as padded as his midsection, and he had his own suspicions about Bogsong Smallwolf and Fistfall Hammerhead!

"I don't think there's a piece left the height of a var," the fourth officer continued. "We're clear, sir, my lord."

Armand slowly rose to his feet, carefully *not* rubbing his back where anyone could see him.

"I think, then, I can leave this to you and your capable crew, Captain Greentrees," he told Cat with carefully managed dignity. "I must take notes on this, to make certain we can duplicate if we need it.

"I will need your assessment as well. Come by my quarters once we are on our course."

Because they were almost certainly going to need the same trick to stand off the Blood King of the Gobvar... and Armand very much needed to talk to Cat in private.

CAT HAD NEVER EXPERIENCED ANYTHING LIKE THE MELD NEXUS. He'd thought he'd understood what he was agreeing to. A sharing of knowledge, using his skills to guide Armand's power.

He'd been wrong. He'd learned more about himself and Armand than he'd expected, but he'd also *lost* himself in the meld. He wasn't even entirely sure what had broken him out of it—the hit on the ship, he thought, but he wasn't *sure*.

It had felt so natural, so unquestionably real. Without the outside interruption of *Void Flyer* taking a blow, he wasn't sure he'd have stepped out of it. That was *terrifying*.

Even more than the realization of not only his feelings for the archmage but that those feelings were *returned*. That should have shaken him to his core, but next to the meld nexus and the risk he now knew they'd taken, it was nothing.

Armand had known and tried to warn him. He hadn't truly understood—but the nature of how deeply he'd just been inside his archmage's head meant that he knew that *Armand* hadn't fully understood the risk either.

He had understood better than Cat had, and he'd *tried* to communicate it, but both of them had underestimated the level of risk. And despite that, part of him already missed the meld, being so close and mingled with another var.

"Do we know where we got hit?" he asked aloud, forcing his fears and distractions aside.

"Toward the lower deck," Brushfire told him. "Masters Axfall and Windheart are sweeping the lower decks with a repair party. I'm worried we've taken damage to the rockets that will either take Alloy to fix or..."

"Or be unfixable," Cat finished for her. He glanced over at the darvar artificer, who was poking at a dial on one of the instrument panels even Cat barely understood. "Alloy? What are you seeing?"

"I don't want to fire the engines again until our gobvar friends report back," Alloy told him. "We've got some strange pressure readings. I *think* the tanks autosealed, but we've definitely lost some fuel. And we had var in those areas, too."

Cat grimaced. That was his two worst fears in one. They couldn't afford to lose fuel—and he wanted to keep his people safe.

"Should you head down to check?" he asked softly.

"We're talking ten decks of piping and tanks, Captain," Alloy reminded him. "I have no idea *where* in those ten decks the problem is. I trust Axfall and Windheart to make a first assessment and tell me what we need to start fixing the mess we've made."

"Thank you," Cat told the darvar. "You have first call on any resources we have, Alloy. We need this ship to fly, or we aren't going anywhere."

"She'll fly, Cat," the artificer said firmly. "We may have lost fuel and we *may* need to cut off an engine to minimize our risks, but we *have* four engines. We can lose one and still get to the Clan Spheres."

Cat gave Alloy a firm nod and turned to his other officers.

"Did Fistfall make it back in?" he asked Brushfire.

She looked up from a quiet conversation with an elvar messenger and nodded swiftly.

"Trueshield here spoke with him," she confirmed. "He was heading straight to the infirmary."

"He didn't look good," the elvar sailor said. "I think he got the edge of the storm-stave bolt. He made it in on his own, but he looked... burned."

Cat noticed Smallwolf stiffen at the report and concealed his sigh. He wasn't entirely sure how Fistfall felt about his youngest officer, but the young elvar was *not* as subtle as she might hope about how *she* felt about the gobvar.

In another place and another time, the concept of an elvar having feelings for and interest in a gobvar would have been a serious problem. Aboard *his* ship, he couldn't care less. Especially out there in the void spheres, halfway to Clan territory.

He'd make sure to warn them about the probable issues if things went further. Court and Kingdoms would not look kindly on such a relationship—cross-var relationships were frowned on in general, but they happened. A relationship between an elvar and a gobvar, though… that would be a very ugly scene with many var.

Cat would do what he could to shield them. Depending on what happened over the next clock-days and dances, that might be quite a bit… or very little. There were many questions.

"You should go check on him, Brushfire," he instructed his first officer. He could not, after all, tell his *fourth* officer to do so. "Come back up to the control room when you're sure he's okay."

That, hopefully, would calm both worried members of his command crew!

The damage could have been a lot worse. It was better than Cat had dared hope when he'd committed his ship and crew to fight an ancient warship twice their length and breadth. The twentysail should have crushed them like a bug.

Unfortunately, *could have been worse* left a lot of room for the damage to be bad enough, and he stared grimly at the roughly hammered-into-place sheet of metal barring the way farther from the stairwell.

"Bear Heartshade and Rosegrace were back there," Axfall said grimly. Neither of the crew—an elvar and a gobvar—they'd lost had been Hammerhead, but that didn't seem to make the Hammerhead elder feel better.

Which was fair. *Cat* certainly wasn't putting any weight on crew being Hammerhead or not. He wasn't putting much weight on any of the crew being *elvar*, let alone which gobvar tribe they were. Everyone aboard *Void Flyer* was his crew.

Even in the moment, though, he appreciated that the rest of the crew clearly felt the same way.

"Did we retrieve them?" Cat asked.

"No. There was no…" Axfall trailed off, the gobvar elder just shaking his head. "We used *up* two air crystals just getting the panel in place to hold the envelope together, sir. I didn't think they *could* be used up."

Bad enough to lose two var. Worse to lose them to the void, with no real chance of ever retrieving their bodies. It was possible that the bodies were still inside the ship, but Cat wasn't sure they'd ever find out.

"How much of the decks have we lost?" he asked flatly. "If we *have* to go into the damaged sections before we reach aether, we have options, but…"

"I haven't heard good things about Fistfall's stunt," Axfall pointed out, then sighed. "About a quarter of this deck is sealed. Half that of the deck below, and two compartments of the one above us. Those were storage, which we've sealed and we *shouldn't* need."

A quarter of one deck, an eighth of another, and roughly a tenth of a third. Cat nodded. A direct hit could have torn all three decks to splinters and ash, but Brushfire firing the rockets at the right moment had left them taking a *mere* glancing blow.

That had killed two of his crew and caused more than enough damage. They'd been unreasonably lucky, but the wraith ship might still have hurt them more than they could afford.

"Cat."

He looked up as Alloy emerged from the stairwell. The artificer had been on the deck below, surveying the damage there.

His face told him that Cat might have been overly optimistic after all.

"Alloy. How bad?" he asked.

"The bolt clipped a fuel tank," Alloy told him. "Some of the magic to seal it and protect it worked. Some didn't. We lost a third of our remaining fuel."

Cat exhaled as if punched. That *hurt*. They'd made their stand to make sure they still *had* fuel when they hit Drinkstar. If they'd lost a third of their remaining fuel, that was almost their *entire* margin.

"So, we have to take it slow through the last two void spheres and no clever maneuvers," he observed. "If we want to land anywhere in the Clan Spheres, anyway."

"If we stick to two leagues a minute here and in Stormfall, we'll make up about half the loss," Alloy told him. "But…"

"But there's still an enemy between here and safety," Cat finished. "And we may need every drop of fuel to get out of here." He sighed. "And the rest of the damage?"

"I'm going to attempt to siphon the remaining fuel to the other tank," Alloy said. "If I can manage that and reroute some of the piping and valves, I think I can keep all four engines firing. It'll be a kludge; we'll need hands on it whenever we fire the rockets."

"We have the hands," Axfall said instantly. "You tell us where you need them and what you need us to do, Artificer, and we will make sure nothing breaks."

"Thank you, Master of Decks," Alloy said with a sigh. "It's going to be a busy clock-day, Cat, and at two leagues a minute it'll be three days before we reach the strait after that."

"What do you need from me, Engines Officer?" Cat asked.

"I may yet ask for volunteers from the mages to go into the breached sections," the engineer replied. "I don't like it and I shouldn't need to do it—I think I can reroute around everything in there without entering them, but I may be wrong. It depends on what she lets me do."

That agreed with Cat's experience of *all* ships. The diagrams and the logic always said one thing was possible… but no ship was what the diagrams and logic said. The impossible might be possible. The possible might be impossible.

The only way to find out was to try.

"Let me know," he instructed. "As Master Axfall says, we have the hands, and we *will* fix whatever we can.

"I have few concerns now in the Warden of Stone, but Stormfall remains between us and the Clan Spheres—and I need this ship as ready as she can be, Alloy. We know what's coming."

"I hope you and the archmage have some more tricks in your pockets," Alloy said. "Because we shouldn't have survived fighting the wraith ship. I'm not sure…"

He trailed off, glancing at the other crew in the room.

"We'll do what we can," he said instead. "*Void Flyer* will be all she can be. You have my word."

But Cat knew what *hadn't* been said, too.

CHAPTER 36

IT TOOK LONGER FOR CAT TO PUT VOID FLYER'S CREW "ON COURSE," as Armand had put it, than he'd expected. Even so, they still weren't *moving* after about eight hours of work. Cat had done everything he could to get the repairs in motion and had drafted the course for once the ship was ready to move.

With all of that done, he *should* have gone to sleep. Years of training as a High Court Navy officer and of duty as the same made the necessity of rest and sleep clear to him.

Instead, he stood outside Armand Bluestaves' door and tried not to feel both foolish and nervous. This was hardly the first time he'd knocked on the door of a man he was interested in, nor the first time he'd done so knowing said interest was returned.

There was a lot more weight to this one, though. If nothing else, he'd never merged minds with someone else before, and that level of intimacy was hard to walk back from. Almost as important, though, was that he was Armand's *sworn servant,* a status with powerful legal implications.

And one he couldn't easily walk away from, even if they weren't on the wrong side of two void spheres from Court and Kingdoms and heading even farther away. If they handled this wrong, if they misstepped and turned good to bad, it could create a lot of problems.

Cat trusted his own professionalism in that case, but his prior relations had been with either civilians or officers of his own rank, to avoid that exact potential issue.

All of his worries held him outside the hatch for a solid minute before he finally disciplined his mind and knocked crisply on the door.

There was no answer for a moment, and then Armand pulled it open and ushered him in silently. The hatch *thunk*ed closed behind them and Armand slid a bar to lock it.

"Want a sweetroll?" the archmage asked, utterly incongruously to Cat's worries, and Cat couldn't help himself.

He stopped in the middle of the room and started laughing.

"What, did you destroy the most powerful warship I ever saw, then come down here and immediately start baking?" he asked drily.

"No," Armand protested. "I took detailed notes to make sure I remembered as much as I could, checked in on the ship and saw you were still working, took a short nap… and *then*, when I found I couldn't focus on anything, I started baking."

Cat shook his head, still chuckling, and smiled.

"I'll take a roll, sure," he conceded. Following Armand over to the kitchen, he saw that these were un-iced and had a moment to worry about whether the archmage had sorted out the issue he'd had with the *first* batch aboard *Void Flyer*.

He shouldn't have. The moment he bit into the roll, he could tell that Armand had fully adjusted to whatever strangeness *Flyer* inflicted on his baking. The roll was just right, fluffy and sweet and cinnamony without any needed glaze.

"So." Armand pulled up a seat, the soft halvar studying Cat carefully. "The meld allows no secrets. We knew that going in. I don't think either of us realized that it would pull the scab off secrets we weren't letting *ourselves* know."

"Current past the sail," Cat said quietly. "We know now. What do we do about it?"

"I…" Armand trailed off. "I am an archmage, Cat. Worse, I am *your* archmage, holder of your oaths and loyalty by your word, *our* magic and the law of Court and Kingdoms. I cannot be the one to step forward and state my feelings. That the meld betrayed me does not change that."

"Do not misread me, Armand, but we both know my oath to you does not compel me," Cat replied. "I follow you by choice, and my oath will not force me to do *anything*. Let alone claim feelings I do not have.

"But the meld laid bare what the mask of my choices would conceal," he said, the words flowing without real thought or planning. "I *do* have feelings for you, beyond loyalty and affection, my archmage. It is not something I would have expected or something I would have *allowed* myself, but it is true nonetheless."

"And my own feelings are equally... frustrating but real," Armand agreed with a smile. "Understand this, Cat: I am not a romantic man. I am also one inclined to self-reflection—it is part of how I became an archmage!

"The meld nexus lay bare certain of my illusions, and I *think* while I bake, Cat. The conclusions are not... unpleasant, I suppose, but they may be awkward."

He reached out to take Cat's hand, his skin soft and warm on Cat's. Cat was suddenly all too aware of his own sharp edges and harsh lines, how everything from his narrow fingers to his long sharp ears contrasted to Armand.

"I am not one to *have* feelings easily," Armand continued. "This is not the first time for me, to be sure, but it is something that sneaks up on me each time. So, it is strange to me to realize the situation is even more complicated than I had thought.

"This"—he squeezed Cat's fingers—"is welcome and wanted. But I cannot promise any... exclusivity."

He sounded so earnest, so sincere and so *worried* that Cat broke out laughing again. When he saw the sudden fiercer concern in Armand's eyes, he squeezed the halvar's hand back.

"Armand, you forget, I think," he said gently. "I am not merely *elvar*; I am *Great House of the High Court* elvar. There are only two kinds of relationships in the Great Houses: formal pair-bonds for bearing children, which require *discretion* for the sake of the children, not exclusivity; and everything else.

"And *everything else* has no rules but those agreed to by those involved. If you say you want this to be on every third day, or off the ship, or never outside this room..." Cat snorted. "Well, the last *I* need to insist on.

"I must command this ship, and to do so I must command *myself* first. This—whatever this is or will become—comes first from a failure to do that."

"I do not believe that *hiding* from yourself constitutes *commanding* yourself," Armand told him, the other var's voice so soft, Cat barely heard him, even as close as they were. "You wear a mask before the crew, but they see past you. You know that, don't you?"

"Maybe," Cat conceded. "But they *expect it* anyway. The Captain must be stable, must be steady. Must be an anchor when everything goes to pieces. They may see past the illusion in the little things, but they need it as much as I do in the big ones.

"And it is only by maintaining the mask in the little things that I *can* hold it in the big ones. I do not expect to *hide* anything between us from the crew, but it still must remain here, in private. Outside this door, you are the archmage and I am your Captain. We can be nothing else, to make certain the crew knows we look to the mission and their safety, not each other."

"I understand," Armand told him. "I can accept that condition, Cat. Mine is solely that you realize that, while I am uncertain of many things, some of those things may... require you to share me."

He patted his stomach with his free hand.

"There is, of course, much of me to go around," he observed with a chuckle that half-melted Cat's heart.

"I can accept that," Cat echoed back. "The repairs are progressing. The course is plotted. I... should probably rest. But you asked me to be here."

"I did," Armand said. "And I have spent our time talking around codicils and complications, rather than the core. I... As I warned, I am not a romantic man. I do not believe I am very good at thi—"

It was less than a full step for Cat to close the distance between them and shut the archmage up in the most appropriate way possible.

CHAPTER

37

BRUSHFIRE STOOD ALONE IN THE CONTROL ROOM, CHECKING THE sextants every so often and glancing out to the void around them. She understood enough of Alloy's usual panel of instruments to see that they still weren't ready to fly—there was a dial marking the pressure of fuel ready to feed into each rocket, and currently, two of the rockets weren't getting *any* fuel at all.

That was why she was alone. Since *Void Flyer* couldn't *fly*, there was no point having extra hands on the control deck, and people were stressed and exhausted. The destruction of the wraith ship had bought them some relief, which would help people sleep.

For herself, Brushfire was already looking to the future. They had no way of knowing if the Blood King was on his way already. They might manage to leave the void spheres before a demigod arrived to bar their way, but she wasn't going to take that bet.

The strange melding spell that Cat and Armand had used had allowed them to take on the ancient twentysail, but she'd *watched* as even their facial expressions aligned perfectly. The merger had been terrifying to stand outside of, and she could tell that something about it had put both var badly off-balance.

Plus, what had allowed them to fight an ancient warship with fundamentally conventional sails and weapons, regardless of how those sails were filled and weapons were crewed, paled against what might be needed to fight the Blood King.

Somehow, from an untold distance away, the King had communicated with the White Mountain, not only learning about them from it but giving the Mountain instructions. From what Cat and Armand had said, the increased danger level of the wraiths had been due to the King's taking direct control.

Worse, the Warden of Stone was fortified. There were fortresses floating throughout the sphere, and while they seemed dead and inactive *now*, so had the mighty twentysail the Blood King had filled with wraiths and sent after them.

It was interesting to her, though, that the wraiths had *needed* the ship. Even when they'd swarmed the landing party on Flame's Gem, they'd come aboveground and been funneled by walls. They might not be physical beings in any sense, but they had limitations as if they were.

Without a world or a ship, the wraiths could not traverse the void. Or, perhaps, couldn't *act* in the void—Brushfire didn't assume that the wraiths had always been aboard the old warship.

It was possible the manifestation had created them there, but it still came back to needing an anchor of some kind. In the void, *Flyer* and her crew had some protection from the hunger of the spell that had destroyed these spheres.

They had no such protection from the spell's *architect*.

It was almost certain that the Blood King had some way to traverse the void spheres. And unlike almost any other var in the spheres, he would know where the strait from Drinkstar into Stormfall was.

There were other connections from the Clan Spheres to the void spheres, of course, but Stormfall was on the fastest route. The Blood King would know that, she presumed, and would almost certainly be able to predict their exact route.

These were *his* home spheres, after all.

All of that meant that Brushfire had set herself the task of locating and flagging any intact-looking warships and fortifications in the Warden of Stone. The forts, at least, were marked on the more-detailed charts of the individual sphere, though a thousand dances almost certainly made for some differences.

Between magic and telescopes, though, she'd managed to locate three concentrations of ships. She wasn't sure they were all warships—some *looked* like ninesails and others like the five-sided ships they'd seen in IronHome, but others were different designs—but they were aether ships.

And she'd started looking around the forts. When she reached the worldlets, she figured more or all of the ships would be merchant vessels. The twenty-odd ships she'd picked out so far were likely warships.

"First Officer Hammerhead."

Brushfire smiled to herself as Smallwolf gave her the full title, then concealed the somewhat-parental expression before she turned to look at the elvar who'd just stepped out of the stairwell.

"Officer Smallwolf," she greeted the younger var. "I believe everyone who isn't involved in the repairs is supposed to be resting."

"I was. Then I checked in on your brother."

Brushfire nodded wordlessly. After what she'd learned about how her brother had felt about everyone's intrusion into his relationship with Petal, she wasn't going to get involved *there* unless asked.

"I assume he's doing better than a few hours ago, when he was still faintly smoking," she said finally. He hadn't been *conscious*, either, at that point. Brushfire wasn't entirely sure how Fistfall had managed to get back into the ship, but she was glad he had.

"He was awake, but Officer Crane wouldn't let me stay long," Smallwolf admitted. "I think he was glad to see me."

Brushfire wanted to close her eyes and count to fifty. She knew *perfectly* well where her Captain and archmage were at that moment—and despite a pang of something she was *not* going to interrogate, she was happy for them.

But Cat and Armand were both experienced adults and well able to make their own decisions, regardless of the difference in their calendar ages. Bogsong, for all that she was roughly the same age as Armand, was *elvar*. An elvar didn't really physically mature until about ten dances later than a halvar or darvar.

Elvar culture tended to hold their children back until they were physically mature, and Bogsong probably wouldn't have started her training as a ship's officer until her thirtieth dance. She'd served on at least one ship before joining their crew, but she was still in many ways younger and more inexperienced than her age might suggest.

Brushfire was bitterly aware that *gobvar* matured at the same rate as elvar, but the pressures put on her people in Court and Kingdoms didn't allow them to keep their children out of work that long. So, while Fistfall was half a dozen dances younger than Bogsong, he probably had more life experience.

"I can't read my brother's mind," she finally told the elvar. "But he's also not very subtle, so if you thought he was happy to see you, he probably was."

There were a long few moments of silence, which Brushfire filled by pointing the magical telescope—the simple version she'd learned from Cat, not Armand's complicated illusory duplicates—back at the largest cluster of ships.

Two ninesails hung in the middle of six of the five-sided ships with their two stave galleries. Another half dozen ships, none that quite looked right to Brushfire, also hung around the fortress they seemed to be using as an anchor point.

"May I ask a... personal question, Officer Hammerhead?"

"I'll trade you," Brushfire said, swallowing a sigh. "You ask a personal question you probably shouldn't, and I'll ask a professional question I should probably know the answer to."

"I'm *supposed* to answer your questions about the ship," Smallwolf pointed out with a chuckle. "But ask away."

"These." Brushfire gestured the elvar mage over to the telescope and indicated the ships she wasn't sure about. "They don't look like ninesails to me, but I wouldn't have figured the five-siders for warships, either, until Cat pointed out the key features.

"What do you make of them?"

Smallwolf stepped closer to the illusion—less than a yard across, it was more shareable than a telescope but still didn't show much detail at a distance of several thousand leagues.

"I don't think they're warships either," she said slowly. "Three sail decks and I don't see any stave galleries. They're beamy ships, as long as the ninesails and even wider. I'd guess cargo, but I've never seen cargo ships like that, and there *are* storm staves on their decks, I think."

"So, not warships, not civilians," Brushfire concluded. "Troopships?"

"I can't think of anything else, sir," Smallwolf agreed. "The more I see of the Ironhands, the stranger I think they are. An entire troopship squadron waiting in the aether, ready to go? To do what?"

"From what Armand has said and we have seen…" The gobvar officer sighed. "To bring anyone who tried to complain back into line. The Ironhands very clearly ruled by force and were prepared to deploy ships and troops with little warning. I don't have the impression they were particularly nice people."

"Even if they were gobvar?" Smallwolf asked.

"Every var has their assholes who should never be given a scrap of power," Brushfire said. "Some of them always end up *in* power. With the spheres all under one banner, as it seems they were in the Ironhands' dances, all the assholes had to do was be born into one family."

And she suspected that, after a certain point, that became self-reinforcing.

"Says something, I suppose, that these spheres just… *went away* and no one cared enough to look into *why*," the elvar said.

"We don't know that. Armand thinks the High Court tried to bury evidence of the Imperium in the Court and Kingdoms, to make their leadership seem eternal." Brushfire shrugged. "Don't get the impression I like the way the Court and Kingdoms work, Smallwolf.

"My people find themselves struggling upwards against a torrent of grazer shit everywhere. On the other hand, the stories I hear out of the Clan Spheres are as bad or worse—and it's not an improvement to know the one shitting on you has the same horns you do!"

Smallwolf was quiet for a few moments, still looking at the ships.

"Six warships, six troop transports, sitting at a fort," she concluded. "Do you… Do you think the Blood King can send them at us?"

"I don't know," Brushfire admitted. "I'm making sure we know where all of the warships in the sphere *are* so that we can keep an eye on them."

She made a note on the chart. *Six warships. Six armed transports.*

"I don't have the impression that the Blood King is going to bother using his powers to send *troopships* with a few storm staves at us," she observed. "The ninesails are probably the biggest threat, unless I spot another big bastard somewhere in the sphere."

She considered the chart for a few moments, then sighed.

"Your *personal question*, Bogsong?" she prodded.

"Right." The slim elvar glanced away for a few heartbeats, then shrugged. "Your brother, Fistfall. Do you… think there's any chance he'd look at an elvar?"

The young were *never* as subtle as they thought they were.

"My brother," Brushfire echoed, then sighed again. "I can't speak for Fistfall on many things, Bogsong. The question I *expected* you to ask, I can't answer. This one, though?"

She smiled at the younger var.

"My brother does not have it in his heart to prejudge anyone by their var," she told Bogsong. "Even *before* joining this crew, when that openness got him in as much trouble as it got him out of, he would judge everyone on their own merits.

"I have no reason to believe that his romantic inclinations are any different." She held up a warning hand. "I will warn you that while his relationship with Petal was more complicated than I think anyone else realized, she *did* die all too recently."

"I know," Bogsong said. "It's… part of why I haven't said anything to him. He saved my life on the Seventh Ward. I'd… already been enjoying his company when we worked together, but I haven't been able to see him the same way since.

"And with him training as a mage, I've only seen *more* of him." She shrugged helplessly. "He's smart and he's kind and he's *funny*, not that he seems to realize *any* of that! But I…"

Brushfire let Bogsong trail off and then chuckled at her gently.

"Fistfall is convinced, from what I can tell, that he is only a pile of muscles and some carpentry skills," she warned Bogsong. "*Some* of that is put on. He has spent most of his life being the single largest var that most people will have met in their entire lives, and making himself appear less of a threat served him well.

"He is not subtle, but he is more self-aware—I *hope*—than it might appear. What I *can* tell you, Bogsong, is that there is only one person you should talk to if you want to know what is going on in Fistfall's head."

And heart.

"Fistfall," Bogsong said, without any prompting. "I know." She smiled and it was a sparkling thing to see. "I just also figured that… well, he seemed the type where *realizing* he couldn't be interested in an elvar would hurt him, too."

She wasn't wrong there. But while Brushfire wasn't going to get further involved if she could possibly avoid it, she also knew her brother. If he *did* think that… well, she figured he'd get over it.

"Fistfall is now in a strange place on this crew," she told the elvar. "He isn't an officer, but he's no longer crew, either. He's a sworn servant of the archmage—as are all of the officers. He is a mage—as are all of the officers.

"So, he can't be crew. But he isn't an officer, either. No one, including Fistfall, has slowed down to see that as a complication because my dear brother is *incapable* of not helping if he sees a task being done.

"But in this crew, with his status as one of Armand's mages, there are no barriers between you two," Brushfire concluded. "The heart wants what it wants. I cannot—I will not!—speak to my brother's heart.

"If you both want the same thing, no one on this ship will bar your way. We will do what we can to protect you when we return to Court and Kingdom, even." She grimaced and didn't even try to conceal it.

"I won't pretend that you're not choosing a hard path," she warned. "Frankly, Bogsong, I don't think you understand just how bad the situation for gobvar is back home. I don't believe that you being elvar will protect him—and I *do* fear that him being gobvar will harm you."

"I… *think* I am prepared to risk that," Bogsong said slowly. "You're probably right. I probably don't know how bad that will get when we go home. But we're a long cursed way from the Court and Kingdoms, and we're not going back anytime soon.

"We might not even make it."

That wasn't a statement any of the ship's officers would make if the crew were present, but they were alone on the control deck still.

"We might not," Brushfire conceded grimly. "Take what you can get, Bogsong. *Ask* him."

"I will," Bogsong told her, her voice determined. "Thank you, Brushfire."

"You are welcome. Now get off the control deck and *rest*. We don't need much of a watch right now, and I have my eyes open."

She… suspected that Bogsong was going right back to the infirmary and, depending on Fistfall's response and level of recovery, *rest* wasn't in the elvar's plans.

That wasn't Brushfire's problem. Even if she felt a *tiny* amount of jealousy that she knew she didn't want to interrogate too closely.

CHAPTER 38

Armand was awoken by the engines. The rockets weren't all *that* loud inside the ship, especially compared to standing in an enclosed space while the ship tried to escape the Seeker holding it in place! Still, it was difficult to sleep while the engines were firing; plus, it was a good sign that things were going according to plan.

He wasn't entirely surprised to realize that he was alone in the bed. Cat had slipped away while he slept, probably to make sure that the engines *were* ready to fire when the time came. Still, he smiled as he recalled his own awkwardness when the elvar had answered his invitation.

Leave it to him, he knew, to turn a romantic invitation and getaway into a discussion of the terms and conditions of them having a relationship of any kind. Cat, thankfully, had seemed to understand.

Snacking on a sweetroll for breakfast, Armand pulled his notes together with a languid gesture and a touch of power. The meld nexus had worked, but it had also been even *more* of a strange and dangerous experience than he'd feared.

Cat hadn't said much about it, but Armand could read at least some of the volumes written by the other var's silence. The revelation of their feelings for each other was one thing, but in hindsight, he suspected they'd fallen deeper into the meld than they could afford.

They probably *should* have been separated, but he hadn't actually told anyone to be ready to do so. The situation had been dire enough that risks were called for.

Now, though, he knew that they needed Brushfire or one of the others standing by if it came to using the spell again. And that they needed another answer.

It would do them no good to somehow break past the Blood King if both Cat and Armand lost their minds! The merger of the two of them couldn't last.

Armand wasn't sure what the failure point of an unbroken meld would be. The author of the book he'd read had talked around the possibility and, like most intelligent experimental magicians, *had* kept someone on hand to end the tests.

He suspected that if they couldn't break out of the meld, it would kill them both.

They needed another option.

After the third card reading, Armand swept the oracle deck off his desk. None of the readings were helpful. It wasn't even that they were saying things he didn't want to see. They weren't telling him *anything*.

The Blood King kept showing up, but not in places or arrangements that made sense. The cards weren't lying to him. His dice hadn't been much clearer.

About the only useful thing the *dice* had told him was, basically, that the only way out was through. The only course that didn't end in utter disaster was *forward*—but *forward* was... blurry.

Unclear.

There were no answers in the divinations. Not even new questions.

Only the reminder that some beings were all but immune to being scried. Armand himself had woven protections over the court and palace of the Golden King of his home sphere, sealing the palace against the very types of intrusion he now tried to wield against the Blood King.

A true seer would be able to find the gaps, to see around the edges and draw upon vision and prophecy to see some answers. With the observer in his tower back home, Armand suspected he could have found a way.

But he'd only truly used the observer once, a scrying that had shown him his death defending the Great Red Forest from an army of dragons. Nothing in *that* vision had warned him he'd come up against the Blood King to stop it.

None of the tools available to him *now* gave him an answer on how to win that fight. On a worldlet, with air in his lungs and ground under his feet, Armand would have been confident that he could at least *fight* the gobvar monarch.

In the void, with a fragile ship providing both his footing and his breath, Armand didn't know where to begin. Fighting a *god* was a far stretch from taking down even an ancient oversized warship, too. Cat's knowledge wouldn't serve them against the Blood King.

Armand needed to shape the battlefield, but he was in the King's territory. Whatever had happened to the void spheres, it had been Oathheld Ironhand that had made it happen. The Last Ironhand had *consumed* his people's core spheres and every scrap of life in them.

A portion of that hunger remained. The King had weaponized that against them already, but Armand suspected Oathheld wasn't inclined to try the same thing twice. The first wraith ship he'd sent had failed.

The vagueness in Armand's divinations told him one thing: the Blood King's answer to that failure was to come himself. It was the presence of the King's protections that made all of his attempts to scry the future useless.

Which, he was grimly aware, meant that the King was not only coming but was *close*. He knew, even with his useless scrying, that they wouldn't reach the Clan Spheres without facing the Last Ironhand.

He didn't know what weapons or powers the Blood King would bring to that fight. More wraiths, maybe. A fleet of the damned instead of a single ship.

Or maybe just his own power. That would be enough, Armand guessed.

He supposed he should focus on what he *could* learn. How the Blood King had fought before. If the King had faced an archmage, and how that had ended.

He didn't even remember pulling Submissive Farmharvest's *A Warning on the Four* from the shelves, but it was on his desk. It wouldn't give him answers, but it *might* tell him how the King would strike at them.

Or, at least, how the Blood King had struck at others in the past.

The book had few reassurances for Armand. Its information had been dances upon dances out of date when the author had written it, and the book had been written almost as close to the fall of the Ironhand Imperium as to the moment.

Still, five hundred dances—or flarings of the Great Fire, in Clan terms—was a lot of history, and while the book was inherently limited in its detail, it told him quite a bit.

The Blood King was rarely directly involved in any particular affair of the Clans. Individual Clans would rarely interact with him at all, in fact. Nonetheless, he was ever-present throughout Clan history, appearing to intervene as he saw fit.

The one pattern that Armand saw was that the Blood King *always* seemed to appear when an event involved two or more large Clans or an inter-sphere conflict. If the Blood King himself didn't arrive, one of his chosen minions did.

According to Submissive Farmharvest, the Blood Guard hadn't existed for the first two hundred flarings or so of the Clan Spheres' existence. They'd come into existence around the same time as the modern border was solidifying—and most non-gobvar were fleeing to the far side of it.

Reading between the lines of Farmharvest's text, Armand suspected that a lot of *gobvar* had fled to the far side of the border too. Three hundred dances between that flight and the book's writing—and eight hundred between then and the current clock-day—left a lot of time for details to be lost.

It was not, Armand had long known, an *accident* that the Quadrumvirate ruled over an empire almost entirely made up of gobvar. He assumed that there were still other var in the Clan Spheres—few elvar, but almost certainly darvar and halvar trapped on worldlets they could never leave—but all anyone in the Court and Kingdoms ever heard of was the gobvar themselves.

Some early decision of the Quadrumvirate had made it clear that the gobvar would be the rulers and everyone else would be ruled or destroyed. Though even Farmharvest's book suggested that life as a gobvar in the Clans was far from easy for most.

The book was old. Armand *hoped* the Clan Spheres would be wiser and calmer now, but two members of the ruling Quadrumvirate were the same as they had been then. There had only been *three* Eldest Sisters since then as well. Her Crimson Sisters were shielded from many of the pressures that robbed even Clan gobvar of their natural lifespans.

The fourth and least member of the Quadrumvirate, the Warlord who earned their place by commanding the most powerful multi-Clan fleet or host, changed more rapidly. Farmharvest estimated that there had already been eighty-four Warlords when he wrote his book.

After a thousand dances, Armand understood the number to be around a hundred and fifty now. *Warlord* wasn't a job title that came with particularly high life expectancy. The rest of the Quadrumvirate provided the stability of the Clan Spheres. The Warlord was simply the current fist.

The Warlord was limited in their power, too. No one *outside* the Quadrumvirate would challenge them, but there were enough forces in the Clans that served the other three members of the Quadrumvirate directly that the Warlord couldn't act with impunity.

The Blood Guard were the second-smallest such faction: fewer than Her Crimson Sisters, who could be found in numbers *everywhere* across the Clan Spheres, but more present and numerous than the Scaled Servitors of Old Bloodscale.

The officers of the Blood Guard served as the voice of the Blood King. *Literally*, it sounded like, with the ancient gobvar able to temporarily possess their bodies from a great distance. Their lower ranks crewed thankfully small fleets of the best ships in the Clans, armed with the best weapons.

The Guard did not, according to Farmharvest, pay for *anything*. Whether it was ships or swords or storm staves or new recruits, they *took* and the Clans conceded. Behind every word of a crimson-cloaked officer hung the immutable and irresistible power of the Blood King himself.

So, the King met *most* issues with the Guard. Sometimes, as Armand had read before, he unleashed what appeared to be a controlled form of the hunger wraiths from the void spheres.

If the Last Ironhand had unleashed his power more directly in the half-millennium Farmharvest recorded, too few had survived for the chronicler—a historical scholar among the Clans before he fled—to have heard of.

None of which gave Armand any answers, and he glared at the book. The being barring their way was over a thousand dances old, commanded the wraiths that had hunted them across the spheres, and led a fleet and army noted for basically *impossible* levels of loyalty.

All of which had been the case five hundred dances earlier. There was no way to guess what had changed or what weapons the Blood King would reach for in the void spheres.

About the only thing Armand was mostly confident of—and even this was only *mostly*—was that the Blood Guard couldn't follow their god into the void. The King would come on his own, and the only allies he would be able to command would be the wraiths of the void.

Armand suspected the King wouldn't need them. Whatever else Oathheld Ironhand had *become*, he'd been an archmage once. It wouldn't take much extension of an archmage's power to make him a barrier *Void Flyer*'s crew could not pass.

A barrier Armand Bluestaves *needed* to pass—but couldn't see a way through.

Each of the void spheres had appeared dead on first encounter, Cat knew, but the Warden of Fire and IronHome had proven to be more complicated.

The Warden of Stone, so far at least, had stayed dead. He could still feel a sense of hunger from where the crystal served as anchor for the strange leftover magic that spawned the wraiths, but nothing in the entire sphere moved.

They'd been in flight for a full clock-day, and he was occupying himself by checking through the clusters of ships that Brushfire had flagged on her watches. There were sixty or so clearly merchant ships hanging around the once-inhabited worldlets, plus around twenty-five warships and as many troop transports.

It felt wrong to him for there to be as many *military* aether ships as there were civilian in the sphere. On the other hand, the Wardens had served as the guardian points against attack on the Ironhand capital. Anything reaching IronHome would come through one of the six Warden spheres.

Six Wardens and, past them, nineteen spheres with ward-fortresses that could sever the straits leading toward IronHome. Given any warning at all, the Ironhand capital would have been invulnerable to any exterior attack.

None of those defenses had protected them against what the Blood King had done, but he could see how they locked together to provide a powerful sense of security, if nothing else. Now, though… all six of the Wardens and half of the spheres holding the Wards had been lost to the void.

The hunger of the ascension ritual remained. The buildings and ships and deep aether structures and everything else built by the hands of var remained… but the var themselves were gone along with the aether that they had breathed.

"I keep expecting something to try to eat us," Windheart said grimly. The old gobvar was managing the half dozen younger crew working around the control room to support Cat. At that moment, though, *managing* appeared to involve standing by the Captain and watching everything.

Given that, some days, it felt like standing and watching everything was *Cat's* entire job most of the time, he understood how that worked. He also understood the fear the Hammerhead elder spoke of.

"I would argue that something already *did*," he told Windheart with a grim chuckle. "That twentysail certainly wasn't coming after us to make friends and snack on the archmage's sweetrolls."

For all of the terms and agreements they'd made, Cat hadn't actually spoken with Armand again since they'd… *initiated things*, so to speak. Things were and would be fine, he knew, but it was still awkward, and he wasn't sure how to handle it alongside commanding the ship.

"You and the archmage handled them," the gobvar said firmly. "And I'm not all that afraid of what this sphere might decide to throw at us, after seeing that. But it being this dead and quiet… hurts the soul."

"It does," Cat conceded. "Charts aren't clear, but there could easily have been four or five million var in this sphere alone. All… just gone."

The High Court, with its sixteen lodeplates and thirty small worldlets, was the most densely populated sphere in the Court and Kingdoms. Over a hundred million var lived at the center of elvar power, and only a handful of the Kingdoms came even close to that number.

The Blood King had killed at *least* that many of his own people. It might have made him a god, or the next best thing, but Cat couldn't *conceive* of that being a price anyone would willingly pay.

"Hurts the soul," Windheart repeated. "And part of it tries to hurt us more directly, too. There's more ships here?"

"Aye," Cat confirmed. "Nothing as big, but we're keeping eyes on them. No sign of wraiths appearing to crew them just yet, but what has happened once…"

"Can be done again," the gobvar agreed. "You and his lordship handled the last one fair enough. We've nothing to fear."

Windheart's confidence was touching—and nerve-wracking, since Cat was not sure that he *could* do the meld again. It had been so strange, so… *dangerous.*

Even if the magic was possible, he wasn't sure his fear would let him.

"We'll see what happens," he said cautiously.

"Something may happen. Something may not," Windheart agreed. "What about the next sphere?"

"Stormfall," Cat said. He was starting to realize that the old gobvar was working to distract him from brooding, but talking out loud about what lay ahead of them wasn't a bad thing, either.

"There isn't much there," he continued. "The usual scattering of rocks and worldlets of various sizes. The Eleventh Ward is the only thing that's left of interest, since the void will have stripped the worldlets of var."

"Rumor has it we're expecting trouble. The biggest kind."

"We are," Cat confirmed. "Our way will be barred and we will overcome."

He shook his head grimly.

"We have reason to believe we have angered the Blood King and will need to find a way past his rage."

The silence was pregnant.

"I was not young when we left the Clan Spheres, Captain," Windheart finally said. "I was not so unlucky as to see the Blood King or His Guard in my own time, but I knew of youths of several Clans and tribes who were taken by the Guard, to join His servants.

"Like Her Crimson Sisters, little choice was given. And like Her Crimson Sisters, the stories said that even if we saw them again, they would not be the same. It was not like your Navy, Captain. To become a Sister or a Guard… They said it took a piece of your soul and never gave it back."

"I had heard much of what Her Sisters do," Cat said slowly. "Mostly of how they guard the border and rile the Clans there to a level of violence even the rest of the Clan Spheres would not allow. They are a known name to the officers of the High Court Navy, but they are rarely *seen* by us.

"They send others to do the dying against our ships. They stay behind to do the *killing* of any who try to get past them."

"Yes." Windheart's single word hung in the air. "They are the whips at the Clans' back, not the ones at the fore."

"If dragons came to rule the Clans, as Armand's visions predict, would Her Sisters be their allies... or a force to overcome?" Cat asked, curious. "I do not think they will be *our* allies either way."

"It depends on where the dragons come from and who, if anyone, they follow," Windheart told him. "If they follow Bloodscale, Her Sisters will see them as a challenge... but in the structure of the Quadrumvirate, they will find a way to work with them. If the dragons have enough strength and power, Her Sisters would adapt.

"It is what they have always done. They are forever a canker on the hearts of the gobvar, in my mind."

"I can see that," Cat conceded. "The Blood King, though. What have you heard of *him*?"

"Less than you may hope, Captain," Windheart admitted. "He is part of the Quadrumvirate. If anyone asked who the king of the gobvar was, it was Him. It meant less to us than most kings in the Kingdoms do to their people, since He was one of four who claimed power over us.

"We knew Him to be immortal and powerful, a magic-user like no other. He was said to be the balance to the power of Her Crimson Sisters, though no one said that very *loudly*. Not where Her Sisters could hear us—and Her Sisters were everywhere.

"I *think*, looking back," Windheart continued with a sigh, "that we hung that small good on Him because there was no one else we believed *could* balance Her Sisters. I do not remember ever hearing anything about the Guard or the King intervening against Her Sisters.

"I don't remember ever hearing about the King doing *anything*," he concluded. "I know His Guard was present on at least one worldlet I was on with my tribe, but it wasn't the Hammerheads they took their new blood from that flaring."

Windheart was silent for a long time, but something told Cat he still had something to say.

"It was Her Crimson Sisters that took blood from us that time," he said quietly. "My then-youngest first-sister, barely twenty flarings old—Brushfire's mother wasn't born until we were in Court and Kingdoms, thirty flarings later.

"Her Sisters took Bushheart from us and killed my father when he objected, without blinking or hesitation."

Like elvar, gobvar didn't distinguish between grades of sibling. If you shared a parent, you were siblings. End of story. Both var lived too long for exclusive arrangements that lasted entire lives to be the norm.

"There are many shadows waiting for us," Cat said grimly. "Along this journey, we may take some small measure of justice for the past. I hope."

"That's not why I'm here," Windheart told him. "I'm here because my tribe is here and I am sworn to guide and protect them." He shrugged and smiled beatifically. "And this clock-day, guidance means I need to go twist Catcher's ear to remind her that wheel does *not* turn that far unless we're doing something *very* specific!"

Cat hadn't noticed the gobvar crewvar misjudging the control she was working—but he would have a moment later if Windheart hadn't spoken, given that the wheel in question was lowering a cloth shade across a good chunk of the crystal panels letting him see to his left!

CHAPTER 40

THE NUMBER OF NOTES, FLAGS, PINS AND OTHER NEW MARKERS ADDED to the detailed map of Stormfall in the chart room told Brushfire that *everyone* was dealing with the reality they were calmly sailing toward.

They would be another clock-day in the Warden of Stone, and she'd given strict instruction for there to be people watching the final set of forts and attached ships short of the strait to Stormfall at all times.

Once the second line of defense for IronHome, the two remaining forts—the charts said there had been six, but the vagaries of void and what she'd have called an aether current elsewhere had scattered the others across the sphere—had been loose rocks just large enough to have natural lodestone cores. They'd been hauled into place by dint of immense effort and then carved and built on to host multiple mighty towers full of weaponry.

Their garrisons were long dead, but that hadn't stopped the void spheres from attacking *Flyer* before—and Brushfire was actively concerned over the trio of five-sided warships still docked at the closer fort.

Time had moved even these forts away from the strait and where they'd originally hung. The charts said the six forts should have formed a three-by-two wall some five hundred leagues across about a hundred leagues ahead of the exit from the passage.

Now the closest fort was almost a thousand leagues away from the passage out of the sphere. They couldn't easily avoid it, not with the limitations on *Void Flyer*'s maneuvering, which meant that Brushfire was focusing on how to deal with it if the wraiths woke up on it.

Once they were into the strait, she'd join the others in worrying about Stormfall. The Warden of Stone wasn't clear for them yet, however dead it felt. Just because they'd encountered threats by this point in each of the void spheres before them didn't mean *this* sphere was safe.

The expected knock finally came on the chart-room door.

"Come in," she told Fistfall without looking up.

He chuckled and walked over to join her at the chart table.

"You knew it was me, first-sister?" he asked.

"No one else on this ship knocks that high on the door," she told him. "Plus, I did send a runner for you. What took so long?"

She looked up in time to see him flush darkly.

"I… wasn't where Sky expected," he admitted. "I… Um. Was in Officer Smallwolf's quarters."

"Anything I should be concerned about?" Brushfire asked him, giving him her best Officer Warning look—which happened to very closely resemble her best Sister Warning look.

"I… Um." He swallowed. "She didn't seem to think so?"

Even as the words came out of his mouth, though, he straightened his shoulders and looked Brushfire directly in the eye.

"If there is a problem, First Officer, I take full responsibility," he said crisply. "I believe Officer Smallwolf understood my status as a mage in training to put me on equivalent status to an officer and avoid any potential concerns."

"She did understand that," Brushfire said, her tone level. "Because I told her so." She grinned at her brother, who took a moment to realize she'd been teasing him.

"I also, I want to make sure you know, told her that she needed to talk to *you* about anything beyond that. I try not to make the same mistake twice, Fistfall," she continued gently. "She and I spoke because she was concerned you wouldn't be willing—or *able*—to see an elvar in a romantic sense."

"I." He stopped, then nodded. "I can see why she would be concerned," he finished. "I would not have even considered the question a dance ago. If asked, I might have said I couldn't. Now, though…"

He shrugged.

"I realize I don't care what var she is. I know *her*."

"If that's good enough for you, Fistfall, it's good enough for me," Brushfire told him. "Do me one favor?"

"Most likely," he said carefully.

"Try to avoid needing a runner to find you in her quarters. This ship isn't anyone's military, and there are, so far as I am concerned, basically *no* rules on this. But the Captain and a bunch of the crew are elvar, and *face* and *discretion* are key for them.

"So, err on the side of discretion," she told him. "Let Bogsong set the pace with her people, and *talk* to her before you set the pace with ours."

"I... need to talk about ours," he admitted. "I know a lot of folk wanted to see me with Petal as much for the chance of new children as anything else. Bogsong and I... don't have that chance."

"You don't, and people will give you grief for it," Brushfire confirmed. "Ignore them if you can; send them to me if you can't. If you really need a stick, remind them that elvar think of relationships in ten-dance cycles."

She smiled gently at him as he stopped to digest that.

"I don't mean she's going to leave you in ten dances, but both of you will live for *hundreds* of dances, little brother. That's time enough to decide you need something else, something different—or to mutually decide to make special arrangements for children, if that ends up important to you."

"And if we don't survive the archmage's quest?" Fistfall asked bluntly.

"Then what matters is that you are happy today and tomorrow," she told him. "I don't *want* you to think like that, Fistfall. But the moment you're in is always the moment you have. Be as happy as you can."

He chuckled.

"And this is why you're the shaman and the eldest sister and *I* am merely a mage-trainee," he told her. "Because I might have magic, but you have actual wisdom."

"Nine-tenths of which, if I'm being honest, is just repeating phrases *my* teachers drilled into my head," Brushfire told him with a chuckle of her own. "It wasn't *just* magic I was learning from aged shamans in smoky caves, little brother."

She gestured his attention toward the chart on the table.

"Now, do you need more sisterly or shamanly advice, or can we talk about what I called you here for?" She smiled gently at him to make it clear the offer was more open than it might sound. "We *have* time for either."

"I am here to help," Fistfall said. "What do you need?"

"How many of the storm staves are ready to use?"

The problem, as Cat had explained it to her, was that the staves recharged by drawing on the surrounding aether. Without aether, they could not recharge—and slowly lost what charge they had, too.

"One," her brother told her. "Just one. I'm not sure what we can do with just one stave blast."

"Piss someone off, probably," she admitted, turning back to look at the updated chart with the two forts and three ships. "So far, everything at the strait into Stormfall appears to be dead, but I don't trust it. I don't think Cat and Armand are able to repeat what they did—but you can't tell anyone else that; am I clear?"

He nodded silently, his steadiness always reassuring.

"Hunter and I have a… an *option*," he said slowly. "We wanted to sort through some more details before we presented it, but we thought we were prepping for something in Stormfall. But you're expecting trouble here?"

"There are two old fortresses and three aether ships still standing at the gateway out of the Warden of Stone," she told him. "Each of those fortresses could easily have as many weapons as that twentysail. They likely will not all work—but the *twentysail's* staves shouldn't have worked.

"I don't know what the wraiths are capable of, but we don't have much choice about sailing past those forts on our way forward. One storm stave isn't going to do anything to them, so I'm open to listening to options."

"Things in the void keep going till they hit something," her brother said quietly. "So, we figure, a ballista bolt will go a long, long way. Won't do much damage on its own, though, but… well, we figured we have all of these stave crystals sitting around that aren't charged enough to fire.

"Doesn't mean they have *no* charge, though."

Brushfire blinked.

"What are you and Hunter suggesting?" she asked slowly.

"A couple of the carpenters are working on a ballista," he admitted. "Back home, a few of the Kingdoms used them on the smaller aether ships, where they stuck all kinds of nasty things on them to make them useful.

"Aether slows the bolt, which limits the range, but void doesn't seem to. And while we don't have a *lot* of options, Hunter says that even a discharged stave failing is massively destructive. Draining a crystal completely is a slow, careful task."

"And the var charged with making sure our staves don't critically fail has a decent idea of how to *make* them critically fail?" Brushfire asked.

"He says." Fistfall looked nervous. "We can't really experiment. But Hunter says he's done it before—though *that* time, he was apparently blowing it in place on the ship."

Her brother coughed.

"He didn't seem inclined to tell me *why* he did that or *whose* ship it was. But we think we can rig the storm stave's thunder crystals to explode on impact. We mount the ballista on the right kind of structure on the hull—Axfall will have to build it; no one else on the ship is good enough!—and I can launch the bolts at our targets."

"That's... an option," Brushfire said, consideringly. "I need to talk to the Captain, I think."

She considered the chart in front of her and smiled at her brother from the corner of her mouth.

"But talk to Axfall and get him started on that mount. If nothing else, I think we *do* need to test the idea, and whether the forts wake up or not, I think they're going to make great *targets*."

Cat listened to her lay out what Fistfall had told her, then sighed.

"I would dearly like to say that sacrificing our storm staves for a handful of shots with a primitive giant crossbow was a terrible idea," he said drily. "And yet, we have one useful stave remaining. Hunter is correct that the others may have enough energy in the thunder crystals to cause major damage to a target, but if we make it through to the Clan Spheres and are once more in aether, we may *need* those staves."

"And if we won't make it through without using them as ballista bolts?" Brushfire asked.

They were alone in his office. *Void Flyer*'s crew had some sense of what they were facing, but there was a level of frankness she still wasn't going to engage in where most of the crew could hear her.

"I would very much like to say I think we will, but I'm not that foolish," Cat told her. "Give me a moment. I want to actually bring Paintrock into this."

He rose from his desk and crossed to the door, opening it in time to see Fistfall standing on the other side, about to knock—with Hunter Paintrock at the big gobvar's side.

"Captain," the blue elvar said brightly. "I had the feeling you were about to send someone for me?"

"I was," Cat agreed. "Both of you. Come in; grab seats."

The office felt a lot less spacious with Fistfall in it, but it still had room for all four of them to sit.

"Lay it out for me, Master of Staves," Cat ordered. "I want to be sure I fully understand and that nothing was lost passing between Fistfall and Brushfire."

"I learned a long time ago to have an ace up my sleeve, sir," Paintrock said. There was a poetry to the phrase that suggested he meant it as part of something else, but Brushfire didn't know what.

"And our storm staves have been leaking power since we left Brokenwright," Cat noted. "So, you have a plan?"

"Not a plan, really," Paintrock admitted. "An idea. An *option*. The thunder crystals, even after firing, still hold a huge amount of energy. They can't fire as storm staves, but they still need to be handled very, very carefully.

"And I *may* have, in another life, learned to rig them to explode. We never thought of *launching* them at anyone, but we turned *other* people's staves into bombs on their ships, if you follow."

Brushfire knew that *Cat* knew that Paintrock was an ex-pirate. So long as the elvar was on their side and *stayed* on their side, she could live with that—and so, she hoped, could her Captain.

"But while I passed even my misspent dances with stave and battlewand, our gobvar crew were more limited in their self-defense tools," the Master of Staves continued. "Fistfall here raised the thought of a really big crossbow."

Paintrock grinned and Fistfall grimaced.

"Turns out there's a *word* for that, but neither of us knew it. *Ballista*." He let the word roll off his tongue like it was his own clever invention. "Couple of the carpenters I roped in had seen them serving in hally fleets."

Presumably *elvar* carpenters, Brushfire knew. The halvar and darvar kings were *sometimes* more open-minded than the elvar, but while gobvar served here and there on merchant ships and traders, *no one* hired them to man aether *warships*.

The elvar had a stranglehold on that particular career path across all of the Courts and Kingdoms. It was part of why the High Court was so powerful—while not all elvar saw it as their primary loyalty, *everyone* knew that the High Court could offer a given elvar more than any halvar or darvar king could.

"So, you have built one," Cat said.

"Mostly," Paintrock said. "Few bits and pieces we haven't quite worked out. *Torsion* is the word my var Shale used. I couldn't find any ropes aboard that quite worked, so we're still poking."

"And the bolts using the thunder crystals?" Brushfire asked.

"I have four bolts ready, but I haven't removed any thunder crystals from the staves," the elvar replied. "It's not a simple process, and while I *can* put the crystals back in, I figured I'd get permission before I went that far.

"And since I couldn't get the *ballista* working…"

"You should have spoken up sooner," Cat said with a chuckle. "Master Paintrock, may I remind you what Alloy Bellowforge *is*?"

There was a long silence.

"An artificer good enough to build this ship," Paintrock finally said. "So, def' one who could sort out torsion."

"Exactly. Brushfire," Cat turned to her. "Take Master Paintrock to talk to our Engines Officer. I'm not certain what they're going to need, but if *anyone* on this ship can take a half-assembled device and a vague concept and turn it into a working weapon in half a clock-day, it's Alloy."

"And the test, Cat?" she asked.

"If the ballista is ready, then I would be *delighted*," he repeated his earlier phrasing with a grin, "to see one of those forts rendered safe to pass.

"Do we think we can manage that, people?"

CHAPTER

41

Alloy apparently took four hours to completely redefine the concept of *ballista* for Cat's crew. Cat himself was only passingly familiar with *crossbows*, let alone their larger cousins, but he was reasonably sure that most ballistae did not involve *quite* so many gears that moved on their own.

"These crystals here hold the stored energy you're relying on," the artificer told Fistfall, tapping a set of six gleaming blue gems mounted along the side of the weapon. "Once they've discharged, you'll need to rotate this wheel *here* to rearm the ballista."

Alloy regarded the massive gobvar listening attentively to him carefully for a moment. "It won't be easy, even for you, to fire it without the crystal charge."

"How many charges?" Fistfall asked before Cat could.

"Twelve. So, more than you have bolts, as I understand," the artificer noted. "I have some thoughts on payloads for bolts, too. They'll take time, though—and we have the thunder bolts already, right?"

"Four of them," Paintrock confirmed, the Master of Staves reentering the space with a cart. "Did you keep the storage— Yes, I see it!"

Two of the elvar stavemasters followed their boss into the room like lost puppies, falling in at a gesture to help him lift the first of the munitions.

The thunder crystals alone were over a yard long. With the casing, shaft and vanes, the bolts were even taller than Fistfall.

"Careful," Alloy warned. "Everything on the ballista is now set up to run from the gears. Once they're in those storage slots, that lever"—he indicated—"will pull the cable back and load the bolt.

"We do *not* want to release this thing inside. Unloaded, the cursed cable might snap. *Loaded*, it will put whatever we've stuck in it right through the hull. I will be much happier once my latest creation is *outside* my ship!"

Cat chuckled, examining the ballista.

It was still clearly exactly what Paintrock had called it: a scaled-up crossbow. Steel arms attached to a steel cable, with heavy hooks in place to draw the cable back and then release it. A crossbow had a handful of gears at most, though, and the ballista was practically *festooned* with mechanisms.

Cat had enough familiarity with clockwork and crystal-empowered arcane devices to be able to work out the components. They couldn't rely on lodestone pull out on the hull, so the bolts were loaded below the bow itself and would be lifted into place once the cable was drawn back.

The same platform that lifted them into place would act as the final guiding channel when the cable was released. The sighting system, just above where the cable would reach its greatest extent, didn't resemble anything Cat had ever seen on a weapon.

It resembled, in fact, the sextants from the bridge sufficiently that he wondered if Alloy had taken one of them.

"We had a spare sextant," the artificer told him, following his gaze. "I dismantled it for parts. Fistfall! This is the most important part."

"I am listening," the gobvar said mildly. He had, from what Cat could tell, been listening all along and paying more attention than Cat would have expected from most of the crew.

Though he was the one who was going to have to stand out on the hull and *fire* the ballista.

"This runs like one of our sextants, but its gears are matched to the ones of the ballista mount," Alloy told Fistfall. "Turn the main wheels; both move. This one left to right; this one up and down. If you release *this* latch, here, you can maneuver the telescope by hand, but it needs to be put back into the cradle *here* to be used for aiming."

"So, leave it in the cradle," Fistfall concluded.

"You may need the telescope to find *where* you're aiming, so I set it up with the option, but yeah… If you take it out, I can't be sure it will work as well after.

"Now, you don't need to worry about drop or even a storm stave's maximum reach," the darvar continued. "Point and release, and it will probably hit. Um. Eventually."

"How eventually?" Cat asked.

"I don't know," Alloy admitted, the words sounding like they were painfully dragged out of him. "There's a lot of different factors, and I haven't had time to do all of the math. Like… ten leagues a minute?"

"We're aiming to fire from five hundred leagues," Cat told them both. "Will it hit at that range?"

"Depends on how big your target is," Alloy said. "It won't even be down to Fistfall's eye at that point. The sextant and the ballista can only get so close. So, uh… aim for the entire fortress, not a particular piece of it?"

"We can aim more tightly as we get closer," Cat conceded. "Let's get this moving. Bogsong, Fistfall. With me."

He was neither surprised that, nor asking *why*, his off-duty fourth officer was in the cargo hold where they were preparing Fistfall's new weapon.

"And, Fistfall," he said quietly to the gobvar as they moved to grab the ballista—there hadn't been time for conveniences such as *carrying handles*.

"Captain."

"If you can, aim for the towers," he told the big var. "One thunder crystal will only do so much… but those towers will have *dozens*."

"Range is now five hundred and ten leagues," Streamwater reported from her sextant.

"Any sign that our wraith friends have found the fort?" Cat asked. He'd picked which of the two forts they were going to pass closest to at random—and deciding they were going to *shoot* at it hadn't changed his thought process.

"Nothing," his second officer told him. "Nothing is moving, nothing is green… except that with the way the light is in this sphere, well, *everything* is green."

He nodded. The bruised purple-green color of the Warden of Stone's crystal was *not* something he'd ever get used to, and he would be glad to leave it behind in about twelve hours. If they'd had the fuel to spend, he could have circled around the forts, staying a thousand leagues from anything threatening.

But he didn't. That was the metric hanging over his head. They'd consumed over two-thirds of their fuel. His math—still guided by Alloy, as it wasn't a *neat* correlation between the gallons of fuel and how many leagues per minute they could accelerate—said they'd reach Stormfall with a quarter of their fuel remaining.

Crossing Stormfall at their planned speed would take a third of that, but he couldn't risk going slower—or spending the fuel to go faster.

There were no good options left, he suspected, so he stuck with the one they'd already decided on. There in the Warden of Stone, he'd planned on the basis of passing the fort at two leagues a minute, a speed where it would be *quite* difficult for any gunner on the ancient battlements to aim at them.

The wraiths might be able to manage it, of course, but it was the best chance he'd thought they had. Now his crew had given him another one.

"Five hundred and four leagues," Streamwater told him. "Two minutes. Assuming he fires as planned…"

"I have full faith in Fistfall to do *exactly* as we discussed unless there is a very good reason not to," Cat murmured. "Much as I would have in you, Faith."

And most of the rest of the crew, without being particularly generous. He would trust Fistfall or Streamwater *most* out of the crew he would trust, but he trusted his crew. He *believed* in his crew.

The ballista wasn't his idea or even Alloy's idea. It was Fistfall and Paintrock who had come up with it, found other crew willing to work on it and then asked—almost too late—for help when they hit a point where they couldn't proceed.

The prophecy might have told him that they needed a trio—Shaman, Captain and Archmage—but if they found the answers they needed, it was the *crew* who would get them there.

"We're running clean and straight," Alloy announced. "No maneuvers; engines are off. She's as steady as she can be for the shot."

Cat took the unspoken hint and released the main wheel. It was locked in place at that moment, but he rested his hands on it by habit when he was on the control deck. Doing so *probably* wouldn't cause any motion to the ship, but it did control the lift crystals.

They needed *this* shot to be perfect.

"There. He loosed," Streamwater announced. "Exactly five hundred leagues. Getting a bead on the bolt for its speed."

At the speed Alloy had predicted, it would take most of an hour for the bolt to land. Nothing *should* move enough to cause a problem, but it was a long, *long* way for the weapon to travel.

"I make it sixteen leagues a minute," she finally said. "That's faster than we expected, right?"

"Like I said, I didn't do the math," Alloy complained. "That was the high end; that cable is tougher than I thought."

"Will it be a problem?" Cat asked.

The darvar hesitated, then shrugged.

"Maybe," he conceded. "Might snap before we get all the shots. I'll warn the kid."

Cat gave Alloy a disapproving look.

"I'll warn Mage Fistfall," Alloy corrected himself, but there was a smile behind it that suggested the artificer was teasing someone.

Possibly Cat, possibly Brushfire. Cat wasn't sure.

"Twenty-seven minutes to impact," the darvar continued.

"I said sixteen leagues per minute," Streamwater countered. "That would be thirty-one."

"You cannot measure a speed relative to anything but this ship," Alloy told her. "The sextants aren't *that* magical. So, if *we* are moving at two leagues a minute and we measure the bolt at sixteen, it's heading toward the fort at *eighteen*, yes?"

Cat hadn't realized that himself, so the explanation was helpful.

"At which point *we* will still be over four hundred leagues from the rock," he noted. "We'll be safe enough."

He hoped.

Cat was sufficiently impressed with his crew's idea and execution that he wasn't going to *tell* anyone he didn't expect the first shot to hit. He did expect the fort to wake up, but the lack of any sign of it so far was letting him *hope* speed would be enough to get them past.

Wraiths might not take as long to wake up and aim well as var, but he suspected that the *equipment* wasn't necessarily in great shape on the ancient fort. Plus, their closest approach was still going to be over a hundred leagues away.

Storm staves *could* hit at that range. Sometimes. The fort likely contained enough weapons to be dangerous at that distance by sheer volume, but speed and distance would make *Void Flyer* safe, even if the bolt missed.

"Fistfall is back inside," a runner reported. "He wanted to know if he should ready for a second shot."

"The first one is about to land," Cat noted. *Or miss.* "Wait here," he instructed the gobvar. "Then you can tell Fistfall if it worked."

"Bolt should be hitting in a few moments," Streamwater told them. Her eye was on the sextant telescope, tracking the fort and watching for any sign—the bolt itself had passed beyond their ability to see it some time before.

The sextant was *good* at measuring ranges and speeds, but it wasn't *perfect*, in Cat's experience. There was enough variability that their expected strike could have been off by as much as a minute in any direction, so he wasn't surprised when Streamwater's *few moments* passed without incident.

He looked up, trying to pick out which of the tiny sparks above him was the fort reflecting the crystal's light. Without a telescope to hand, he was about to conjure a magical one when it suddenly became *very* clear, as one of the sparks flared with a brilliant blue-white light for a few heartbeats.

"Streamwater," he said calmly. "Take a moment for your eye to recover, then tell me what you saw."

His second officer stepped back from the sextant, blinking rapidly. She'd been looking right at the fort when the explosion had occurred, and they hadn't been expecting *that* big a result. The sextant had darkening lenses to allow an officer to look close to a crystal or an ember, but they hadn't been in place.

Fortunately, it had *some* magical protection and elvar eyes were tough.

"I can't say I saw the bolt hit," she admitted. "But there was a backfire chain in one of the fort's towers. Maybe sixty crystals went up? None of the blasts were much on their own, but…"

"But sixty storm staves backfiring wrecks the tower and does damage to the fort itself," Cat agreed. *Now* he conjured his telescope, looking at the fortress rock while Streamwater recovered.

There had been four towers on the side of the fortress facing them. Now there were three, but two of the remaining towers had been devastated by the destruction of the fourth. Only one of the four firing positions was intact enough to still be a threat, and Cat nodded in satisfaction.

"Tell Fistfall he did good," he told the runner. "We won't need a second shot."

The gobvar vanished at a run and Cat turned back to the control crew.

"We're going to adjust course slightly," he told them. "Engines won't be needed. With a bit of lift-crystal work, we can make sure we pass on the defanged side of the fort. Even if the wraiths *do* show up, Master Fistfall's clever idea just bought us clear passage to Stormfall!"

He'd stay on the control deck until they hit the strait. After that, though, it was time to start putting brains in one room. Everyone had been poking at plans for when they met the Blood King, but he realized they'd all *assumed* they'd do so in Stormfall.

A dangerous assumption, as shown by the ballista not being ready for this task until Cat and Alloy had intervened. That same intervention showed the other problem: ten individual half-complete plans weren't worth a tenth as much as one *complete* plan supported by everyone's resources.

And there wasn't going to be time to *experiment* when they found their way barred by an angry god.

CHAPTER

42

Armand looked around his main sitting room and considered the people who had carried him this far. He'd sought out Cat himself originally, because the elvar had been one of the few to see in person the dragons that Armand had seen in his vision of the future.

Brushfire they'd recruited because they'd needed a crew for their ship and because Cat had a prophecy from his old ship's seer that he needed to be part of a trio—Shaman and Captain, Captain and Archmage.

There'd been a lot more than the prophecy to recommend her and her tribe, and everything Armand had seen told him they'd *underestimated* how capable and useful the gobvar were going to be. *Void Flyer*'s crew was two-thirds gobvar, and while they lacked the education Armand was used to in his companions, he was learning that other skills were just as valuable.

Alloy hadn't been sought out or predicted, but Armand *knew* that the artificer was just as much a part of what the seer had predicted as the other three. His own divinations had confirmed that Alloy would be as critical in finishing the mission as the rocket ship he'd built had been in getting them there.

The rest of the crew and officers were important, but somehow Armand knew that *these* three—four counting him, of course—were the critical point. Their relationships, friendships and combined power and knowledge would be key.

He wished he had the divination skill to be surer of *how* or *why* that would be the case, but he knew it to be true.

"It appears we were a touch overzealous about the forts at the strait," Cat told the others. "We blew one of the four towers on the closer fort to shards and wrecked two others before we passed the rock, but nothing moved on the rock or the ships by it as we sailed by."

"Whatever intellect controls these things may have decided that the damaged fort wasn't worth it," Brushfire suggested. "We think that's the King, but it might just be the same manifestation that threw wraiths at us in Warden of Fire, right?"

"It might," Armand agreed. "Certainly, the manifestation of the hunger of the void *is* present here, but it seems much less capable on its own. Crewing and sailing the twentysail required the Blood King's power and focus.

"And I fear *he* decided not to attempt the same trick twice." Armand shrugged, looking over at Cat to draw some support from his Captain. *His* Captain… That had a slightly heavier weight now, he thought.

Or it might have had that weight for a while and he hadn't realized it. He was certainly having suspicions about the way he thought of Brushfire as *his* shaman.

"So, he'll do something different," Alloy said. "Do you think he knows what we did to that fort?"

"Almost certainly," Armand admitted grimly.

"These void spheres are his in a way that I don't think we can quite understand, let alone describe," Brushfire added. "He killed them to become a god, but I *think* that in doing so, he made them part of him forever."

Armand wouldn't have thought to phrase it that way, but she was entirely correct, and he nodded to her.

"Exactly. Which is part of why he is coming to deal with us himself."

The room was silent, and his three companions each took a bite of the cake he'd served them—so perfectly synchronized it couldn't have been planned.

"You're sure," Cat said. It wasn't a question.

"Divination can be blocked," Armand observed. "But that our divinations *are* blocked tells us something. Something I can't see bars our way, and I can't scry anything of the Blood King himself. Knowing that the White Mountain told him we were present, I see only one conclusion."

"Which leaves us with one *question*," Cat said. "How do we get past a god? We can't outrun him, we can't *fight* him… I know we have all gone over the Stormfall charts. I know we have all looked at everything this ship is capable of.

"I know I have at least one foolish, probably suicidal plan that almost certainly won't work," the Captain observed. "I doubt I'm alone. As Fistfall and Paintrock phrased it when they presented Brushfire and me with a half-built ballista and the idea of using thunder crystals as *projectiles*, we need *options*."

There was a long silence, and the somehow *extra* dark void of the strait beyond the arcane "windows" didn't help.

"Can't you and Cat do what you did before?" Alloy finally asked. "The meld seemed extraordinarily powerful and flexible."

"It is, but it comes with a cost," Armand warned. "We should have been more careful. Cat and I were both almost lost to the meld, which I… do not believe, now, that we would have survived."

He gave Cat an apologetic look.

"I did not realize the risk was that great," he confessed.

"We would have had no choice but to take it anyway," his Captain replied. "There *were* no other options to defeat the twentysail. And if you tell me there are no other options now, I will risk it again to protect our crew."

"I think you and I *specifically* cannot risk it again," Armand warned. "Part of the danger was the emotional connection neither of us realized existed, which has not gone away. But because we already almost slipped into an unbreaking meld once, I fear our risk is even more elevated now."

He held Cat's gaze levelly until the elvar nodded, then he looked around at the other two.

"Plus, it wouldn't be enough," he admitted. "Cat's *skills* were what I needed to take out the twentysail. Against the Blood King, skill is insufficient. I can master enough of what I learned in the meld with Cat to be *able* to fight him from *Flyer*, but he is a god or near enough to make no difference to us!

"I am an archmage, and despite what some think, that *does not* mean a god," he concluded. "Alone, I do not think I can even hold him off. And adding another mage's power to that will not make enough of a difference.

"A direct magical confrontation with the Blood King of the Gobvar will only accelerate our demise."

Alloy grunted, though something in his expression was still thoughtful.

"We have the ballista now," the artificer observed. "While I have adjustments I would love to make, they would require bringing it back inside, and I don't believe that is a wise choice."

"Nine shots," Cat noted. "The bolts fly faster and truer than I'd dared hope, but it is not a weapon that will threaten a *ship* at distance. And I am not even certain that the Blood King will arrive on a ship.

"Or need said ship if he *does*."

"He will arrive on a ship," Armand told them. He'd taken time to track down the handful of members of the gobvar crew who remembered stories of the Blood King and compared them against the limited texts he had and his own assessment. "He has never arrived in a sphere without a ship and an escort. Half a dozen ninesails, at least, crewed by the gobvar of the Blood Guard."

"He can't bring his Guard into the void spheres, can he?" Brushfire asked.

"It is possible he could," Armand warned. "He has enough power and enough *control* over the void spheres to carry a bubble of aether with him. I..."

He paused, thinking through that and assessing the drain on *him* of maintaining his own bubble of air when needed. Aether would presumably be easier, though he didn't know anyone who'd ever *tried*. Prior to this journey, he'd never heard of anyone attempting to enter the void before.

"I *think* even he would struggle to maintain such a bubble around more than one ship," he told his mages. "I... believe he would not need a crew to operate a ship in the void spheres, since he could summon wraiths to do the same."

"The question is whether he would switch var for wraiths in Drinkstar... or when he was forced to drop the bubble and abandon his Guard to their deaths," Cat said flatly.

Armand shivered at the implication of what Cat said, and he wasn't the only one. He couldn't argue with Cat's assessment, though. If they pressed the Blood King at all, the immortal would almost certainly abandon his var to focus his power on them.

No one expected the being who'd killed untold millions to ascend to godhood to care about a few hundred var loyal to him.

"If he arrives on a ship, the ballista may work… but he will come on a real warship, and our chances of surviving long enough to even see if we hit are low," Cat continued. "Fistfall and Hunter's clever idea and Alloy's construction have given us a real weapon, but it is limited in several ways—and *they* will have a ten-stave broadside. At least."

"And then there was your second question, Cat," Brushfire said. "Does he *need* the ship? Will it even slow him down if we destroy it?"

"Slow him down? Yes," Armand told her wearily. "Kill him? No. Destroying whatever ship carries him would buy us time, I think, but potentially not even enough of that."

"What about pinning it in place? Along with him," Brushfire asked. She reached across the chart on the table and tapped a symbol that Armand had barely considered. "The Eleventh Ward is there. We don't know what condition it's in, I know, but the Seeker turned the Seventh Ward into a trap, one that nearly pulled us back to the rock."

"I am not sure how she did it," Armand admitted.

"It was also a thing of the aether currents," Cat warned. "I'm not certain that it would do *anything* in the void, even if we could duplicate what she did."

The room fell silent again.

"I think the Ward still may be our best asset," Armand said slowly. "It is a powerful ancient device. If nothing else…"

He trailed off, considering what he was about to say with some degree of fascinated horror.

"If nothing else," he repeated, "I suspect we can duplicate Fistfall's destruction of a defensive tower on the Eleventh Ward and open enough of a hole to hit the central abyss. While I don't *know* what would happen if we detonated a thunder crystal on that piece of arcana, there is a great deal of energy tied up in it.

"Rupturing that abyss would be…" He stretched for a word.

"Impressive," Cat suggested. "I'm not certain we can arrange a situation where we are close enough to trigger a rupture while the King is close enough for it to matter where we are not destroyed by either the King or the rupture itself."

Cat held up a hand before Armand said anything in response.

"I agree that the Ward is an asset we cannot ignore," he said. "Our options will be limited by time, distance, fuel and the presence of the enemy. Given time, I think I can see several ways that we could turn the Ward into a trap that would buy us time to bypass the King.

"What we do not know is how much time we have. It will be two clock-days to reach the Eleventh Ward, adding three clock-days in total to the journey through Stormfall and increasing our fuel costs in the system by half.

"It gives us options and might be worth it, but may I suggest we find a better plan than *blow it up while we're there*?" Cat asked drily.

"If nothing else, being near the Ward should make the Blood King hesitate," Alloy noted. "*He* knows what it can do far better than we can. While we don't have the hands to man the fortress's weapons, we also could potentially *acquire* some of them to augment our thunder-bolt supplies."

"Assuming that the King can't awaken wraiths there, too. The *real* problem, though, is that if we have the time to do much preparation at the Eleventh Ward, we might have the time to *escape* Stormfall," Brushfire pointed out. "Wouldn't we be better served getting clear of the void spheres rather than preparing to fight the Blood King?"

Armand grimaced and let the silence hang for long moments before he put into words what he figured they were all thinking.

"No matter what we do, the Blood King is going to pursue us," he told her. "I don't think we'll get past Drinkstar at best before we face him—and if we face him in Drinkstar, there will be few opportunities for us to gather additional resources.

"We will have much the same limits on our crew and *Void Flyer* facing the King in Drinkstar... and *he* will have his fleet.

"While I am certain that he wields more direct power of his *own* here, I think we are better off fighting him in Stormfall, away from the Blood Guard, than in the Clan Spheres with a fleet behind him."

CHAPTER

43

BRUSHFIRE WAITED IN THE SILENCE AFTER ARMAND'S DARK pronouncement, considering the situation as her archmage laid it out. Their options were bleak: try to run, and possibly face a god backed by a mortal fleet—or try to lay an ambush for the same god in his own territory.

"We set our course for the Ward, then?" she finally asked. "And see what kind of trap we can rig? If he gives us enough time, we may be able to find the regular access to the abyss and set up something with timers and a thunder crystal, to rupture its arcane structure on *our* schedule."

"It's an option," Cat said, his tone exhausted to her ear. "And we've too few of those. But it's better than fighting an entire fleet."

Brushfire didn't want to point out that said fleet might *still* be waiting for them if they somehow handled the Blood King. Everyone knew that. But they could only handle one problem at a time—and the one in front of them was trouble enough.

"We can scavenge thunder crystals from the old fortifications, too," she suggested. "Expand the ammunition for our one weapon and set up whatever trap we need without using our own stocks."

"They may not be intact," Alloy warned. "Those on the Seventh Ward weren't, from what I heard from His Dark Brothers."

Brushfire hadn't *forgotten* that Alloy had been held captive on the Seventh Ward, but she hadn't connected that to giving him knowledge they might use.

285

"That was with aether to wear them down, though," Cat pointed out. "We've seen here already that things left to the void are more static than things left to the aether. They aren't intact, but they are more so than they should be after a thousand dances.

"Some things may be intact on the Eleventh Ward." He shrugged. "Or the entire thing could be useless, its abyss long-faded into memory. We have to prepare for all possibilities."

"We're coming up short on most of our thoughts," Brushfire told him gently. "What are yours?"

He chuckled.

"Ram the bastard, to be honest," Cat admitted. "If we come in fast enough and straight enough, *Void Flyer* is a smaller target head-on than any stavemaster has trained to hit. The front of the ship is the most reinforced piece, so we have a chance of surviving punching through a ninesail and coming out the other side intact."

"Not a very *good* chance," Alloy said after a long moment.

"No," Cat agreed. "Like I said, *my* idea was foolish and probably suicidal. I'm drawing a blank on options that aren't, though. We speak of not merely defying but *fighting* a god."

"The Blood King is not a god," Brushfire snapped, her tone a surprise even to her. "He has forced my people to regard him that way for a thousand dances, but he is *not* a god. Gods do not walk the spheres or require ships to move them between worlds.

"Gods are a *source* of power; they have not stolen the lives of millions to wield it. He may be powerful beyond any archmage, and he may even be immortal, but he is no god."

"And gods, perhaps importantly, do not fear," Armand added, the archmage's voice thoughtful. "The Ward presents the greatest danger in the system. The Blood King has sacrificed *everything* that most var would value to become immortal.

"While I don't know if the Ward's abyss could threaten that immortality, I am not sure *he* would, either."

"And with all he has done to be immortal, he must fear death more than anything," Brushfire guessed, following Armand's thought. The stories of the Blood King her tribe had passed down were terrifying things, tales of violence wrought for little or no reason. The Blood King seemed to appear as much to make sure the gobvar remained afraid of him as anything else.

Which fit with what Armand was saying. The Blood King *used* fear, but he had also feared death *so much*, he had committed the greatest atrocity in history to avoid it. When faced with that fear again, what would he do?

"It's not much, but it may give us more time," she continued. "If he believes we are in place to use the Ward against him, then he may hesitate. He may attempt to wait us out."

"He can probably wait us out," Cat pointed out.

"The biggest problem with shooting his ship from a thousand leagues away is that a ship is moving, isn't it?" she asked her Captain with a suddenly cold smile. "If he takes a position to blockade us, well…"

"He's not moving," her Captain conceded. "And in *that* case… a single backfiring storm stave can cause a lot of havoc on a ninesail. If we hit a stave gallery, even a single shot could destroy his ship."

"And near-god or not," Armand said in satisfaction, "he is unlikely to be able to *catch* us without a ship."

It wasn't much of a plan, Brushfire knew. But at least it wasn't all down to one throw of the dice. They might be able to use the Ward as a weapon. They might be able to shoot the Blood King's ship down.

As Cat had said… it gave them *options*.

Hopefully, one of those options might even work.

CHAPTER

44

CAT KNEW PERFECTLY WELL HE HADN'T BEEN GETTING ENOUGH SLEEP. From the moment they'd opened fire on the fort outside the strait to when they'd entered the strait, he'd needed to be on the bridge. First, because the threat of the fort was only *reduced*, not destroyed, and second, because he was the only one aboard capable of finding straits in the void.

None of his officers shared his sense for the aether. They could manage to stay *in* the strait—the glow of Stormfall's outerlight shell was visible at the far end to provide a navigation point—but entering it was up to him.

The planning meeting had consumed a third of the time they'd been in the strait. He'd managed a nap after that, but he was back in the control room for their entrance into Stormfall.

The universe expanded around them as they passed out of the narrow passage, and Cat conjured his own telescope in front of him as Brushfire and Streamwater set to scanning the system with the sextants and telescopes.

After a quick scan to be sure their immediate surroundings were clear, Cat had eyes for one place: the area of void where their charts said a strait should link to the Clan sphere of Drinkstar. If their enemy wasn't waiting right outside the strait, the Blood King had to be either along the route from Drinkstar or, well, not there yet.

He absently noted that the strait into Drinkstar, at least, was *visible* in a way that the straits between the void spheres weren't. Aether leaked through from the sphere on the other side of the strait, though it dispersed far too quickly to have any effect on the larger sphere. A small area of very thin aether wisped around the strait, but it was enough for him to *see* it.

That was reassuring in one particularly morbid way. They couldn't go *backward* without him, but if the worst happened in their conflict with the gobvar monarch, his people could get *out* of Stormfall and into a regular aether sphere without him.

He didn't know how they'd get home from there—but then, he admitted to himself that he wasn't entirely sure *Void Flyer* was going to be an option for getting back regardless. With the threat in front of them, he'd barely thought that far ahead since they'd left the White Mountain.

At that moment, though, the key point was that while he could see the strait, he couldn't see anything *else*.

"Faith, Brushfire. Are you seeing anything moving in this sphere?" he asked his officers.

"Nothing," Streamwater replied. "I've checked two spots where there *should* be straits into other void spheres—not that we can tell if they're there!—and two of the worldlets. Nothing seems to be alive."

"The strait to Drinkwater is clear," Brushfire confirmed. "We can even see it, too. Nothing on the Eleventh Ward, either."

Cat nodded as she continued.

"I'm trying to get a feel for the state of the Ward. The Seventh Ward in Brokenwright was worn down to nothing outside of His Dark Brother's monastery. This doesn't look like it's in quite as bad shape, but…"

He turned his own scope with a gesture, the panel in front of his face not actually moving as his magic picked up light from another angle. He knew where the Eleventh Ward was relative to their emergence, but it still took him a dozen heartbeats to truly get it focused.

The asteroid fortress looked almost identical to the one in Brokenwright, which said quite a bit about both the resources of the Ironhand Imperium and their determination to defend their core spheres. Reshaping rocks in the aether was *doable*, but it required a lot of either magic or labor and was something reserved for only the most critical of purposes.

Or most egotistical, he supposed, considering some of the places he'd seen.

The Wards were shaped like drop spindles, wide disks on one end narrowing into long spikes pointing toward the strait they were built to control.

Cat saw the problem the moment he settled his view onto the entire old fortress. At some point in the last thousand dances, a natural rock that looked large enough to have its own lodestone heart had drifted close enough to the Ward to get caught in the effect of its larger lodestone core.

The stone—a dozen cables long compared to the asteroid fortress's three hundred leagues—had struck with some force, embedding itself in the lower spike about a hundred leagues from the tip. At first glance, it was an odd mountain on the greater worldlet, and that *might* be all it was.

But while Cat didn't pretend to understand how the magic of the Wards worked, he suspected that it was a careful balance, and having another rock stabbed into a key portion of the asteroid might be a problem.

"Any sign of the Blood King anywhere?" he asked softly.

"Nothing," Streamwater confirmed. "This sphere is dead as a tomb."

"Except for the usual," Brushfire added. "We can all feel it. The hunger is the weakest I've felt it yet, but it's still… terrifying."

Cat nodded grimly.

They didn't know why Stormfall had been swept up in the ascension ritual and Brokenwright *hadn't* been. Possibly because Stormfall had a strong outerlight sphere and livable worlds, where Brokenwright's ember had been a sad and weak thing even during the Imperium's rule.

The Ward had been the *only* thing in Brokenwright that the Imperium cared about, but Stormfall had been home to millions of var. Var that the Blood King had murdered.

"We'll set our course for the Ward as planned," Cat said. "We'll keep our eyes and minds peeled for the wraiths, but there is only one thing in this sphere of use to us. Let's go check it out."

He considered the view above him for a moment, then conceded that he was too tired to make sense of anything.

"I'm going to rest," he told his officers. "Wake me *immediately* if anything moves."

Because there, in the last of the void spheres they had to pass through, the only things that were going to move were the enemy.

Cat was honestly surprised by the time on his clock when he woke up. He'd expected to be woken up by his crew at some point, but it seemed he'd slept for a full half-clock-day.

His own training and instincts would normally have woken him up after about eight hours, so he'd *definitely* overdone it. Probably not helped by two nights of… not really *sleeping*, exactly, in the last few days.

If no one had woken him, then he likely had the time to take this at a slow pace. He washed and dressed at a steady pace, assembling the components of his no-longer-military uniform. The colors had changed, but the stiff-shouldered tunic was fundamentally the same.

Where he'd worn gold braid as a Navy officer, though, he had the blue trim of an archmage's staff. A bright blue sash went over the dark blue jacket as well, a uniform marker he didn't need aboard *Void Flyer* but had made part of his personal uniform regardless.

The fight ahead wasn't going to need a sword, but his focus went everywhere with him. A few minutes left his long hair clean and organized, and he felt ready to face the spheres.

He rushed the process most mornings at this point. He kept his hair more simply than he had as an elvar officer, and the clothing was all of a simpler design than the High Court Navy uniform. The *cut* was similar, but the buttons and seals and such were all designed to be easier to handle.

The Navy assumed an officer would *make* the time to be perfect. Face and decorum and respect all required it. A civilian ship, especially one like *Flyer* that sailed under an archmage's pennant, didn't have nearly the same games of face and expectation.

Even the elvar among his crew would regard High Court standards as a joke. The only person aboard *Void Flyer* who expected Cat to live up to them was Cat himself.

But it was part of how he commanded, even if he'd allowed himself to relax enough to *recognize* that it didn't matter to anyone else.

Something told him that this was going to be a clock-day where *he* needed to be fully confident in himself, in his ability to command his ship, his crew... and himself.

"Officers Hammerhead and Streamwater went to rest three hours ago, sir," Bogsong Smallwolf reported as he entered the control deck.

She and Alloy were holding down the watch, accompanied by a half dozen gobvar and Alloy's oldest daughter. Cat hadn't seen much of the Bellowforges, and he had to admit that he'd thought the girls were younger than she *now* appeared.

"Captain," Alloy greeted him. "My daughter Electrum. I am training her on the control-deck instruments." He grinned. "Or, at least, explaining what her father is doing most days."

"There are spaces on this ship only darvar can easily fit," Electrum said cheerfully. "My honored father is not as spry as he once was. While Heart is too young, I hope to learn enough to help."

"Plus, you were bored," Alloy said with a gentle smile.

"Plus, I was bored," the young darvar agreed.

If Alloy had asked, Cat would have guessed Electrum was all of maybe twelve dances. Now he saw her away from her tormentors and learning the arcana around her, he realized he'd misjudged her—not least because even *Alloy* wasn't much taller than a preteen elvar.

She wasn't an adult, he judged, but she was definitely no longer a child, either. An adolescent, one who should have been in school, chasing boys, not aboard a ship about to fight a god.

They'd had no real choice, he knew. Their aether ship, *Star*, hadn't been in any shape to go back to the Court and Kingdoms. *Void Flyer* was too unusual. A strange ship manned mostly by gobvar would have drawn too many questions and eyes, and their divinations had warned that even Armand's status wouldn't have broken them free.

Not in time, at least.

They didn't know what time limit was hanging over them, only that there *had* to be one. Only one of the visions Armand had seen had been of the past: the battle where Cat's career had ended.

The other visions had been later, of a war already in progress... a war already being *lost*. At some unforeseen hour, the dragons would muster their gobvar slaves and invade. Without knowing *when*, they had to move quickly.

Taking Alloy's wife and children back to the Kingdoms hadn't been an option. But the reminder of everyone they were risking sent a chill down his spine. There was no turning back, but where they'd ended up...

It wasn't good. They had a plan, which he wasn't sure was going to work. And they had a lot of people who were going to die if it didn't.

"Everyone can help," he told the adolescent. "And perhaps, since you know your father, you'll understand his instruments better than the rest of us."

"Who don't even know what filtration pressure *means*," Alloy grumbled.

"Who don't even know what... that means," Cat echoed with a chuckle. "I just know that if *that* dial"—he gestured at the one that measured filtration pressure on decks one through ten—"goes into the orange zone, I send people to check the filters on deck six."

He *didn't* know what *filtration pressure* meant. But he knew which dials were measuring it and which ones were for each deck and what to do if there was a problem. Which was, for the Captain of the ship, enough.

To start, at least. Given time, he'd learn everything about his ship. It was what he'd done with ninesails, and it was what he'd do with the *Flyer*.

And any other ship fate and Armand saw fit to need him to command!

BRUSHFIRE TOOK THE TIME TO MAKE SURE THE OTHER OFFICERS WERE resting before she returned to the control room. The last few clock-days had been hectic, and the *next* few clock-days were going to be worse. They had a clock-day and a bit left before they reached the Eleventh Ward, and she had no idea what they would or wouldn't be able to achieve there.

The control-room crew had changed over since she'd left to rest herself—they *should* have swapped twice, since she'd been out for half a clock-day after sleeping and checking key parts of the ship.

The only person she'd *known* she would find there was Cat. She stopped at the entrance to regard her Captain for a few moments, trying to ignore the feelings running through her head still.

She'd rested too long, she judged, and her emotions were getting the better of her. She wasn't *jealous*, she didn't think, of Cat and Armand. She wanted both of them to be well and happy, too much so to really begrudge them finding comfort in each other.

It was a surprise that she was as close to doing so as she was. She'd figured out *Cat's* proclivities early on, after all. She would never have expected him to be interested in a gobvar, but she also knew that he was only attracted to his own sex.

Armand she'd found harder to pin down, and in her more honest moments she had suspected there *was* something there, both on her side and his.

She wouldn't have *expected* that if someone had asked her. Her previous encounters had been with her own var, almost exclusively intended with at least an *intent* at children. That was, after all, part of how the scattered tribes and clans of gobvar in the Court and Kingdoms avoided inbreeding.

Brushfire suspected that part of why she'd never found anyone she was interested in a life or even term partnership with was that she'd never really had a chance to get to know anyone outside her tribe except her shamanic teachers.

Her tribal elders had, with her consent, arranged meetings through other tribal elders. Some of those meetings had gone as well as could be expected, though no children or even second encounters had come of any of them.

And now she found herself standing at the door to the control deck of her void ship, complaining to herself that her Captain and her archmage had sorted things out between them. She was happy for them, she told herself determinedly.

Jealous wasn't the right word. *Envious* was.

Either way, it was time to get to work.

Cat gave Brushfire a smile and a nod that made her wonder if he realized she'd paused in the stairwell door. He might have—he certainly seemed to have a preternatural sense of the space around him at all times—but he said nothing more.

"Everything quiet?" she asked.

"So far, Stormfall remains a tomb," he confirmed. "What you did in the Warden of Stone was a good idea, so I took a stab at it here."

There was a crude copy of their chart of the sphere spread out next to the control dais. It had the markers, to Brushfire's eyes, of something created with magic—not *conjured*, exactly, but using a set of magically guided charcoals and brushes to duplicate the key information of a more detailed and ornate chart.

The process couldn't exactly copy *anything*, not without a mage who was far more skilled at the spell than Cat clearly was, but it gave them a lot of the key information without retreating to the chart room.

"There are about three dozen definitely civilian aether ships scattered between the worldlets our chart says were occupied," her Captain told her. "Plus what looks like four of the Ironhands' five-siders over the capital."

"Bad enough but could be worse," she murmured.

"That's just what's at the worldlets," he warned. "There's another squadron of four five-siders, this one with a ninesail in company, at the strait toward Ashflow."

At her raised eyebrow, he shrugged.

"Another void sphere, home to the Twelfth Ward," he explained. "Irrelevant to us, really. It links into the Warden of Stone, and while it theoretically links to the Clan Spheres, no one *lives* in the spheres it links to, so we couldn't refuel there.

"Drinkstar is our only way forward, and thankfully, there are no ships there. Our possible problem is the *third* squadron of five-siders and the second ninesail."

Cat pointed at where someone—presumably him—had added a set of flags to the chart. They weren't *quite* at *Void Flyer*'s destination, but Brushfire judged that they probably had been positioned above the Eleventh Ward.

"The Ward was moved by the asteroid strike," he told her. "Its defensive squadron wasn't, but they're still close, and if the wraiths wake them up, they can bar our way."

"So far, so good?" she asked, crossing to a sextant and using it to narrow in on that squadron. Five ships, as he said. A ninesail and four five-sided warships. Even the ninesail was small and under-armed compared to the High Court Navy, but *Void Flyer* had few defenses.

Even one of the five-siders could probably end their voyage if they didn't find the right tools. They had the ballista, but Brushfire didn't think they could manage to hit an evading target with it.

"So far, everything remains dead," he agreed. "But we need to keep an eye on everything, and it's starting to make my eyes hurt spreading them so far."

Brushfire chuckled and stepped back from the sextant to grin at him.

"Well, I'll keep my eyes on the Ward and you keep your eyes on the strait, and then no one is trying to make one set of eyes see two places, right?"

"Agreed. Thank you."

"That's the job," she told him. "Make the Captain's life easier!"

"If only all first officers realized it," he told her in a martyred tone that earned him another chuckle and a warning finger-wag.

Still, she turned back to the sextant, arranging its rangefinders and telescope to give her the distance and motion of the Ward and its trailing defenders. They still had a lot of distance to cover before they reached their destination, and while the *biggest* danger was still absent, it was always possible for the wraiths to wake up on their own.

Armand might be convinced that it would take the Blood King's attention for the hunger of these spheres to operate an aether ship, but Brushfire didn't want to take that chance.

After all, her entire family was on this ship!

"Cat," Brushfire said quietly some time later, as her examination of the Ward drew her to an unfortunate conclusion. "We may have made an assumption about the Ward that's going to be a problem."

"What is it?" he asked, shifting his magical telescope panel to match her sextant view.

"I think we were all assuming we'd be able to get around on the surface of the asteroid," she told him. "But the Seventh Ward, back in Brokenwright, didn't have an air envelope. It had aether right down to the surface... and Stormfall has no aether."

Her survey of the Eleventh Ward told her that it *also* had no air envelope. And while she'd hoped and checked for a similar envelope of aether, drawn by the abyss at its heart, she hadn't found anything.

Cat studied the illusory telescope in front of him in silence for several moments.

"That's going to be a *pain*," he finally said. "We might get lucky and find there's air inside, which would help, but..."

"We can rig up tents and covered sections that we pump air from *Flyer* into," she told him. "That's how we got Armand into the Seventh Ward, after all. It's a question of scale and what we have supplies for."

"And time in the void," Cat pointed out. "I have every faith in Axfall and Windheart's ability to build just about anything we ask for, but it will take two mages for every crewvar to keep enough air going to allow them to work.

"It will slow us down, and time is already a problem."

"What choice do we have?" she asked.

He said nothing, his illusory telescope vanishing as he looked up at the crystal panels above them, showing the sphere outside *Flyer*'s hull.

"None," he finally admitted. "We need to rip apart at least one of the Ward's towers for thunder crystals. We may need to go in with just us mages for that, get a sense of what we *could* seal off."

He shook his head grimly.

"After this long, I *should* remember we're in the cursed void," he told her.

"Every place we've needed to land so far has had air," she pointed out. "It took magic to be on the hull in flight, but the places we've landed on have all been easy enough to move around on.

"I don't think we forgot we were in the void, Cat. We just didn't think about the difference between the Wards and a worldlet. Not least because the cursed things are larger than any asteroid fortress I'd seen before this."

He nodded silently, staring blankly at the void above them for a few long moments.

"We'll do what we can," he finally said. "I'm not convinced the Ward's abyss is going to be as useful as we hope, but I'm not seeing any *other* options."

Brushfire nodded silently, turning her attention back to the sextant and the darkness outside the ship. She wasn't sure herself what they'd be able to manage with the abyss, but... she was *good* at duplicating magic she'd seen others perform. While she hadn't seen the Seeker weave the spell that had trapped *Star* above the Seventh Ward, she'd been *inside* the spell.

She hadn't wanted to promise anything, but she thought—she *hoped*—that she could duplicate the magic if she was standing in the same place the Seeker had stood. The Wards had been meant to do *one* thing, she knew—but the abysses the Ironhands had created to block the straits were terrifyingly powerful presences.

"It's funny."

"Sir?" she asked Cat, looking up from the sextant again.

"I could feel the Seventh Ward from a long way away," he told her. "But there was aether in Brokenwright, and I could feel it moving. Here, though? All I can feel is the hunger trapped in the light. The pull *out* to the outerlight shell is stronger than anything the Ward is doing."

"Do you think the abyss might… not be there anymore?" Brushfire asked.

He shrugged.

"We are forty-five hundred leagues from it," he pointed out. "Over a clock-day's travel still. I suspect that His Dark Brothers woke the one at the Seventh Ward up from some kind of slumber, and we may need to do the same.

"Even if the abyss proves useless, there's no greater concentration of weapons to take parts from in this sphere. It's still our best chance—and one that may make the Blood King hesita—"

Cat cut off like he'd been punched in the gut, air rushing from his lungs in a burst that brought Brushfire rushing to his side.

"Cat?" she asked. "Captain?"

In answer, he summoned his illusory telescope and expanded its viewing pane. The strait to Drinkstar was visible, a red-purple-blue smear of fading aether ten thousand leagues distant.

And rising from that smear, her sails as full as if an aether current were behind her, was a black-painted ninesail with blood-red sails. Even with the magic, details were hard to pick out, but Brushfire didn't see any var on the rigging or the deck, even as the sails twitched and the warship settled onto a new course.

One that, unless she misjudged, was heading *directly* toward *Void Flyer*.

"That's… him," she said. She could feel it now, a presence in the back of her mind, a pressure weighing down on her skull, her magic and her soul.

"It has to be," Cat agreed. "We're out of time, Brushfire."

Out of time still left them with roughly three clock-days until the ninesail reached them, if they followed their plan. And enough time for the four key mages to gather once more in Armand's windowed quarters.

Armand didn't want anyone to panic, which meant *he* couldn't panic, which meant he was baking.

Because he was on the edge of panicking. The others, he knew, could feel the Blood King's presence through their magic. *He* could feel the Blood King's presence through the Source. It wasn't simply the pulsing beat of another archmage's link that he'd feel in their presence.

It was a *worldquake* through the entirety of the Deep Magic. The very fabric of the spheres *thrummed* with the power of the being who had come to Stormfall to hunt them. He had known that everyone called the Blood King a god or demigod. He had *known* and *accepted* that the Blood King was more powerful than any mage he'd ever faced, of an entirely different type and nature of power.

It was something else to *feel* it. Armand Bluestaves could draw on the Deep Magic to fuel his power, with a constant connection that lived underneath his heart.

From what he could feel through the Source, the Blood King was basically *made* of the Deep Magic, every piece of him linked to the Source and the Weave that underlay all reality.

If he wasn't a god—and knowing where he'd come from, Armand didn't *want* to call him a god—Armand wasn't quite sure what a god would be.

The being calmly sailing a crewless ship toward them was close enough for this purpose. Close enough that defying him could only lead to their deaths—but Armand didn't think that the Blood King was coming to *negotiate.*

"What do we do?" Brushfire asked, her voice surprisingly calm. He appreciated that, since *he* wanted to run in circles.

"First, we have to understand what is going to happen if we do nothing," Cat said. There was a grim certainty to Armand's Captain's tone, less reassuring than Brushfire's level calm.

"Oathheld Ironhand destroyed a dozen spheres to become immortal," Cat continued. "These spheres were never meant to be seen by anyone other than him after that. I don't know if our presence here is a threat to him—or a reminder, or just an annoyance.

"But he is going to destroy this ship and kill every member of the crew."

Cat's pronouncement hung in the air and only added to Armand's desire to panic—which he focused into checking on the oven.

"So, we need to stop him," Cat continued. "Our crew. Our families. Our *people* are on this ship—and I will neither stand by and quietly go to my death nor quietly permit my crew's.

"If we fail, he will kill us. But if we do not try, he will kill us anyway."

Armand exhaled a long breath and nodded slowly to Cat. His Captain was right. They *did* have to face that, because it put a lot of options on the table that he wouldn't consider otherwise.

"So, how do we fight a god?" Alloy asked. "We're still heading to the Eleventh Ward, but will we have time to do anything of import there?"

"Maybe a day or two, but probably not enough," Brushfire said. "There's neither air nor aether around the Ward."

Armand shivered and conjured an illusion of the old fortress. He could, if he thought about it for a few moments, pick out which light reflected in the distance was the Eleventh Ward, but this gave them a greater level of detail.

"The Ward is not the threat to us," Cat said. "The problem is..."

Armand barely even realized he *had* conjured the oracular spirit before the critter swooped into a section of empty air by the illusion of the asteroid and screamed at him. It circled in that air like an angry cat, then screamed again.

"I think your spirit wants you to look at something," Cat said, looking up at the creature after the interruption. "And I'm afraid I know what. Armand?"

Armand nodded and gestured, shrinking the scale of the illusion and expanding its scope. He'd already shrunk three hundred leagues of rock down to about a yard of translucent gray magic. Now he shrank the image of the Ward again and expanded the illusion to pick up the void around it.

Most of it was empty space but, exactly where the oracular spirit's angry screaming fit would have been on this scale, something shimmered.

The spirit dive-bombed that shimmering, hissing angrily as it passed harmlessly through the illusion.

"What is that?" Alloy asked.

"Can you show us just that area?" Cat asked quietly.

Armand did—but he'd guessed what he was going to see even before the five aether ships grew to a size where they could be identified. After a moment, the five ships—the largest of them not even a cable long—filled the space above his baking counter.

Green light covered their decks and a vague red mist filled their sails—and they were moving.

"From spheres upon spheres away, the Blood King could command wraiths to crew a single ship," Cat said quietly. "Now he is *here*, and I think every warship is the system has been awoken against us.

"We can't fight all of them. But... Armand, this magic. Would it survive him?"

"The wraiths would," Armand said instantly. "They are a thing of the hunger he instilled in these spheres, not of his magic. He commands them, but he is not creating them. But the wraiths can't sail without aether.

"It is his rage that fills their sails, his will that moves them forward. If we... somehow remove the Blood King, they will no longer be able to pursue us, at least."

"So, Alloy and I need to get to the control room," Cat replied. "We need to change course."

"To go where?" Alloy asked.

"Right at the bastard," Cat said flatly. "One way or another, we must face the Blood King. Now that he has arrived, everything else he will conjure is to drive us to him.

"He did not come this far to not finish us himself—and I believe we can set a course where we will reach him before any of the other ships can reach us."

"And what do we do when we reach him?" Armand asked softly.

He certainly didn't see any solid options. They could get lucky with the thunderbolts—and he had some ideas for using their magic to improve the chances of that—but it *would* be luck. The skills Armand had borrowed from Cat in their meld didn't make him any more of a master of aether war than he had been before, but he could see the limitations of that weapon.

If nothing else, hitting a *dodging* target wasn't going to be possible at more than the less than a league where real combat usually took place. Armand understood better now why aether battles always took place at straits and worldlets: *Void Flyer*'s three leagues a minute put most aether-sailing ships to shame, but they still sailed long distances at speeds where no mortal var could *hit* a ship.

They needed to fight while moving more slowly, which meant defenders sought places attackers *had* to go and attackers sought places defenders *had* to protect: straits and the worldlets var lived on.

Void Flyer's need to minimize changes in course made her more predictable as a price of her potential greater speed. The seventy thousand leagues of void they'd crossed since leaving Brokenwright had taken them over thirty days to travel—but an equivalent distance through regular aether spheres in *Star* could have taken twice that.

"I don't see any reason to slow," Brushfire suggested, her thoughts following Armand's. "Can he hit us if we fly past him at three leagues a minute?"

"With regular var and storm staves?" Cat asked. "No. With wraiths and storm staves? I'm not sure. With his own power? Almost certainly."

Their Captain shook his head.

"Passing him is not an option," he said firmly. "He will pursue, if nothing else, and we cannot outrun a demigod.

"I need to go set our course in motion. We have a clock-day to consider our plans. If nothing else... well, *Flyer*'s prow is steel where that ninesail is built of wood. I don't know if *we* would survive ramming his ship, but she won't!"

Alloy and Cat headed for the control deck to set the final movements into motion, leaving Armand alone with Brushfire and his baking. He checked the oven once more. The muffins were almost done.

"Do you *always* bake when you're upset?" she asked from behind him.

"I always bake," Armand said with a chuckle. "My mother once said she could tell how stressed I was by the *quantity* of the baking and how sweet the results were."

He eyed the muffins.

"Of course, I've run out of frosting ingredients and a few other things, so these muffins are sweetened with dried fruit and some of my last molasses," he noted. "My mother's metric probably requires me to have access to a full pantry."

"You aren't eating all of what you're baking," Brushfire observed, walking over to stand next to him. Her presence was steady and reassuring, a warmth in his life as important as Cat's.

Armand wasn't quite sure how to deal with that particular realization. It was part of why he'd made clear to Cat that their relationship couldn't be exclusive, because he had feelings for so few people in his life, he was unwilling to let even one go.

He had the same problem with Brushfire as with Cat, though: she was his sworn servant. In some ways, the situation was *worse*, since as a gobvar, she needed his protection in the Kingdoms more than Cat did—and his protection was extended over her entire tribe at this point.

It probably wasn't going to matter. They had a clock-day, and then they were probably going to die, because Armand Bluestaves had led everyone to disaster.

Brushfire's hand fell heavily on his shoulder, turning him to face her wordlessly and not quite forcing him to meet her gaze and scrutiny.

"Hey," she said quietly. "I did imply a question you didn't answer before you started staring into the oven like your muffins would explode. What *are* you doing with all of your baking?"

"Been trading it to Faithful for gossip," he admitted. Faithful Hammerhead was the second-oldest member of the Hammerheads. "I walk the ship a bit, but she's been keeping me up to date with everyone's stories."

He grinned at a thought.

"It's *amazing* how much people tell the var who feeds them," he observed. "Not harmed, I'm sure, by Faithful being... well, Faithful. I presume you understand?"

Faithful Hammerhead was kind and clever and a brilliant cook—though not so good a *baker*, which was part of how Armand had recruited her as his spy. She also did not think about consequences, long-term planning or much beyond the current moment and task in front of her.

"Faithful is very precious to us and very *useful*, but even she recognizes her limits most of the time," Brushfire agreed. "But I learned when I was quite young not to underestimate her *memory*."

"Exactly," Armand agreed. "She knows everything about your tribe, and while she has some sense of discretion, she is... well, her. So, I know, for example, that Fistfall and Bogsong have sorted out their awkwardness to mutual satisfaction."

"To be fair, no one on this ship is as subtle about their relations as they think," Brushfire told him drily. "And yes, that includes you and Cat."

"The meld nexus leaves us few secrets," Armand said quietly. He hadn't wanted to keep anything secret—especially not from Brushfire—but something in her tone warned him to walk carefully. "Both of us, I think, would have denied our feelings to ourselves given our situation.

"The nexus took that choice from us. Our feelings became part of why the meld was so dangerous to us. Made it easier to fall into each other and risk our sense of self, of identity."

He shook his head.

"If you were to meld with another mage, it would be safer?" she asked.

"I have a better sense of the precautions needed now, too," he told her. "And I am not convinced that being an *archmage* didn't cause as many problems as any emotional entanglement."

"Is that our best option, then?" Brushfire asked. "You and I should be able to meld safely, which would give us more power to fight the Blood King?"

While Cat was probably the most *skilled* mage aboard *Void Flyer*, Armand's archmage nature made him the most *powerful* without question. Brushfire, though, was the most powerful *after* Armand, with inner reserves and energy channels greater than the elvar Captain's.

And Cat was far from a weak mage. He was easily stronger than the rest of the officers, though Alloy was skilled enough in his own way to make up much of the difference. The other officers were decently strong mages, but they didn't rival Brushfire's natural power or Cat's trained expertise.

Fistfall was a wildcard, where it was difficult to judge the novice mage's strength so far. His lack of *skill* put him behind the ship's original officers, though, where Brushfire's power and exceptional learning speed put her above the others.

Really, it was those three, Alloy, Brushfire and Cat, who would deliver survival or victory when they met the Blood King. But there were problems, and Armand sighed at Brushfire's suggestion.

"I do not know that you and I would be much safer," he confessed, letting her interpret that as she wished. "I *do* know that adding one mage, even one of *your* power, to the meld nexus doesn't add much in terms of magical strength to my own power.

"The meld nexus with Cat was necessary to make up for skills I lack. I remember enough of what we did in that nexus to repeat much of that on my own, and it was *my* power behind our defeat of the twentysail."

He shook his head gently.

"No, Brushfire, I don't think the meld nexus is our answer. I fear the answer falls to me... and I have no concept of how a single archmage may defeat a demigod."

He turned to check his muffins again, realizing he'd let them sit too long, and cursed softly as he pulled the oven open and calmed its heating crystals.

He didn't hear Brushfire leaving.

He certainly didn't notice that she'd taken a book.

CHAPTER 47

AFTER A QUARTER-DAY IN THE CONTROL ROOM BROUGHT CAT NO answers and an abortive attempt at sleep proved a waste of time, he retreated to the chart room and studied the maps with a dire expression.

One of the crew had added flags for the three groups of warships, all heading slowly in their direction. None of them would reach *Void Flyer* before the void ship intersected with the Blood King's own vessel, but their threat continued to herd them toward that confrontation.

Which was their purpose, of course. Cat doubted that the Blood King had come all this way to watch his wraiths tear their ship apart. More likely than not, the King wanted to tear them apart with his own magic.

Or he figured they had some weapon that would destroy the ships without much fighting. They *had*, after all, taken down the largest warship Cat had ever seen. *He* knew that had been luck and taking utterly reckless risks, but he wasn't sure how much the Blood King knew of what had happened to his distant minions.

The thunderbolts weren't going to do them much good against the Blood King's ship, he knew. They'd *try* anyway—it was sufficiently out of the ordinary that the gobvar demigod might not see it coming, and until he started *dodging*, they still had a chance to hit.

Cat had to focus on destroying the ninesail, but in the back of his mind was the constant niggling thought that destroying the ship might not even kill the Blood King. *Immortal* was pretty specific, after all, and the ship was probably a *convenience* to the King, not a necessity.

His only real hope was that they could leave the Blood King drifting in the void while they blazed past him to Drinkstar. Without the ship, he hoped that it would take the old gobvar a long, *long* time to make it back to the Clan Spheres.

Sighing, Cat picked up and shuffled the oracle deck. The cards moved readily under his hands, their magic warming to his touch.

"Give me... an option," he told them, and dealt a card onto the table.

The card bounced twice and fell flat. The Blood King.

"Not helpful," he growled, and dealt a second card. It landed on top of the first, showing an impossible face: the Blood King again.

There *was* only one Blood King card in the deck.

He dealt a third time. Another Blood King joined the first two on the charts, and he swallowed a curse as he turned the deck over and fanned it out. Like *that*, the cards looked normal—but their magic protested at the indignity.

He turned it back over and dealt a fourth card. He wasn't surprised when a *fourth* Blood King landed on the chart, though.

"We're too close," he muttered. "Whatever effect he has on scrying, we're *inside* it now."

Cat shook his head and shuffled the cards back into the deck. He needed to talk to Fistfall and Alloy. Between those two, he might get a sense of how far away they could fire with the ballista.

The one thing his quarter-day of watching the cursed ship had given him was that it *wasn't* really maneuvering. Just charging directly toward them at a speed no regular aether ship could match.

That gave them a chance, after all.

He only made it halfway to the door before a mental blow drove him to his knees, as a *presence* swept over his ship and drove spikes of power and anger into his mind.

Cat struggled against the power in his mind, finding the strength to push back against it magically, mentally and physically. He rose to his feet, struggling for breath, and then released the breath in a curse.

"*Void take you*," he snarled.

"It did that long ago," a smooth voice said, echoing around the chart room. "And I took it in turn. And created it. Forged it. From the void you curse, I created arms and armies. From the void you curse, I drew forth power.

"Through the void you *violated*, I became a god."

The accent was strange to Cat's ears, with the cropped sibilants he would associate with the Gobvar Clans, but the paced syllables and smooth tone he associated with High Court nobility.

"You are Oathheld Ironhand," he told the air.

Anger spiked through him, nearly driving him to the ground again.

"That var died a long time ago," the voice replied. "Twelve spheres the pyre for his murder. Twice and tenfold repaid upon the hands that threw him forth. *I am your King.*"

Somehow, Cat remained standing despite the force of the ancient Will that pushed against him—the power, the arrogance, the *rage* that defined the being projecting onto his ship.

"I am an elvar of the Great Houses, sworn to the High Court and the Sixteen," Cat snarled. "I kneel to no gods, no kings. *I am of the High Court. Let kings tremble!*"

He mustered his power on a subtler field than he was used to. He focused *his* will and forged it into a mental shield, driving the presence around him back.

"You dare defy me? You, who have violated my home and stolen a dead name from the words of the White Mountain? Beg for mercy, little elvar, and I will make your death quick."

"Get away from my crew," Cat shouted, throwing the shield outward. He could *feel* the presence pushing against him as he drove it away—and he didn't stop at the chart room. He drove his shield farther out until he encompassed the control room as well.

Then he felt Faith Streamwater and Alloy Bellowforge's magic spill out from the control room, their mental shields less refined than his but real enough. He layered them into his magic, linking spells in the old-fashioned way, and expanded the shield again, sweeping through deck after deck.

Bogsong's addition to the spell from her quarters was fitful to start but picked up after a few moments. She was a weak mage, but she was learning to make up for it with skill—and he realized the *fits* had been her walking Fistfall through the same process.

The young gobvar lacked skill but he had *enthusiasm*, adding two more mages to the shield that now spread through the kitchens and dormitory decks.

Brushfire's power came in late, her will rising from the officers' deck alongside Bogsong's and Fistfall's. Their combined power drove the Blood King's presence from their ship, deck by deck, room by room.

They drove it from the infirmary, and Crane failed to join them. Cat *knew* that meant he'd have to send a runner. He'd felt enough of the Blood King's power that he feared what that lack meant.

And his fear spiked harder as they pushed the expanding shield through the observatory deck where Armand's quarters lay. The archmage's power didn't join them—and Cat had been *relying* on it.

Even with four other mages, he didn't know if they had the strength to shield the entire ship without Armand. He pushed. He *pushed*, sweeping more decks, but the counterpressure was growing.

Three-quarters of the ship was shielded against the Blood King's power now, but that left key decks and sections of the engines unprotected—key *var* unprotected.

Then, suddenly, Armand was there. The archmage's power wove beneath the quilted shield of the other four mages, providing a supportive layer that allowed them to push out again. There was a sense of surprise and anger from the Blood King's overwhelming presence... and then it was gone.

A single thought hung in his head and he knew it wasn't his.

Impressive. But you have mere hours, elvar child, until you are in the reach of far more direct magics. You have trespassed where no mortal var should walk, seen what no mortal var should see.

These are my spheres—and for breaching them, you will die.

BRUSHFIRE CLOSED EMBERLIGHT CRANE'S STARING EYES and gestured for Sky to pull a cloth over the *Flyer*'s third officer and doctor. The only person on the ship who might have been able to confirm what had killed Crane *was* Crane, but Brushfire could guess.

The Blood King hadn't even really been attacking them. It had been more than an attempt to communicate, but she suspected that if the demigod could act directly at that distance, they would all be dead.

Even so, the fear and stress had been too much for their doctor—and not *just* Crane. Six others had died before the mages had driven the gobvar King's power from their ship.

Including Faithful Hammerhead, which tore at Brushfire's heart. Her mother's cousin had been present through her entire life. Never one to lead, Faithful had still lived up to her name and been a rock of support for the whole tribe for Brushfire's entire life.

Now she was gone and Brushfire didn't even have time to go see her body, because every minute that passed, they were half a dozen leagues closer to the Blood King. One of the officers had needed to check on Crane, to be certain they'd lost one of their mages, but even that was taking more time than she could justify.

"Take care of them, Sky," she told the sailor. "Thank you."

"We've got them, sir," Sky told her. "We're going to get the bastard for this, right? And for the others?"

Brushfire bared her teeth in what *no one* would mistake for a smile.

"Or we'll die trying, Sky; you have my word," she told the elvar. "No more."

There was only one answer left. Well, other than *ramming* the bastard, anyway—and if her plan failed, they'd probably get to that one, too.

She strode from the infirmary to find Armand waiting outside, his blue robe in his hands as he worked it like a stubborn lump of dough.

"Brushfire."

"Armand. Come with me," she told him.

He did, adding a touch of confusion to his clear distress.

"I have a plan," Brushfire continued. "What did you want?"

"I… don't know," he confessed. "I feel like everyone is looking to me, but I don't have any answers."

"You do, I think," she said bluntly. "You're just afraid of them, and we're past time for fear."

He didn't argue with her, just keeping step with her as she reached the stairwell.

"What's your plan?" he demanded at last, something in his voice telling her he was guessing part of it.

"Well, first, *this*."

She was enough taller than Armand that kissing him required half-stepping, half-hopping to a point two steps lower than him on the stairwell. His surprise bought her enough time to do that, but he didn't attempt to pull away, either, though his surprise was clear.

"Oh."

"Yeah. You and Cat aren't the only ones whose emotions are going to fuck up the meld, are they?" she asked him.

"No. My feelings for… both of you complicate matters and could render the meld nexus extremely dangerous."

"And one mage wouldn't add enough," she agreed. "But I read the book, Armand. Each mage is a multiplier, not an addition. Two regular mages working together are more like two and a quarter. But *three* is more like *five*.

"Adding us to *you* isn't much, but where adding *one* regular mage—or one and a quarter—wouldn't make much difference, adding *four* mages' worth of power?" she asked. "We will not quietly lie down and die, Armand. I think you *have* to be the anchor, but it needs to be all three of us.

"Shaman and Captain, Captain and Archmage. *Three.* Against *him.* I'll back those odds if you'll try them. If you have the strength."

"I have the strength," Armand told her. "But I am afraid. Of losing myself... Of losing Cat. Of losing *you.* Of losing us all. Of *failing.*"

"If the Blood King kills us all, I think we fail," Brushfire pointed out. "Wouldn't you rather die *trying?*"

"I do not think you understand what we risk," the archmage said, but he was starting to move up the stairwell. "Death will come, eventually. But first we would lose everything we are into a slurry that might not contain *anything* of *any* of us once the damage is done."

"Or maybe there's something beyond the line where this experimenter panicked," she told him. "Something he was afraid to risk enough to try—or something that the presence of an archmage might change."

"I doubt it. But we have no choice," Armand agreed with a sigh. "We must try."

Armand was more than a bit dazed by the sudden turn of events as he trailed Brushfire onto the control deck. All four of the ship's surviving officers were now present, though Streamwater and Smallwolf both looked clearly distressed.

Cat, somehow, only seemed calmer and more certain of things as things grew closer to the knife—and Alloy had settled into a frozen mask of imperturbability that was clearly a mask but otherwise revealed nothing.

"Range?" Cat asked, glancing back at Armand and Brushfire and giving them a welcoming nod.

"Four hundred leagues. Closing rate just ticked up to seven," Streamwater reported. "That's not on our side, which means he decided to push that ship up to four leagues a minute."

"I wouldn't expect her masts to take that for long," Cat observed. "Long enough, I suppose. Any word from Fistfall?"

"He sent a runner saying he was going out onto the hull five minutes ago," Smallwolf reported. Her voice almost broke as she said her lover had stepped out into the void, but she bore on steadily.

"We've discussed the plan," Cat told her. "At this point, he's to fire whenever he thinks he can hit until he's out of bolts—and to be back inside the hull before we reach a hundred leagues."

"Is he going to hit anything?" Brushfire asked.

Armand was still trailing in her wake but stopped at the edge of the central circle dais holding the sextants and main control wheel. Streamwater and Smallwolf had the sextants, and Cat, of course, held the wheel.

Alloy was seated at the instrumentation panel off to the side, and Armand moved to join him. Somehow, he knew that he needed to be on the control deck. Whatever happened next, he needed to be *there*.

An hour left until things were decided, he judged.

"There is a chance that he will hit *once*," Cat told Brushfire, loudly enough that everyone could hear him. "Right now, the Blood King is splitting his focus across over a dozen ships. All of them are flying straight courses, with no maneuvers.

"That means we *might* hit. And that hit might be lucky—but as soon as the Blood King realizes what's happening, he will maneuver that ship so we won't hit a second time."

Armand stood silently, waiting for Brushfire to make her pitch.

"What range is he going to be able to hit us at?" she asked—and it took Armand a moment to realize she was asking him.

He coughed to clear his throat, then shrugged as he recognized his complete lack of knowledge.

"*I* wouldn't be able to stretch past a couple of leagues, even with what I have learned from Cat," he told them. "We would be well served to assume he could strike at ten—or even a *hundred*—times that."

"Well, we'll try to get you to that couple of leagues," Cat promised. "I have a few tricks up my sleeve to make him miss his first few tries."

"Fistfall has fired," Streamwater reported. "Fourteen leagues a minute compared to us. Twenty-one leagues relative to the Blood King's ship. Eighteen minutes to contact."

"So, we wait," Cat declared.

Seconds ticked by like molasses, interrupted only by Streamwater reporting the continuing sequence of Fistfall firing. He'd had five thunderbolts loaded into the magazine on the ballista—plus four spares—and he'd emptied the magazine in a pattern that would hopefully give them a hit.

They waited. Armand knew what Brushfire's plan was. He knew that he *could* probably wreck the ninesail if they got close enough, but he doubted they would manage it.

He was surprised that she hadn't said anything. His shaman stood next to his Captain, silently watching the stars where they couldn't even *see* the enemy.

"I prefer it when I can see the people coming at me," Cat said aloud. "Or at least their ships."

"Enough of our ways to see that ship are magical that we wouldn't see *him*," Armand pointed out. "His shield against scrying would block any of the magical telescopes."

There was very little to the magic Armand had seen Cat use to survey a sphere—or the telescopes in the sextants, for that matter—that would count as *scrying*. But it would still be blocked. The shield around the Blood King was the strongest Armand had ever sensed.

"I figured that when my oracle deck stopped drawing anything *except* the Blood King," Cat pointed out wryly. "Time, Streamwater?"

"Should be about… now."

There was nothing. A strike by even a single thunderbolt would have been visible as a brighter star above them, but a bolt that missed would just continue on into the void. Four more bolts were in the void, closing the distance behind the first, and Armand tried not to hold his breath.

"*There*," Streamwater suddenly snapped. "Last bolt hit one of the masts!"

"Damage?" Cat asked.

There was a long silence, one that stretched on past Armand's liking.

"She lost two of the three masts on one deck, but it doesn't look like there was any hull damage," Streamwater finally reported. "He's slowing down to balance the sails and maneuver, I think. Looks like two leagues a minute."

"Well. Let's get some maneuvers of our own in play," Cat ordered, reaching for the ship's wheel. "We're out of time and out of clever ideas. We dodge whatever we can, get the archmage into range for *his* magic, and then we ram them."

"The prow is made of steel, but it's not particularly reinforced," Alloy warned. "I don't know if we'll survive that."

"We won't survive doing nothing," Cat replied. "So, we do what we can."

"There is one more option," Brushfire said, finally pulling the book she'd apparently taken from Armand's tables out of her jacket and laying it on the secondary instrument panel next to Cat. "I've gone through the meld ritual you and Armand did, Cat.

"The effects of additional mages act as multipliers," she told the Captain. "Adding just me or you to the mix doesn't change much for Armand, but adding *both* of us does.

"Especially since we're all using foci from the same archmage. The original tests found *that* helped, but didn't have access to an archmage to test. But since Armand made his own foci and you and I have foci from him…"

Cat looked back at Armand, who raised his hands palms upward in a shrug.

"She's not wrong," he told the elvar. "And we're out of other choices. The three of us will be more powerful than the two of us, and it *should* help stave off the effect of our having melded before."

"If three is good, four is better," Alloy interrupted grumpily, stepping into a conversation that had excluded the rest of the room with clear intent. "And, well…"

He gestured around the three of them.

"*Emotions* fucked up the first meld. The bloody emotional polyhedral the three of you have going on isn't going to help this one any better. You need someone involved in the meld who *isn't* tied up in each other's bits; you get me?"

Armand couldn't help laughing, shaking his head at the darvar.

"He's… not wrong," he admitted with a sheepish smile. "But you know the risk you're taking, Alloy?"

"Loss of self, loss of mind, loss of life?" the darvar reeled off. "Yeah. But *that*"—he gestured at the red-sailed ship approaching them—"is definitely going to cause loss of life. So, we fight."

Alloy nodded firmly. Brushfire met Armand's gaze and nodded too, leaving the archmage holding Cat's gaze.

"I don't see any other way," he told his Captain. "And I don't know that even the four of us together can take him. But I *know* that the prophecy put you and me and Brushfire together for more than just making sure we had the right crew for this trip.

"And Alloy, I'm realizing, was always meant to be here. The four of us, as one, against the void. It was meant to be."

Cat nodded slowly.

"You're right.

"What about us?" Streamwater asked, gesturing at Smallwolf. "Four mages good... but six mages?"

"Someone has to fly the ship if this goes sideways," Cat told her. "Someone has to finish the mission. That will fall to you two and Fistfall, to take care of our crew and find out what's going on with the dragons.

"Understand?"

From the second officer's expression, she hadn't been thinking about *that* part of the task before them. Just surviving the next twenty minutes.

Which, to be fair, was what all of this was about.

"Foci," Armand instructed. Each of his sworn servants produced their foci. With all of them made by him, they had a resonance he didn't normally pay attention to. As the three other mages gathered around him, that resonance seemed to hum around him.

He took Cat and Brushfire's hands, covering Brushfire's focus as he did so, and watched as they took Alloy's hands.

"Let us... *begin*."

He closed his eyes... and *they* opened theirs.

Four became one with a smoothness that made the merger of Cat and Armand seem rough and unsteady. Two of them knew the meld nexus now, and while the pull between the three emotionally entangled with each other was strong, that knowledge and Alloy's calm steadiness stabilized the entire link.

When two had become one, the pull together had been ever-present and dangerous, even if they hadn't realized it at the time. Now, with *four*, that pull was balanced. The fears passed aside into certainty.

Other certainties spilled out around with that. Armand and Brushfire's feelings for each other came crystal clear alongside Armand and Cat's feelings. The complexity of the *emotional polyhedral*, as Alloy had named it, was laid bare and naked.

Brushfire's feelings for *Cat* were there too, but even the four-as-one were surprised by how little concern that raised. Cat didn't return them as she did, but they were not unwelcome.

Three-as-one or even a normal conversation might have sorted out their issues. Or maybe it was Alloy's calm outside perspective on it that allowed the polyhedral to be assessed, weighed, *decided on* and put aside for future resolution.

The realization that the meld nexus could become useful to relationship counselors across the spheres brought a smile to all of their faces, but then the moment of threat was upon them.

With Cat's sense of the aether and Armand's sense of the weave of magic, the void around them fell into clear patterns. They conjured an illusion of their enemy, alongside a constant steady sense of the distance between the two ships.

But while the scrying illusion couldn't *see* the Blood King, their senses could feel him. He was too powerful, too immense a pool of magic and emotion, to hide at this distance. Somehow, his rage, his anger, his *hunger* combined to register on Cat's aether sense—almost an *anti*-aether, unlike both void and aether.

It was the same sensation he'd been able to track the wraiths and the hunger of the sphere with across four void spheres, but so much denser and fiercer as to make its structure and nature clear.

The Blood King and the ritual of his ascension were antithetical to the very nature of the aether spheres. He had been born of a wound in the aether. The wound remained, and its damage had pursued them across their journey, but *he* was the blade that cut the fabric of reality.

They wrapped the power of an archmage around *Void Flyer* in a shield of power and will. The power of an archmage *multiplied*—but as their ship passed a hundred leagues, they faced the truth of their enemy.

The bolt of power crossed the distance between the two ships in a moment, a blaze of bruised fire whose mere *presence* tore at their souls and magic. The shield they'd summoned held, and they tightened it in places they didn't know *existed* before, driving back the subtler warping effects before they could harm the crew.

It was a shock when the four-as-one realized they could *feel* the Blood King's frustration. Either the ancient gobvar was unused to concealing his emotions at all, or the mages who could sense the aether—and his emotions through it—were rarer among the gobvar than anyone thought.

Or perhaps it was an intersection of not only being in the void—removing the background sensation of an aether sphere—but being in the very void where the King had ascended. *There,* he was unguarded.

There was no one to guard against except them, after all, and he was very determined to kill them.

The Blood King's next step was an entire salvo of the same bolts, bruised purple-green fire hammering against the shield the four-as-one held around *Void Flyer*. Again and again, two or three or four at a time, blasts that should have shattered their fragile ship hammered against the shield.

Not as many struck as could have. The four-as-one couldn't spare the attention to fly the ship, but Faith Streamwater held the wheel, and if she wasn't as good a navigator or pilot as Cat Greentrees, few were.

She ran the lift crystals at full power and spent fuel the four-as-one wasn't sure they could *afford*, but she dodged almost half of the bolts. Not by seeing them coming but by simply not being where the Blood King thought *Void Flyer* would be.

Without those maneuvers, the four-as-one knew they would have been overwhelmed. *With* them, they held against the King's wrath for ten leagues. Twenty. Thirty!

But seventy leagues remained, and the meld nexus couldn't strike from much farther away than Armand on his own could. The Blood King ceased his strikes, and they could feel his angry contemplation at a distance.

A whole minute passed in silence. Two. Ten more leagues of distance vanished before the King struck again, and this time, there were no games or distractions.

Pure dark power, the essence of the void itself, suddenly hammered against their shield from every direction. Force and energy pressed in on *Flyer* and their shield, trying to crush ship and crew and meld nexus alike.

They threw open the link to the Source that beat under Armand's heart, drawing on the substance of the universe to defy the attack. As the Blood King brought void and nothingness, they drew on the aether and the Weave, the Source of all reality, to protect them.

And the Source answered them. Power flowed from Armand's link like a torrent, supporting their shield and allowing them to push back the Blood King's pressure. A precarious balance hung in the void as they guarded the ship and he continued to try to crush them.

Another ten leagues passed while the balance hung in, then all of the void pressure suddenly collapsed into a single point, a spear of force stabbing directly at the control deck where the meld nexus stood.

Their enemy had been paying attention—but so had Faith Streamwater, and in the same moment the encompassing sphere of force vanished, she hit the engines at full power.

A spike of force aimed for the tip of the ship struck close to the base. Weakened and deflected by the shield as well, it tore through metal and decking with crushing force—and where the engines had thundered a moment before, there was only silence.

The four-as-one had all of Alloy's knowledge of the ship he'd built, and their illusory eyes gave them the knowledge to judge the damage.

It was bad. It was *really* bad. The only *good* news was that the fuel lines that had been torn apart alongside a third of four decks were the ones that had been cut out from earlier damage. But machinery was shattered, supplies thrown into the void and var killed.

And there were more var still on those decks, var who *would* die as the air escaped into the void. They drew on the Source once more—reckless; they *all* knew there were debts to be paid drawing from the Source and only hoped they could spread it across all four of them instead of leaving it on Armand—and slammed a new shield into place.

Not to shield against the enemy but to hold the air in while their people got out. Nine var were dead, but another fourteen were on the other parts of those four decks, already running for the stairwell that *should* still hold air.

At the same time, their main shield tightened, weaving a barrier that should hold against even the void lance that had broken through the engine decks.

Moments later, it *did* hold, as another spearpoint of void drove at the control deck, and *this* time, the engines couldn't answer Streamwater's commands. They couldn't hold both, but not all of the crew were safe.

For a few moments, seemingly eternal, the four-as-one faced the choice between abandoning half a dozen var to their *preventable* deaths or possibly losing the entire ship.

And then someone *else's* magic was there, taking over the barrier keeping air in those decks. Fistfall Hammerhead couldn't *create* enough air to fill four decks of *Void Flyer*, but he could keep the air that was already *there* inside the ship. He stood outside the stairwell on the lowest of the four broken decks, his wand in front of him as he channeled his power into protecting the crew.

The meld nexus left him to it, refocusing all of their power in time to stop a crushing blow of void and force that tried to slam the entire ship sideways and force it onto a course of the Blood King's choosing.

A course, they calculated instantly with Cat's skills and knowledge, that would have kept them outside any mortal mage or archmage's reach of the Blood King's ship.

They pushed his blow aside, keeping the ship on course as *Flyer* crossed more leagues. A mere twenty leagues separated them now, but the nexus couldn't reach that far.

The demigod could, but they could *feel* that they had him spooked. No one and nothing had ever withstood the power of the Blood King of the Gobvar this long. His power was forged of blood and murder, stolen from the fabric of the spheres and reforged through some ancient thing of the void.

And with the Source itself buoying their power, the meld nexus defied him. Every strike was blocked or deflected as they closed. Every attempt to shunt them aside defeated.

Each league they closed, his blows grew stronger and more desperate. Their own defense grew equally desperate, drawing more and more dangerously on the Source as Armand's link became the only thing that could sustain them.

The other mages multiplied how much power the four-as-one could command at once, but they were far beyond the reserves of any mortal mage or archmage. Only the Source and the Deep Magic could sustain them this far.

Ten leagues, and they risked the impossible. A bolt of lightning formed at the very point of *Void Flyer*, as far away from them as they could manage to create it, then struck across the void in the blink of an eye.

They'd aimed at the main hull, but the Blood King's power flared almost casually, deflecting it away. He was *too* casual, and the bolt still struck home, tearing away another set of sails.

He tried harder next time, but the nexus allowed for that. Not quite enough—but enough that more sails were lost. His ninesail was now down to about *four* sets of sails, and the wraiths crewing his ship didn't know how to manage the imbalance.

The Blood King's ship dove forward, beginning a long, helpless curve that threw off his next strike. Only half a dozen leagues remained between the two ships, and the meld nexus leaned on Cat.

Even Alloy didn't know as much about how an aether ship was put together. But it was his knowledge of the weaknesses of key components that matched with Cat's knowledge of the ships to recognize the chance.

It was Brushfire's knowledge of the exact mechanisms and structures, of the maintenance and workings of sails and decks, that gave them the angle.

And it was Armand, with his power, his knowledge and his link to the Deep Magic of the spheres, that gave them the strength to strike.

Half a dozen wisps of light—each the size of a var, though distance rendered them mere sparks—appeared around the decks of the Blood King's ship. They dove toward the decks in a carefully managed sequence, the first explosion sending debris scattering in every direction as it opened the hull for the key strikes.

The Blood King saw them and acted. Three wisps were smothered before they could explode. But one made it into the starboard stave gallery, the explosion scattering but failing to rupture the storm staves along the gallery's deck.

The three headed for the staves had been a distraction. One of the real threats had been squashed, but one made it to the very core of the ship—where it *merged* into the main lodestone keel, the length of magical metal that both held the ship's length together and gave it a sense of *down*.

For a single heartbeat, the wisp suffused the keel with its energy, saturating the central *third* of the cable-long lodestone beam.

And then it exploded—and those seventy yards of magically dense lodestone exploded with it. The chain reaction turned the entire keel into shrapnel, scything through the ship with speed and energy that drew more from the lodestone's nature than the explosion that fueled it.

Now storm staves ruptured, first one deck and then another and then the third detonated in blue-white flashes of electricity and fire. The very arcane powers and devices that held together the gobvar warship were torn from their careful balances and unleashed.

Four catastrophic explosions grew until they consumed each other and only one strangely colored explosion thundered across the void, barely a league from *Void Flyer's* flank as they blazed past it.

CHAPTER 51

Is he dead?

The question echoed across the meld nexus, four minds thinking it as one as they turned their senses to the fate of their foe. The destruction of the Blood King's ship was one thing, an unquestionable victory, but the Blood King claimed immortality and had *proven* it more than once.

How much of those stories were just that—stories—was impossible to know. Brushfire knew the tales from her people. Armand had old histories, and Cat had newer reports and intelligence assessments, but all of it was based off what other people had seen.

There were no firsthand accounts of the Blood King shrugging off death. Just enough stories to convince most that there had to be some truth.

It took a dozen heartbeats or more to confirm the truth. The Blood King was dead, the presence that weighed on their minds and senses slowly fading away, scraps of his essence scattering across the void.

But *something* told the four-as-one not to release the nexus yet. It might, they knew, be the danger of the meld. They might be unwilling or unable to step back from the merge at this point, even as they were victorious.

Or it could be the instincts that kept guiding them in the right direction, even when formal divination failed.

They felt the scraps of the Blood King's essence scatter, spread across leagues of empty void by the force that had broken his physical form.

That was likely *what* they were feeling, they realized—his body had been destroyed by the explosion, rendered into pieces now scattering with the debris of his ship.

And then those scraps of essence began to move on their own, changing direction as they began to draw toward each other.

They had killed the Blood King, but just *killing* him wasn't enough. He was re-forming, his energy gathering back together at speeds no ship could match.

Void Flyer's speed was taking them away from the site of his death at speed. The four-as-one were rapidly passing out of their reach of the re-forming King's essence and form, but if he could reach them as he had while he was aboard his ship, they were going to be in real trouble.

The shield re-formed with a shared thought, but they could feel their shared depletion. Even drawing on the Source might not be enough to carry them out of the King's range, but they would defend their ship and their people until either everyone was safe or the four-as-one died.

The pieces were converging, scraps of energy forming into chunks large enough to radiate new emotion—a level of anger that dwarfed the offended self-righteous rage that had driven the Blood King so far.

Now he was *truly* furious with them, and they couldn't see any way to stop him re-forming and coming after them.

What do we do?

That the question was even consciously asked was its own answer. No one in the nexus knew. They were the only hope for *Void Flyer*'s crew. The only hope for the quest to save the spheres from whatever the dragons were up to in the Clan Spheres.

But if what they had already done couldn't destroy the Blood King, they had nothing left. Without the extra force of releasing the pent-up energy inherent in any aether ship, they couldn't strike as hard as they already had.

The void.

The void hung around them, every place between worlds and rocks and the outerlit sphere robbed of its aether and left with only emptiness.

And, permeated through it like a bruise upon the skin of the spheres, the sickly hungry energy left of the Blood King's ascension.

The hunger.

The wraiths were merely a manifestation, but the four-as-one knew the feel, the magical *scent* of the wraiths now, and they grabbed the ribbons and remnants of the Blood King's crew. They were too far away to summon light and damage the wraith remnants, but they didn't want to this time.

This time, they pulled those remnants together, guiding the hunger wraiths' own nature to form them back into a single ball of green mist. The nexus formed that mist into ribbons, strips of energy and essence to achieve the impossible.

Pieces of the Blood King's own ascension ritual became the bindings to hold his fragments apart.

A net forged of wraith essence caught the closest piece of his essence before it could reach another chunk, pulling it away—and then something *clicked*.

The nexus lost control. They'd been using the net to catch the Blood King's essence, but suddenly, a *new* power had control.

For a moment, the four-as-one thought the Blood King had reassembled enough to exert control over his wraiths… and then the fragment they'd captured *vanished*, the mist-like trap they'd caught it in compressing with sudden speed and hunger.

Oh, gods. It ate *him.*

New dancing ribbons of purple-green light swept across the void now, forming out of nothing but the light from the outersphere as the *hunger* that defined the void spheres finally found a meal that could sate it.

A swarm of dancing lights converged on the largest piece of the Blood King's essence, and for a moment, they could *feel* the struggle as the fragments of the King's Will tried to exert control on the hunger he had created and controlled for a thousand dances.

But the shards were not equal to the whole. The Will that had dominated the hunger of the void spheres to his commands failed, and fragment after fragment of the Blood King just… popped out of existence, consumed in reverse by the very ritual that had created him.

The four-as-one watched in fascinated horror as their enemy's immortal essence was eaten by the same wound in the spheres that had created it.

We can let go now.

There was a moment of fear that they wouldn't be able to. It was slow and delicate, separating one entity into four.

A single mind became four.

A single magic became four.

And one synchronized heartbeat became... *eight?*

CHAPTER 52

Cᴀᴛ ꜱᴛᴜᴍʙʟᴇᴅ ʙᴀᴄᴋᴡᴀʀᴅ, ɢʀᴀʙʙɪɴɢ ᴏɴᴇ ᴏꜰ ᴛʜᴇ ꜱᴇxᴛᴀɴᴛꜱ ᴛᴏ hold himself up as he drew in a deep staggering breath and tried to find his equilibrium. His center.

Except his center was off-balance. He used his heartbeat to balance—he used a carefully trained heartbeat and breath to count *time* away from a clock!—and now his heartbeat was accompanied by a second pulse, a half-moment later, in perfect rhythm.

He focused on his breath, touching his chest and trying to find a physical sensation of the second beat. It was... both there and not there, even to his hand, and he finally realized what he was feeling.

He'd spent enough time in Armand Bluestaves' head now to know how the archmage felt his link to the Source. *A second heartbeat, a comforting presence nestled under his heart.*

It wasn't an organ that was beating. It was a rhythmic pulse of power. It was the Source, the Deep Magic. It was the link that divided mage from archmage... and Cat Greentrees hadn't *had* that link when he'd entered the meld nexus.

He touched it mentally and it cheerfully responded to him, a gentle rush of power that eased the fatigue in his limbs.

For now, at least. He knew enough about archmagi to know he'd pay a price later. He'd just...

He'd been *forbidden*, by elvar law, from standing the Archmage Trial. His sister had passed, so the expectation was that *he* would have children to allow that potential to pass down the next generation.

In denying him the Trial, the elvar had kept a powerful regular mage that they might have lost in the Trial *and* someone who could theoretically have children with the same potential.

And now the pulsing link of an archmage lingered in his chest. He looked up at the other three and smiled wryly.

"Not just me, I'm guessing," he told them. "What *happened*?"

"We opened my link too far," Armand said. "Somehow... instead of killing me, that woke something up in each of you. I..."

"The Source *wanted* us to win," Brushfire said into the silence. "The Blood King's power was something... oppositional to the Deep Magic. To the spheres themselves. So... the essence we were drawing on was *trying* to help."

"I have the distinct feeling that *forming a meld nexus to fight a god* isn't that much more survivable a training method than the traditional Trial," Alloy said, his voice shaky. "What... what do we *do*?"

"For now, we need to rest," Cat declared. He turned to Streamwater and reached out to clasp his second officer's shoulder.

"Your maneuvers, Faith, saved us all," he told her. "We couldn't have held against his full power. You made all of the difference."

"I... had to do *something*," she whispered. "What *happened*?"

"We fought him. We killed him. He tried to... un-die, and then the void spheres *ate* him," Brushfire laid out flatly. "The very hunger that created him destroyed him. There was nothing left of his essence by the time we broke the nexus. Do you feel anything now, Cat?"

He considered his aether sense, an old friend that felt a touch strange at that moment.

"Nothing," he told them. "Not... even the hunger now. It's like the sphere is sated by consuming him. At least for now."

"Or by returning his essence to the wound that created him, something has begun to heal," Armand said—a guess, Cat knew. "Even if that's the case, though, it will take a thousand dances for the damage done to these spheres to heal."

"Better healing, however slowly, than forever injured," Brushfire said. "If we all have a link to the Source now... what does that even *mean*?"

"That I will swiftly need to give you all as much of the training you would have received prior to the Trial as we can pass on," Armand said grimly. "There are dangers to what you have gained, and you have none of the training for them.

"You are *archmagi* now." His smile was still grim—but real. "I guess *Shaman and Captain, Captain and Archmage*, just became even *more* incomplete."

"I think you are still our archmage, Armand," Cat promised. Not just in the personal sense, either. If nothing else, Armand was the only one recognized by the Academies in the Court and Kingdoms. Without that recognition, the link alone wouldn't give, say, Brushfire protection against the usual bigotry against her var.

"We need to see to the damage," he declared. "Streamwater, did Fistfall get everyone off the damaged decks?"

"He did. How did you... Never mind." She shook her head. "That nexus was weird to see, sir. I'm glad to have you back—and I'm glad you took the bastard down.

"We've pulled everyone above the damaged decks, which leaves us with the lower eight decks abandoned. We will need to send people down to repair piping or we won't have *engines*, but that can wait.

"You all look exhausted. Fuck, I think *everyone* is exhausted," she said.

"You're right," Cat allowed. "Can you hold down the watch, Faith? For a few hours, at least. You need to rest too, so I will relieve you then."

And they had two clock-days before they needed to slow down to enter the strait. They had space to breathe.

He hoped.

CHAPTER

53

It took Brushfire a few moments to realize where she was when she woke up—and even then, she found herself focusing internally, half-expecting the second pulse to have vanished along with the link to the Source.

The pulsing link remained. It had shifted slightly, in her perception. Moving upward from where it had started—exactly where Armand felt it, she realized—to now rest slightly above her heart.

She suspected they'd received a *copy* of Armand's link in many ways, one that would grow and adjust to match them over time.

Other things, she knew, would be growing and adjusting. The fact that she was waking up in Armand's bed in his observation-deck quarters, with the outerlit sphere's light blocked by curtains and a command to the magical crystal panels that faked being windows, spoke to some of those things.

Armand was still asleep, she realized, and she let her hand rest on his shoulder. Like this, he seemed so small and vulnerable, her hand covering his entire shoulder and feeling awkwardly huge.

Somehow, the size disparity hadn't been an issue the previous night. *Exhaustion* had been, but new chances and decisions had left both of them wanting to consummate things right then.

Now her archmage slept.

She wasn't sure how the sudden awakening of three other mages to the same level of power would go in the long run, but there was no real question that they were following Armand. It was his vision that had brought them there—both his literal vision of a future they had to stop and his plan for a *way* to do so.

And somehow, they'd killed a god.

Now that the Blood King was no more, she'd allow that title. One-quarter of the Quadrumvirate that ruled her people was gone—and part of her wondered if his death would help prevent the future Armand had seen or *create* it.

Armand shifted, starting to snore softly, and she chuckled.

The academic might be able to sleep more—and she knew they could both *use* the sleep—but she was a sailor and was awake enough to know that there was work to do.

Brushfire wasn't expecting to find Verdant Bellowforge and Electrum standing at the access to the damaged decks, directing traffic. The two darvar didn't seem entirely comfortable doing so, but Axfall Hammerhead stood just behind them, the Master of Decks' silent commentary more than enough to keep the crew moving and listening to Alloy's wife and daughter.

"Axfall, Verdant, Electrum," she greeted them. "Where are we at?"

"Rough," Axfall told her. "The fuel lines we capped off before are just *gone* now, but the other ones are damaged somehow."

"We're not leaking fuel," Verdant said. "Thank the Builder for that. But fuel isn't getting to the engines, and we can't slow down without them."

"Have we got in to check on them yet?" Brushfire asked.

"We're working on it, but we're only up to about a quarter of the damaged decks having air," Axfall warned. "And not the quarter with the fuel lines we need."

Two elvar popped back up from the lower decks, Windhook leading the way and giving the collection of supervisors a respectful nod.

"Sirs," he greeted them. "We managed to clear the block and we're into the engine rooms. There's air, at least, so we can start inspecting shit and seeing if it's working."

He blinked at the young darvar and flushed.

"*Stuff*," he corrected. "We can start inspecting *stuff*."

"You have heard my father talking about his projects, yes?" Electrum asked sweetly. "I've heard worse, Windhook. If it's safe, I'll come take a look at the engines?"

"You've as good an eye at this as I do," Verdant agreed instantly. "Master Windhook?"

"We've shored up the collapsed section of the stairwell, but we're only so certain of what *broke* it," Windhook warned. "It was after we pulled everyone up into the top bit of the ship."

"Aftershock damage happens," Axfall observed. "But there shouldn't be any *more* of it. If the stairwell and engine decks have air now, it should be safe."

"If something happens, Paintrock will kill me," Windhook said plaintively. "It *should* be safe, but she's one of the *kids*."

Brushfire was a touch surprised to hear that it was the Master of Staves the elvar was concerned about. Though, she supposed, Alloy was *probably* less likely to kill someone in a fit of paternal rage.

Hunter Paintrock, for all of his virtues and loyalties, did not have what most people would regard as an appropriate value on var life. He *probably* wouldn't kill someone for being there if Electrum was injured in an accident.

Probably.

"It's her call," Brushfire told Windhook, who inhaled firmly and nodded. He might have also realized that referring to an adolescent var as one of *the kids* was probably only slightly wiser than letting one of said kids get hurt.

"All right, sir," he told the darvar. "You know the arcana in this stuff better than most of us. Follow me."

"Smart var," Electrum said with a smile, and set off down the stairs.

The three older var watched them go, and Brushfire heard Verdant chuckle.

"I know *some* of this ship, just from listening to my partner," she noted. "But, really? I am here because no one is going to listen to Electrum otherwise, and she knows this ship better than anyone except Alloy."

She paused, thoughtfully.

"Maybe Captain Greentrees, at this point," she added. "The Captain has been determined to learn as much as he can."

"Can everything be fixed?" Brushfire asked the two var.

Axfall's face told her the answer before he even said a word, his grim expression far too familiar to her.

"We'll be able to get the engines back on, I'm pretty sure," he told her. "Windheart has some plans for using sail fabric to seal the outside sections of the damaged decks to let us get air back into them, but… we'll need to abandon these decks in the strait or when doing heavy maneuvering."

"I know this ship well enough to know that *heavy maneuvering* isn't a thing we can do with the decks like this," Verdant warned gently. "I am a metallurgist, not an artificer or a mage," she explained. "Picking and creating the alloys that make up *Flyer*'s hull was a major project for me, back before the Brothers kidnapped us."

"And?" Brushfire prodded.

"This hull isn't made of those alloys," Verdant said bluntly. "It's regular steel, with a few additions they let me sort out, but nothing much. Without a proper foundry and press, it lost a lot of what strength it *should* have had."

Brushfire was suddenly even *more* glad they hadn't rammed the Blood King's ship.

"And the damage?" she asked.

"We could plate over it and contain air, but the structural damage to the ship can't truly be repaired," Verdant explained. "There is stress fatigue along key structural components. The hull was only… six-tenths, maybe, as strong as the one I wanted. It would *survive* most uses, but it had a limited lifespan to begin with.

"With the additional strain? We lost half of the strength we had. We will need to accelerate carefully and *turn* even more carefully."

"We can't finish our mission in this ship, can we?" Brushfire asked.

"No," Verdant said calmly. "This ship doesn't have another journey in her, Officer Brushfire. Her next landing will be her last."

CHAPTER

54

A RMAND'S NOTES ON THE MELD NEXUS WOULD, EVENTUALLY, RIVAL the original thesis he'd brought with him from the Great Red Forest. Especially once he recorded the experiences of the other three var— now archmagi all!

Their *exact* circumstance wasn't replicable. No one else was ever going to fight a demigod fueled by a wound in the nature of the spheres. One of the realizations Armand had come away from the battle and its accompanying changes with was that the Deep Magic was more aware than he had thought.

Archmagi drew on the Source and knew it more than any others alive. They knew that it could be temperamental and unpredictable at times, but it did so inside certain boundaries. More like water or weather than a creature, let alone a var.

But against the Blood King, the Deep Magic had clearly chosen a side. A power draw that should have left Armand with a lethal debt had been spread across four var—which was what he'd *hoped* for but hadn't truly expected—and muted even then.

There were ways to manage a theoretically lethal energy debt and Armand had been willing to take the risk to protect everyone else.

But instead, the four had been exhausted when the nexus collapsed, and that was *it*. Even spread across all of them, the magic they had drawn from the Source should have left them exhausted and battered for *days*.

Magic that was normally lent had been *given*, and Armand had only heard of anything like it once or twice—and, if he was being honest, he'd

341

dismissed those stories as flights of fancy from archmagi who should have known better.

But those stories had been of similar, if less *explicit*, struggles to stabilize or restore the fabric of the spheres. The Deep Magic was the underweave of all of the spheres, and it appeared—now that Armand had seen it in action—that it sought to protect and restore itself.

None of the stories, including his own, spoke to clear and obvious actions that would have drawn on some kind of balancing energy toward equilibrium. For what they had experienced to occur, the Weave had to have a sense of what they were intending and what they were doing.

It had *chosen* to support them. And it had left its mark on the var involved—as either a consequence of its support or as a reward for helping it? Armand wasn't sure of the *why*, only the what.

He couldn't suggest the meld nexus as a new way of bypassing the Archmage Trial. But he *could* theorize ways that it could be used to make the existing Trial *safer*. A Trial, after all, had four results—an aspirant could lose all of their magic, or could become a far stronger mage but still without a link to the Source, or they could become an archmage... or they could die.

And even among the elvar, who seemed to have a far clearer sense of who had a decent chance, more died than the other three results combined.

But Armand *thought* that if the aspirant was linked to an archmage in a meld nexus, the archmage could provide a more direct guidance—and, potentially, sense when it was going wrong early enough to save the aspirant's life.

It was a theory. One that would take a lot of careful study before he would ever test it—and he certainly wasn't going to test it until *well* after this mission was done. If four archmagi couldn't overcome whatever scheme of dragons they faced, a chance of gaining a fifth wouldn't be worth the risk of losing the mages they already had.

What four archmagi couldn't manage, *five* wouldn't do much better at!

His notes were for later, for when he'd saved the future and had a chance to put his mark on Academies and aspirants and the course of magic through the Court and Kingdoms.

If he was *right*, not only would they stop the slow bleed of their most powerful students that the loss of aspirants entailed, but they might be able to put *more* students to the Trial—and raise the proportion of aspirants who became archmagi, as well.

While Armand doubted that the experimenter whose book he held was the *first* to test the theory, the meld nexus was an esoteric magic, one with too many risks for its purposes. But those risks could be limited, he judged, and the events aboard *Void Flyer* suggested a value that had never even been *considered*.

The engines kicking in was a relief, though Armand could tell things weren't *quite* right. The rumble seemed muted, as did the pressure of maneuvering.

Still, they *were* maneuvering, which meant they'd hopefully manage to enter the strait when they reached it without further difficulties. And *that*, he knew, would finally see them to the Clan Spheres and where his mission could actually *begin*.

As Brushfire had pointed out to him, the detour through the void spheres was the only way they could bypass the border held by Her Crimson Sisters. It hadn't been a shortcut or even an easy journey, but it had been the only way.

Suspecting that the others would be free enough of repair work to begin their lessons, he began to clear away his own notes and sort out a rough teaching space. He'd held enough lessons for the junior mages aboard during their journey to know what could move where in his rooms to make that possible.

Brushfire was the first to arrive, knocking politely on the door and entering when he called.

"Need a hand?" she asked, watching him shuffling a desk across the floor with as judicious a use of magic as he could manage.

"Please. We need enough space for everyone to sit for some parts and stand for others," he told her. "I forgot that I had Fistfall for all of the other lessons, and that boy moves furniture like... well, like *that*."

Brushfire had picked up the desk without even slowing down, carefully balancing it to keep its contents on top—though he could feel that *she* was using a touch of magic to help with that.

"Where do you need it, Armand?"

He pointed, and she moved the piece of furniture in a tenth of the time it would have taken him. Armand had almost an entire deck of the ship to himself, which meant he had plenty of space and only a *few* things had drifted into the lesson space.

Mostly, he'd needed a couple more tables to spread his notes out on. It helped make sure he didn't repeat or contradict himself if he just needed to turn and look at a page rather than sorting through a pile of paper.

Alloy and Cat arrived together just as Armand was sliding the fourth chair into place—ignoring Brushfire's clear-but-silent message that she could do it faster and was concerned he would hurt himself.

That two of his key people were now also his lovers was going to add some interesting *flavor* to things going forward, he suspected. But they all understood what they were doing and why they'd come this far.

"Have a seat," Armand told the three new archmagi. "We're going to have to have a lot of these sit-downs in the future. There is a great deal of training you should have received as aspirants before there was ever a chance of you becoming archmagi.

"Since, it seems, the Source has a mind of her own, I will do everything in my power to teach you in days what should take a full dance or more," he promised. "We won't be touching on making foci for a while, either. Without a properly secured facility—on *rock,* if you please—we can't risk that practice.

"But there are a great many oddities and tricks to being an archmage that you will need to learn—and dangers, especially of overdrawing on the Source."

"I think we've all experienced the discomfort of overuse of magic," Cat said. "I've seen you do far more magic than I ever could, even before it seemed you were drawing on the Source.

"But when you draw on the Source, it gets pulled back, right?"

"Yes and yes," Armand confirmed. "You will find that the mere existence of your link to the source expands both your channels and reserves. You can wield more power at once, and you can wield more power from your own energy before you reach your limits.

"Having access to the Source will allow you to *exceed* those limits, as well, and the increase to your natural reserves becomes dangerous," he warned. "You need to know when you are drawing on your link, to make it a conscious thing rather than an automatic reaction.

"Without knowledge and training, you *will* do it automatically," he told them. "And since you no longer know where your natural limits lie, you will find yourself in energy debt far too easily.

"And while that debt is not all taken back at *once*, it will drag on you for both magic and regular activity until it is repaid." He shrugged. "It is an easy choice, frankly, to draw on it when it is needed. But to draw on it by *mistake* can be just as harmful."

"How do we tell?" Alloy asked. "Or... is it going to be different for each of us?"

"It's going to be different for each of you," Armand confirmed. "But we have ritual and practice that help us find out what those signs will be. Tonight, we will discuss what that entails. The actual ritual itself will knock you out for a clock-day or so, in terms of magic at least, so I think we should refrain until after we are in Drinkstar."

"Three clock-days," Cat told him. "We need to take it far more slowly than we have been. *Void Flyer* is no longer up to the maneuvers we have put her through."

From the other three's expressions, that was only news to Armand at this point.

"How bad?" he asked.

"We can reach Drinkstar and land *Flyer* on a worldlet," Alloy said with a sigh. "But then we will need to find a new ship, one way or another."

"Then, I think, it is absolutely critical that we make sure you are all as capable with your new gifts as you can be," Armand said firmly. "There are few things in the spheres I would expect to have difficulties with as a *single* archmage. With four of us?"

He smiled.

"We'll sort out a ship," he promised. "And everything else. But first... I am afraid you are going to need to learn some more theory."

THE STRAIT INTO DRINKSTAR DIDN'T REQUIRE CAT TO GUIDE THE ship in. For the first time in clock-days upon clock-days, his crew could see the strait as well as he could. The aether around *Flyer*'s hull was still wispy and barely half-present, but it *was* there.

Since it was spilling out from the mouth of the strait, everyone could see it. That allowed Smallwolf to hold the wheel, the youngest of his officers carefully guiding the void ship toward her exit back to regular spheres.

"We're on the line," Streamwater said aloud. "Steady goes it, Bogsong."

There were still hierarchies and chains of command among Cat's crew. Those were a *necessary* component of keeping them all alive when the nearest water and food were weeks of travel away.

But the edges of those hierarchies had been smoothed away in their journey. His people had faith, both up and down the chain, and that allowed for a degree of informality and comfort that Cat had never seen in the High Court Navy.

Of course, the High Court's Navy would never have *allowed* it, even on ships where that two-way faith and loyalty existed.

It wasn't what Cat was used to, and he kept himself *mostly* apart from it, but he didn't discourage it among the rest of the crew. The longer his mixed crew of elvar and gobvar—plus one halvar and four darvar!—worked together, the more they became both a crew and a family.

He feared for the rude reminder his gobvar crew would get when they returned to the Court and Kingdoms. On the other hand, they were a *long* way from that—and the spheres they entered now belonged to the Gobvar Clans.

Cat and the rest of the elvar crew would need to rely on their gobvar crewmates to shield them from prying eyes now.

"And we're in," Smallwolf declared aloud, sounding both surprised and pleased with herself. She was more than capable of navigating an aether ship, but this was the first time anyone other than Cat or Alloy had helmed *Flyer* into a strait.

Normally, there was no real sensation to passing from a sphere into a strait. This time, though, Cat *felt* the aether flow in around *Void Flyer*. It permeated her hull, the underlayer of its presence slipping through the air they kept the ship filled with and taking away a lack he'd barely noticed now.

His aether sense could feel it all, and it felt like a warm blanket. Like coming home. Even the rest of the bridge crew, none of whom shared his navigator's sense, visibly relaxed as the aether swept in over them.

Now, even in the worst case, they could actually go out on the hull!

"Well done, Officer Smallwolf," he told the young elvar. "You can see the rest of the strait?"

"All the way to Drinkstar, sir," she confirmed.

"Then you have the helm," he told her. "Alloy will manage the rockets, but you keep us pointed at that exit. We are out of the void at least, my var, and I'd rather not get lost at the last moment!"

Cat didn't go far, just to the chart room. Their charts of Drinkstar were an eclectic mix. The old Ironhand charts were useless now—a thousand dances of var living in a place could change orbits or even see entirely new structures of wood and stone take shape in the aether.

The High Court charts were nonexistent. They knew the sphere *existed*, but no High Court ship had *ever* been this far into Clan territory. There were no detailed charts in the formal atlases from the Court and Kingdoms.

Somewhere—and Cat wasn't going to ask too closely—they had acquired a set of Clan charts that were only about a hundred dances out of date. Those showed him a few worldlets, one big enough to *supposedly* have a level of shipbuilding.

He wasn't sure that gobvar shipbuilding would live up to his needs—but the last choice they had left was which rock in Drinkstar they put *Void Flyer* down on. She was done after that. No more journeys for the rocket.

So, Whiskyfire it was. If all they could get was a merchant version of the crude galleons he'd seen the gobvar use to attack the border, so be it.

That, too, was assuming that their money and resources could buy anything there. Gold and silver were gold and silver, but their main asset was Armand's ability to produce foci. While those had to be just as valuable—if not more!—in the Clan Spheres, Cat worried about the attention it would draw them.

Landing in the Clan Spheres was going to be an interesting prospect. They *would* draw attention—*Void Flyer* was a very unusual ship—which could be good or bad. He wasn't sure.

His *plan* had been to keep the elvar, halvar and darvar components of the crew concealed inside *Flyer* and transfer over to whatever aether ship they bought well away from prying eyes. Keeping the presence of the elvar crew and the halvar archmage secret could have been valuable.

But that was no longer an option, so they would be discreet and quiet. But they were going to have to move their var from ship to ship on Whiskyfire and hope that wasn't enough on its own to draw attention.

Cat focused on the planning sufficiently that he misjudged the time, looking up from his charts to see the clock ticking down the final few minutes before they emerged from the strait. The distance through a strait was always a *bit* variable, and he expected it to be even more so with the void strait. He'd planned to be back in the control room at least a quarter-hour before the scheduled arrival, just to be certain.

The impact that knocked him from his feet as *Void Flyer* lurched around him told him they'd exited early... and that he *needed* to be at the controls!

CHAPTER

56

Fortunately, the chart room was only a few steps from the bridge. Close enough that only the most immediate of crises would be a problem.

Unfortunately, the spheres had presented them with one of those most immediate of crises, and by the time Cat was back on the central dais, he didn't even need to *ask* for answers.

His officers were reporting aloud as they dug into their new situation.

"Four ships," Streamwater declared. "They were waiting around the strait, watching for anyone to emerge, then..."

"Hit us with *nets*?" Smallwolf finished, the young officer sounding confused. "We've got a net across the main bow." She gestured up at the crystal panes above them, where a pattern of webbing was *barely* visible against the sphere beyond.

"We've got more nets wrapped around the guidance fins, and I *think* they link all the way back to at least two of the ships," the elver concluded.

"Boarding nets," Cat told her. "Not something the gobvar have managed to try on the High Court in the last few dozen dances, but it's definitely in their lexicon.

"And since they were watching for someone to come out of the strait, the usual problem of range isn't an issue."

He was scanning the ships as he spoke. Four ships, as his second officer had said. Two bigger, two smaller—ninesails and galleons, he judged—all with the same black hull and blood-red sails of the ship the Blood King had sailed into the void spheres.

"They're Blood Guard," Windheart said flatly, the old gobvar stepping onto the bridge a pace behind Brushfire. "The Blood King's personal escort, the ones he must have left behind to enter the void spheres to find us.

"Unbreakably loyal, unstoppably vicious." He looked up at the ships, and Cat could *see* the fear in his Master of Sails' eyes.

"And we just killed their King," Cat said grimly. "I... Why aren't they already boarding us?"

The four gobvar ships were easily a cable away, but he would have expected the Guard to be swarming across them already.

"Because they have no idea what they've caught," Brushfire told him. "This ship is unique, Cat. More, though, in *our* spheres, we at least have darvar paddlewheels around, so we're familiar with the concept of an enclosed ship with air held inside.

"The Clans would never permit halvar or darvar to build ships of their own. And while the *Clans* might be convinced or bribed, Her Crimson Sisters would not. The Guard have no idea what *Void Flyer* is."

Or what it carried. Cat looked back to see Armand and Alloy step into the bridge, the darvar a couple of paces ahead of the halvar.

Four archmagi versus four aether ships wasn't a winning fight for the aether ships. On the other hand, though...

"They really don't know what they've caught in their net," he agreed. "And it would serve *our* needs to take one of those ninesails intact. Hard to do at range."

"What are you thinking, Cat?" Armand asked.

"Between us, we can take out that fleet," Cat said with certainty. He was reasonably sure that, given the level of surprise he expected, *he* could take them out on his own. Probably without *Void Flyer* even getting hit.

"They have to figure they've caught a ship, so they won't be surprised if we send people out to talk to them," he continued. "They *won't* talk to an elvar—if any of my var step out onto the nets, they'll try to kill us all.

"But Brushfire can cross to one of the ninesails and talk."

"*Talk*," she echoed grimly. "You mean kill them all."

"If we obliterate the ships, we're already killing them all," he pointed out. "I know taking the ship won't be *pleasant*, but we *need* an aether ship, and that's our best chance of capturing a ninesail."

"And sailing under the Blood King's banners will prevent a lot of trouble before it can even start," Windheart said slowly. "*No one* will get in the Blood Guard's way. Even more than sailing under the blue flag of an archmage in the Court and Kingdoms, we would be clear to go almost anywhere we want."

"You're the only one who can, Brushfire," Cat told her. "I won't—"

"I'll grab Fistfall and go out through the midship exit," she cut him off. "Be ready. I don't plan on starting anything… but from what I know of the Blood Guard, none of us will have to!"

CHAPTER

57

Brushfire understood where Cat's confidence in both the four archmagi's ability to handle the fleet *and* her ability to handle the crew of an entire ship came from. She wasn't entirely convinced he was *correct* in that confidence—but he was also right that an elvar stepping out into the aether from *Void Flyer* would cause the Blood Guard to immediately unleash their storm staves.

That left her and Fistfall carefully climbing out of the battered rocket ship's hull and onto the netting connecting *Flyer* to the Guard ships.

"That one has a bunch more gold on the aftercastle," her brother pointed out, gesturing toward the slightly more distant of the two nine-sails. "I'm guessing that means it's the more important one?"

"I'd guess the same," she agreed, hanging on to the netting with one hand and surveying the two ninesails. The galleons were slightly closer—and having seen Ironhand five-siders recently, Brushfire could see the lineage, with the missing weapon deck and the ships being barely two-thirds the length of the ninesails—but she had never expected to go to one of them.

She needed a ninesail, and the Guard would expect her to go to the commander *anyway*.

"Let's go," she told Fistfall.

For the first few yards, where *Flyer*'s lodestone base still had an impact, it was almost climbing. After that, there was no real pull at all.

Brushfire made sure to keep a hand and a foot hooked into the netting at any given moment, and knew she wasn't moving nearly as fast as she'd like.

She could think of a couple of ways she could use magic to accelerate the process, but she didn't want to be *obvious* in bringing two mages over. The foci would make that clear as they boarded the Blood Guard ship, but that couldn't be helped.

Hand over hand, foot over foot, they pulled their weightless selves along the net toward their destination. No one called out to them to give directions or instructions or *anything*, though she could see sailors on the decks of the galleon they passed closest to.

She couldn't see *faces*, she realized. All of them wore full helmets, built around their horns, that covered their faces with stylized masks of predators. She could tell roughly where they were looking, but that was it.

She could *also* tell that the storm staves and flamethrowers on the galleon were definitely trained on *Void Flyer*. The nets were set up to board, but the Guard were taking no chances.

It *shouldn't* be enough, not with three archmagi back aboard the ship to protect her and strike back, but Brushfire knew she was *supposed* to see the aimed weaponry.

"Subtle they're not," Fistfall murmured, barely loud enough for the aether to carry it to her ears.

"There's a reason they're making us come to them," she replied—though she marveled at the Guard's patience. It took them far longer to cross the netting than she would have expected them to wait.

Her var were not known for their patience—and stereotype or no, there was some truth to that claim. The stories she'd heard of the Guard didn't give the impression that they were any *more* patient than anyone else, either.

The ability to demand whatever you wanted didn't lend itself to patience, she suspected.

Still, the four ships waited, their weapons trained on *Void Flyer*, until Brushfire reached the end of the webbing and swung herself onto the ninesail's deck. Just as they'd picked out the ship by the gold filigree on the aftercastle, she picked which of the three sail decks they touched down on by *which* of the three aftercastles had the *most* filigree.

A dozen masked gobvar in long crimson cloaks were waiting for her, their uniforms and halberd-wands identical.

"Surrender your foci," the closest barked, leveling their halberd at her.

"No," she told him. "You will explain yourselves. You have captured my ship without cause, and I will *not* be ordered about like a common sailor!"

Brushfire channeled her memories of Armand and Cat's anger at the elvar who had treated all of their crew as criminals solely on the basis of being gobvar.

"Take them!" the same gobvar snarled, and Brushfire acted.

Despite the *plan*, something wasn't sitting quite right, and she didn't leap immediately to complete destruction. She didn't even *draw* her focus, her fingers on it enough for her to channel her power for now as she tore the halberd-wands from their owners' hands, clattering them to the deck in a relatively neat pile.

"I said *no*," she repeated, like she was speaking to one of her tribesvar who had been particularly stupid. "I will speak to your commander."

"You will—"

"Speak to me," a new voice interrupted. There was a gravel and dignity to the voice the first var didn't have, a combination of tones and accents she'd never heard in her life.

Give Brushfire and Fistfall another dozen dances of being senior and respected crew and mages, they *might* begin to approach that combination of calm authority, dignity and the intonations of gobvar culture and voice boxes.

In many ways, the new gobvar sounded like *Cat* to Brushfire—but he was definitely gobvar. He was as tall as the tallest of the Guards who'd intercepted her, but it wasn't *physical* power that made the greeting party split at a tiny gesture.

His uniform was the same as the others, but standing next to them, she could now see the differences. His long tunic, cloak and leggings were the same cut but a finer fabric.

With the comparison of the commander, she saw now that the guards *did* have insignia: a red blood drop embroidered into the tunic where neck met shoulder. The stranger had a *ruby*, carved into the exact same shape, sewn into his uniform at that place. And while the masks of the sailors had shown some predator she'd never seen, the stranger's mask was unquestionably the face of a dragon.

"You command here?" she asked, as if it wasn't obvious just from the body language, let alone the uniform.

"I am Lord Commander Fallen Sky of Broken Ash and the Stone-shine," Fallen Sky introduced himself crisply. Name, then Clan, then sphere. "I serve the Blood King of the Gobvar as Lord Commander of His Guard.

"So, yes. I command here," he told her, his tone a touch wryer than she honestly expected.

The squad of Guards who had met them as they boarded pulled back now, their body language embarrassed at being quite so easily disarmed—and cautious, as all of them *also* had backup swords and battlewands.

More Guard appeared at speed, a circle taking shape around Brush-fire, her brother and the Lord Commander. Before she managed to say a word, a second masked gobvar stepped through the circle of soldiers.

This one's uniform was unmarked, without any embroidery at all to either decorate or indicate rank—and their mask was flat, plain metal with no decoration whatsoever. Unlike even the Lord Commander, though, they carried a wand focus in a scabbard tied tightly to their tunic, though they didn't draw it as they took a place one step back and to the left of the officer.

"What is the meaning of your attack on my ship?" Brushfire finally asked, forcing herself to ignore the armed var surrounding her and even the strange mage. "We entered the sphere and were immediately seized by your ships."

"You believe you are innocent? That our capture of your ship is unjusti-fied?" The sardonic edge to his voice was biting. "You *do* realize that strait leads into the void, yes? Beyond that passage, nothing lives. It leads to nowhere and nothing—and your ship certainly didn't enter it from *here*.

"So, yes, we captured your ship. And you *will* answer our questions. We are the Blood Guard," he concluded. "We serve the Blood King's voice, and *He* has authority over all gobvar and everything in these spheres.

"You *will* explain what your ship is and how you came to leave that strait."

Brushfire smiled thinly, giving him her most disdainful look.

"My vessel is built for the void, Lord Commander Fallen Sky," she told him. "Travel through the void sphere beyond this strait was her *purpose*, and that is what we have done. We have transited into and out of a void sphere, leaving through a different strait than we entered, following an old chart."

All of which was true enough, though it missed that they'd traveled through *four* void spheres and started in the Court and Kingdoms.

"I see," Fallen Sky said. He sounded more amused than anything else now. "Then I suppose I shall have to seize your ship for His Glory. You should be *honored*, Captain, to have created something He will see value in."

No one moved. He wasn't giving orders to his var, which told Brushfire he was... hunting for something.

"I believe I must decline that honor," she said calmly. "I should return to my ship."

She started to turn, only to find the blank-masked mage suddenly in her face. They were short for a gobvar, though the horns emerging from their helmet were impressive, but that didn't stop them barring her way.

"Games and stories tell no tales," they told her in an odd singsong. "Blood burns but truth reveals. In darkness, hunger. In spherelight, fear. Speak."

"What do you *want*?" Brushfire snapped.

"He isn't talking to you," Fallen Sky told her, and his voice was strange. Tired? "Your name, please, Captain?"

The title felt stiff and awkward to her ears, but she realized he meant her. She hadn't *quite* realized that was the persona she was putting on.

"I am Brushfire of Tribe Hammerhead," she told him, not turning back to him, still facing the strange mage, and hoping to get some clue of what was going on with them.

"Then, Brushfire, I ask for the truth you have spoken around," the gobvar commander said. "My Guards are on edge, their steel showing."

"Steel on steel will veil the feel but leave no answers in the falling."

Oh. *Oh.* The second stranger was a *seer*.

Brushfire had never actually met one, not of *her* var, but she'd heard Cat and Armand talk about them. Divination was one thing, a focused skill. To be a *seer* was to see *prophecy*. To know what would be, not what was.

But not, as she understood it, ever particularly clearly or usefully.

"If one of us makes the wrong move, var will die," Fallen Sky told her. "You do not appear to believe that will include *you*, which is fascinating to me, but I would rather, today, avoid any dying."

That was so far outside what she had expected from a Blood Guard officer that Brushfire considered her next step very carefully. She could push past the seer, use her magic to throw aside the Blood Guard and sever their nets with ease.

On the other hand, she and Cat had expected her to be attacked and for her to seize the ship. Provoking the Guard would certainly get them to *that* goal.

"What do you want?" she asked, carefully, still facing the seer not Fallen Sky.

"His touch on her soul, a shadow of blood marked by fire and *hunger* in the *void*," the seer said. Their words were nonsense, but the urgency to them told her that the var was drawing on prophecy—probably intentionally, which she doubted was overly safe at the best of times.

"A moment, Stonekind of Gloryherd," Fallen Sky instructed. The seer stepped backward, one step.

Just one step. They were still barring her way.

"The Blood King entered that strait some clock-days ago," the Lord Commander said. His tone was slow, stiff, dignified—yet there was an edge of pain and anger, too. She wasn't sure she'd have picked it up without long experience around Cat, though.

It seemed the Blood Guard and the High Court Navy followed similar schools of thought on command. They certainly used the same clock-day and *language*... and she wondered if the traditions of the commands were *also* inherited from the Ironhand Imperium?

"I learned His destination in time to remove the crew from the ship He was on," Fallen Sky continued. "He entered alone, as only He could. Now, where the Blood King entered, *you* leave.

"Our King should have returned by now. So, tell me, Brushfire, what did you see on the far side of the strait?"

She *heard* the seer—Stonekind of Gloryherd, she presumed—inhale to speak before stopping. Slowly, she turned to see that Fallen Sky had held up his hand, ordering the seer to remain silent.

"Speak true, Brushfire Hammerhead," he told her—and the way he structured her name told her he'd seen through at least *one* part of her deception. She'd tried to imitate how he'd structured his own name, to avoid the impression that she was from the Court and Kingdoms.

She'd clearly failed, and that suggested she was running out of chances to do anything except grab her wand and start blasting. She could *feel* Fistfall's tension beside her, her brother following her lead but not sure what her plan was.

Which was fair, given that *she* wasn't sure what her plan was. But if it was down to tell the truth or start killing… well, the truth wasn't going to save her, but they were at a point where she didn't think it could *hurt*, either.

"Your King declared us trespassers and attacked us," she said calmly. "We destroyed his ship… and the void spheres themselves *consumed* him."

The silence rippled out from her like an inverted explosion, her words sinking into each of the Blood Guard and almost freezing them in place.

"*Impossible*," one of the guards around her snapped. "He was a *god*."

"And we know He is dead," Fallen Sky snapped back. "Stonekind?"

The seer was silent for long heartbeats, and Brushfire knew that the var around her had to be checking weapons. This time, though, her attention was focused on Fallen Sky.

They already knew the Blood King was dead.

"She is marked," the seer finally said, their tone more natural, if stilted. "His power has fallen on her, but it does not remain. The hunger of the void… stains her. And the Song of the Spheres fills her.

"One archmage could not defy our King. But I can taste the shadow and ash on the aether current, and she is not alone."

Even the less-prophetic words were still… not as clear as Brushfire suspected the Lord Commander hoped. *She* could piece together the meaning, but she *knew* what had happened.

"You fought the Blood King?" Fallen Sky asked.

"I did. I was not alone," she conceded.

"And you are an archmage?"

"I am," she confirmed. It was *far* too late for them to do anything that could contain the power of an archmage, after all—and the other three archmagi on *Void Flyer* would end the Guard if something happened to her!

"What do you mean, *the void spheres consumed him*?"

Brushfire had been expecting to be attacked. Defiance. Rage. Denial. By declaring the death of the Blood King to his people, she'd figured she was kicking off the fight she'd come there to have. The Lord Commander's questions were *not* what she'd expected.

"The spheres beyond that strait were once ordinary spheres," she said slowly. "Everything in them was consumed by the Blood King to fuel his ascension. But a stain of that magic remained, an enduring and insatiable hunger.

"When the Blood King was weakened, the sphere's hunger... consumed him," she repeated. "What he stole was taken back and he is no more."

The Guard shifted around her.

"*Impossible!*" one of them screamed, the sound turning into a lunge toward her—whether to shut her up or strike her down, she would never know.

Fallen Sky moved faster than she did. The Lord Commander sounded old, but he hadn't slowed down at any point. She hadn't recognized the ruby on his uniform as a focus until he called on it, magic moving him at a speed no ordinary var could match.

There was a flash of steel and power—and the attacking Guard was on the deck, pinned beneath Fallen Sky's boot.

Brushfire couldn't even tell if the var was alive.

The Lord Commander stepped away from his soldier and glared around his people.

"Do *we* owe anyone vengeance?" he snapped. "Do *we* owe *that* being vengeance? It is not in our bonds. It is not in our oaths.

"I will not avenge the Blood King."

Brushfire... didn't understand, but she wasn't going to interrupt as the gobvar stared down his own people.

"*I* command here," Fallen Sky declared. "Our bonds are broken. Our oaths released by death. But *I* command here. Will you follow... or be broken?"

At least half of the ninesail's crew had to be on the deck, Brushfire judged. Potentially a bit less, given that he'd said they'd taken the crew off the Blood King's ship—and Fallen Sky's specification that *he* had arranged that, not the Blood King, suddenly echoed in her mind.

The Blood King hadn't even *thought* about the fact that sailing his ship into the void would kill hundreds of his var. Not until one of his chief minions had taken action to prevent it.

And whatever bonds and oaths Fallen Sky spoke of being broken, one thing rapidly became *very* clear on the deck of the Blood Guard ninesail.

Regardless of what bound them all to the Blood King, *these* var would follow Lord Commander Fallen Sky anywhere.

"We will follow," Stonekind declared, the seer the first to speak. The first to go to one knee in fealty before Fallen Sky.

With hundreds of gobvar on the sail deck, they were far from the last.

BRUSHFIRE STOOD STILL AS THE GOBVAR SHOWED THEIR ALLEGIANCE, her fingers still on her focus. She didn't think this was a bad thing, but she wasn't sure. They'd killed the Blood King, but it seemed like his top commander was, at least, not going to hold it against them.

"You have questions," Fallen Sky said to her. "Speak."

"You served the Blood King. He is dead. What happens now?" she asked.

There was a long silence, and the Lord Commander made a wave-off gesture. The Guards slowly rose to their feet, dispersing back to other duties and giving them a growing area of privacy.

Then Fallen Sky reached up and released a hidden latch at the bottom of his helm. Several clearly audible latches released in sequence, and he pulled the mask away to allow himself to lift the helmet off.

Underneath the helm was a gobvar probably between Axfall and Windheart's age, easily over two hundred dances old. His hair was stark white and close-cut, with the characteristic roughness of someone who cut their own hair. Possibly with a knife.

"Every var on these ships was given to the Blood King as tribute at their sixteenth flaring of the Great Fire," he told her. With the helmet removed, his voice was clearer, but that only seemed to increase his calm authority and dignity.

"He marked us. Claimed us in a way I barely understand now, two hundred flarings later. We could not defy Him. Could not refuse Him.

His orders defined and drove us, and such that we always knew our actions were not our choice.

"For two hundred flarings of the Great Fire, Brushfire Hammerhead, my will has not been wholly my own." He met her gaze and she knew there was no way she could fully understand what that meant.

"Now the Blood King is somehow dead and my mind is my own and I can *choose* what I do now," he continued. "I will not fully deny that choice to my Guards, but for them to lose their guiding light will be difficult. In exerting my authority, I hope to give them focus until they can find their footing beneath themselves."

"To see if such will work is beyond even such as me," Stonekind pointed out, the seer the only var still within easy earshot. "Tell me, Brushfire Hammerhead, must you still take our ship by force?"

With a literal mask over his face for most of his career, Fallen Sky clearly hadn't learned not to show his surprise on his face.

"I am deciding," Brushfire admitted, realizing that lying to the seer was probably pointless. "It depends on whether you will let my ship go."

"You think you can take this ship on your own?" Fallen Sky half-asked, half-growled.

She looked at him assessingly. *If* he reached her before she drew on the Source, he *might* manage to stop her. In which case Cat and the others would destroy the ship.

"If I cannot take control of this ship, then it and the rest of your fleet will be destroyed," she told him calmly. "You are not an archmage, Lord Commander. None of your crews are. We are not the ones outmatched here."

There was a long silence.

"What brings *one* archmage across the void?" Fallen Sky finally asked. "I did not believe there *were* gobvar archmagi in elvar spheres." He paused. "Stonekind already told me there were more of you, didn't he?"

"I did?" the seer asked, then cough-chuckled. "You forget, my old friend, that *I* do not always remember what I have spoken. She is an archmage. And..." They sniffed the air. "Yes. The scent of His shadow and the ash that burned it wafts in a way that carries the Song of the Spheres. There is another archmage on her ship."

"What brings *two* archmagi here?" Fallen Sky asked. "Your ship is unusual, but now you claim to need mine?"

"What would you have me say, Lord Commander?" she asked. "That the spheres themselves linked the Source to multiple mages to allow us to fight the Blood King? That destroying your king and monarch wasn't even part of our plan? That we seek to stop a greater threat, one that threatened to enslave all var, and your former master simply got in the way?"

"Not two archmagi, then," the gobvar officer noted. "More. You killed a *god* by *accident*?"

"Killing him was intended, I will admit," Brushfire said drily, *hearing* her brother choke next to her. "But we did not plan to fight him at first and did not know our route through the void spheres would bring us into conflict with him.

"We are following a vision of a future where all var—elvar, gobvar, halvar, darvar, *all* var—are broken and enslaved to the will of a host of dragons. Our senior archmage saw a future of war and conquest, where gobvar were at best first among slaves and all var knelt.

"And we set ourselves on the course to stop it." She shrugged. "Our void ship is damaged. We need an aether ship to continue our search. The answer, we believe, lies in spheres once called the Radiant Realms."

"So, you would take *my* ship by force, would you?" Fallen Sky asked.

"I am prepared to trade or negotiate for it," she said drily. "We *knew* the Blood Guard would fight. The Guard are known for their violence, after all."

"That was His will. We can... choose something else now," the Lord Commander told her. "It will take me time to deal with the other ships, to sort through my var. But I think..."

She stared at him as he fell into silence, until Stonekind clapped their hands and giggled.

"A quest for the once-damned?" the seer asked. "Hitch your star to the archmagi four, command a fleet in the pursuit of salvation for your soul and all var alike? Will those who helped break the Clans save them?"

"You see, I think, why seers are rarely popular," Fallen Sky said drily. "But I owe Stonekind's father from long ago… and them, themselves, for more recent service.

"And they are not wrong. I *think*, if you give me a clock-day or two, I can give you more than one ship, Archmage Brushfire Hammerhead.

"We are lost souls now, cast adrift by the death of our enslaver at your hands."

He smiled.

"I think the least you owe us is a *quest* to provide us a new beacon, don't you?"

ABOUT THE AUTHOR

GLYNN STEWART is the author of Starship's Mage, a bestselling science fiction and fantasy series where faster-than-light travel is possible—but only because of magic. His other works include science fiction series Duchy of Terra, Castle Federation and Vigilante, as well as the urban fantasy series ONSET and Changeling Blood.

Writing managed to liberate Glynn from a bleak future as an accountant. With his personality and hope for a high-tech future intact, he lives in Canada with his partner, their cats, and an unstoppable writing habit.

CREDITS

The following people were involved in making this book:
Copyeditor: Richard Shealy
Proofreader: M Parker Editing
Cover Artist: Elias Stern
Faolan's Pen Publishing: Jack Giesen

And a sincere thank you to Glynn's Patreon subscribers!

Jonathan Hamm ✳ Jordan Placer ✳ Joseph R. Garrett II ✳ JW Lack
K Nakamura ✳ K. R. S. ✳ Karen M ✳ Karl M. Drewke
Kelly G Smith ✳ Kerry aka Trouble ✳ Kory Christensen
Larry Edwards ✳ Liz Broadwell ✳ Lou Dakin ✳ Marci M Matthews
Mark Kurta ✳ Marshall McGowan ✳ Martyn Smedley
Matthea W. Ross ✳ Matthew Gerboth ✳ Matthew Peloso
Maxime de Hennin de Boussu-Walcourt ✳ Mazi Melton
Michael Brown ✳ Michael D Smith ✳ Michael Esparza
Mitch Collins ✳ Mo Moser ✳ Mr. Natbar ✳ Nathan Ciaio
Nic Thompson ✳ Nicholas Kristopher Forrester ✳ Nick Burrows
Patrick Dalziel Lewis ✳ Patrick Hunter ✳ Paul Buckingham
Paul J Stone ✳ Paul Smith ✳ Paul Zagieboylo ✳ Peter Blom
Phil Adkins ✳ Phyxius ✳ R. Randall Hall ✳ Randy Murphey
Read Fenton ✳ Richard Morgan-Ash ✳ Rob Lazenby
Rob MacGregor ✳ Rob Steinberger ✳ Robert Brown
Robert T. Alford Jr. ✳ Robyn Weimer ✳ Ron Lugge
Ryan McMurphy ✳ Sam Stoliker ✳ Sam Willis Fischbeck
Sarah Woodson ✳ Scott Smith ✳ Scott W. Shippee
Sebastian W.H. Moon ✳ Shultzman ✳ Skye Sisk ✳ sonicthe
Susan McKilligan ✳ Susan Weber ✳ Thomas Lambert
Thomas M. Murtola ✳ Tommy Kanary ✳ Travis Bass ✳ Trevor Rivet
Vespry Family ✳ Vincent K. Miller ✳ Wayne Hamilton

OTHER BOOKS
BY GLYNN STEWART

For release announcements join the mailing list
or visit **GlynnStewart.com**

STARSHIP'S MAGE
Starship's Mage
Hand of Mars
Voice of Mars
Alien Arcana
Judgment of Mars
UnArcana Stars
Sword of Mars
Mountain of Mars
The Service of Mars
A Darker Magic
Mage-Commander
Beyond the Eyes of Mars
Nemesis of Mars
Chimera's Star
Ambassador for Mars
Chimera's Fall
The Lies Arcana
Shadow of Mars(*upcoming*)

Starship's Mage: Red Falcon
Interstellar Mage
Mage-Provocateur
Agents of Mars

Starship's Mage Novellas
Pulsar Race
Mage-Queen's Thief

HOUSE ADAMANT

The Exodus Gambit
The Old Guard
The Valkyrie Strategem
Regent's Mate
Broken Prince(*upcoming*)

EXILE

Exile
Refuge
Crusade
Ashen Stars: An Exile Novella

CASTLE FEDERATION

Space Carrier Avalon
Stellar Fox
Battle Group Avalon
Q-Ship Chameleon
Rimward Stars
Operation Medusa
A Question of Faith: A Castle Federation Novella

Dakotan Confederacy
Admiral's Oath
To Stand Defiant
Unbroken Faith

VIGILANTE

(WITH TERRY MIXON))
Heart of Vengeance
Oath of Vengeance

**Bound By Stars: A Vigilante Series
(With Terry Mixon)**
Bound By Law
Bound by Honor
Bound by Blood

AETHER SPHERES
Nine Sailed Star
Void Spheres
Fated Skies (*upcoming*)

TEER AND KARD
Wardtown
Blood Ward
Blood Adept
Adept's Path (*upcoming*)

CHANGELING BLOOD
Changeling's Fealty
Hunter's Oath
Noble's Honor
Fae, Flames & Fedoras: A Changeling Blood Novella

ONSET
ONSET: To Serve and Protect
ONSET: My Enemy's Enemy
ONSET: Blood of the Innocent
ONSET: Stay of Execution
Murder by Magic: An ONSET Novella

STANDALONE NOVELS & NOVELLAS
Seekers in the Void: A Space Opera Novel
Children of Prophecy
City in the Sky
Excalibur Lost: A Space Opera Novella
Balefire: A Dark Fantasy Novella
Icebreaker: A Fantasy Naval Thriller

www.ingramcontent.com/pod-product-compliance
Lightning Source LLC
Chambersburg PA
CBHW021338310726

48971CB00001B/182